Praise for *All That Shimmers*

"This book is ingenious in its exploration of life's complicated layers. The vibrant settings reflect the tension between hope and tragedy . . . stolen kisses, giddy first love, and new friendships happen and matter even as death swirls beyond them . . . prose is both raw and elegant . . . bittersweet ending mingles uncertainty, grief and hope . . ." – **Foreword Reviews**

". . . a spectacular and bittersweet saga of loss, hope, and love . . . a well-written, atmospheric, and alluring fantasy that transports readers to a world of beauty and mysticism . . . highly recommend this captivating tale to all fantasy fans." – **Readers Favorite, Makeda Cummings (5 stars)**

". . . a whimsical journey packed with dazzling creatures, hope, heartbreak, and, ultimately, a winsome ending . . . complex characters . . . Ambrose is skilled at tinting even the harshest realities with lovely hues. Comparable title . . . Heather Fawcett's *Emily Wilde's Encyclopaedia of Faeries.*" – **Publisher's Weekly BookLife**

"Tragic and hopeful in equal measure, this is a heartfelt, character-driven romance that tugs at your heartstrings from start to finish . . . a must-read for readers of historical fiction and fantasy." – **Readers Favorite, Pikasho Deka (5 stars)**

"Historical romance and fantasy readers will relish the interwoven elements of history, love, and magic . . . Ambrose excels in drawing together a satisfying blend of magic, social change, and psychological insight." – **Midwest Book Review, D. Donovan, Senior Reviewer**

"Kady Ambrose masterfully weaved the elements of fantasy and romance to create an enchanting story that readers of both genres will enjoy. I highly recommend it as it's a five-star book and more." – **Readers Favorite, Carol Thompson (5 stars)**

". . . an enchanting and emotional story of innocence to experience . . . a darker version of *Anne of Green Gables* meets the mischief-makers of Shakespeare's *A Midsummer Night's Dream* . . . I loved it!" – **Allison Morse, author of *Fallen Star***

"Libraries . . . will welcome *All That Shimmers* into their collections. It's an exceptionally poignant examination of one twenty-something woman's shifting options . . . against [a] . . . challenging social and political atmosphere . . ." – **Donovan's Literary Services, D. Donovan, Editor**

"Perfect for fans of the historical fantasy of Heather Fawcett and Sarah Addison Allen, *All That Shimmers* is thoroughly charming and utterly enchanting." – **Sarah Vance-Tompkins, author of *I Put a Spell on You***

"I wolfed down this beautiful book. I was charmed, engaged, and completely lost in the cleverly crafted story . . . stunning characterizations, witty dialogue and a structure that leaves you feeling complete . . . and yet still wanting a sequel. Bravo." – **Colette Freedman, author of *The Affair***

". . . a must-read for anyone who enjoys beautifully written and emotionally resonant fantasy romance." – **Cordia Pearson, author of *Iridesce***

"Spot on details of the setting and hardships the vulnerable young heroine faces, plus a magical dip into a bit of fantasy, make this book unique. A true delight." – **Meg Mims, Spur Award-winning author of *Double Crossing***

All That

Shimmers

A Twin Birch House Novel

Kady Ambrose

ANQA PRESS

for Annie

who made everything sparkle

This perfect day with joy my being fills, here could I dream and
let a lifetime pass . . .

Charles Henry Lüders

Chapter One

— SEPTEMBER 1868 —

Ezra's mind popped and crackled with ideas on how he'd spend his new-found riches. It was a sultry summer night in New Hampshire's White Mountains, but the stone passage he crept through was refreshingly cool. Bent at the waist on account of the tunnel's low ceiling, he made his way through the short entrance with an empty flour sack gripped in one hand, a lantern held high in the other.

After emerging from the passageway, he straightened. A soft, pearly light that seemed to come from everywhere and nowhere bathed the wooded glen before him. The golden light from his lantern reflected off a strange dew covering the grass, trees, and bushes, making everything sparkle. Indifferent to the glen's otherworldly glitter, he beelined across the small clearing toward a pond near its center.

Earlier that night, his lantern had lit the wheelwright's nicely dimpled daughter leaning over that same water with a giant blue butterfly on her finger. Squashing the twinge of guilt roused by the memory, he held his light over the pond and peered past the lily pads floating on the surface. The treasure was still there on the bottom, gleaming up at him through the crystal clear water. It was real, even if Prudence hadn't taken any notice of it.

He whistled through his teeth and hitched up his pants. Truth be told, he didn't mind not having to share the booty with her.

"Welcome back, Ezra."

He stumbled backward, almost dropping the lantern. The sound of giggling seemed to come from the pond itself, but how could that be?

"Who's there?" Sweeping the lamp right and left, he scanned the wood.

"Down here." The second girl's voice was different than the first. More giggles followed.

He swung the light back over the pond, now filled with a dozen or more comely young ladies, all standing up to their waists in the water. To his shock and delight, not one wore a stitch of clothing. They all had long hair flowing over their shoulders, covering them up pretty good, though. "You . . . you're those nymphs Prudence was goin' on about."

"That's right," replied a willowy blonde with a crown of crocus blossoms.

"Where is she?" asked a redhead with white tea roses woven into her curls.

His eyes roamed from one beauty to the next. "I . . . I came back alone."

"For these?" An ebony-skinned girl with a daffodil tucked behind her ear swept her arm over the jewels and gold nuggets twinkling below the surface.

"Ye . . . yes." Collecting the booty might be a little more complicated than he'd reckoned on. "Are they . . . yours?"

"They're in our pond, but they mean nothing to us," replied a toffee-skinned brunette wearing nothing but morning glories.

They beckoned him with inviting gestures. "Come in with us. The water is warm . . . and you can take what you wish."

With eyes darting from one sweet face to the next, he determined that joining them was an excellent idea. He placed the lantern down carefully so he wouldn't lose sight of the ladies as he tore his clothes off as fast as he could. The cool air was bracing, but the water was every bit as welcoming as the naiads promised.

The nymphs surrounded him as he slipped into the pond and tilted his head back. His eyes drifted closed as he took a long, deep breath. The blossoms gave each naiad's soft hair its own special perfume.

Before long, he plumb forgot the treasure below his feet. Time faded as his body relaxed in watery pleasure. He'd never known contentment like this. Even as his head slid beneath the surface, he sensed nothing but the water sliding over his skin . . . through his skin. He was floating, drifting.

Under the water . . . part of the water . . . one with the water.

Chapter Two

Vanessa's terror was so profound it gave her a peculiar calm. As long as the children remained missing, she had to keep her seething hysteria imprisoned deep in her belly. She cupped her hands on either side of her mouth for the fifth or sixth time. "Edna! Walter!" In the fading light, even the wood's noises had changed. The rustle of leaves, soft and welcoming earlier, now sounded like the whispering of conspirators. She searched the forest clearing in an ever-widening circle. Surely her two young charges were simply hiding, playing a trick on her. Out of character for these two, perhaps, but it wouldn't be the first time pampered children had tormented a new nursemaid.

"Walter! Edna! I give up. You win!" The enormous sapphire butterfly that had lured them so far from the hotel reappeared. Forcing her gaze from the creature's extraordinary beauty, Vanessa raised her quavering voice. "Don't you want to go back and finish our picnic?"

She could already picture herself stepping off the train back in Boston. Unemployed and penniless. Or worse, still in the woods after dark, huddled under a tree all alone, encircled by wolves.

A sharp *crack* cut through the woodland noise. She froze, her gaze darting back to the butterfly, which had settled on a nearby branch and appeared to be watching her. Deepening shadows pressed the forest in closer. Something flew over her head. Goosebumps rose on her arms as she fought back tears. "Children?"

"Right here!" The voice was masculine, with a hint of forced cheer.

She spun around. A young gentleman of medium build stood between two mossy boulders—Walter and Edna in hand. They were all smiling, the little ones appearing none the worse for wear.

"Oh! Thank God." Dizzy, she turned her back to hide the tears she could no longer contain.

"What's wrong, Miss Perkins?" Six-year-old Edna's genuine confusion made Vanessa's reaction seem ridiculous. How long had they been gone, for goodness' sakes? A few minutes?

Lifting her apron to pat her face dry, she forced a smile into her voice. "Nothing, sweetheart." She turned to face them. "I was just a little worried when I couldn't find you."

"We found Avuhwy!" Three-year-old Walter gazed up at the young man with adoring eyes, clearly smitten.

Vanessa gave her head a slight shake, wincing in embarrassment. She'd let her imagination run away with her . . . again.

The "Avery" fellow pushed his spectacles up his nose as he drew near, his hand extended. "Nice to meet you." Guilt tinged his angular face.

A spike of anger pierced her gut. Refusing to shake, she squeezed her intertwined fingers together at her waist. "I take it this little game of hide-and-seek was your idea?"

"Not at all." He crossed his arms. "I was painting when they came upon me. I brought them back directly, I assure you."

"Oh." She glanced down at Edna and Walter's innocent faces. Either he was telling the truth, or the children were extraordinary actors. "I see." As usual, her tendency to make hasty decisions was making a fine mess of things. She extended her hand. "My apologies."

"None required." A smile tugged at the corner of his mouth as he uncrossed his arms and shook her hand. "As you've heard, I'm Avery." He cleared his throat. "Avery Nolen."

"Vanessa Perkins." As her composure returned, her gaze ranged over his shaggy, light brown hair and the worn leather satchel slung over his shoulder. He seemed too relaxed to be staff . . . and too disheveled for a guest. From town, perhaps? She recalled Mrs. Wainwright mentioning a local doctor who treated the children. "Are you any relation to Dr. Nolen in the village?"

Avery's face clouded. "He's my father. And I take it you're the new nurse-maid." His brows arched as though his statement was a question.

Her hand flew to the white cap pinned to her hair, though there'd been no judgment in his tone. "That's right."

His voice lowered. "Edna tells me Miss O'Neill is serving abroad as a nurse."

She raised her eyes. "Seems most of the families staying at the hotel have sons or staff members over there." Biting her tongue, she refrained from asking why he wasn't in France, fighting "Woodrow Wilson's War." He appeared only slightly older than her, early twenties maybe. Rare for a fit young man over twenty-one to be left behind.

"Yes." His gaze shifted away. "So many have gone." As he stared into the distance, there was sorrow in his big brown eyes. They were the color of dark molasses, their soft warmth at odds with the sharp edges of his nose and cheekbones. After a moment, he waved his hand, as though brushing the war itself away, and turned to the children. "Are you two going to be in the Flag Day parade?"

"Yeth." Walter beamed, while Edna nodded in silent agreement.

"We're just on our way back to the hotel now." She tried to sound casual. "Would you care to accompany us, Mr. Nolen?"

"Of course." He gestured them forward, a flush of pink creeping up his neck. "But you can call me Avery."

"Only if you call me Vanessa, and please, you lead. I'm sure you know the way better than I do."

First names already? Her emotional afternoon had apparently left her as gushy as a society girl.

"Happy to." His smile was fleeting, but spectacular. A burst of sunshine piercing the clouds. "Come along, Miss Wainwright. Let's get you to that parade." He took Edna's hand and led the way.

Vanessa released a deep breath as he swung the little girl's hand. Whatever the reason, she was glad they'd dispensed with formalities. If the children were so fond of him, he must be alright.

"Up, pwwease." Walter reached for her with both hands. Her own legs were a bit shaky from all their mountain climbing. He had to be exhausted.

"Upsy-daisy." After lifting the boy onto her hip, she gave him a quick kiss and followed after their new guide. Without a doubt, coming to Twin Birch House as the Wainwright's nursemaid was the best thing that ever happened to her. All she could do was pray the children didn't complain to their parents about her nearly losing them in the woods.

Chapter Three

Lachima flapped her sapphire wings gently as she settled on the hotel roof to watch Vanessa and Avery lead Edna and Walter across the emerald lawn.

What fun she'd had, flitting around the nursemaid's picnic with the Wainwright children, then leading their trio into the woods so Vanessa and Avery could meet.

As one of the three Fates, Lachima had always been responsible for every mortal's timeline between birth and death. Her two sisters determined each life's beginning and end.

But when humankind abandoned most ancient deities, their faith had also shifted away from the Fates, or "fairies," as they'd come to be known. So Lachima was limited, at least for the time being, to small interventions . . . like organizing for Vanessa Perkins to catch the eye of both Avery Nolen and a handsome hotel guest named Ned Cooper.

Content as her reduced circumstances would allow, Lachima let out a delicate butterfly sigh. Thanks to her maneuvering, it promised to be an interesting season at Twin Birch House.

Chapter Four

Grateful the Flag Day parade was over and the children were tucked in their beds, Vanessa passed through the crowded staff dormitory. Dozens of girls chatted as they changed clothes in the single, large room not unlike the dorms at the Girls Home, the orphanage in Boston where she'd grown up. It was one of the few familiar rituals she experienced since entering the dazzling world of Twin Birch House.

Her bunkmate was still in her chambermaid uniform, reading a letter on the bed above Vanessa's. With fleshy limbs, plain features, and limp, dirty blonde hair, Gladys was no beauty. But her unguarded smile and sensible nature had penetrated Vanessa's defenses in the two weeks since they met . . . and explained the volume of letters the girl received from her devoted fiancé.

Vanessa poked Gladys playfully. "Aren't you coming to the dance?"

Gladys held up a finger. "Almost done."

With a loud sigh, Vanessa sank onto her lower bunk and pulled off her muddy boots and sodden black hose.

"Tough day?" Gladys still sounded distracted.

"More like a roller coaster."

"I don't know how you nursemaids do it. I'd strip a million beds before I'd wipe runny noses all day long."

Vanessa thought of Walter's arms around her neck that afternoon, and the grassy smell of Edna's hair when she kissed her goodnight. "You can keep your duster and wash bucket. I'll stick to my grimy kids." Her reply came out snippier than she'd meant. Gladys was a good egg, and she'd hate to offend her. She stood and jerked her chin at the pages in her bunkmate's hands. "Sweet nothings from your beau?"

Gladys rolled onto her side, propped her head up with one hand and waved the letter's thin sheets. "Why does he bother to write? He says so little! 'Received your letter of May sixth, keeping busy, glad you're well, write soon, somewhere in France.'"

"I'd guess he doesn't want the Army censors reading all his mushy love poems."

"Ha! The day Chester writes a love poem is the day I sprout a tail." Gladys sat up, tucked the letter back in its envelope and swung her legs over the side of the bunk. "I'm not sure I believe you don't have a beau."

Vanessa shook her head. "I really don't." Never even had a crush before. In all her years in the Girls Home and in servant quarters, she hadn't had much exposure to young men. Especially the handsome, educated kind that populated Twin Birch House as both guests and summer staff. And never anyone like Ned Cooper . . . or Avery Nolen, for that matter. She did a mock pirouette in her bare feet along the deep green floorboards. "But the season is young!"

Several nearby girls broke from preparing for the dance to clap in friendly agreement.

"Bachelors beware." Clara, a fine-boned blonde in the next bunk over, shook out a sheer party dress with a floral-print skirt. "Nursemaid on the prowl."

Vanessa's eyes narrowed. College girls like Clara mainly helped out at the front desk or were waitresses at the hotel's less formal dining services to help pay their way through some fancy school like Vassar, Mt. Holyoke, or Smith. Others were simply earning pin money while enjoying the resort for the summer. None needed their jobs like she and many of the other girls did, to keep a roof over their heads and food in their bellies.

"And what's wrong with that?" retorted a curly-headed girl as she unfastened her black maid's uniform at the waist. "You can't deny that many a wedding has followed a season at Twin Birch House."

The girl's encouragement buoyed Vanessa's mood. She understood that a relationship with Ned was unlikely and could be . . . misconstrued. But it didn't stop her from fantasizing about spending the evening on the dance floor in his embrace. Nothing improper about that.

Arms aloft, she waltzed up and down the aisle between the rows of wooden bunks. She could almost feel the light pressure of Ned's hand on her waist and see the lopsided curve of his lips as he gazed down at her. "Dances on the beach, picnics by the lake, live music. It's a dream come true. Anything can happen here!"

"Unless your dreams include Ned Cooper," drawled Clara.

Vanessa's arms drifted down to her sides. Like most everyone else, she was aware the Cooper clan owned a whole bunch of companies and resided in Boston society's top tier. But since meeting him in person, she'd discovered Ned was one of the hotel regulars, his family one of the many elites from Boston, New York, and Philadelphia who summered in New Hampshire's White Mountains every year. Yet he had picked her for his special notice. Had waltzed with her three times at the prior week's dance. More than with any other girl. Surely that meant something.

"I'll dream as I please." She turned and strode toward her bunk, pulling the pins from her uniform cap.

"Unless the fairies intervene," said Clara, "best remember Ned Cooper's kind don't consort with the help."

"Not for very long, anyway," added Clara's equally snooty bunkmate, earning snickers from a few other girls behind Vanessa's back.

"Ignore them." Gladys scowled as she wiggled herself into an unflattering sleeveless beige dress.

Vanessa untied the back of her apron and jerked the strap over her head. Even if Clara and the others were right, they had no business suggesting she wasn't their equal for no reason but a childhood beyond her control. She pictured Edna and Walter waving their little flags in the parade. They were in America, weren't they?

Gathering her dignity, she turned to face Clara. "I'm touched by your concern." Her imitation of Mrs. Wainwright's elegant posture and silky intonation was pretty good. "But who says the fairies won't intervene? For all you know, by the end of the summer, I just might not be just 'the help' anymore."

Clara's eyebrow arched. "Your employers might be interested to hear about those ambitions, Nursemaid."

Vanessa's jaw tightened as she balled her apron and threw it on her bunk. "The Wainwrights are quality people who would only wish me the best, I'm quite sure."

She turned her back on Clara to find Gladys biting her lip, her eyebrows lifted high. Oh, no. Had she gone too far yet again? Had she let what the warden at the Home called her "excessive exuberance" distract her from what really mattered—protecting the children and keeping her job?

She tossed her head and pulled her own dress off its hook at the end of the bunk. "Give me a minute to get ready, Gladys." She raised her voice, determined that Clara could hear. "Then let's go have some fun."

Chapter Five

Candlelight and fireflies flickered in the dusk as Vanessa hastened across the hotel grounds with Gladys, her cheeks aflame from her quarrel with Clara. Music wafted from the ballroom—the heavenly sound of Knecht's Dance Orchestra, brought in all the way from New York City. She needed to recover her composure before showing up at the staff dance down at the beach. "Let's listen a moment." She tugged Gladys from the gravel path onto the grass and into a run. Laughing, they came to a halt in a circle of light surrounding the hotel's glittering ballroom.

Inside, stylish guests swirled on the dance floor or clustered at the bar, their laughter as light and bubbly as their champagne. Waiters and bartenders in white uniforms plied their trades with as much elegance and grace as the dancers. Her eye was drawn to a large oil painting on the central wall. A radiant young couple smiled from the colorful canvas, Twin Birch House in the background. The woman was a striking redhead in wide hoop skirts. The man was handsome, with smiling eyes, his arm protectively around the woman's waist. Vanessa pointed. "Who are they?"

Gladys looked toward the portrait. "Paul and Riona LaFontaine. The hotel's original owners."

"The painting looks like it's from before the Civil War." She turned to Gladys. "I didn't realize the hotel was that old."

"Positively ancient. Built in 1852. My great-grandmother worked here when it first opened. Oh, look!" Gladys pointed through the open French doors to a beauty in her late twenties waltzing with her husband, a diamond tiara sparkling in her mahogany hair. "That's Sarah Gardner."

Vanessa recognized Ned Cooper's elegant sister from *The Boston Globe*'s society pages.

Gladys elbowed her in the ribs. "As pretty as her brother."

"How can you say that?" She batted Gladys's arm with a grin. "Ned is much prettier."

Gladys's voice hushed with genuine admiration. "And don't your employers look fine tonight?"

The Wainwrights danced close together, dozens of wall sconces burnishing the couple with their golden glow. No surprise Vanessa's adorable charges were so beautiful coming from such a handsome pair . . . their mother's strawberry blonde hair exquisitely offset by her silky green dress; their father's trim form on display in perfectly cut formal wear. They were so romantic. So in love.

A lump formed in Vanessa's throat. A perfect family. Her nails dug into her palm. Regardless what Clara said, she had no intention of giving up her dreams of having her own perfect family one day.

"Come on." She grabbed Gladys's hand and they half skipped, half ran down the lawn to their own party at the grand hotel's private beach. All guests were welcome at the hotel's formal ball, but, luckily for her, young single ones—like Ned—usually preferred the more casual lakeside mixers.

The band of student musicians kicked off the dancing with a Grand March and Circle. Even though the amateurs couldn't compete with the talent at the hotel proper, their tune set Vanessa bouncing on her toes. She didn't even mind being jostled as couples rushed to the wooden dance floor pressed into the sand.

Clara gave Vanessa an icy look as she passed by with several of her college girl pals. After a tentative survey of the rich girls' outfits, Vanessa relaxed about her own. The dress was top shelf. Expensive beading on the transparent bodice and sleeves, satin trim along the plunging neckline. Never mind the piece was a cast-off from her prior employer, marred by a nearly invisible wine stain near the hem. And her hairstyle came right from the pages of Mrs. Wainwright's latest issue of *Vogue*. The thin bandeau around her forehead was the height of fashion.

Freed of her nursemaid uniform's heavy black dress and long apron, it was possible she might be mistaken for a girl from a good family . . . or even a hotel guest. At least that's what she hoped.

Her eyes swept over the crowd again. "Do you see Ned?"

Gladys shook her head. "Nope."

Vanessa twisted the ring on her right hand. It was her only inheritance . . . and proof she'd once been more than a poor orphan. "Let's keep looking."

She and Gladys wove through the circle of candles set in paper sacks weighted with sand, careful to keep their calf-skimming hems from the flames. The air was scented with Bay Rum wafting from the smattering of young men's freshly shaven cheeks. The sparse collection of males included a blend of the locals and college men on staff, and a handful of high society hotel guests. It was a social mix unheard of in Boston, but Gladys had assured her it was common at all the White Mountain grand hotels. Many of the summer employees and young guests went to college together, so it was natural for them to mix while on vacation.

"Don't be such a stiff, Karl."

Vanessa clutched Gladys's arm and froze at the sound of Ned's voice.

"You own the place, don't you?"

Ned's voice simply oozed privilege and confidence. Vanessa and Gladys stood directly behind him and his particularly well-dressed companions.

"That would be my father, Ned," Karl responded. "And he wouldn't appreciate me booking a Harlem jazz band any more than most of our guests would."

Keeping hold of Gladys, she inched forward to get a better view of Karl Fiske, the heir to Twin Birch House. She'd heard he was running the hotel alone that season, without his father. Tall and thin, he wore his blond hair parted on the side. His tight-lipped expression matched his tone of voice.

Ned waved his hand to include the other young men. "We're all listening to jazz in the city. How do you know the other guests wouldn't like it, too?"

"I *know* they wouldn't, Ned." Karl looked down and kicked at the sand. "And you do, too."

From her new vantage, Vanessa had a clear view of Ned's square-jawed profile. Willing him to look in her direction, she made sure it wouldn't appear she was staring, but kept him in her peripheral vision. If he turned to her, she'd know she hadn't imagined the bond between them.

At that moment, as if by magic, Ned turned his head directly toward her and smiled brightly. She threw her own bright smile back at him, then lifted her chin as she turned away. She'd observed the art of flirting while watching plain-looking housemaids and kitchen girls. The best of them used wiles alone to snare chauffeurs and deliverymen. Ned Cooper was no hireling and she'd had little practice, but she still hoped her efforts would be equally successful.

"I've got to get back," Karl said somewhere behind her.

A moment later, a hand touched her elbow. Her breath caught. She composed her smile, her heartbeat racing in delicious anticipation.

"Excuse me." It was only Karl. He squeezed past her without a glance and continued through the crowd.

Maintaining her smile, she relaxed her grip on Gladys's arm. She mustn't lose her nerve. If it were meant to be, Ned would make his move, sooner or later.

Then she spotted Avery dancing with Irene Seward, the groundskeeper's daughter. When she'd met him earlier that afternoon, he hadn't mentioned he was coming. But then, why would he? Perhaps he and Irene were sweethearts. They'd make a good match. Both locals, both kind and rather . . . dignified.

Her flicker of disappointment made no sense. Ignoring it, she raised her arm and waved, then turned to Gladys. "Do you know Avery Nolen?"

"Avery's here?" Gladys craned her neck. "He doesn't usually come to dances."

"Let's go say hello." Vanessa wrapped her arm around her friend's waist and headed over, glad to have Ned see she had more to do than wait on him.

It pleased her more than she expected to be greeted by warm smiles from both Irene and Avery. "I thought I'd make some introductions," she said, "but it seems you two know each other already."

"So terribly long we're in danger of boring one another." Irene laid the side of her head against Avery's shoulder. "Right, Avery?"

"Too right. I was just stifling a yawn." He tugged at his shirt cuff with a shy smile. "Happy to see you've returned this season, Gladys . . . and good to see you again, Miss Perkins."

Slightly magnified by his wire-framed spectacles, Avery's brown eyes were as warm as Vanessa remembered in the woods. While Irene and Gladys hugged, Vanessa wagged her finger at her new acquaintance. "I agreed to call you Avery, but you're not holding up your end of the bargain."

"Yes, of course. My apologies . . . Vanessa."

The angles of his face were sharper and his movements stiffer than they'd appeared in the woods. Though shy and artistic, he seemed grounded. Solid, like the mountains around them.

Irene's gaze bounced from Avery to Vanessa and back again. With wavy brown hair and womanly curves, Irene seemed older than nineteen. And even though they were the same age, in their few encounters Vanessa had felt young and silly in comparison.

"You should dance with Vanessa." Irene withdrew her arm from Avery's. "Not fair of me to monopolize one of the few unattached men."

"It would be my pleasure." He turned to Vanessa and gave a slight bow.

Unattached? Vanessa suddenly had mixed feelings about dancing with him. What if Ned saw them and assumed they were together? She didn't want the dashing Mr. Cooper to lose interest. On the other hand, the most successful flirts she knew seemed convinced a little competition worked magic for their appeal . . .

The orchestra launched into "Lady of the Lake." "Come on." Irene linked arms with Gladys. "I heard your Chester is overseas, too."

"Oh, no." Gladys's eyes rounded. "Was Roy drafted?"

Irene nodded. "I miss him like crazy."

Their voices faded as they headed toward the refreshment table swapping tales of their distant beaus in uniform. Avery held out his hand. He had a quiet charm and didn't make Vanessa feel all jittery and excited like Ned did. She followed him onto the dance floor, where the tune was upbeat. He led surprisingly well. She hadn't figured him for a dancer, given his reserve.

About halfway through the song, her pleasure dancing with Avery became vaguely uncomfortable. Was she the kind of girl whose heart could so easily slide from one man to the next? She made a casual sweep of the crowd . . . and spotted Ned.

When their eyes met, he grinned, making her insides feel like chocolate syrup sliding down a scoop of ice cream. Despite the distance between them, the devastating dimple on the left side of his mouth and his long lashes were clearly visible in the mixture of candle and moonlight.

What beautiful children he'd father.

Suddenly feeling guilty for searching out Ned while in Avery's arms, Vanessa focused her smile back on her dance partner. Though she didn't want to lead him on, she certainly didn't want to be disrespectful. It was all so confusing. Only a week ago, she'd been so disinterested in boys that becoming a nun had actually crossed her mind. And here she was, all atwitter for one young man and strangely intrigued by another. Quite disorienting, to say the least.

Avery returned her smile, his brow slightly furrowed, before lowering his eyes to the region of her knees. His smile was fleeting. Like when she'd first seen it in the woods. But it still made her miss a step. Something she rarely did since an employer's daughter taught her to waltz at the age of fifteen. He gripped her hand tighter as she recovered, but otherwise, seemed to take no notice of her mistake.

When the song was over, the musicians stood and stretched, putting their instruments aside.

"Thank you for the dance, Miss . . . I mean, Vanessa."

"You are more than welcome, Avery. You're a magnificent dancer."

"It's you who's magnificent . . . dancing . . ." He coughed and pushed his glasses up his nose. "Would you . . . care for a refreshment?"

She took his hand. "That sounds lovely."

Some young men who worked in the boathouse cranked up a Victrola as she and Avery wound their way back to Irene and Gladys. Moments later, they were treated to Peter Dawson crooning "A Bachelor Gay." The very tune she'd been humming to herself all week while thinking of Ned. By the time she and Avery rejoined the others and he'd gone to get them drinks, the final lyrics hung in the air: ". . . and he loves her as he's never loved before."

She accepted a glass of cool punch from Avery and took a sip, her eyes flitting over the crowd. And there Ned was, sparkling eyes fixed right on her. He slicked a stray lock of dark hair along the crown of his head and winked.

Anticipation fizzed in her belly like she was on a roller coaster at Norumbega Park, click-clacking slowly toward the ride's summit. Happiness mixed with fear, excitement mingled with doubt. She wasn't fully prepared for whatever came next, but was determined to see where the path led, regardless of what Clara or anyone else thought.

With icy fingers, she lowered her glass to the table. Taking a steady breath, she looked down and ran her thumb over the deep red gem on her finger for luck, and raised her eyes back to Ned . . . just as a cloud of blonde hair appeared at his shoulder.

Blood rushed to Vanessa's face as Ned turned and took the stylish young woman in his arms. Within moments, he was gliding across the dance floor to the strains of "Poor Butterfly" . . . with Clara.

Chapter Six

Vanessa spun around, turning her back on the dance floor and put her hand to her throat, pretending to cough. Let Ned dance with Clara. She'd give the girl no satisfaction by appearing to care.

"Are you alright?" Irene rubbed Vanessa's shoulder.

Surprised by the maternal gesture, Vanessa nodded, hoping her false smile didn't come off as a grimace. As she picked her glass back up and took a sip, Clara's bunkmate's taunt echoed in her ears. *"Ned Cooper's kind don't consort with the help."* It had been ridiculous to pin any hopes on a man like that.

"Are you enjoying your stay at Twin Birch House?" Avery's question startled her.

"Please forgive me." She lowered her glass with a sigh. "Despite years of scolding, it seems I'll never outgrow daydreaming."

"Nothing to forgive." The corner of his mouth twitched upward. "I would never have known your mind was off adventuring had you not confessed."

"You're too kind. It's my questionable tendency to 'adventure' that got me lost out in the woods today. You truly rescued us this afternoon."

He ducked his head. "No need to exaggerate."

Of course he couldn't appreciate how foreign and confusing the forest had been. Not to mention the high, tinkling sounds and odd shimmers of light that Walter called "faiwheeze" in his adorable lisp. Growing up, the closest she'd ever come to nature was the trampled grass of the Boston Common and the neat rows of trees lining its pathways. The city's threats she understood . . . and more importantly, knew how to avoid.

"No need to be modest," she teased. "I bet you've played knight in shining armor to plenty of dizzy nursemaids."

A slow flush rose from his neck to his face. "You're definitely the first."

Moments earlier she'd virtually ignored him, swept up in silly thoughts of Ned Cooper, and now she was simpering like a desperate flirt? Talk about a dizzy nursemaid!

"I . . . I just wanted to thank you properly." Her voice deepened as the true terror she'd experienced when Walter and Edna disappeared washed through her again.

"Of course." His tone matched the seriousness of hers. "And you're welcome."

"And in answer to your question . . ." She turned her eyes up the lawn toward the hotel. "Yes, I'm enjoying my stay at Twin Birch House."

Moonlight bathed the hotel's multiple chimneys and cupola-topped tower. A balcony swept around most of the second floor, while peaked roofs crowned sections containing the third and fourth floors. On the ground floor, a wide porch lined with rocking chairs wrapped around the front three sides, giving guests a breathtaking view of Lake Lakona. She imagined the guest cottages and outbuildings behind the main structure like a village, all supported by the hotel's dedicated farm, which in the daytime was visible in the distance. "It's like a storybook palace."

"Postcard perfect," he agreed. "I forget whenever I've been away for a while."

"All that's missing is a moat."

"And a dungeon."

His deadpan delivery made her laugh, rekindling her hopes for a wonderful evening.

The final bars of "Poor Butterfly" sounded from the phonograph and Irene took the punch glasses from Gladys and Avery's hands. "Now it's Gladys's turn."

Gladys's thick fingers flew to her face. "Oh, no. I couldn't."

"Nonsense." Irene pushed their friend toward the dance floor. "Every girl deserves to waltz with Avery at least once in her life. He dances like a dream."

"I do love this song . . ." Gladys blushed and allowed Avery to lead her away.

As they went, Vanessa pressed her fist to her chest. Avery had treated Gladys with the same formal respect he'd extended to her. Silly to think his gentlemanly behavior had anything to do with her.

Vanessa's head bent toward the grass as she made small semi-circles in the grass with the toe of her hand-me-down shoe. From two men to none, and all in the blink of an eye. Maybe they'd been right at the Home.

Orphans with dreams were on the express train to heartbreak.

<h1 style="text-align:center">Chapter Seven</h1>

Lachima flapped her wings gently on the corner of the boathouse roof, where she had an excellent view of the candlelit dance on the beach below. She was particularly enjoying the ups and downs of Vanessa's unfolding drama and congratulated herself for orchestrating it.

An emerald butterfly with veins of silver etched on his wings emerged from the shadows and landed next to her. "Lachima." The tone of her brother's greeting warned he was annoyed.

"Morniero."

Her brother contracted into a pinpoint of light, followed immediately by a modest flash as he expanded into his humanlike form, shimmering and transparent.

They could both transform more freely on summer evenings when their bursts of light were mistaken for the blinking of fireflies. Once in their human form, they were invisible to actual mortals . . . unless they chose to show themselves, of course.

Featherweight as he sat on the roof next to her, Morniero frowned and gestured to Vanessa down below looking stricken. "You promised Mother."

Preferring to be the same size when he challenged her, Lachima shifted into her own human form and tossed the mass of white hair floating around her head. "I haven't said a word to the girl."

He arranged his liquid silver cloak over his shoulder. "Yet you deliberately moved events along this afternoon, leading her up to the Wood."

"I'm free to perform my function as I see fit." She relaxed back on her elbows. "And helping with introductions is one of my only entertainments."

Morniero raised a brow. "Is this one a pet or victim?"

Lachima shrugged. "That would be up to her, I suppose."

He shook his head with tight lips, his dark green vest and black boots dappled by moonlight. "Just don't drive this one mad."

"Vanessa's always been imaginative. Even if I did choose to . . . present myself, she'd come to no harm, I'm quite sure."

Her brother's skeptical expression drove her to sit upright. "If you weren't able to visit them in their sleep, you'd be just as tempted to involve yourself as I am."

As the god of dreams, her brother saw aspects of the humankind Lachima longed to share. Though sometimes, there was a haunted look in his eyes that made her worry the mortals' nightmares were more harrowing than she could imagine.

"I'm sure you're right." Morniero took her hand with a sigh. "But Mother is, too. Interacting just brings trouble, for them and for us. We haven't gotten mixed up in half the complications we did when they believed in us." He swept his arm to include Lake Lakona, the expansive grounds of Twin Birch House, and the surrounding forest. "And out here, it's easy to avoid entanglement with them if we try."

Lachima pulled her hand away. "We're not meant to be apart from them. I know you agree."

"The humans made their choice." He crossed his arms. "And they're the ones suffering for turning their backs on us."

"But we're suffering, too." She examined her slender fingers. "Mother knows that."

"Which is why she allowed us to give this experiment of yours a try." He ran his palm over his white, slicked-back hair. "Living amongst the mortals, but not involving ourselves with them."

He was right, of course. But some days were harder than others.

"Just be happy we're still permitted free contact with children and the very old." He nudged her with a sly smile. "That's something at least."

Refusing to be jollied, she brushed at her simple, lavender-gray silk gown. "I suppose."

He leaned back on his hands and looked toward the Wood. "And Willow's lucky Mother hasn't found out she's hanging on to that Avery of hers."

Lachima whipped her head to face him, her eyes flashing. "Don't you dare tell her. It would break Willow's heart to lose him."

Keenly aware of the gentle wood nymph's tragic background, Lachima had always felt especially sorry for the tender-hearted nymph.

"No consultations with your little Vanessa, and it won't be me who alerts Mother to Willow's indiscretion with Avery." He extended his hand. "Agreed?"

Lachima scowled and shook her brother's hand. "Agreed."

As soon as they released hands, she resumed her butterfly form and flew toward the hotel ballroom. If Morniero insisted on being so bossy, she preferred to listen to that excellent orchestra from New York alone.

Chapter Eight

With a shake of her head, Vanessa raised her chin and surveyed the festivities. Staff girls dancing with each other, a wrestling match some of the younger boys started on the grass, and the gentle pulsing of fireflies hovering over a bench at the edge of the lawn. She'd never seen the miraculous creatures in the city, and half-believed they were actual fairy lights . . . until Edna caught one and showed her it was an insect.

If only she could share all this with Ruth.

She inhaled sharply as she was assaulted by intrusive memories of those first years in the Girls Home. The hunger. The cold and coughing. Her little sister dying in her arms, specks of blood on her ragged pinafore. Battling the memories away, she breathed carefully through her lightly parted teeth.

Up the lawn, glowing spots of orange signified guests smoking cigars on the long porch. Golden light poured past the porch roof from various windows on all three floors. No telling if she'd ever get back to a paradise like Twin Birch House again. She owed it to herself . . . and Ruth, to enjoy it while she could.

Patting her damp upper lip dry with her fingertips, she vowed not to waste another minute of the magical summer feeling sorry for herself. When the orchestra returned, she took the dance floor enthusiastically with both Irene and Gladys. Then she took a spin with each of Irene's younger brothers. Playful young men of few words, Nelson, Frank, and Denis were like a pack of bear cubs wearing clothes for the first time.

Between dancing with them and accepting every invitation from the young men on staff, she'd stopped thinking about Avery and had nearly gotten over Ned Cooper. Though it gave her no small pleasure that Ned never danced with Clara again.

"Last dance!" called the bandleader.

Avery headed in her direction, and she was grateful. Her previous partner had been more energetic than skilled. Dancing with Avery would end the delightful evening on an up note.

"Save the best for last?" Ned's breath was warm on the back of her ear, his scent a risqué blend of booze and wintergreen mint. His lips so close to her neck sent a shiver up her spine.

But Avery was drawing closer every second.

She cursed Ned for waiting so long, even as every fiber of her body reached for him. Buying time, she composed a perfectly demure smile, made a quarter turn and stepped back, leaving the two men facing each other. "I'm flattered to hear you describe me that way, Mr. Cooper."

Ned grinned. "Spunky. I like that." Up close, his eyes suggested a private party going on inside his head. Invitation only. He shifted his focus to Avery. "Hello there, Nolen. It's been a while."

Avery's smile was taut, his eyes dark. "Evening, Cooper."

Ned shook Avery's hand. "We'll have to catch up later. Miss Perkins and I are about to take the last dance."

"Perhaps my arrival interrupted your invitation." Avery's tone grew hard as granite. "I didn't actually hear one."

"Nor did I," Vanessa added saucily.

Ned's smile did nothing to soften the steel in his eyes as he and Avery locked glares. "Guess that leaves the choice up to you, Miss Perkins."

The rivals turned to face her. Her eyes widened and she gulped. Of course she was dying to dance with Ned . . . but hated the idea of Avery feeling passed over or slighted in any way. Yet dancing with Avery would be a disappointment, knowing she could have ended the evening in Ned's arms. "Now this is hardly fair!" She put her hands on her hips, pretending an indifference she didn't feel. "Forcing such an impossible choice."

"If we want to consider fairness . . ." Ned managed to appear simultaneously humble and confident. "I believe you did already dance with Nolen at least once." He drew out his last word with a charming grin.

She bit her lip as she addressed Avery, genuinely wishing she didn't have to choose. "That is true . . ."

Ned grinned. "Surely you wouldn't begrudge me my own opportunity, old friend?"

Avery clapped Ned's arm. "It's only fair." The flint in his expression diminished when he turned toward her. "Good night, Vanessa." He gave her a brief nod. "Very glad to have met you."

"I feel the same, Avery." She clasped his hand. "Thank you for . . . everything."

He nodded again and disappeared into the crowd.

Breathless over the sudden turn of events, she returned her gaze to Ned and took his extended hand. The desire in his eyes and warmth of his touch made her feel like Cinderella being selected by the Prince at the ball. Thank goodness the first strains of "The Missouri Waltz" relieved her of any need to speak. In moments, his arm was firmly around her back as they glided across the floor.

"I hope you didn't think I was neglecting you all evening." His tone fell in the hazy territory between sincere and mocking.

"Were you?" The urge to both combat him and surrender to him made for a delicious thrill. She lifted her chin. "I must have been too busy dancing to notice."

His laugh was deep and spontaneous. "My sister would approve. She, too, makes a point of keeping me in my place."

"I like her already." Vanessa's skin tingled with the shock of her audacity, speaking of Sarah Gardner as though they attended the same finishing school.

Ned didn't react at all. Like it was quite a natural thing for her to say. Flying through the sky in an aeroplane couldn't have been more exhilarating. They danced in silence a few moments, his eyes twinkling down at her. At the prior weekend's dance, he'd been flirtatious, but this time, his interest felt more specific. Like he was seeing her for the first time. He was nothing like she expected, and she wondered if he was thinking the same of her.

"Perkins." His head cocked. "You wouldn't happen to be a relative of Isabel Anderson's, would you? I'm quite sure she's a Perkins."

Isabel Anderson? The heiress?

Vanessa's tone remained playful, her eyes locked on his. "Anything's possible, Mr. Cooper."

Chapter Nine

The next morning, Avery crisscrossed the tip of his paintbrush on the yellow cube in his watercolor set, then swirled it into the smudge of blue on his pallette. He was in a hurry to capture the exquisite sapphire hue of the butterfly's wings before it flew away like it had the day before, when Walter and Edna Wainwright had appeared so unexpectedly.

In all his years visiting the "Enchanted Wood," as he called it, he'd never seen anything like the brilliant creature. It now perched on a cattail by the nearby lily pond but had flown into the glen through the stone passageway . . . from the outside.

Yet it was so big and bright, it strained credibility that it came from the regular world. Certainly not a species he'd ever observed in the mountainous habitat surrounding the Wood.

He frowned, then added a bit of black to his mixture on the pallet in order to deepen the blue.

He'd nearly dropped his brush when the children called his name yesterday. But at the sight of their ecstatic faces, his frustration had dissolved into happy memories of when he and his sister shared this magical place, where all the colors were supersaturated, and everything sparkled as if sprinkled with fairy dust.

"Do you think the Wainwright children saw you yesterday?" He tilted his head toward the wood nymph swaying over the ornately carved stone bench he sat on to paint.

Willow's smooth skin was decorated with whorls of grain, like finely polished furniture. Leafy fronds sprang from the top of her head, arching up and curving over to drape her shoulders, the ends swaying around her waist. "No." Her voice was enriched by sap and suppressed laughter. "They only see the fairies."

He chuckled. "Of course. Walter's 'faiwheeze.'" The little boy's face was so open when he explained how he and his sister were led through the hidden stone portal, Walter clearly assumed Avery shared his familiarity with the mythical creatures. Unfortunately, though tales of their sighting had been passed around Twin Birch House and Adamsville his whole life, Avery had never had the pleasure of seeing one, even in the Enchanted Wood.

"Judging by their nursemaid's reaction when I returned her missing charges," he added, "I'd say she wasn't included in the fairies' invitation."

"Was she startled to see you exit the passage?" Willow's leafy fingers twisted, her delicate brow crinkled.

"Thankfully, her back was turned when we came out."

"Oh, that's good."

It certainly was. Otherwise, poor Vanessa would have thought they'd materialized out of thin air. His fist clenched around the handle of his brush. Mistake to let his thoughts wander to Vanessa Perkins—even though her eyes were the exact color of the butterfly whose image he was attempting to capture. Enormous blue eyes that had seemed so . . . inviting. But later gazed up at Ned Cooper like the guy was a matinee idol and war hero all rolled into one.

Avery clenched his jaw in an effort to drive away the image. He'd gotten the distinct impression Vanessa returned at least some of his interest, first in the woods when they met, and later at the hotel, when they'd chatted with Mrs. Wainwright on the lawn. And last night, when they'd danced, she'd seemed a little self-conscious. Had even made a little misstep, like she was as nervous as he was. But less than two hours later, she fell into Cooper's arms like she belonged there. The girl was a complete riddle.

Gritting his teeth, he forced his attention back to the watercolor propped on his portable easel. He'd only gone to the stupid staff dance to make sure Irene wasn't too lonely, what with Roy being overseas and all. As he applied the newly mixed paint he'd carefully blended, the butterfly rose from the cattail and flew into the passageway.

He pushed his glasses up his nose and checked his wristwatch. Eleven already. Just as well his subject ended their session. His family would be returning from church soon and he'd promised to join them for dinner.

An hour later, Avery strode up the geranium-lined walkway to his house, his satchel bumping against his thigh. Despite his regular returns for the Christmas and summer holidays, the two-story saltbox seemed smaller than when he left for college.

"Till the Clouds Roll By" blared from inside. Hattie must have come home from church alone. Their parents always lingered to socialize.

After pressing the front door closed as silently as possible, he paused in the entryway. His sister and her best friend, Paulina, romped around the doily-draped sofa in the living room, singing along to a wildly popular duet blasting from the phonograph next to the fireplace. He grinned at Hattie looking like a schoolgirl in a wide-collared blouse that hung low over her knee-length skirt while singing along off-key to Ann Wheaton's part. Paulina hammed up James Harrod's lyrics in a more sophisticated calf-length dress.

Their shoes were off, and though they were both sixteen, Paulina wore her dark hair in a loose coil at her neck, while his sister still fastened a big bow behind her head, a single, deep auburn braid swinging down her back.

No wonder Vanessa seemed so familiar. Her reddish-brown hair and spritely energy were so much like his sister's. From a distance, he had even taken the nursemaid for just a girl. But when he neared, she looked to be at least nineteen or twenty. And . . . breathtaking. Tendrils of hair falling from her bun gave her a vulnerable quality. The imperfections of her face—eyes set a bit too wide, nose a bit too long—only made her seem more accessible . . . and appealing . . . to both him and Ned Cooper.

What happened to change girls from being normal and relatively easy to understand when they were young, to being such frustrating mysteries as they grew older?

Hoping not to embarrass the girls, Avery stepped lightly across the wood floor. On the stairs, his footsteps were muffled by the worn oriental runner padding the treads.

"Avery! You're home!"

So much for his noble effort. He rested his hand on the newel post as Hattie ran toward him, her cheeks flushed pink from her musical exertions. Her eyes were brown, like the rest of the family, and her face was much rounder than Vanessa's.

"Just got back." He waved toward the living room. "Hi."

Paulina flushed crimson as she waved and mumbled some sort of greeting. Evidently not over the crush she'd developed on him when he was in high school, which he'd always pretended not to notice. Too bad he didn't have the same effect on Miss Perkins.

Hattie fluttered her fingers against the back of his hand. "Didn't you see your letter? It's still on the kitchen table."

"From Bess?" He hadn't seen his twin since Christmas, but it felt like longer.

She shook her head. "From Dartmouth. I'll go get it."

He stepped back down the stairs as she dashed into the kitchen. Who'd be writing him from school? He already had his diploma, so there was nothing he was waiting for them to send.

Letter in hand, Hattie beamed as she slid across the polished wood floor in her black hose. The front door creaked open behind him.

"Harriet." His father's voice trembled with irritation.

Hattie's eyes widened as her feet skidded to a stop inches from Avery's boots.

"We've told you a thousand times." Their mother's stern tone was undermined by her twinkling eyes.

"I know." Hattie thrust the letter into Avery's hand and scurried to the living room. "I'm sorry." She lifted the needle off the disc, abruptly silencing the music, while he jammed the letter in his pocket and crossed the foyer.

"It was my fault." He kissed his mother's plump cheek. "I asked her to turn it up."

A snort escaped from somewhere behind his father's thick brown mustache flecked with gray.

"I did," he protested, wishing he could lie as convincingly as Bess.

"That's my Avery, always to the rescue." His mother removed her light coat and pulled the felted cloche from her head. "But we're not feebleminded yet." She hung her things on the coat rack just inside the door and waved him toward the dining room. "Now set the table for dinner. I've got ham in the oven."

The letter would have to wait.

Chapter Ten

Vanessa took a deep breath on her way to the Wainwrights' quarters. The air smelled of pine. Fresh and light. Matching her mood. She hummed as she glided down the path, her footsteps falling into the one-two-three tempo of a waltz. With a little imagination, she could still conjure the smell of Ned's cologne when he'd leaned over and whispered in her ear, "I'll find you tomorrow, after church." Remembering the heady scent of his breath and the heat of his cheek against hers propelled her effortlessly forward.

A-one-two-three.

Though it was her day off, she had volunteered to take Walter and Edna to the pony rides when the family got back from the village church. She already regretted the offer, too distracted by hopes of encountering Ned again to be decent company.

A-one-two-three.

But she'd never let the children down. They were such darlings.

"Miss Perkins, a word?" Mrs. Juneau swept up the path from the kitchens, her brass key ring jangling at her side.

"Yes, ma'am." She chewed on her thumbnail and waited on the walkway that branched between the hotel's main structure and collection of the outbuildings clustered behind it. Though not her boss, the Head of Housekeeping was effectively in charge of the girls working for private families at Twin Birch House whenever they were off duty.

"We haven't been properly introduced." The observation sounded like an accusation.

Vanessa shook Mrs. Juneau's hand. "There were so many of us at the orientation meeting . . ."

Sunlight pierced the web of tree limbs overhead, painting craggy shadows across Mrs. Juneau's face as she withdrew her hand. "You're a Home girl, aren't you?"

"Yes . . ."

The woman's expression firmed. "Then you should know, I make it my business to look out for my sisters."

Blinking a few times, she frowned. "You're from the Home?"

"Left on the doorstep in the proverbial basket, but that was many years ago."

She struggled to imagine the formidable figure before her as a little girl, shivering in one of the thin smocks the Boston Girls Home considered adequate clothing for orphans. Mrs. Juneau patted her temples, where gray spread into her otherwise light brown hair. "Rumor has it you've caught Ned Cooper's eye."

Vanessa tilted her head back and smiled up at the azure sky. How gratifying to learn his attentions were newsworthy beyond the gossips in the women's dorm. Something unusual existed between them. Strangers could see it. She lowered her chin and clasped her hands together in an effort to appear nonchalant. "Is that so?"

"You must realize the Coopers are a serious family. To people like them, marriages are more business merger than fairy tale."

"I'm well aware of gentlemen who are no gentlemen, if that's what you're implying." Her nails dug into the knuckles of her intertwined fingers as she tried to keep her memories at bay.

Mrs. Juneau's tone softened. "An employer?"

She nodded, her mood blackening. "The oldest son in my last position."

"He didn't . . ."

"No. I was lucky." Vanessa closed her eyes, reliving those horrible moments on the backstairs. The wooden step digging into her spine, his hand squeezing her breast so hard it brought tears to her eyes. She'd never forget the sickly sweetness of after-supper port on his breath as he pressed his mouth against hers, muffling her screams. Only his poor choice of location prevented him from completing his mission. The upstairs maid came upon them, a tray with hot milk for the lady of the house in her hands.

"I left before he got another chance. Set about finding myself a new position right away." Her voice trembled as she strove to fold the memory back up and bury it again.

"And the Wainwrights took you on."

"After a month as a hideaway back at the Home." It hardly seemed possible that only a few weeks earlier she'd been sleeping on the kitchen floor at the Girls Home, her only sanctuary after fleeing her prior employer's mansion. Doing pre-dawn food prep to bribe the cook into letting her stay. Scrambling to find a new post before Boston society abandoned the city for the summer.

Mrs. Juneau nodded, grim satisfaction etched on her face. "So you know how to wheedle favors . . . and make do."

Vanessa's cheeks warmed to hear her act of survival described in such cold terms. "I guess you could say that."

With hands folded, her new "sister" peered over her glasses. "Just keep one foot on the ground while you reach for the stars."

Vanessa lowered her gaze. "And remember that summer promises tend to shrivel with the autumn leaves." She spoke in a singsong voice while sweeping an arc in the gravel path with the toe of her boot. When she looked back up, Mrs. Juneau's lips were trembling in an apparent effort to suppress a smile. "I may not have much experience," Vanessa continued with a sigh, "but Boston libraries stock plenty of novels."

Narrowing her eyes, Mrs. Juneau recovered her firm demeanor. "Perhaps you don't need my little lecture, Miss Perkins, but we must protect the good name of the Home, now mustn't we?"

"Because the Home protected us so well, after all." Vanessa made no effort to disguise her bitterness. She had an ideal position with the nicest family she could ever hope for. Yet the terror of slipping back into the conditions she endured at the Home still plagued her.

Mrs. Juneau pursed her lips. "Whatever troubling recollections you may have, there are worse fates to befall a girl with no home and no family."

Her eyes dropped again. "I know."

Wasn't it the lingering fear of those very fates that worried her still? Ending up like the sunken-eyed girls back in the city, selling themselves in the shadowy alleyways of the wharf?

It was ironic the Home had been her only refuge after her recent ordeal. The debt of gratitude she owed the place chafed alongside her well-tended resentment.

"And crude sarcasm's not the style of Ned Cooper's set," said Mrs. Juneau. "Surely you've noticed their barbs come sheathed in velvet."

Vanessa's head snapped up and hope swelled in her voice. "I'll keep that in mind."

Mrs. Juneau scowled. "It's not meant as encouragement, child. I'm serious about protecting the good reputation of the Home. It's the only advantage most of those poor girls will ever have. Now on your way."

"Yes, ma'am." She turned back toward the front lawn. How many times had she been told to get her head out of the clouds? To stop believing wishes could come true? To remember she was a worthless orphan lucky to even have a job?

Vanessa added the waltz tempo back into her footsteps. At least she sounded better educated than the typical ward of the Boston Girls Home. In the brief time they'd had together, her schoolteacher mother had insisted she speak proper English. Maybe it was time she stopped listening to those voices.

A-one-two-three.

It's not like she'd be the first penniless girl to ever marry a charming, wealthy man and raise a family of her own in comfort and security.

A-one-two-three. A-one-two-three.

Why not her?

Chapter Eleven

After dinner, Avery sank onto the edge of his single bed, which was still draped with the plaid spread from his childhood. He reached for the letter opener on his desk and slit the envelope from Dartmouth open.

The letter was from his college advisor, the botany department chair. Remaining concerned for Avery's future, his mentor had sent a pamphlet from the Forest Service with a list of positions opening for trained botanists in the newly formed White Mountain National Forest—and an application.

Avery's grin widened as he read and reread the material. The new national forest practically surrounded Adamsville. An opportunity to work in his field, and so close to home? It was fantastic. Almost too good to be true.

He moved to his desk, yanked the drawer open and pulled out a pen and bottle of ink. Smoothing the application against the desktop, he prepared to write.

Then he pictured his father's face and his hand stilled.

He leaned back and stared at the wall. So many of his watercolors were secured there with thumbtacks, he could barely see the striped pattern of the navy and cream wallpaper. Some works were new, others so old their edges curled.

Since he'd been a boy, it was understood he'd take over his father's medical practice one day. Majoring in botany had been a pleasurable way to earn a science degree, but now it was time for his real training in med school to begin. The idea he'd follow in his father's footsteps was so firmly fixed in both their minds it wasn't until recently that he'd admitted the truth to himself. He didn't want to be a doctor. His unexpected admission to Harvard Medical School had delighted his father . . . and made leaving the path to medicine even more difficult.

He ran his fingers over the application. If he was going to break his father's heart, it wasn't going to be on a whim. With a heavy sigh, he re-capped the fountain pen and returned it to the drawer, along with Forest Service materials. He owed it to his father to at least give medicine a try.

The chair screeched against the floor as he pushed it back and crossed to the window. After lifting the sash, he leaned out and drew a soothing breath of summer air. Times like this made him miss Bess the most. She always knew when to make a joke or tease him out of a sour mood.

The prior day's encounter with the Wainwright children made him especially nostalgic for his and Bess's time together in the Enchanted Wood. Back when they were small. Before she lost her ability to see the stone passage . . . or even keep hold of his hand to follow him through the tunnel.

The smell of freshly mown grass wafted from the neighbor's house, reminding him of his own neglected chore. His gaze moved to the lake. Dinghies darted about its choppy surface, their sails bright white against the green of the forest behind them. Puffy white clouds floated against a deep blue sky that matched the color of Vanessa's eyes.

He pulled back inside and slammed the window down.

Enough with Vanessa Perkins's eyes.

Chapter Twelve

I t'th my turn, it'th my turn!" Walter thrust his arms over his head toward the potbellied stable hand.

"Right you are, young sir."

Vanessa smothered her grin as the weathered old man lifted the tot onto a tranquil pony and led him away. Raising her hand to her brow to block the sun, she waved at Edna, who sat atop a sable pony on the other side of the corral. With identical blond hair, freckled cheeks, and stormy blue eyes, the Wainwright children could easily be mistaken for twins.

After lowering her hand, Vanessa ran a finger over the spot on the back of her hand, the one Ned's soft lips had kissed when the musicians played their last note.

"Well, hello, Miss Perkins."

She spun around with a gasp. Ned's outfit was impeccable. A straw boater at a jaunty angle atop the long hair he wore slicked back, sides cropped short. His linen suit was freshly pressed, his tan suede shoes perfect for a day of summer leisure. Less expected were the two children holding his hands. The boy appeared to be about seven, the girl a bit older. Both were dressed in spotless whites, their expressions vaguely bored.

"Pleasure to see you again, Mr. Cooper." She struggled to appear friendly, but not overeager. "And who might these angels be?"

"We'll forgive the confusion since you've never met them." Ned's arch delivery left no doubt he was teasing. "These little *devils* are my niece, Cecile, and my nephew, Albert."

The little girl rolled her eyes. "Uncle Ned!"

He dropped her hand and patted her head. "Oh, don't pout, my sweet. Devils are far more fun than angels."

Cecile scowled up at him as she straightened the giant blue bow fastened at the back of her hair.

Vanessa extended her hand, pleased to be off duty and not wearing her uniform. Hoping for just this encounter, she'd worn her favorite white blouse with a pleated front and a flattering, high-waisted forest green skirt. "Pleasure to meet you both. I'm Miss Perkins."

Well-bred, each child shook her hand, but they scarcely glanced at her as they mumbled their perfunctory replies. Albert frowned at the corral. "I want to ride a horse, not a stupid pony."

Ned summoned a stable boy holding some ponies' reins. "Uncle Ned's not going to take the blame if you fall off a horse and break your neck." He clasped Albert's shoulders from behind and gave them a squeeze. "Today you'll ride a pony."

Cecile stood on tiptoe and waved to another girl across the corral. "There's Rose!"

"See, Albert." Ned winked at Vanessa. "Everyone who's anyone is riding ponies today."

The boy crossed his arms, but quickly unfolded them when it was his turn to be helped into the saddle of a dappled gray mount.

"Sweet of you to be looking after them." Vanessa kept her eyes on the children as they were led away.

Leaning close, Ned whispered conspiratorially, "I saw you heading over here with your charges and improvised. Their crabby old nursemaid was happy to let me take them."

With his features fully illuminated, he was even more handsome than he appeared in the moonlight. His nose was strong and straight, his smooth skin lightly tanned, and his aquamarine eyes sparkled in the sunlight. Judging by his scent, he even used the same expensive aftershave as Mr. Wainwright and a number of the other gentlemen guests. He couldn't be more perfect.

"Well, aren't you quick on your feet?" She glided toward a nearby bench as she imagined "Mrs. Ned Cooper" might do, pretending she and her magnificent husband were watching over their own adorable brood.

"Not as quick as you." He followed. "I could barely keep up last night."

"You'll just have to practice." She favored him with her sweetest smile.

Flirting seemed to be getting a little easier.

Settling down next to her, he draped his arm over the back of the bench. "That sounds too much like work."

"Surely you work, Mr. Cooper."

"Oh yes. My father is a big believer in learning every aspect of our company's businesses. Just finished a four-month rotation at our shoe factory."

"But you're still allowed a summer vacation?"

He turned to her in exaggerated surprise. "Father's not a monster!" She laughed and he leaned back again. "I have a few weeks before my next assignment. Then it will be down to weekends for me, like the rest of the domesticated males. Slave all week in the city, then relax in the mountains with the family Saturday afternoon to Sunday eve."

Struggling to keep the laughter from her voice, she played along. "Does sound absolutely horrific."

"It is, it is," he moaned in mock misery.

"No military service?" Though still teasing, her tone grew a bit more serious. "You seem older than twenty-one."

"Twenty-four in July. But I, my dear, am exempt. An essential worker."

She raised a brow. "And what, exactly, makes you so indispensable to the war effort?"

"That shoe factory now makes soldiers' boots. My father made clear how disastrous to the entire operation it would be if I were pulled away."

These people really did live in another world. Part of her railed against the injustice, and sympathized with the labor organizers, fighting and dying for workers' rights.

And, she hated to admit, a conflicting part yearned to find shelter in that privileged world and the protections it offered. To be freed from her ball and chain of anxiety . . . to float up to their cushioned realm of perpetual safety and comfort.

He extended his other arm over the top of the bench and gazed toward the lake. "Truth is, I worried I'd be lonely this summer."

"What about all your friends?" She spread her fingers over her knee, where he might notice her ring. A reminder to them both she hadn't always been poor.

"What friends?" he replied with a snort. "Everyone's overseas, covering themselves in glory. There's no one here but Karl Fiske, and he's too busy to play. And kind of a bore, if truth be told." He clasped her hand. "But you're here." He sat forward and gazed into her eyes. "A hidden gem discovered within these mountains of granite."

She pulled her hand away with a laugh. "And a poet, too?"

Little Walter waved from atop his tiny steed. Vanessa waved back, searched out Edna, and gave her a hearty wave, too. Ned sent Albert a brief salute, then tilted his head toward her. "What can I say? You inspire me."

She rolled her eyes nearly as high as Cecile had earlier. "How many nurse-maids have heard those lines, I wonder?"

Her breath caught. The same joke had landed so awkwardly with Avery.

He clasped his hands to his heart. "You wound me!"

No need to worry. Ned and Avery were quite different.

"Besides," he continued, "I had no idea of your position here when we first met."

She narrowed her eyes. "Yet . . . you assume Walter and Edna are my charges."

"Touché, my clever one. But I've known the Wainwrights since they were born, as well as their former nursemaid. Miss O'Neill, I believe her name was. Don't have to be Sherlock Holmes to deduce you're their new nanny."

Despite her best effort, the laughter rippling beneath his commentary made her smile. But her mouth's betrayal only stiffened her resolve to resist his charms. "So, what's your plan, Mr. Cooper? To come slumming with the staff for the season, since you have no proper friends to entertain you?"

He winced. "Ouch."

"I'm sorry if I sound harsh, but surely you understand my concern." Best to let him know she was no patsy. "I've already received explicit warnings."

He shifted his gaze to the corral. "I understand." The humor had drained from his voice, leaving it sounding detached. Blasé. "What respectable business would a young man in my position have with someone in yours?"

She turned away. Just as well. He'd given her some delicious memories, but the flirtation would end now. Without shame, without humiliation. "Thank you." She rose, keeping her back to him. "For not . . . taking advantage."

He took her hand before she could step away. "But there's more to me than my position."

Moved by the sincerity in his voice, she left her hand in his grip.

"Just like there's more to you than yours." He released her. "Continue keeping me in line with your ruthless honesty, Miss Perkins, and I promise you honesty in return, if nothing else."

Honesty. She stared into his eyes, his gaze unwavering. That was all an honorable man could promise, wasn't it? She took a deep breath and extended her hand. "Deal."

He shook. "Deal."

A mischievous grin appeared as he patted the bench beside him. "Now, how shall we begin our season of honesty?"

She returned to her seat, silenced by her surprise. Whatever she'd imagined it would be like to converse with him in private, it was never this . . . real.

Her original attraction to his handsome face and rarified status was more akin to mooning over some cinema star, like Rudolph Valentino or Richard Barthelmess. This was so much better.

Leaning back, he crossed his arms over his chest. "A game of croquet, perhaps?"

With an arched brow, she pretended a calm she didn't feel. "With the children?"

"Of course! I can't be trusted without a chaperone." He flashed another of his winning grins and winked. "Or four."

At that moment, she wanted to kiss him so badly, she wasn't sure if four chaperones would be enough to protect her reputation.

Chapter Thirteen

Still sweaty from mowing the lawn, Avery stood over the kitchen sink finishing a bowl of cornflakes. He'd outgrown the moving picture booklet available to anyone who bought two boxes, but they were still one of his favorite snacks.

After rinsing the bowl and spoon, he put them in the drying rack and turned to the table behind him. As usual, a stack of mail sat on the corner of the ivy-patterned oilcloth next to the wall.

His eye was drawn to an envelope on top of the pile. The Harvard Medical School seal was printed beside the return address. He picked it up, hope fluttering in his gut. It was possible they'd written to say things had changed. More qualified applicants were coming back from the front and they regretfully needed to withdraw their offer of admission.

He turned it over. The envelope had already been opened. Though it was addressed to his father, it had to be about him. Feeling justified, he pulled its folded contents out and scanned the neatly typed message.

No luck. Just the tuition invoice for his first semester. Classes started Monday, September ninth.

After tucking the letter back in the envelope and returning it to the pile, he ran his hands over his head. Maybe he'd be conscripted before then. He'd turned twenty-one in May and registered for the draft as soon as he got home from college. But, so far, he hadn't heard anything. Almost wished they'd call him up. Get him out of this mess.

Then Avery pictured Dewey sitting at the kitchen table, his legs spread wide and his chair tipped back. How many times had the two of them eaten cereal together on that green and white tablecloth?

He couldn't remember not knowing Dewey. Irene's oldest brother had been one class above him and Bess at school. Avery'd been nearly as happy as Bess their freshman year when she and Dewey had started dating. It was like he finally had a brother. A popular, fun-loving brother who didn't care that Avery was quiet and preferred drawing and reading to hunting and sailing.

Honestly, which was worse? That Dewey lay dead somewhere in France? Avery slammed his fist on the table. Or that *he* remained alive, doomed to perpetual guilt that his problems would forever be dwarfed by Dewey's ultimate sacrifice?

The front door creaked open, followed by multiple footsteps in the entryway. His parents back from their bridge game at the neighbors'.

"Avery?" His mother's voice often had an edge of concern lately. Like the draft board might have snatched him during her brief absence.

"In the kitchen!" Still breathing hard from recollections of Dewey, he could hardly blame her for worrying.

His mother entered, her eyes drawn to his bowl on the drying rack. "Wish you'd joined us. The Hansons recruited their deaf aunt to round out our foursome."

"Sorry. The lawn couldn't wait."

She patted his shoulder and pulled her apron on over her muslin blouse and long plaid skirt. "Oh! Is this a new one?"

His grin widened as she reached for his latest watercolor, propped above the sink. "You like it?"

It was the one of the brilliant blue butterfly he'd started that morning. He'd finished before mowing the lawn, so it was still a little damp.

"Oh, Avery." She spread her fingers across her bosom. "It's simply lovely. I must show your father."

His hand flew up to stop her. "That's alright . . ."

But she was already on her way to the living room. He followed, steeling himself.

"Darryl, isn't Avery's butterfly exquisite?"

Settled in his worn leather armchair by the fireplace, his father had his right leg up on a brocade footstool. Though he didn't like seeing him in pain, Avery was glad the bum knee his father had gotten in college kept him from joining the troops overseas, where so many other doctors had gone.

His father left off stuffing his pipe with tobacco to take the watercolor she handed him. His mustache twitched, then he passed the artwork back. "Nothing wrong with a man having hobbies."

She pursed her lips and held the picture up to admire again. "Simply outstanding."

Avery's jaw tightened. "I'm glad you like it, Mother."

She glanced at his father, whose head was tilted down over his pipe again, and seemed to recognize her defeat. "Supper's in an hour." She turned back toward the kitchen, jabbing her finger on Avery's arm as she passed. "And you best not have spoiled your appetite with those cornflakes."

Once his mother was gone, he walked over to the sofa and sat facing his father. "I've been thinking."

The leather chair creaked as his father leaned back. "Yes?"

Avery rested his elbows on his knees and leaned forward, his gaze fixed on the old braid rug covering most of the floor. "Instead of working at the Cullens's store this summer." He raised his chin to meet his father's dark eyes. "Why don't I volunteer at the hospital? Get a little head start for the fall."

The relief and pleasure that swept over his father's face confirmed Avery's belief he was doing the right thing, as hard as it was.

"Good idea, son. The hospital's especially short-staffed lately." He reached for his box of matches. "Should even be able to get you on the payroll."

"Excellent." He stood. "I'll let Mr. Cullens know."

He'd just have to find a way to make it work. That's all.

His father nodded. "It will be nice having you around, son. I look forward to showing you the ropes."

"Me too, Father." He grimaced as his father put the pipe in his mouth and lit a match, but hoped his expression passed for a smile. "Me, too."

Chapter Fourteen

Waltzing across the grounds again after returning the Wainwright children back to their parents, Vanessa passed the quaint sitting garden on the hotel's south wall.

Inside the garden's low iron gate, Irene Seward draped woven flower necklaces over a pair of statues standing in a stone niche against the wall.

Vanessa stopped and took hold of the garden fence with a laugh. "Those baubles are a bit wasted on those two, don't you think?"

Irene turned with a gasp and clutched her side. "You near scared the teeth from my head."

"Sorry about that." Vanessa let herself through the gate. "But how can you bear to make such beautiful creations and not wear them yourself?"

Irene's smile faded as she fingered the floral loops in her basket. "It's just . . . something my mother used to do."

"Oh." Vanessa blinked several times. There was a powerful undertow of loss in Irene's voice, and she recalled hearing that the groundskeeper, Irene's father, was a widower.

As though realizing the effect her sorrow was having, Irene brightened and continued draping necklaces on the statues. "These fine gentlemen are called 'lares.'"

Vanessa bent forward to examine the bronze figures more closely, eager to follow Irene's lead toward happier thoughts. Both statues were about four feet high. Curly haired boys in short togas standing on tiptoe, like dancers. Each held a drinking horn up with one hand, a shallow dish on the upturned palm of the other. "They're quite fetching." An expression she borrowed from Mrs. Wainwright.

"Mother said they protect the house."

"Twin Birch is an awfully large house." She nudged Irene with her shoulder. "You sure these two little fellas are up to it?"

Irene laughed, but it was sudden and scratchy. Like she hadn't done it in a while. Inspired by the whimsical lares, Vanessa realized the caretaker's daughter was the ideal person to relieve her growing curiosity. "So, tell me. What's the story with fairies around here? People keep mentioning them like they're as common as squirrels."

Irene gave her an enigmatic smile as she laid the last of the blossom wreaths on the statues. "Everyone loves those rumors."

Vanessa's breath caught. That wasn't a denial.

How she longed for fairies to be real. For her lifelong sense of hidden creatures and mythical worlds to be more than just her imagination. "Have you seen them?"

"Yes. No. Maybe." Irene shrugged and stared at the twin statues. "Fairies. Nymphs. Angels. Who knows? I was a child." She brushed flecks of pollen and flower debris from her blouse. "And when you grow up, you don't know if certain things you saw are true memories . . . or just parts of a dream." She cocked her head. "Was it the same for you? In the city?"

"In a way." She thought back to those horrific first years after her parents died. "At the Girls Home, the veterans liked telling the new ones that every child who died there wandered the dormitory at night, trying to find her bed. Everyone seemed to believe it, and before long I was seeing and hearing them, too. Now

I'm nearly certain it was my imagination, like you said, or nightmares. Still, I couldn't swear those ghosts weren't real."

"That's simply awful. I'm so sorry."

She flapped her hands. "It's alright. I didn't mean to get morbid." Rubbing her thumb over the stone in her ring, Vanessa drifted further into her memories. Back to when she was three or four. Playing on the grass while her mother sat on a bench. In a little park. Ruth just a baby in her pram. It did seem she had visitors then. Friendly ones, not unlike that gorgeous blue butterfly that led her and the children to Avery. But these thoughts she kept to herself. Too vague and private to share. She grinned. "Whether they're real or not, I find the idea of fairies delightful. Especially after seeing Mary Pickford in *Cinderella*. Did you see it?"

Irene nodded. "At the new theater over in Bethlehem, a few years back."

"The forest here reminds me so much of that scene where the fairies helped Cinderella collect firewood."

"Right before she meets the Prince on his hunting expedition." Irene gazed into the distance. "It was magical, wasn't it?"

Vanessa clapped her hands. "Oh, yes. I dreamt about it for weeks after. And my charges are firm believers in fairies, that's for sure."

"Well, if there are mythical creatures here . . ." Irene continued to stare in the direction of the lake. "They couldn't have found a better home than Twin Birch House."

Vanessa sighed with pleasure at how the late afternoon sun burnished the entire landscape a warm, golden hue. "You can say that again."

"Well, if there are mythical—"

Vanessa's sudden laughter interrupted Irene, who threw her a crooked smile and bent over to retrieve her empty basket.

"I'm so glad we're friends." Vanessa twirled in a circle, arms in the air. "This summer just keeps getting better and better."

A shadow crossed Irene's face. "It would get better if this horrible war would finally end."

Vanessa's feet slowed and she lowered her arms. Powerless to take any loved ones from her, the war often slipped her mind. She touched her fingers to Irene's arm. "Yes. We're all praying for that."

Chapter Fifteen

A month after Avery's decision to spend the summer at the hospital, he planted himself on a stool next to Irene at the counter of the Adamsville Drug Store. The black leather was slick from years of patrons sliding over its surface and the wooden counter was smoothed from countless arms rubbing its edges. Chocolate malt became his regular order when the soda fountain was first installed, and seeing Irene through the window had whetted his appetite for one now.

"Well, hello there, stranger." Her straw swirled around in the remains of her strawberry ice cream soda as she sucked up its final dredges. She never ordered anything else.

"Good to see you." He glanced at his reflection through the gold curlicues painted on the mirror behind the counter, ran a hand through his messy hair and thought of his twin. If she'd ever pry herself away from DC, Bess would insist he cut it. He nudged Irene's elbow. "How've you been?"

Irene shrugged, leaning on her elbow. "No news from Roy in a while." The floppy collar of her striped blouse just missed the wet spot her soda left on the polished wood.

"I'm sure it doesn't mean anything." Avery tried to sound reassuring as the druggist slid him his malt.

Irene's fiancé had been her older brother's best friend. The idea of Roy dying over there after she'd already lost Dewey was more than Avery could imagine. "Doesn't mail get backed up over there pretty regularly?"

"Yes . . ."

"You see. A bundle will probably show up tomorrow."

"Could happen." She propped her head in her hand. "Hear anything from Bess?"

Reaching over to pull a straw from a glass canister, he considered his twin's latest letter. "Not much more than we see in the papers. She and her suffragette friends are livid their bill got filibustered in the Senate a few weeks ago."

He took a long draw of his malt. "She didn't give any details, but hinted they were planning some big protest in August, so hang on to your hat."

"Nothing more . . . personal?" Irene toyed with her empty soda glass. "Like when she's coming home?"

Avery's jaw tightened. How could Bess be so selfish? Not even telling her best friend she wouldn't be returning home after college graduation? Dashing off to Washington without a thought for all the people in Adamsville who missed her?

"Nothing." He shot Irene a sideways glance. "Mother keeps talking about Christmas, but I'm afraid it might be based more on wishful thinking than Bess promising to come."

Irene frowned. "I'm sure she believes she's doing the right thing." She straightened up, smoothing her skirt over her knees. "But with Roy and all those other boys overseas, it's not the right time to divide us here at home."

"Surprised she's not in France herself." He snorted. "She'd have an easier time getting the Huns to surrender than getting those blowhards in DC to give women the vote."

Irene laughed harder than the joke deserved. "So what about you?" she asked. "How are things going at the hospital?"

Another pull on his malt allowed him the time to muster a fake smile. "Great. Learning a lot. And the hotel? The guests all behaving?"

"Quiet this season. More empty rooms than we've ever had." Her brow creased as she played with her used straw. "Pa says it's more than the war. That big places like Twin Birch are going out of style."

He put his hand over hers. "Don't worry, Irene. After the war, everyone will be in the mood to celebrate and come flooding back. You'll see."

Her glance betrayed her doubts, but she smiled. "I'm sure you're right."

Ignoring her transparent effort to jolly him, he tried to make his next question sound as casual as his first. "And how about that new girl, Vanessa? See much of her?"

"More than I expected." She threw him a wicked grin. "And she's succeeded in upsetting the college girls, which is always fun to watch."

He was struck with the protective urge to run up to the women's dorm and set things straight with anyone harassing the wide-eyed young nanny. "How so?"

Irene leaned close and lowered her voice. "By nabbing Ned Cooper."

"Cooper?" His grip tightened around his malt. "Nursemaids aren't usually his style."

She shrugged as she slid off her stool. "Well, I guess Vanessa's charms proved a match for his." She gave his cheek a quick peck. "You should come up more often. The dances suffer terribly without you."

He tried to drown his jealousy with another draw of his soda as she left, the bells above the door jangling at her departure. Despite his efforts, the chocolate grew bitter on his tongue as he pictured Vanessa twirling under the stars in Ned Cooper's arms.

Chapter Sixteen

S itting on the bench in the garden, Vanessa stared at the afternoon sun reflecting off the bronze cheeks of Irene's lares. The prior Sunday, Ned had found her reading here after church. She hoped he'd return to the same spot today. Strictly speaking, the garden was not part of the hotel available for staff use, but she'd never seen any guests there and figured she could feign ignorance if anyone raised a fuss.

When she'd arrived earlier, Irene had been there, draping the twin statues with flowers again. But she'd left a few minutes later. Off to her weekly visit with her beau's parents. They owned Cullens' Market, Adamsville's only grocery store.

Though Vanessa held the latest in the *Anne of Green Gables* series open in her lap, the image of Irene with her eventual in-laws made it nearly impossible to concentrate on the words. It was a niggling reminder of how flimsy the foundations of her current happiness truly were. She certainly enjoyed the games she and Ned played, finding a way to discreetly spend at least a little time together every day. But, really. What was her own gossamer connection with him compared to the substance of what Irene had with her Roy? Or Gladys with her Chester? If Ned were serving overseas, she and his parents would not comfort each other, reading snippets from his letters aloud, holding hands and praying for his safe return. The idea was laughable.

No longer defending her pride against Clara and the other girls in the dorm, she could more easily admit how little chance there was for their romance to progress any further than it already had in the last four weeks. Whatever bond she and Ned had developed, marriage was too much to hope for. Now she almost wished he wouldn't come . . . or would tell her he'd lost interest. That way she could cry her eyes out, mope around a bit, and eventually get over him. Despite her pessimism about their future, she couldn't see breaking things off herself. Ned made her laugh too hard. And he smelled too good. Made her feel too special. The end of the relationship was likely coming, but she'd do nothing to hasten its demise.

Movement by the lares caught her attention. If it weren't ridiculous, she would have thought it had been the statues themselves that shifted. Clearly another illusion provided by her overactive imagination. Most likely a bird simply took off from the vines on the wall behind their heads.

"And what are we reading today?"

She closed her eyes at the sound of Ned's voice. What had she been thinking? She never, ever wanted him to break things off with her. *"Anne's House of Dreams."* She kept her tone cool and made a show of concentrating on the book as he let himself through the gate.

"What appropriate reading, here at the charming Twin Birch House."

She glanced up to discover him standing with his back to the closed gate, the vulnerability in his eyes more exciting than his most practiced sultry smile. If it were physically possible, she'd swear her stomach did an actual flip, but she didn't dare let on how much he affected her. "And what are *you* reading this week?"

"The latest *Sherlock Holmes* installment." He waved the book as he headed toward her. "Can't get enough of the fellow."

Perhaps she'd imagined that vulnerability. Or merely wished for it to be there. She glanced up as he slid next to her and leaned close, landing a quick kiss on her lips. She straightened her spine and whipped her head toward the lawn. "Ned! People can see us!" But she couldn't help grinning.

He sat back with a gentle laugh. "There's hardly anyone in sight, and no one's bothering with anyone as insignificant as the two of us."

Her chest felt too small to contain the fireworks exploding within its confines. He'd kissed her! But even as she celebrated, she ignored a tiny lump of regret in her stomach. She'd imagined a more romantic event. Had pictured him looking deep into her eyes, holding her hands and gently kissing her lips, followed by murmurs of how much he loved her . . . and couldn't possibly return to Boston without her.

"And I have wonderful news." He was almost childlike in his delight.

"Which is . . . ?" She held her breath.

"I've figured out a way for us to spend much more time together."

Her fingers clamped around the edges of her book. "How?"

"I managed to persuade that killjoy tending my sister's children to return to Boston." He took her hand in his. "Family emergency was the agreed-upon excuse. Lord knows where she'll spend the 'incentive' I had to give her."

Vanessa's brow knitted as her breath released. "What does that mean?"

"What it means, my darling, is that my sister is in desperate need of a nurse-maid for Cecile and Albert." He grinned. "It will be so much easier for me to see you this way. It's getting a little tiresome to constantly try and figure out where you'll be."

"But, what about the Wainwrights?" Her stomach knotted as she remembered the children's bedroom just the night before, the entire family listening to her story about a misguided castle mouse who'd collected gems instead of nuts for his winter store. The rush of love she felt for all of them made her heart ache. "I couldn't leave them."

"I thought you'd be pleased." Ned's grin faded. "That you were feeling the same way I do."

"I do, it's just that . . ."

Lifting her hand, he pressed it to his chest, his eyes pleading. "You want to spend more time with me, don't you?"

"Yes, yes, of course . . ."

"Then seize the day, my glorious Vanessa. This is our chance." He rose, still holding her hand. "Let's go find Sarah before she solves the problem on her own."

Pulled to her feet, she followed after him. When he released her hand to unlatch the garden gate, she clutched her book and straightened her spine, despite the fluttering sensation in her stomach. "What I meant, Ned, was what does this mean for *us*?"

His hand rested on the gate as he turned to face her. "Why, just what I've said. We'll see far more of one another." He brushed a tendril of hair from her cheek. "And the family will get to know you better, see all the qualities I see."

A magician may as well have split her chest open, releasing a flight of doves to soar heavenward. "Oh." She tilted her face down to hide her smile, which quickly faded. "I still need time . . . to consider."

"Of course. It was impetuous of me." He ran his hand back over his head. "I should have consulted you first." He took her free hand in his. "You were so irresistible at church this morning. I had to do something."

How could she not be flattered? Moved, even? "Thank you. It's certainly a wonderful opportunity. I can see that. Please don't think me . . . ungrateful."

"Never." He lifted her chin, his eyes tender. "Mrs. O'Malley leaves on the morning train. If you want the job, meet me at the platform and I'll take you to my sister."

He glanced around, then moved her behind the enormous lilac bush growing next to the gate. Once they were shielded from view and enveloped in the lilacs' seductive perfume, he wrapped his arms around her and kissed her properly.

The kiss was nothing like anything she'd experienced before. Firm, but not too hard. Moist, but not too wet. Alive, but not too active. It was . . . perfect.

She didn't know where he learned a skill like that and didn't care. She knew she would remember her first real kiss forever . . . and that lilacs would always be her favorite flower. But she still wasn't certain. Was Ned's offer an opportunity to be seized? Or a temptation to be resisted?

Chapter Seventeen

Vanessa remained at the garden gate after Ned left, contemplating her dilemma. It was a strange experience . . . having a choice to make. When had she ever had the luxury of options? Escaping the home of her assailant may have been a choice, but it didn't feel like one at the time. Other than in that one, extreme situation, she'd simply taken whatever job she'd been assigned . . . or been fortunate enough to be offered.

Hugging herself, she turned and paced. If only there was someone to talk to. That's probably what normal people did at moments like this. But who? Gladys was profoundly practical and would simply tell her she was crazy to consider leaving the Wainwrights. She stopped and considered the twin lares. Irene? Perhaps. She seemed to have a sympathetic ear, but in truth, they weren't actually that close. And Irene was off visiting her sweetheart's parents anyway. Mrs. Juneau? No again. Though she was a fellow survivor of the Girls Home, she had practically forbidden her entanglement with Ned in the first place. Reverend Tiller at the village church? She pictured the kindly, eighty-year-old minister's face as she explained her unlikely relationship with one of the scions of Boston society. "Ha!"

She threw the latch on the garden gate and hurried across the lawn toward the woods. She needed to get away. Sort out the tangle of emotions wrestling in her chest.

In a few moments, she entered the well-groomed path that most hikers used to begin their treks. After several minutes of intense marching up the sloping hillside, she stopped to catch her breath, leaning her hand against a granite outcrop. Her agitation had driven her up the hill so fast she was closing in on a group of five or six casual hikers from the hotel.

With a sigh of irritation, she cut off the footpath and pushed through the woods. Swiping away a low hanging branch, she forged through a cluster of ferns, her skirt catching on a spindly root poking from the base of a long-fallen tree. After several more minutes, she realized she had unwittingly returned to a familiar scattering of distinctive boulders covered in moss. It was the exact spot where Walter and Edna had disappeared weeks earlier . . . only to reappear with Avery Nolen.

She took a deep breath and surveyed her surroundings. Despite the horrors of those moments when she couldn't find the children, it was as good a place to sit and think as any.

After brushing dried pine needles from one of the rocks, she settled on its relatively flat surface. Pressing her book against her knees, she contemplated the cover. In the couple of chapters she'd managed before Ned arrived, Anne was back at Green Gables preparing for her wedding. Was that what she really hoped for with Ned? To assemble a trousseau, like Anne? Plan a European wedding tour, like the one Anne's friend Jane took?

No. She wasn't a girl who fantasized about a fancy wedding day. The girls she knew married working class boys in simple affairs, wearing dresses that could be worn again. Savings were spent on moving into an apartment together, not on hotels and cruise tickets.

But being able to kiss Ned whenever she wanted? To dance with him like the Wainwrights in the hotel ballroom? In a few years' time, to sit with him in the nursery, telling their children bedtime stories? That sounded positively divine. Cautiously, she allowed herself to seriously contemplate being part of a family, surrounded by love and cherished by a ridiculously handsome man. But as the tension in her chest softened, the risk of acknowledging those desires wrenched her thoughts back to reality. There was no escaping the truth. She was a penniless orphan from the working class, no matter how refined she tried to appear.

She sprang to her feet and dropped the book on the rock. This decision needed to be made with her head, not her heart. Irene might be convinced to help Mrs. Wainwright with Walter and Edna for the rest of the summer, but was a temporary position with the Gardners a good enough opportunity to lure her from the security of the Wainwrights? On the one hand, the Gardners were higher up the social ladder, so their recommendation should assure her another post back in Boston. But on the other, no family she'd ever served had been as fair and kind as the Wainwrights. Whoever came after the Gardners were unlikely to be as good to her, and children sweeter than Edna and Walter probably didn't exist. Yet . . . the Wainwrights could always fire her on a whim, in which case she'd regret not taking a hand in shaping her own destiny.

"Phooey!" She paced in front of the boulders, glaring at a cluster of beech trees growing on a sunlit mound where the rocks tapered down to resemble a low, stone ruin.

How had Anne described the beech trees on the Green Gables property? "Ivory columns in a fairy palace of twilight and stars." The thought made her laugh, despite her foul mood. What was it about Twin Birch House that prompted references to fairies at every turn?

Chapter Eighteen

From her perch in a tree branch above the mossy boulders, Lachima grew increasingly agitated as Vanessa fretted down below. The girl's distress reverberated with unusual power, nearly impossible to ignore.

Though Lachima didn't have as much influence on human lives as she once did, the threads of all their lives still spooled through her fingers, each white hair in the massive cloud growing on her head representing a current mortal's lifetime. A new strand sprouted with each birth, and with each death, a strand fell out, dissolving back into the ether. With so many human lives to consider, it was the rare mortal who attracted so much of her attention. Yet Vanessa always had . . . from the moment she was born.

Lachima smoothed her lavender dress and glanced around. Morniero was nowhere in sight.

Just a quick intervention, she promised herself as she floated to the ground. Nothing more than a little talk to calm the poor girl's nerves.

Chapter Nineteen

Vanessa heard the familiar tinkling, like tiny crystals rippling in the breeze behind her somewhere. The sound had become as much a part of the woods as birdcalls and wind in the treetops. But the shimmers of light that usually accompanied the barely perceptible noise always disappeared whenever she tried to catch a glimpse. She frowned. It was irritating to constantly play the toddler reaching for a toy, only to have it yanked away just before her outstretched fingers could reach it.

"Hello." The voice was feminine and impossibly high, yet gentle. Like the sweetest of violin notes.

Vanessa turned to find a breathtakingly beautiful womanly creature floating a few inches off the ground. She recognized the glimmer radiating from the apparition's head. It was the same light that had teased the corners of her eyes for all these weeks. But this time, a dazzling figure appeared in full view. A silky sheath hugged her slender, six-foot frame, the fabric the color of pale, gray pearls. Her expectant expression suggested she was waiting for Vanessa to reply to her greeting.

"He . . . hello."

The apparition was vaguely translucent, and the way her white hair glistened and floated made it appear she was underwater. "So, Vanessa," the figure trilled. "You're worried about your future. You have questions."

The creature knew her name! Despite the stories and what the children said about seeing fairies in the woods, Vanessa had definitely not expected to share their experience. Had she wished for it, though? Had the absence of guidance in the real world sent her to the forest in hopes of just such an encounter?

Or was she imagining the whole thing? No denying the creature appeared quite like the fairy godmother in the *Cinderella* film she and Irene had talked about. Minus the wings. But in the motion picture, the fairy was clearly an actress holding a staff with a cutout star stuck on top. Whatever floated before Vanessa now, it was far more awe-inspiring than even the most impressive Hollywood illusion. "Are you . . . one of Walter's fairies?"

"It's not what we call ourselves, but 'fairy' is one of the many different names your kind has given us over the centuries." The fairy glided closer, her eyes darting around the glen. "But I'm afraid we don't have much time. Suffice it to say that I know a lot about your future. What would you like to know? What would ease your troubled mind?"

Vanessa blinked. Of the infinite number of questions she might have, how could she decide which to choose? And what did she really want to know? Surely some things about one's life were best left uncertain.

The fairy's beatific face smiled from under her crown of delicate silver twigs embedded with dots of white, sparkly light. "I'm sorry. I'm sure you're overwhelmed. I used to be able to ease into these kinds of encounters more gracefully." She glanced around again. "But circumstances have changed."

"Th . . . that's alright." Vanessa felt a little ridiculous, reassuring the stunning, magical creature.

The fairy placed her hand on Vanessa's shoulder. The touch warmed her deep beneath her skin. "I can't promise you a life free of pain and sorrow," said the beauty in her ethereal voice. "For that is the lot all your kind share."

Vanessa nodded, her voice coming out in a squeak. "Of course." Her whole body now tingled, as though hot mint tea flowed through her veins.

"And I'm assuming your current troubles are related to your romantic prospects. Those are what trouble most people your age."

Vanessa nodded again, raising her clasped fingers to the middle of her chest and wondering if she was going mad.

"I can't give you any details, but I can say this." The fairy leaned closer and whispered. "Your match is a man of true worth. A man of sterling and gold."

Vanessa squeezed her eyes closed. Surely the creature was a figment of her imagination. How else could she have known exactly what Vanessa longed to hear? That she *was* destined to find a man who could offer true love and protection. That a brighter future *did* beckon, as she'd always hoped, but hadn't dared believe. When she opened her eyes to find the fairy still there, hope flickered that the creature was actually real.

Allowing herself to believe, even just a little, that she was truly receiving a magical prophecy prompted a deep sigh. The knot of fear that lived in her belly loosened. Not entirely, but enough to provide genuine relief. Her lips trembled. "Thank you."

The fairy bent down and kissed her forehead. "When you're ready, he will appear before your eyes." The soothing sensation of her breath on Vanessa's skin remained as the fairy shrank into a flash of light and disappeared.

"Thank you!" She reached her hand out, but there was nothing left to touch. Her arm fell back to her side and she sank onto the rock again.

Could that have just happened? Was it possible that the world was far more complex than it appeared? That so many of the stories passed off as fairy tales spoke to actual events? She reached for her book and clutched it to her chest. How wonderful that would be! If those dim memories of companions who were neither human nor animal were as real as those of her mother singing while giving her a bath . . . or sitting on her father's lap, his hand wrapped around her fist, guiding a pencil in the shape of letters.

Still tingling from the fairy's touch, Vanessa thought of how the orphaned Anne of Green Gables had ultimately recognized Gilbert as her true love after years of confusion. Why not believe that her life could turn out as happily as Anne's did? What was to be gained by denying the experience she'd just had?

She rose, took a deep breath, and focused on the sky. It was settled. As far as she was concerned, fairies were real. She'd just seen one, felt her touch. And no matter what the odds, she determined to reach for the future with her heart in the lead. To act out of hope, rather than fear.

Still a bit dizzy, she made her way back to the mountain path, heading for the Sewards' house. With any luck, Irene would be back from visiting. Vanessa needed to speak with her right away.

Chapter Twenty

C hildren." Mrs. Wainwright sounded cool and formal sitting on the settee, Walter perched on her lap. "Miss Perkins is leaving us and wanted to say goodbye."

Sunlight shining through lace curtains dappled the family with dancing spots of light, giving them all a rather saintly quality. Clutching her sweating palms together at her waist, Vanessa bit her lip when Walter's face crumpled and he rubbed the collar of his shirt between his thumb and forefinger. It was a trick she'd taught him to resist sucking his thumb. Seeing him do it now nearly made her change her mind.

Edna scooted forward on the opposite sofa, where she sat with her father. "But why? Where are you going?"

"Not far, sweetheart." Vanessa's throat pinched. "The Gardner family's nursemaid had a . . . family emergency and had to go back to Boston. And, umm, well . . . since the children already know me . . . their mother was quite insistent that I take over."

"What about our bedtime stories?" Walter's voice was high and anxious.

Vanessa fought back her tears. "I'll have to put the Gardner children to bed, darling." Dropping to one knee, she gazed into his eyes. "But, I'm sure we'll still see a lot of each other, and I'll tell you stories whenever I can."

The little boy slid off his mother's lap and ran to her. "Don't go!"

When he threw his little arms around her neck, Vanessa's throat clamped so tight it ached. She'd known them less than two months. How could it hurt so much? Looking at Edna over Walter's shoulder, she blinked back tears and tried to make her tone light. "The good news is that you already know your new nursemaid. And she's quite kind."

"Who is it?" The girl sounded skeptical.

"Irene Seward, sweetheart." Her mother's voice was calm and reassuring. "You know, the groundskeeper's daughter."

Irene had questioned Vanessa hard about her decision to pursue the opportunity Ned created for her, but ultimately agreed when it was clear Vanessa's mind was made up.

Edna's brow smoothed. "Oh. She *is* nice."

Vanessa struggled to keep her expression cheerful. The children would clearly be over her faster than she'd be over them.

"Miss Seward will take care of you part of the day," added Mrs. Wainwright, "and the rest of the time, I'll look after you myself."

Both children appeared confused. Edna's eyes widened. "You're going to be our nanny?"

Mrs. Wainwright smoothed her skirt as she and her husband exchanged a glance. "Not your nanny, sweetheart. Just your mother."

Vanessa gave Walter's silky hair a quick kiss, then rose before the tears overwhelmed her efforts to hold them back. "Thank you all for your understanding." Her voice cracked. "You're the best family I've ever worked for."

"Well, it's just too bad it had to end this way." Mrs. Wainwright's smile was small and tight. The time didn't seem right to ask for the reference Vanessa hoped to obtain before leaving.

Mr. Wainwright walked her to the door, his tone clipped. "We wish you all the best, Miss Perkins."

A moment later, she was alone in the corridor. When the door snapped shut behind her, it took all the willpower Vanessa had to congratulate herself for braving the steps to make her dreams come true.

Chapter Twenty-One

"Psst." Ned's eyes twinkled in the light of the hallway sconces. He leaned from inside the dining room and gestured for her to join him.

Vanessa stopped, careful to keep her tray with two glasses of warm milk steady and her voice low. "What are you doing here?" They were in the "Beech cottage," the four-bedroom house where the Gardners stayed. Ned's family had quarters in the hotel's main building.

"I miss you."

She smiled. Only an hour had passed since she'd last seen him. After a quick glance over her shoulder toward the kitchen and then up the stairs to her left, she slipped into the dining room. Once she was safely inside, Ned slid the pocket door closed while she put the tray on the table.

He took her hands and whispered, "Well? How was your first day?"

"Wonderful. Truly."

"Sarah's been civil?"

"Absolutely."

His concern was endearing. She'd never have guessed such generosity lay beneath the air of bored indifference he cultivated for public display. "You were there most of time, after all," she added with a quiet laugh. They'd passed the entire afternoon together as he lounged with his sister and her family on the lawn. It was marvelous. Everything he'd promised in arranging her move to the Gardner's employ.

He pulled her close, his lips brushing her ear. "But the important things happen between people when no one is watching."

She slid her arms up and around his neck. "She's been perfectly nice, even in private. I promise." If only it were possible to stay entwined with him like this forever.

"Good." He gently kissed her ear lobe. "I've wanted to do this all day."

As he nuzzled her neck, she was reminded of the fairy and her prophecy. "Speaking of things happening when no one is watching . . ."

He pulled back, a wicked grin tugging his lips. "Yes?"

"Have you ever encountered any fairies here at Twin Birch House? I keep hearing about them and am beginning to wonder if there isn't some truth to the stories."

"Fairies?" Ned laughed. "Unfortunately not. I know they're the unofficial mascot of the hotel, but I assure you, they are purely fictional."

Disappointment and concern wrestled in her mind. How she would have loved to share her incredible encounter with him. But worse than having to keep the fairy a secret, she couldn't help worrying that she'd made the whole thing up. That being imaginative was slipping toward being delusional.

The sensation of Ned's lips brushing her neck was enough to distract her from those unpleasant thoughts. The warm tip of his tongue caressing her earlobe dispelled them entirely. Being so close all day while pretending there was nothing between them was more difficult than she'd anticipated.

True, he'd included her as often as he could, but it was clear his sister and brother-in-law had no interest in having their children's nursemaid join their conversation. Vanessa honestly couldn't see how their social divide would ever be bridged. But for the moment, she was enjoying Ned's kisses too much to care.

After finally detaching herself from Ned, Vanessa entered the children's bedroom with their milk. Placing the tray on the table between their beds, she prayed her lips didn't appear as swollen from kissing as they felt. How would she explain their alarming condition?

She needn't have worried. Cecile and Albert were far more interested in their bedtime treat than whatever she'd been up to before reaching the nursery. After her new charges finished their milk, brushed their teeth, and slipped between their sheets, she knelt on the striped cotton rug between their beds and set a lit candle on the floor in front of her. It was her favorite time of the evening, surrounded by the scent of beeswax and the chorus of croaking frogs wafting in the open window.

The story she'd picked for their first night together was one of the Wainwright children's favorites. Edna and Walter had praised her stories so much, their parents had taken to sitting on the children's beds to listen themselves. "Our very own Scheherazade," Mr. Wainwright had called her.

"Once upon a time," Vanessa began, "a beloved princess was traveling with her family on a tour of the kingdom when she got separated from her parents during a terrible storm. A raging wind tore the crown from her head and the rain left her gown tattered and covered in mud. When the sun came up the next morning, the little girl rolled out of the ditch where she'd fallen asleep to the smell of bread baking. Following her nose, she walked into a nearby village, straight to the baker's open door. 'I'm Princess Giselle,' she said. 'Can you please give me some bread and help me back to the castle?'"

Holding her hands in front of the candle, Vanessa formed the shadow of praying hands on the white wall. "But the baker pointed at her raggedy clothes and scoffed. 'You're no princess—'"

"Can you read *The Tin Woodman of Oz*?" Albert's tone suggested it wasn't a question.

Vanessa stared, tempted to scold him for interrupting. She held her tongue only from concern that she might sound defensive.

"Father brought it up this weekend." Cecile jumped out of bed and retrieved the book from the shelf near their rocking horse and multiple chests of toys. "It just came out."

Albert snuggled into his pillow. "We've got the whole set at home."

"Of course." Vanessa couldn't decide if the boy was trying to impress her or remind her they were accustomed to getting whatever they wanted. Given her past experiences with him, it was more likely the latter. She picked up the candle and rose to her feet. "I love those books, too."

"You can sit there." Cecile handed her the book and pointed to a chair in the corner.

After setting the candle on the side table, Vanessa ran her hand over the cover, doing her best to ignore her disappointment. The book was new. Naturally they were excited. "How will you see the pictures?"

"We've seen them plenty of times. Mrs. O'Malley read it to us." Back in her bed, Cecile crossed her arms behind her head. "We can just listen this time."

"Goodnight, darlings." Their mother sailed into the room in a cloud of perfume Vanessa recognized as Chypre de Coty, a favorite with Boston's smart set. Sarah Gardner and her husband were off to an evening of cards and cocktails in the hotel's enormous lounge.

As Mrs. Gardner kissed the children in their beds, her husband moved closer to Vanessa's chair. "I wanted to thank you for stepping in on such short notice."

Her tingling lips prompted a twinge of guilt, reminding her of the real reason for Mrs. O'Malley's sudden departure. "My pleasure, Mr. Gardner."

"You're from the Boston Girls Home, I understand."

Her fingers tightened around the picture book. "Yes, I am."

"Fine institution." He straightened his vest. "Every girl my family ever hired out of there has been of excellent character."

"Thank you, sir." She kept her voice warm and courteous, though it grated to be reminded the Gardners thought of the Girls Home as nothing more than a place that produced reliable labor.

She stared down at the book's cover illustration—two smiling tin men made a seat with their bent elbows for a little boy in a feathered cap. Apparently happy servants, the tin men grinned while the little boy gripped each by their long noses. Vanessa bit the inside of her mouth. It was so easy for others to accept their place. Why was it so hard for her?

Girls from the Home were all groomed for service in high-society households and were lucky for the work. Most openings for domestics were filled with Irish girls from enclaves like Charleston and South Boston. So why was she the only one who seemed to feel like an impostor? Like she was meant for something else? Or someone else.

As the Garners swept out of the room, Vanessa raised her gaze to the candle flame and thought of Ned. A man of sterling and gold, without a doubt. If she were destined to become Mrs. Edward Cooper, it would certainly explain her growing dissatisfaction with the life of servitude the Girls Home had prepared her for. The reassuring thought stiffened her resolve to make the very most of the opportunity Ned's audacity had provided.

She opened the book and looked over at the children. "Shall I start at the beginning?"

Chapter Twenty-Two

Vanessa shifted her bottom on the hard pew in the village's Unitarian chapel. Sitting next to Gladys, she stared at the back of Ned's beautiful head. Two weeks of working for his sister had proven him right. They saw much more of each other and had grown even closer.

Sunlight streamed through the window, illuminating tiny particles of dust in its rays, providing a natural spotlight on the vase of blue hydrangeas set in front of the minister's lectern. Their heavy scent and the light snores of the village's old schoolteacher made the warm room even more comforting. Like she imagined Sunday afternoons might have been like with grandparents, if she'd ever known hers.

"'He that tilleth his land shall be satisfied with bread: but he that followeth vain persons is void of understanding.'" Reverend Tiller looked up from under his snowy brows. "Psalms 12:11."

Ignoring the flicker of concern the minister's words inspired, she tapped her toes on the smooth stone at her feet, the prior night's final waltz still playing in her head. No matter who else they danced with earlier in the evening, she and Ned made a point to be together for the last dance. It was the highlight of her week. But was he her "man of true worth" the fairy had promised? How could she know for sure?

"Stop that," Gladys whispered, pressing her hand on Vanessa's thigh. "You're worse than the children."

Mrs. Juneau raised her eyebrow at them from down the pew. All three of them sat in the back of the chapel, along with the rest of the staff from the hotel. Vanessa smiled apologetically and Gladys gave a little wave, then they both stared straight ahead. After giving Gladys's hand a squeeze, she folded her hands in her lap and allowed her eyes to wander over to the Wainwrights.

When she still worked for them, Walter and Edna had babbled to her freely about their fairy friends. Their parents had played along, too. Had they simply been indulgent, or had they seen the fairies themselves? Who knew?

Missing the Wainwrights more than she cared to admit, Vanessa shifted her gaze to the windows. She had yet to enjoy a return visit from the fairy, despite several trips back to the mossy boulders. Cecile and Albert never mentioned mythical creatures floating around Twin Birch House. Nor did their parents.

Nonetheless, since her magical encounter, more of Vanessa's own misty memories had surfaced from those days in the park with her mother and baby sister. Between those dreamy images and the ethereal tinkling she still heard in the woods from time to time, she felt . . . attended to . . . for the first time since her parents' death. Less alone in the world. She focused on the painting of a dewy-eyed Jesus smiling down at the congregation, his hands clasped in prayer. Maybe that was the feeling everyone was after.

Vanessa's gaze returned to Ned and his family. His parents sat pressed together. His sister and her family formed a tight cluster to his mother's left, while Ned sat alone to his father's right. A bubble of space surrounded him, well separated from his father on one side and the end of the pew on the other. It was a sad tableau.

Was that what she did for Ned? Made him feel less alone?

After the services, Vanessa left Gladys to her private prayers in the chapel. It was hard to see her friend so glum. News from the front was encouraging for the Allies, but the poor thing hadn't received a letter from her beau in weeks. Vanessa stepped into the sunlight, needled by guilt for being grateful Ned was safe at home, out of harm's way.

Lingering on the lawn outside the church, she longed for him to acknowledge their relationship in front of his family for the first time. When she was on duty and in uniform, his reluctance to include her in conversation with his parents was understandable. But Sunday offered the perfect opportunity for at least a brief chat with them, to demonstrate her refined manners. In her white linen dress with blue pinstripes, white hat, and lace gloves, she felt especially presentable.

A flash of light caught her eye. Sunshine reflected off Avery Nolen's glasses as he emerged from the church next to a middle-aged man with similar spectacles and a thick mustache. The man had to be his father, the local doctor Mrs. Wainwright had mentioned. The two men followed a doughy woman in a conservative brown jacket and matching skirt, her arm linked with an auburn-haired girl with a braid down her back. Avery's mother and sister, no doubt.

Vanessa smiled at Avery as he and his family drew closer. Her heart ached strangely at the way his face lit up after he spotted her. She hadn't seen him again after the day they met . . . the night he ceded that last dance to Ned. Six weeks had passed since then. The dread slumbering in her belly raised a sleepy eye. The summer was slipping away too fast.

"Good morning, Mr. Nolen."

The entire family turned, his mother with a smile that mirrored her son's, his sister with open curiosity and his father with raised eyebrows. Avery returned her smile. "Mother, Father, allow me to introduce Miss Vanessa Perkins."

She shook their hands. "Delighted to meet you."

The girl thrust her hand out as soon as Vanessa's hand was free. "And I'm Harriet, but you can call me Hattie." She was probably sixteen or seventeen.

Her light blue top had a white collar with a loosely knotted necktie, the nautical look that had become so popular in recent years. Vanessa liked her immediately.

"I'm so happy to meet you." His sister's coloring was the same as Avery's, but whereas his brown eyes were soft and warm, Vanessa noted that Hattie's were bright and sparkly. "Your brother is my hero."

His father glanced at Avery, eyebrows raised even higher. Hattie covered her giggle with her slender fingers.

"I was hopelessly lost in the woods . . ." Vanessa's voice faltered as Ned and his family passed behind the Nolens. ". . . and he appeared out of nowhere, like an angel, and returned me to safety."

Though apparently listening to something his father was saying, Ned managed to glance in her direction and wink.

"Oh, my dear!" Avery's mother pressed her gloved hands to the sides of her ruddy face. "What were you doing wandering out there by yourself?"

"I . . . uh." Vanessa tore her eyes from Ned's retreating figure. She didn't want to appear rude . . . or daft.

"She was with the Wainwright children and not at all far from the hotel." Avery shook his shaggy head, his tone lightly scolding. "It wasn't nearly the dramatic rescue you give me credit for, Miss Perkins."

"So, you work for the Wainwrights, do you?" Dr. Nolen focused on her more intently.

"I did, yes."

Her eyes snuck back to Ned as he and his family moved farther away.

"Fine people . . . the Wainwrights," said the doctor.

She got the distinct impression Avery's father wasn't convinced *she* was such "fine people." "I agree, though I'm with the Gardner family now."

Her chest tightened under the man's scrutiny as she returned her full attention to his face. "But I know how much the Wainwrights appreciated the tonsillectomy you gave Edna last summer."

The doctor's expression softened. "Yes, well, it's a simple procedure."

The Cooper family joined the Gardners for the walk back to the hotel. As they departed, Vanessa's earlier buoyancy leaked away.

"We're heading home for dinner." Mrs. Nolen tilted her face up at Avery, her expression hopeful. "Perhaps your friend would like to join us." Her head swiveled from Avery to Vanessa and back again.

Hattie clapped and bounced on her toes. "Oh, yes. Do come for dinner."

Avery's brown eyes were magnified in his glasses. "If you're free . . ."

The invitation was appealing. The warmth in his expression relaxed Vanessa. Made her feel she didn't need to perform for him. But Sunday afternoon had become her and Ned's special time in the sitting garden. She was reluctant to miss their rendezvous. It was when they had their most lengthy conversations. And kisses.

"I'm so sorry, I'd love to, but I have another commitment today."

"Yes, well, another time then." Avery's father took Mrs. Nolen by the elbow.

"Yes, dear. Another time." Avery's mother extended her hand. "Such a pleasure to meet you." She linked arms with her daughter again. "Come along, Hattie."

"Thank you, Mrs. Nolen, Dr. Nolen. The pleasure was all mine."

Hattie grinned over her shoulder as she skipped away next to her mother. "See you soon, Miss Perkins!"

"I promise!" She smiled. The girl's bubbly enthusiasm was contagious . . . and she seemed so familiar. Vanessa's hand flew to her throat. Harriet was who Ruth could have been, if she'd had the chance to grow up.

Avery grabbed her elbow. "Are you alright?"

She blinked up at him, then patted her eyes with the heel of her gloved hand. "Yes, yes. Your sister just reminded me of someone. That's all."

"That person must have meant as much to you as Hattie means to us." The concern in Avery's eyes nearly spilled her tears.

She laughed and tossed her head. "Indeed. She meant the world to me." She didn't speak of Ruth to anyone. Ever. So the sudden recollection of her lost sister was alarming. It made Vanessa feel as if she were standing before a creaking dam, its groans threatening an unwelcome flood of memories and emotions.

"But enough of that." Vanessa clutched her fingers together as though in prayer, the pressure distracting her from the tightness in her throat. "I was hoping to see more of you this summer." The truth in the statement took her by surprise. "No more dances?"

Avery's expression remained solemn, but he followed her lead into easier terrain. "Oh. No. I don't usually go to those."

"But you dance so well."

He blushed and ran his fingers back through his wavy hair. "My sister made me practice with her."

"Hattie?"

"No, no. My twin. Bess."

"A twin? Do you know, you're the first person I've ever met with an actual twin. What a wonderful thing that must be."

"I wouldn't know." He seemed to take the matter seriously. "I've never experienced anything else."

She bowed her head and smiled. "Well, I suppose that makes sense."

"We're quite different." He contemplated the ground for a moment, then peered up, his tone lighter. "I'd introduce you, but she headed straight down to Washington with her suffragette cohorts right after graduating from Bryn Mawr." He shook his head. "No telling when we'll see her again."

"And brothers?" She hoped this was a happier line of inquiry. "Any others to carry on the Nolen name?"

To her dismay, Avery's mouth tightened. "Afraid I'm the only one."

Good thing she'd declined the dinner invitation. The conversation was going as well as the Titanic's maiden voyage. Seeming to share her assessment, Avery gave her a strained smile and extended his hand. "Please don't let me keep you." He pushed his glasses up his nose with his free hand. "I know you have plans."

The pleasure of his lightly callused grip dissolved the tension of their awkward interchange. "Goodbye, Avery. I hope to see you again, and sooner this time."

"Goodbye . . . Vanessa." His lips turned upward, but he stopped short of the radiant smile she remembered from their first encounter.

Forgetting her disappointment at missing Ned's parents, Vanessa watched Avery hurry after his family. Her chest ached and eyes grew misty once more.

Family.

Since arriving at Twin Birch House, she'd been constantly surrounded by families whose qualities she admired. The loving warmth of the Wainwright foursome. The energy of the Seward clan. The solidity of the Nolens. All of them reminded her that she was an outsider. A feeling even Ned's personal attentions had so far done nothing to relieve.

Her fists clenched. Avery's twin was mad to take that family for granted.

Chapter Twenty-Three

Y ou're right." Ned stood in a shaft of sunlight in the clearing with the mossy boulders, hands on his hips. "This is a delightful patch."

"It's my favorite place in the forest. My private getaway." Vanessa caught a shimmer of light in the corner of her eye, and heard her telltale sound, but so far, no visible fairy.

Ned had found her in the garden after church. Having missed walking back to the hotel with his family, she'd hoped that bringing him to the mossy boulders might prompt the fairy's arrival. Anything to bolster her flagging confidence that Ned was the fulfillment of the fairy's prophecy.

He peered into the forest behind the enormous rocks. "Is that a pond over there?"

"I don't know." She rose and joined him. "I've never gone past this point." Sure enough, there was a small pond about twenty yards away, edged by a clump of cattails.

"Let's go see." He took her hand and they walked over.

The water appeared shallow, and there was a flat-topped, weathered rock sitting next to it that made a perfect seat. He took his jacket off and laid it down on the stone surface. "Shall we?"

Vanessa nodded, her disappointment at the fairy's failure to appear replaced by anticipation of the delicious kissing sure to come. He sat on his coat and gently pulled her onto his lap. "Our little hike was a superb idea."

"I quite agree." She wrapped her arm around the back of Ned's neck. In the privacy of the wood, she felt freer to surrender to the pleasure of his lips, to press against his chest, breathing in his now-familiar scent. She shivered as his warm palm traveled over her breast and down her side, working its way along her leg.

Actually, it was probably best no fairy appeared to interrupt them.

Avery was relieved to finally emerge from the stone tunnel into the Enchanted Wood. Seeing Vanessa at church that morning had stirred him up, making dinner with the family nearly unbearable. An afternoon spent with Willow and the other wood nymphs, lost in his paints . . . that would be the best way to drive away thoughts of the sweet-faced nursemaid who clearly did not return his interest.

He stepped into the Enchanted Glen's magical light, looked toward the pond, and froze.

Ned and Vanessa were on his bench . . . in a passionate embrace.

Willow swayed above them, her hands clutched together, her eyes wide as she peered across the clearing. "They can't see or hear you," she called to him. "They didn't come through the passage."

Dazed, he remained rooted in place. The picture was excruciating . . . yet mesmerizing. Ned's arm wrapped around Vanessa's back . . . his lips pressed against hers . . . his other hand now moving up from her ankle to caress her calf.

His stomach knotted and he turned away, ashamed to have spied on their intimacy. And of his own jealously. Bending over, he escaped back into the passage, wishing he'd never seen that image. A vision he knew would flash before his eyes every time he saw or thought of Vanessa again.

"Seems like your Vanessa has two admirers," said Morniero from his perch on an oak branch overlooking the Enchanted Wood, or "Fairy Glen," as some earlier locals had called it.

On the tree limb next to him, Lachima brushed locks of floating white hair back with her long fingers. "Not surprising. She's an extraordinary girl."

Morniero raised a brow, his gaze still fixed on the tableau beneath them. "I'm afraid Willow isn't taking the news so well."

The nymph's back shook as she curled into her tree trunk, her sobs muffled in its depths.

Lachima understood why her niece transformed girls into wood nymphs rather than let them be caught by the lusty brutes pursuing them. Nonetheless, the result of their rescue seemed nearly as cruel as the fate the girls narrowly escaped. And little Willow had only been nine when Artiana snatched her from the clutches of her drunken father and turned her into the wood nymph she was today.

"Poor thing," said Lachima. "Avery does seem oblivious to her feelings."

Morniero crossed his arms behind his head. "Willow brought it upon herself, allowing him access to the Glen for so long."

Lachima swatted her brother's thigh. "You feel as bad for her as I do, and you know it."

Down below, Vanessa pulled away from Ned, her face flushed. "We . . . we should go."

He removed his hand from her leg and placed it against her cheek. "I wish we could stay here forever."

The wistful note in Ned's voice drew Lachima to lean forward to get a better view.

"Don't you think one location might get a little dull after an eternity?" Vanessa replied with a laugh as she slipped off Ned's lap.

"Not if that eternity were spent in the right company." Ned's tone of flirtatious detachment was back in place as he rose and kissed her again.

"And speaking of access to the Glen . . ." Morniero gestured toward the pond with his chin. "Your little lovebirds down there best not tempt the naiads into their old ways."

The water nymphs giggled and dipped in and out of the water, their eyes fixed on Vanessa and Ned as the two departed, hand in hand.

Turning to her brother, Lachima mustered a hopeful smile. "How will we know if the water nymphs can be trusted with the humans if they never have a chance to prove it?"

Staring at her with narrowed eyes, Morniero folded his arms across his chest, but made no reply.

Chapter Twenty-Four

Later that night, Avery lowered himself into his desk chair and stared up at the array of his watercolors pinned to the wall. Some were of the local flora and fauna. Chokeberry and sweetfern. Gray dogwood and scarlet elder. Just rolling their names over his tongue calmed him down. Restored his equilibrium.

Others were more fantastical. Images of the wood nymphs stretching branched arms from tree trunks, giant exotic flowers, and snow laden trees sparkling with flecks of diamond. These were scenes from the Enchanted Wood. In all the years he'd been visiting, he'd refused to think too deeply about the place. Unable to discuss it with anyone and wary of losing it, like Bess had, he simply accepted it at face value. Fantasy or reality, it pleased him, and that was enough.

But now, looking at the images as he imagined Vanessa might, he was inspired to dream, to remind himself that anything was possible. She certainly seemed to be a dreamer, attaching herself to a blue blood like Ned Cooper. Despite Irene's revelation of their relationship at the soda fountain, it was an entirely different matter to witness their intimacy himself.

Yet, despite what Avery had seen, he refused to believe that Vanessa was the kind of girl to play mistress to a man like that. He trusted she had higher hopes for the relationship, no matter how far-fetched the idea.

He pictured her outside the chapel earlier that morning and realized that it was more than her beauty that moved him. It was . . . the bounce in her step. The openness of her face. There was a hint of childlike innocence there. A part of her that still seemed to believe anything was possible.

She made him feel lighter himself, more optimistic. Opening his desk drawer, he pulled out the well-worn pamphlet his department advisor had sent weeks earlier. He ran his finger down the list of new positions with the White Mountain National Forest. The document was dog-eared and creased from his constant handling, but remained blank.

If a nursemaid had such faith in a brighter future for herself, why not him?

He reached for his pen and ink. It was time to fill out the application.

<h1 style="text-align:center">Chapter Twenty-Five</h1>

The next day, Avery was still thinking about Vanessa and Ned as he pushed an empty cane-backed wheelchair down the hospital corridor. After breakfast, he'd gone straight to the Wood to paint, trying to capture Vanessa's image outside church while it was still fresh in his mind . . . and replace the vision of her kissing Ned Cooper that still plagued him.

He arrived at the treatment room, where his father was just smoothing the last layer of plaster onto the leg cast of an elderly woman. The way the light from the dusty window shone through the woman's yellowed hair reminded him of the sunlight in the Enchanted Wood reflecting the dozens of auburn shades in Vanessa's hair, from mahogany to cherry to copper.

Gently lifting the old woman from the examination table into the wheelchair, he thought of his efforts to replicate all the colors of Vanessa's features. Her lips, the blushing pink of a dogwood tree in blossom. Her eyes, the deep blue of sapphires, reflecting light and wit.

Wheeling the old woman down the corridor to her family in the waiting room, he tried to remember any girl affecting him like this before. He'd had a crush on Pearl Jenkins in high school, but never got close to asking her out. At Dartmouth mixers, he'd been a popular dance partner, and even dated one girl from Hanover he met at Winter Carnival his junior year. But no one had ever consumed his attention like this.

Once his father's elderly patient was safely transferred to her family's care, he pushed the wheelchair slowly back to the storeroom, its wheels squeaking on the hospital's linoleum floor.

It was foolhardy to be so taken with this girl he hardly knew.

His grip on the chair's handles tightened as he remembered how she smiled when Ned Cooper whispered in her ear on the dance floor earlier that summer. How she'd declined the invitation to join his family for dinner . . . and wrapped her arms around Cooper with such passion. There was no reason to hope Vanessa shared his feelings.

He yanked the storeroom door open and jammed the chair into place.

Best to simply finish her portrait and add it to the collection of artworks on his bedroom wall. A lovely image that had nothing to do with the real world of artificial lights, the smell of ammonia, and the groans of restless patients.

A few hours later, Avery lifted a patient off his soiled sheets and waited for Nurse Hutchins to stretch fresh ones in place. The old man coughed bloody phlegm onto the sleeve of Avery's uniform, but there was nothing Avery could do but stand there with clenched teeth.

As soon as the nurse finished, he laid the gentleman back on the bed and dashed out the door. Reaching the back steps, he vomited into the bushes, tore his white tunic off, and threw it to the ground. Having dropped his Forest Service application off at the post office on his way to the hospital, he found his work today nearly intolerable.

Any lingering doubt about his future in medicine was eliminated. He couldn't stand being trapped indoors day and night. Making small talk with patients while gagging from the smell of their blood and excretions. And worst of all, watching those his father couldn't help succumb before their eyes.

"Avery?"

He turned to find Nurse Hutchins standing behind him, hands on her ample hips.

"Your father wants to see you. In his office."

Avery stood silently in front of the wide maple desk as his father finished writing in a medical chart. How many hours had he remained in this spot over the years, waiting for his father to acknowledge him? His fists clenched as his eyes wandered the immutable landscape of his father's dominion. The crammed bookshelves behind his father's back, the aged "Illustrations of the Human Body" chart with an advertisement for J. R. Stafford's Olive Tar running down the center, diplomas yellowing in their frames. The humble office screamed "death" even louder than that old man's phlegmy hack.

After a seeming eternity, his father recapped his fountain pen, closed the file, put it aside and folded his hands on the leather blotter. Only then did he look up. "It's time for you to go home now."

Avery's gut twisted. He knew this tone. His father was furious. "Sir?"

"Mr. Griffin informed me that you threw him on his bed, and Nurse Hutchins said you ran from the room looking ill."

"I didn't throw him." It was a boy's response and shamed him more than the truth of his possible insensitivity with the elderly patient.

"I thought this was going to be an excellent opportunity. A chance for you to gain some experience, give you a head start." His father pinched his nose with is fingers. "But you've made it clear enough you don't want to be here, disappearing every time there's a moment for me to demonstrate a skill or talk through a patient's symptoms."

His father lowered his hand revealing sorrowful eyes. "Or maybe you think my ways are old-fashioned. You'd prefer to start fresh with whatever they're teaching at medical school these days."

"It's not you, Father. You're an excellent doctor."

"Then what's the problem, son?"

Closing his eyes, Avery tilted his head back. It was time. Ignoring his galloping heart, he took a deep breath . . . and spoke. "I don't want to go to medical school."

As soon as the words passed his lips, his eyes flew open as the weight of an entire oak lifted from his shoulders.

His father blinked. "What?"

"It's the truth, Father. I don't want to go."

"What do you mean?" His father appeared sincerely confused. "Of course you're going to medical school. You got into Harvard, for God's sake."

"I don't want to be a doctor. I've never wanted to be a doctor." Avery's spirits rose with every word.

"What are you talking about?" His father stared, his palms flat on his desk.

Avery was shocked at the magnitude of his father's surprise. Had he guarded his secret that well? Or had his father fought seeing the truth? "I never, ever wanted to disappoint you."

"You . . . you're going to join my practice. Take it over one day." He'd never seen his father so lost and confused, aging right before his eyes.

The guilt of it buckled his knees. He sank into the wooden chair in front of his father's desk. "I can't, Father. I just can't."

"I knew something was wrong." His father shook his head, his eyes fixed on his hands. "I knew there was something you needed to tell me . . ." He stared up at the ceiling, his lips shaking as though he started to say several things before reconsidering his words. After a number of excruciating moments, he lowered his head, his shoulders sagging. "So what do you want to do instead?"

"I've applied for a job with the Forest Service, in the new national forest."

His father squinted. "You want to be a *forest ranger*?"

It had been foolish to harbor that flicker of hope his father would approve. "Not exactly. More like a researcher. Doing inventory of what's currently growing there. It would be outdoors . . . and nearby."

"God gave you the brains and the hands to be a doctor. A healer. A man who can save lives." His father rose to his feet and leaned across the desk, eyes blazing.

"And you want to turn your back on all that so you can hike around in the woods and take notes?"

Avery nodded, blood draining to his feet. It was everything he feared. The reason he'd avoided telling the truth for so long.

"Well, it's an abomination. A waste of human talent, and you won't get my blessing for it." His father pounded the desk with his fist. "You won't!"

Avery pushed himself to his feet, turned and left the room. Dizzy, he reached for the wall as he made his way along the corridor. The sensation of lightness he'd felt at admitting the truth had morphed into something more akin to weightlessness. Like being an untethered balloon, losing contact with the earth.

Chapter Twenty-Six

"Tell me about your sister's house in Boston." Vanessa smiled up at Ned as they waltzed across the dance floor on the beach. "I don't believe I've ever seen it."

It was the last day of August and the last dance of the season. She wore her finest dress, the gauzy one with beading, hoping he remembered it from the night he'd whispered in her ear about "saving the best for last."

"The place is a monstrosity." He swung her around to head the opposite direction across the dance floor. "Larger than anyone could ever need."

"I can't wait to see it." She peered up at him through her lashes. "When we're all back in the city."

He had yet to speak of their future together, though most guests were already packing for their return to their homes in cities along the East Coast. It was giving her stomach aches. She'd hardly seen Ned since he'd returned to work, coming out on the train with the rest of the men on weekends only. This evening was the first time in weeks they'd had a chance to talk privately.

He pulled her close against his chest. "Don't remind me the summer has come to an end. I never want to leave this paradise."

She laughed. "So not such a terrible time without your friends after all."

"Thanks to you, I didn't miss them a bit." Ned led her off the dance floor by the hand. "Hasn't the season been grand?"

"Oh, yes! Better than I ever imagined." The months had passed in a blur. Her hours were long, but time spent with the children was generally pleasant.

They walked to the dock, where he leaned his back against the railing, still holding her hand. "Cecile and Albert have behaved themselves." He pulled her close. "Haven't they?"

She stood between his outstretched legs. "They've been no trouble at all."

It was true. There was nothing about working for the Gardners to complain about. The children had eventually tired of their picture books and now enjoyed hearing her original bedtime stories. Still, she missed her candlelight evenings of the early summer, weaving tales for the much sweeter Walter and Edna.

But ever since she'd joined the Gardners' staff, her true passion had been for what came after her charges were in bed. When he wasn't in Boston, that was when her private time with Ned began. They visited their rock by the pond when they could, his hands roaming with greater abandon, addicting her entire body to his touch. Once he caressed her bottom with his palm as he kissed her, which caused an explosion of sensation in her loins that was almost painful. When he was gone, she daydreamed of his fingertips caressing and exploring, which was sometimes enough to make her insides quake . . . and the weeks fly by.

The moon hung behind Ned's head, casting him in silhouette. Her breath came fast and shallow as he traced a spiral on her upturned palm. "It's been the best summer of my life," she whispered.

The raw truth of it was bittersweet. Needing a distraction from her desire to throw herself against him and kiss him in front of the entire gathering, she pulled her hand from his clasp and placed it on her hip. "And to think, in June, when I got on the train to come here, I thought Twin Birch House might be some enormous tree house, and imagined the staff had to sleep in tents, trying not to get eaten by bears."

Still holding her other hand, Ned laughed. "Eaten by bears! That's what I love about you. Constantly saying the most charming and unexpected things."

All she heard was *"what I love about you . . ."* Joy leapt from her belly to her throat. How she'd longed for him to confess some deeper affection for her. "Do you really?"

"Really what?"

Her heart seemed to beat against her collarbones. "Love me?"

He became quite serious, searching her eyes as he held her shoulders. "If that's the word for thinking about someone all the time when you're not with them, and wanting to kiss them all the time when you are."

She gripped his arm for fear she'd float away from sheer happiness. Could she define love any better? How did anyone know when they're in love, anyway? All she knew for certain was that he'd just described exactly how she felt about him.

As the weeks had flown by with no sign of the fairy and no declarations from Ned, she'd nearly given up hope he was her "man of sterling and gold." But the tiny flicker that remained now roared into flame.

The tinkle of high-pitched laughter floated over the water. She cocked her head with a smile, for the delicate sound seemed to promise wedding bells. The sparkles of moonlight on the lake brought to mind the rice that would fly outside the church on their happy day.

"Come with me," Ned replied in a husky voice. His fingers intertwined with hers as he led her past the ring of candles circling the crowd. She bit the inside of her cheek to keep from grinning like an idiot as they headed up the sloped lawn.

When they bumped into Avery and Irene coming down from the hotel, she bubbled with giddy delight. "Hello!"

"Hello to you, too." Irene sounded serious. "We've been looking for you."

"So glad you found me!" She glanced up at Ned. "Or, rather, found us."

The men said each other's names in clipped tones and briefly shook hands.

Vanessa laid her hand on Avery's arm. "It's been ages! I'd hoped you'd come up to more dances." She hadn't seen him since late July, when she'd met his family at the church.

She'd meant to ask Irene if she knew how he was doing, but a vague discomfort held her back. Her commitment was to Ned, making her continued . . . thoughts . . . about Avery feel somehow disloyal.

Avery ran his fingers through his adorably messy hair. "I've been working at the Cullens's grocery store recently."

"Saturday nights?" She meant to sound teasing, but it occurred to her that he might have genuinely been avoiding the hotel.

Ned coughed. "Pleasure seeing you both, but would you excuse us a moment?" He wrapped his arm around her shoulders. "There's something I need to discuss with Vanessa. Privately."

Speculation about Avery's motives for skipping the dances melted in the warmth of Ned's embrace. She squeezed her lips together to keep from grinning and turned to follow him, but Irene grabbed her by the wrist. "Have you seen Gladys?"

"Not since supper." Vanessa squinted back toward the dance floor. "She must be here somewhere."

"You two have a pleasant evening." Ned's voice was as firm as his grip on her upper arm.

Avery's eyes narrowed at Ned, then focused squarely on her. "We'll see you later, I trust?"

"Absolutely." Ned squeezed Vanessa's shoulder. "I'll have her back in no time, safe and sound."

"We'll be holding you to that." Avery sounded quite serious, though Ned laughed as if he had made a joke.

As Ned led her away, she turned back. "Wonderful to see you again, Avery!"

He waved, his mouth a slim line. The light from the circle of candles reflected off his glasses, making him appear rather fierce.

Irene stood at his side, hands on her hips, face obscured in Avery's shadow.

Vanessa turned back to Ned, who clasped her hand and quickened his pace. Soon they were running together toward the woods, her jangled nerves sending her into a giggling fit. "Where are we going?" she managed to say after they slowed and she caught her breath.

"Our spot. I need to ask you something."

Ask her something? Her breath caught in her chest. It could only mean one thing. Everything she'd been dreaming of all summer.

She and Ned quickly reached the pond, where the moon shone down on its smooth surface. Strange to think how frightened she'd been in these same woods only a few months earlier. As usual, he pulled off his coat and laid it over "their" flat rock. "A throne for my queen."

After a quick curtsey, she took his hand and lowered herself onto his jacket. Between the scent of his cologne and anticipation of his pressing question, all thoughts of her earlier fears were forgotten.

He sat next to her, leaning on the arm he'd placed behind her back. "You are beautiful, Vanessa."

His finger trailed along her hairline and over her ear, making her shiver. Her face lifted toward his, her lips eager for his kiss. He tilted her chin toward his mouth with the lightest touch and pressed his mouth against hers. Her conscious thoughts faded as she surrendered to the pleasure of their tongues meeting in a playful dance. The cool night air made the heat of his hand gripping her waist that much warmer.

"God, how I want you," he murmured as his fingers slipped under her beaded bodice and caressed her hardened nipples over the silk layer beneath. She slid her hand up his sleeve, reveling in the feel of his muscle flexing beneath his shirt. Their tongues danced between their mouths as he swiftly unbuttoned the side of her dress. His touch made it hard to think as his palm ran over the bare skin at the base of her ribs . . . then glided upward to cup her breast.

She breathed her words out between kisses. "What . . . did you want . . . to ask me?"

"I think you know . . ." he whispered in her ear, lightly nibbling its curved edge.

"I . . . I think I do . . ."

He kissed her more passionately as he slid his hand lower, atop the folds of her skirt, his palm warm through the thin fabric as he kissed her neck, making her gasp again and close her eyes.

Aside from the backstairs attack she endured, her only sexual experience beyond Ned involved a handful of brief kisses with a shy delivery boy and having her chest groped a few times by a roguish stable hand. She'd never gone this far.

Never felt such need, experienced her body arching toward a man, as though it had a mind of its own. The intensity left her lightheaded and breathless.

Ned leaned over and slipped his hand slowly down to the bottom edge of her dress. Once he'd reached beneath the hem, he pressed his mouth against hers and began gliding his hand from the top of her ankle up toward her knee.

Overwhelmed by the avalanche of sensation, she rolled her head away from his lips' reach. Dread and excitement wrestled in her belly as his fingertips crept farther and farther up, eventually reaching the inside of her thigh.

Only then did a little voice begin to protest, to warn her into action. Mustering every ounce of determination to resist her own desire, she forced herself to grab his wrist. "Ned."

He nibbled her ear. "Yes?"

"We can't." She gently guided his hand out from under her dress. "We're not even engaged."

He stilled, his breath heavy on her collar bone. "Engaged?"

"Yes."

"Don't do that, my angel." He pressed his lips to her eyelids and cheeks in slow, deliberate kisses.

She leaned her head back as he bestowed more kisses on her neck. "Do what?"

"Spoil our last night together . . ." He moved his head down to kiss her chest at the lowest point of her satin-trimmed neckline. "With talk of what we can't have, when we should enjoy what we can."

Her head cleared in an instant. The chill in the night air became unpleasant, despite the warmth of Ned's breath on her exposed skin. "Our last night?"

He turned his head, disappointment creeping into his voice. "We return to Boston in the morning. You said so yourself."

Scooting back, she clamped her knees together, turning them away from him. "But I'm coming with you . . . I mean, with your sister . . ."

Still propped on one hand, he placed the other on her knee. "Mrs. O'Malley is waiting for them in Boston. I couldn't keep her at bay indefinitely."

Nauseated, she began refastening the side of her dress. There'd been no promise, of course. Neither Ned nor his sister had said anything about the position being permanent. Only her own denial had allowed her to think otherwise. "I just assumed . . ."

"She's been with them forever, though I don't know what they see in her." He caressed her knee. "I would have done more if I could. You have to know that."

"Your sister hasn't said anything about me leaving her service." She knew she was grasping at straws, and worse, that no one had misled her more than herself.

His expression held sorrow and pity in equal measure. "I've kept my word all summer, Vanessa. I've been completely honest."

The horrible truth sapped her strength. "But . . . you wanted your family to see my qualities . . ."

"And they did. I've no doubt my sister will provide an excellent reference. You'll be sought after by all the best families."

She covered her mouth to stifle her moan, then lowered her fingers enough to murmur, "So . . . your question?" Blinking back tears, she cringed at the pleading in her voice.

He turned away and propped his elbows on his knees, his eyes on the ground between his shoes. "I'm a gentleman. I wouldn't force myself on you." He turned toward her, looking genuinely hurt. "And I thought you wanted me, too. I'm sorry if I . . . misunderstood."

The forest seemed to bend and twist around her, as though reflected in the funhouse mirrors of a traveling circus. She squeezed her eyes shut and covered her face with her hands.

"We've had the most magical summer together, don't you think?" His tone was nearly as pleading as hers had been.

She whispered through her fingers. "You said you loved me."

He sighed and hung his head. "What do our feelings have to do with it? What future could we have?"

Lowering her hands from her face, she turned toward him, her jaw tightening. "We could get married, Ned. There's no law against it."

He raised his chin and stared a moment, his eyes growing cold. "And here I thought it was me you cared about, not my family's money."

Crack!

Her palm tingled from slapping him, her heartbeat thundering in her ears.

He blinked as his hand cupped his cheek. To her surprise, he appeared confused. Hurt, even.

She scrambled to her feet, tears spilling down her scorching cheeks. Without looking back, she headed toward the lights of the hotel, just visible between the tree trunks and underbrush.

Idiot. Fool.

As she tripped and stumbled through the dark, her palms scraped against rough bark. Low branches clawed at her dress and hair.

Silly goose.

Her heart had warned her that Ned had no thought of marriage. Gladys and Irene had both hinted at it. But she hadn't wanted to listen. Didn't dare listen—for it meant that leaving the Wainwrights had been a catastrophic mistake. But was it the fairy who'd been wrong . . . or was it her?

She arrived at the edge of the woods and stopped, taking a moment to run her fingers through her hair and straighten her dress. Eyeing the dormitory across the lawn, she stepped onto the grass and began her beeline for the sanctuary of her bunk. Forcing herself to walk, she held her breath, praying that no one would notice her.

"Vanessa!"

It was Avery. She closed her eyes at the sound of his voice, her feet slowing beneath her. Plastering a smile on her face, she turned to find him jogging toward her.

"Leaving the party?" He slowed as he drew near.

Turning toward the dorms, she yearned to be magically transported to her bunk. "I'm rather tired . . ."

He stopped a few feet from her, half his face illuminated by the light pouring from the dorm windows, the rest cloaked in darkness. His eyes roamed her face and his brow furrowed. "Are you all right?"

"Yes, of course. Just been a long day."

Looking into the distance behind her, he crossed his arms. "Where's Ned?"

"Oh, we've said our goodbyes." Her smile took every ounce of effort she possessed.

He reached out for her shoulder, his grip tender and light. "He didn't do anything . . . to upset you?" His voice hardened. "Did he?"

"No, no. Just said goodbye." She lowered her eyes to the grass as they threatened to fill with tears. "We'd become rather . . . friendly . . . over the past few months."

His hand lifted from her shoulder. "Well, I wanted to be sure to say goodbye as well." He sounded nearly as disappointed as she was.

She glanced up, a lump forming in her throat. "Thank you. I'm sorry we didn't see more of each other this summer."

How different things might have been, had Ned not whispered in her ear just before that last dance back in June. What would the season have been like if she had shared that last waltz with Avery instead?

"Me, too." His tone allowed her to imagine he was asking himself the same question.

After a moment of awkward silence, she extended her hand. "Please do take care of yourself."

He clasped her hand in both of his. "You, as well."

Losing control of the tears burning her eyelids, she turned and raced for the dormitory, no longer caring who saw her go.

Chapter Twenty-Seven

With smooth flaps of his silver and green wings, Morniero followed Vanessa across the lawn. Lachima had shown far too much interest in Vanessa's encounter with Ned by the pond earlier that evening.

As much as he wished he could trust his sister, he needed to do some testing of his own.

He popped into his humanoid form as he followed her into the dim light of the deserted women's dorm, lined with wooden bunk beds and washstands topped by pitchers and bowls.

Though he was loath to admit it to Lachima, Vanessa did have an unusual allure. He'd visited the dreams of the nursemaid's charges. They were full of imaginative stories and memories of playful moments spent with her. The kind of happy scenarios he wished he found in every child's nocturnal visions.

So, although he had never visited Vanessa's sleep before, he'd seen so much of her in the children's dreams, she already felt familiar to him. Settling on the bunk across from hers, he watched as she threw herself onto her bed and sobbed into her pillow.

Feminine voices reached him through the open window. Girls returning from the lakeside festivities, no doubt. He feared the new arrivals might try to comfort Vanessa and postpone her going to sleep. Plus, he wished to ease her suffering.

Glad Lachima wasn't there to see him, he crossed over and laid his hand on Vanessa's head. A minor infraction of the rule against interacting with the mortals, he assured himself. As anticipated, Vanessa's sobs quieted into the gentle rhythm of slumber.

Closing his own eyes, Morniero leaned over and touched his forehead to hers. She'd only just entered her dreamworld, so it was still jumbled and disjointed. He heard Ned Cooper's final words by the pond again. Felt the comforting pressure of Walter Wainwright's arms around her neck . . . and little Ruth's arms from years earlier. Witnessed the twin monsters of cold and hunger leering at her through a broken window with sallow faces and bloodshot eyes. And then he experienced the tingle of Lachima's hand on Vanessa's shoulder, promising her "a man of sterling and gold."

Pulling his head abruptly away, he returned to himself just as several young ladies entered the dorm, giggling and stumbling from the effects of the mixer's spiked punch. But he didn't care about them. He was too angry Lachima had broken her word. And more importantly, that she hadn't been able to resist the temptation of communicating directly with a human.

The whole experiment had been Lachima's idea. If she couldn't control herself, what hope was there for the rest of them?

Chapter Twenty-Eight

❧

The following morning, Avery dressed for church, staring into his bedroom mirror as he slid his necktie around his collar. He was still agitated from the night before. Something had gone wrong between Vanessa and Ned. She obviously cared for the bastard as much as he'd feared, if not more. As he flipped one end of the tie over the other, a part of him worried that her distress was more than sorrow at parting from Cooper.

After tugging a Windsor knot into place under his chin, he leaned both hands on the wall and blew his breath out hard. What if that selfish cad hurt her . . . physically? Or, God forbid, dishonored her? The blood rushed to his face. He'd never felt so protective, so capable of violence.

With a snort, he pushed himself away from the wall. He'd never been in a fight in his life, and now he wanted to be the hero? For a girl who barely knew he was alive?

Reaching for his jacket, which hung on the back his desk chair, he saw the Forest Service logo. It was on the corner of an envelope sticking out from beneath a pile of folded laundry. His mother must have put it there when she left the clean clothes.

He tugged the letter out. It had to have arrived Friday. Hattie wouldn't have understood its importance, and his mother must not have either. That meant both he and his father had kept the fact he wasn't going to medical school from his mother. His father probably hoped he'd change his mind, while Avery had maintained the secret in hopes of breaking the news to her with a job offer in hand, as he'd originally planned to do with his father.

He slid a finger under the envelope's flap and tore it open. Holding his breath, he unfolded the enclosure and scanned it quickly. There it was. The word he was looking for. "Congratulations."

He exhaled and grinned as he read the text again more slowly. ". . . welcome you to the Service . . . telephone as soon as possible to discuss . . ."

"Hurrah!"

He grabbed his coat and bounded down the stairs, letter in hand. Hattie and his parents were already by the front door.

"Avery, dear?" His mother pressed her hat onto her head. "What is it?"

His father's eyes moved to the paper in Avery's hand and his shoulders drooped.

A lump rose in Avery's throat, but it couldn't be helped. Hopefully his father would come around one day. "I have some important news, Mother." He gestured her into the living room, struggling to contain his excitement and anxiety. "You'd best sit down."

Her soft eyes blinked in confusion. "But we'll be late for church. Can it wait?"

"Oh, come on, Mother." Hattie pulled their mother by the arm. "Didn't you hear him shout? We can't wait all the way through the service to hear what he's so excited about."

"Well . . ." His mother shot him a worried look. "I suppose you're right."

She dragged the hat from her head and allowed Hattie to lead her toward the sofa. His father clutched the rim of his derby with both hands and headed for his own chair.

As Avery followed his family, his thoughts returned to Vanessa. He now realized that most of his reluctance to pursue her during the summer had been because his future had been so unclear. He hadn't felt like he had anything to offer. And now it was too late. Today marked the peak of the pre-Labor Day departures from the White Mountains. No doubt Vanessa left on the morning train with the Gardners, along with most of the other hotel guests and their personal staff.

He sat on the edge of the upholstered chair next to his father and faced his mother and sister. Taking a deep breath, he scanned their expectant faces. Though he couldn't imagine Hattie cared deeply about him becoming a doctor, his mother would likely be as devastated as his father, even if she hid her feelings better.

His gaze fell to the letter clutched in his hands. After he told his family the news, he'd skip church and go straight to the Enchanted Wood. At least he could be sure Willow and the other nymphs would share his happiness.

Chapter Twenty-Nine

After a restless night of unsettling dreams, Vanessa awoke to find the dorm bustling with excited girls. Many of them were packing to catch the early train to Boston with their employers. Most of the college students on staff were leaving as well.

Sitting up, she wiped the crust from her bleary eyes and placed her feet on the dark green floorboards. She shuffled to the washbasin and splashed cool water onto her face. Patting her cheeks with a linen towel, she turned back toward the bunk and froze.

Gladys's bed wasn't just empty, it was stripped bare. All her belongings were gone.

Vanessa's stomach twisted as her eyes swept the dorm. Irene's question the night before echoed in her ears. *"Have you seen Gladys?"*

At the adjoining bunk, Clara's blonde head was bent over her open suitcase, her hands busy folding and packing garments. Not Vanessa's first choice, but as the nearest person who might know anything, she would have to do.

"Clara." Vanessa strode to the girl's side. "What happened to Gladys? Where did she go?"

The blonde straightened, her eyebrow arched. "You didn't hear?"

"No." The knot in Vanessa's stomach began to ache. "What did I miss?"

"Her beau." Clara's face softened, her eyes misting. "He was killed."

She sank onto Clara's bunk beside the open suitcase. "Chester?" His name came out in a croaky whisper.

Clara nodded. "A letter arrived from his mother. Gladys read it last evening after supper." Her voice trembled. "Mrs. Juneau arranged for the hotel car to take her directly home. Guess she doesn't live far from here."

Nodding, Vanessa stared at the whitewashed walls without seeing them. "Moultonborough."

She tried to remember the last time she'd given Gladys her full attention. Weeks? Picturing the girl at supper the night before, she realized how much weight her friend had lost since they first met. The poor thing was literally sick with worry . . . and then her worst fears came true.

Vanessa covered her face with her hands and moaned. Thinking of no one but Ned, she'd been no help in Gladys's darkest moment. Not even there to say goodbye.

Clara's hand rested on her shoulder. "Have you got someone over there, too?"

Vanessa shook her head, then lowered her hands. There were tears on Clara's cheeks. "You?"

Clara nodded and she withdrew her hand. "My brother."

"I'm so sorry."

"I pray for him every day." Clara wiped her tears, rubbed her palms on her skirt, and resumed packing.

Vanessa's eyes returned to the floor, sympathetic toward her nemesis in a way she'd never dreamed possible. "You were right, of course. About Ned."

Clara's hands stopped moving. She straightened and met Vanessa's eyes. "You were, too."

Surprised, Vanessa tensed for the snide remark sure to follow.

"Why should you pass up a chance at love?" Clara's eyes drifted to Gladys's stripped mattress, her voice leaden. "You never know how long you have."

This was not a sentiment Vanessa ever imagined hearing from Clara. Was there *anyone* she'd judged correctly this summer? Irene? Avery? Ned's sister?

She looked at Clara's suitcase and sucked in her breath. What if Mrs. Gardner *wasn't* letting her go? Anger flared in her belly. She sprang to her feet, barely avoiding hitting her head on Clara's upper bunk. Ned's sister had never said a word about leaving Vanessa behind. Made no mention of a final paycheck. Nothing.

What if Ned was wrong . . . or lying?

"I've got to go!" Vanessa dragged her bag from under her bed, and tossed in her hairbrush and books from the little shelf over her bed.

"With the Gardners?" Clara kept packing.

"I certainly hope so." She hurried past Clara, her bag bumping against her leg.

"Good luck."

She ignored the skepticism in Clara's voice. "You, too!" After pulling her hat and coat off the wall hook, she rushed out the door.

Chapter Thirty

Vanessa pushed her way through the porters and masses of guests, their children, and staff. The sea of people moved along the gravel path from the hotel's main building to the private train platform at the rear of the property. The spur line led down the mountain to the Boston & Maine railway stop in Conway.

She stood on tiptoe near the peak-roofed shelter, pressing her hat to her head as she scanned the crowd.

"There you are, Miss Perkins." It was Ned's sister, calling from somewhere behind her.

Relief loosened Vanessa's shoulders when she turned and found Cecile and Albert standing next to their parents, smiles on their faces. Sarah Gardner's lips were pursed and she let out a little huff. "We thought you'd come by the cottage this morning."

Vanessa drew closer to the family. "I'm sorry. I wasn't sure where you wanted to meet."

Mrs. Gardner fluttered her hand. "Never mind that. Just glad to see you now. Mr. Gardner has your check."

Vanessa's fist clenched the grip of her valise as her employer pulled an envelope from inside his jacket and handed it to her. "I thought . . . I might be staying on with you. The children and I get on so well."

She smiled down at Cecile, who was watching with apparent interest, twirling a lock of hair in her finger, and Albert, busy digging something from his nose.

"Oh, darling, they have enjoyed your company, too," cooed Mrs. Gardner. "But as it happens, their regular nanny's family crisis has passed. She's waiting for us at home." The elegant brunette tilted her head slightly. "I thought it was clear this was just a summer arrangement."

"No, Mrs. Gardner." Vanessa squared her shoulders. No matter how slim the chances she could turn the situation around, she needed to try. "When your brother convinced me to leave the Wainwrights, I believed my position with your family had the potential to become permanent in nature."

"Oh, dear. That is unfortunate." Mrs. Gardner's effort to appear sympathetic was anemic at best.

Vanessa's lungs felt like they were turning to stone, making it harder and harder to breathe. "Can I at least get a reference?"

"Hardly anything to say, you were with us such a short time . . . but if you find you absolutely *need* it, come by the house and I'll see what I can do." Her eyes warned against taking her up on the invitation.

Mr. Gardner checked his pocket watch. "Come along, Sarah, children." He gave no indication of having the slightest interest in Vanessa's fate. "Time to get aboard."

Cecile gave her a quick wave before skipping after her father and brother. Ned's sister gathered the folds of her pleated top-skirt in one hand. "You're a clever girl, Miss Perkins. I've no doubt you'll land on your feet."

Vanessa grew lightheaded as Ned and his parents joined the Gardner family boarding the wooden railcar. When their eyes met, his sad smile gave at least the illusion he harbored regrets.

"Mith Perkins!"

Before Vanessa could turn around, her knees were almost knocked out from under her as Walter threw himself against her legs. She dropped her suitcase, scooped the boy up onto her hip and closed her eyes as she kissed his hair. "Hello, little man."

"We haven't theen you in foowehvuh." Walter pouted but didn't loosen his grip.

"I know." Her voice cracked. "I've missed you."

"Good morning, Miss Perkins." Mrs. Wainwright approached holding Edna's hand. Her former employer's frosty tone inspired Vanessa to gently lower Walter to the ground.

"Good morning, Mrs. Wainwright. Back to the city?"

"Yes. Edna will be starting school this week."

Vanessa smiled down at the little girl. "That's wonderful, Edna. What a big girl you are."

The girl beamed back. "Are you coming on the train, too?"

"Well . . . actually . . ." A glance toward the carriages confirmed the Gardners and Coopers were no longer in sight. She turned back to Mrs. Wainwright. "My place with the Gardners was only for the summer, so I'm free again."

She smiled with hopes of appearing carefree and gay, but inside she was begging on her knees.

Mrs. Wainwright glanced over her shoulder at her husband walking beside the porter and their mountain of luggage. "Children, go see if your father needs help."

Once Walter and Edna had scampered back to join their father, she focused on Vanessa, her brow knitted. "Miss Perkins, you should know that every family of note in Boston has already heard, or will soon hear, of your thoroughly unprofessional behavior this summer."

Vanessa stopped breathing as her idol and role model publicly upbraided her. Despite Mrs. Wainwright keeping her voice low, other passengers and staff were beginning to listen.

"First you leave me and my family in the lurch, then you throw yourself shamelessly at Ned Cooper? Frankly, it embarrassed me to no end that I brought you here in the first place." Mrs. Wainwright clutched her gloved fingers together. "I'm telling you this because we were all once so fond of you. I wish to save you the humiliation of seeking a position with any respectable family in Boston, as you will never find a place amongst us again."

The experience was so shocking, it almost seemed to be happening to someone else. Any lingering fantasies that Vanessa might one day be welcomed in high-society's ranks were crushed for good. But to be branded unsuitable to even serve them? It was her worst nightmare brought to life in broad daylight.

Standing in the ashes of her life, forming a reply was beyond her capacities.

As Mrs. Wainwright turned her back and rejoined her family, Vanessa once more perceived the crowd surrounding her. Left and right, she swiveled her head. But the view was the same in every direction—the smug, smirking faces of Boston's elite, enjoying the spectacle of her social destruction. She barely noticed the more merciful among them. The ones who turned away before meeting her eye.

As disjointed as Pinocchio, she picked up her bag and walked off the platform on wooden legs. The loud buzzing in her ear was reminiscent of when the warden at the Home boxed her ears. The memory called forth instincts from her youth, when showing weakness meant your blanket got stolen while you slept.

She swallowed her tears and held her face immobile as she pressed against the current of departing guests, making her way back toward the hotel. But halfway to the main building, her steps slowed. No place remained for her at Twin Birch House. She'd been ejected from the Eden that had been her home since June.

She came to an abrupt halt. An island amidst the flow of people moving around her, recomposing their groups once they'd passed.

What could she do? Where could she go?

The questions kept repeating in her mind, but no answers came back.

Chapter Thirty-One

Unable to stand in the pathway indefinitely, Vanessa forced her feet to move. Getting away from the crowd was her only goal. She crossed the hotel lawn, her mind vacant as she focused on nothing but her next step.

She passed the tennis courts, then the pony stables and the Sewards' house. From that point, there was nowhere else but the woods. Crossing from the sunshine into the shade of the forest, she stepped into the woodland's cool, green embrace. It wasn't long until climbing the mountain felt right. The only thing to do. A way to clear her mind of the realities she'd left behind on the train platform. The wreckage of her life.

Perhaps she would get lost in the forest. Actually get eaten by a bear. No one would note her disappearance. Gladys was gone. Irene and Mrs. Juneau might think it odd she didn't say goodbye, but wouldn't be looking for her. They'd assume she took the train back to Boston with everyone else. And no one in the city awaited her return.

The completeness of her isolation, her utter lack of connection to the world was a burden too heavy to bear. Too depressing to contemplate.

The time that had passed since she left the Twin Birch House grounds could have been three hours or fifteen minutes. She couldn't tell. But the effort of climbing uphill brought her back into her body. She began to notice the roots and stones pressing through her soles. The growing weight of her satchel in her hand. The dampness under her arms and perspiration beading on her upper lip.

She sat on a fallen log to catch her breath. Shoulders rising and falling, she listened. The voices and noises of the hotel were too far to hear. There was nothing but the breeze in the treetops, a woodpecker rapping out his persistent beat in the distance.

Glancing around, she recognized where she was. Without planning to, she'd returned to the same spot the sapphire butterfly had led her to . . . and she'd been drawn to all summer. The path she'd followed this time was completely different than the one she normally took; yet here she was again.

Or was she? The mossy boulders seemed just as she remembered, but the clearing had changed. She stood up, staring around in confusion. There was a much higher outcropping of rock behind the boulders, and many more stones leading down the hill from them, forming a low wall that tapered down to a scattering of stones at its tail end.

Completing a slow circle, she confirmed that everything surrounding the mysterious new rocks was just as she remembered. She was, indeed, in the same place where she'd met Avery and the fairy . . . and later brought Ned. Nothing was different except the rocky additions to the landscape.

She neared the old, familiar mossy boulders. As she drew closer, she discovered they now obscured some sort of passageway through the new, taller rock behind them. The passage was roughly four feet in diameter. Just large enough for an adult to walk through hunched over.

Powerfully drawn to enter the strange tunnel, yet wary of where it might lead, she backed away and walked several yards along the newly arrived wall, stopping when the piled stones were as high as her knees.

Sure enough, the pond and its surroundings appeared exactly as she'd last seen them. The elaborate passageway evidently led to the same place anyone could reach by stepping over the sloping rock wall.

So where did the wall of rock come from and why was it there?

The mystery of it was a welcome diversion from her private misery. Returning to the tunnel opening, she placed her hands on her hips and contemplated the situation.

Did it have something to do with the fairies?

She couldn't imagine turning around and leaving without seeing where it went. The unsatisfied curiosity would torture her . . . and she had nowhere else to go. If she never returned, at least someone might find her bag and launch a search for her. Leaving the bag behind, she took a deep breath, stooped over, and entered the passageway, one hand stretched in front of her, the other holding her hat in place.

The passage was only about twelve feet long, dry and smooth, as though carved from the stone with intention. Its floor was packed earth, topped by smatterings of broken acorn tops and dried leaves that crackled under the soles of her boots.

Reaching the other side, she exited and stood up. Her jaw dropped and eyes widened in wonder. It was essentially the same clearing she and Ned had visited several times, but *everything* about it was different.

The pond was there, but it was now bursting with emerald green lily pads spotted with enormous pink blossoms. The trees were where she remembered them, but now they shimmered and sparkled, as though sprinkled with pale glitter. The sky was the color of robin eggs, the outlines of the brilliant white clouds brushed in silver. The sunlight seemed to come from everywhere and nowhere; the golden orb itself was missing.

Placing each foot cautiously, she made her way over a carpet of lush green grass to the pond. The flat rock she and Ned used to sit upon was now a swirling, curved bench carved out of a single slab of granite. She took a seat, breathing in the mysterious, floral scent of the air.

Closing her eyes, she was transported to her childhood bed. She felt the weight of her mother sitting next to her, brushing a strand of hair from her forehead. It was her mother who told her stories of magical lands, fairy princesses, and flying dragons.

It all made sense now. The safety and warmth of her parents' love and the worlds of her imagination were real, just hidden from view by tricks of dimension and time.

She half expected the world to have returned to normal when she opened her eyes, but it hadn't. It was still there, as real as the Girls Home, the Boston mansions where she'd worked, and Twin Birch House. And as different from each of those locations as they were from one another.

"Welcome back, Vanessa." The voice was high and delicate.

With a sharp inhale, she whipped her head from side to side, but saw no one. A chorus of giggles burst from the pond, drawing her attention to a dozen or so human-size figures swimming and floating on the water's surface, in and amongst the lily pads.

Blinking several times, she clutched the bench and stared. Once again, she was reminded of the wood gathering scene in Mary Pickford's *Cinderella*, where the forest fairies were girls of all different ages and hairstyles.

But these were beautiful females of *all* ages and races, from a young girl with reddish-brown skin, black eyes, and straight black hair to a slender teen with ebony skin and white flowers woven into a swirling crown of braids. A plump redhead with turquoise eyes to a wrinkled woman with almond eyes and flowing white hair. One moment they seemed to be made of the water itself, the next they appeared fully formed, like real humans.

"You . . . know me?" Vanessa let her breath out as they dipped under the surface and re-emerged, their hair instantly dry, or merged with the water and reappeared in another form.

"You've been here before, haven't you?" asked a nymph with freckles and a cap of curly blonde hair.

"Yes . . . and no. I mean, I've been to the pond, but it was nothing like this."

The nymphs giggled and splashed. "We saw you. That's why we opened the portal. So you could see us, too."

"Th . . . thank you." She gazed all around the sparkling garden. "It's beautiful here."

A toffee-colored nymph laughed. Her green, watery hair matched her eyes. "We're glad you like it."

"Are you . . . water nymphs?" She'd read about them in mythology books, and even seen pictures in some of the illustrated ones. "Or do you prefer 'naiads'?"

"We have many names."

"The fairy said that, too. Do you know her?"

The nymph shrugged, then melted back into the water.

Gripping the cool stone of the bench, Vanessa stared, her breath shallow. After Ned's unambiguous reaction to the idea of their marriage, she'd decided the fairy was a fantasy, along with the magical visitors of her childhood. But this place . . . and these nymphs . . . it was too much to be imaginary, even for her. "So . . . I'm not making this up?"

This prompted another wave of laughter. "Not at all."

"So . . . anyone who comes here can see you?"

"Children sometimes can and sometimes can't." They laughed. "But we only open the passage for grown-ups we especially like."

Vanessa blinked back tears and attempted to smile. "Hate to say you're just about the only ones who like me at the moment." The self-pity in her voice made her sick. She wouldn't have lasted a day in the Girls Home with an attitude like that. Seemed the comforts of Twin Birch House and the fairy's assurances had made her soft.

"But I appreciate the invitation," she added in a firmer tone. Rising from her seat, she squared her shoulders and gestured around with a wave of her hand. "It's . . . dazzling."

A woman with a snow-white bun and kindly blue eyes glided toward the pond's edge. "Then why are you so sad?"

They'd seen her before . . . so they must have seen Ned, too. Their intimate moments on the flat rock . . . that was now the elaborate stone bench she'd been sitting on. Her cheeks warmed at the memory of Ned's hands on her bare skin, and the idea they hadn't been alone. "Perhaps you saw what happened here . . . last night?"

A wave of giggles burst from the other nymphs. "With Ned?" they cried, their voices echoing one another as they repeated his name.

Their giggling suddenly seemed a lot less friendly. She frowned slightly. "Why, yes."

"He's delicious." The arch of their brows and curve of their lips left her certain they had indeed been privy to her and Ned's most intimate moments.

Eager to change the subject, Vanessa did a slow turn. "Well, I'm a little overwhelmed by all this."

The other naiads melted away, leaving only the woman with the white bun. "Don't mind our appetites. We're just hopelessly fond of men . . . especially men like Ned, with appetites of their own."

"That is a good description of him." A wry laugh escaped Vanessa's lips. "I am feeling somewhat devoured."

The other nymphs returned. "You won't get sympathy here." A redhead splashed water in her direction with a pout. "*You* have power we can only dream of."

"Me? Powerful?" Vanessa snorted. "Afraid you don't know much about my world."

"Just open your eyes." The nymphs spoke in a single voice. "You'll see." Then they all disappeared under the surface in a single motion.

Just open her eyes? Not terribly helpful advice, if that's even what it was.

After a few moments, Vanessa stepped closer to peer into the pond. There was nothing but black beneath the patches of water between the lily pads. Either the bottom was very dark or very deep. It was impossible to tell.

She returned to the bench, where she sat and clutched the edge, twisting around as she gazed about the enchanting world some more. A flowering vine wrapped its way around the thick trunk of a willow tree behind the bench. Taking in the exotic scent of flowers she couldn't name, Vanessa trailed her finger along the petals of the vine's giant, lavender blossoms. The willow had gently arching boughs. Its branches formed an umbrella-like canopy that covered the bench and draped partially over the water, reminding her of the short skirts worn by ballerinas. The glen was unnaturally quiet with no breeze to rustle the trees. Just the soft burble of water feeding the pond.

Maybe she'd just stay there forever. Perhaps that's what she was meant to do. The reason nothing seemed to work out for her in the "real" world. At the thought, fatigue weakened her limbs so quickly she was reminded of the first *Wizard of Oz* storybook, when Dorothy was drugged into slumber by the cheery red poppies. She curled on her side and tucked her hands under her cheek, surrendering to whatever fate had in store. Somehow, it felt more promising than what she'd left behind.

Her eyes drifted closed and she dreamt of Christmas morning with her parents and Ruth. Her sister was still a baby, sitting upright on a blanket, banging her little fists against chubby knees. A fire crackled in the fireplace, the scent of pine needles filled the room and her mother's lap was soft and warm.

When her eyes fluttered open again, her stomach rumbled and her back was stiff from lying on the hard stone. Sitting up, she swung her feet to the ground, relieved to see she was still in the mystical garden. It was real. Perhaps a portal or bridge between the imaginary world she'd known as a child and the ordinary world she inhabited now. Real and unreal at the same time.

Spending time with her family had restored her spirits, even if it was only in a dream. Rays of optimism poked through her gloom. It was over with Ned, but her life wasn't over. The Wood was a perfect example of a surprise she never could have anticipated when standing on that train platform just hours earlier.

Her stomach rumbled again. Kneeling by the pond, she leaned over, seeing her reflection in the water's smooth surface. "Hello! Are you still there?"

The water shimmered and slid over itself as the nymphs returned. "Did you sleep well?"

And she hadn't imagined the naiads.

"I did, but I'm hungry now. Is there more to this world? Places to live? Something to eat?"

Their radiant smiles faded as their eyes swept the confines of the lightly wooded clearing. It was bordered by the entryway boulders to her right, the mountainside behind her seat, and a thickening forest behind the pond to her left and facing the stone bench. "What you see is all there is." They turned their lovely faces to her in one motion. "Only your world offers what is needed to fill the void."

"So . . . I'm not meant to stay here."

They burst into laughter once more. "Not unless you want to be hungry forever."

"No, thank you." A lump rose in her throat. "I've had enough of that for a lifetime."

Chapter Thirty-Two

On her way down the mountainside, Vanessa shook her head with a smile. She still had no idea what she was going to do, but she no longer felt so alone.

When she arrived at the edge of the woods bordering the hotel grounds, she stopped. As always, the beauty of the scenery below moved her. The midafternoon sun sparkled on the lake, creating a bed of diamonds for the handful of sailboats zipping along its surface. A few older couples strolled on the lawn—those with no need to return to the city for work or the start of school—and the ponies swished their tails in the corral. Shadows moved across Irene's flower-draped lares in their stone niche, making the dancing boy statues appear to be swaying to their own music.

Whatever setback Vanessa currently endured, that single summer at Twin Birch House had provided some of her life's happiest moments. Telling bedtime stories to Walter and Edna. Allowing herself friendships with Gladys and Irene. Waltzing under the stars . . . with both Avery and Ned.

Her grip tightened on her bag. Between the comforts of the hotel and the magic of the Enchanted Wood, there was no place in the world she'd rather be.

And she hadn't gotten herself this far to let a handful of entitled snobs crush her spirit now.

A tall, blond man stepped off the hotel porch and headed in her direction. As he drew closer, she recognized Karl Fiske, the hotel owner's son. His stride was purposeful, his lean legs flinging out in front of him in coltish bursts.

She shrank back into the shadows of the trees. He wasn't heading exactly for her, but rather toward a bench nestled into the edge of the tree line. A quiet place where she and Ned had often sat in the dark, watching the moon. Her heart flinched at the memory as Karl settled on the seat and let out a deep sigh.

It was likely a relief to have most of the guests go, along with their staff. She turned her attention to the hotel, imagining herself its owner, rather than a worker or guest. How different everything appeared through that lens. The lawn became a mowing chore. The boathouse—wooden decking to be stained and varnished. And the adorable ponies? Mouths to feed through the winter.

Yet the newly imagined responsibility wasn't oppressive. To her surprise, it tugged at her maternal instincts. The resort was a demanding child. Delightful and needy in equal measure.

"Just open your eyes." That's what the nymphs had said. Well, her eyes were open. And who appeared before them? The hotel owner, or his son, at any rate.

She'd heard bits and pieces about Karl and his family over the summer and remembered overhearing Ned pressuring him to bring a jazz band to the resort. Her lips pursed. Knowing Ned, it was a wonder the Original Dixieland Jazz Band hadn't already replaced the hotel's in-house orchestra.

As he struck a match to light a cigarette, she smoothed her skirt, ran her finger under her eyes and tucked a loose lock of hair back up under her hat.

Was it possible Karl Fiske being the first person she saw after leaving the nymphs meant her future was somehow tied to Twin Birch House? Wouldn't that be wonderful?

She stowed her valise under a bush and strolled toward him. What did she have to lose? "Why . . . hello there, Mr. Fiske." Hopefully she sounded surprised.

He turned toward her, not looking especially pleased. "Hello, Miss . . ."

"Perkins." She gripped the back of the bench, hoping he hadn't been informed about the scene at the train platform. "Vanessa Perkins."

His mouth curved downward, as though he smelled something vaguely unpleasant. "Oh, yes. The Gardner's nursemaid."

She slid around the edge of the bench and sat next to him. "You remember. With all these guests and their staff, in addition to your own employees, I can't imagine how you keep everyone straight."

"It's nothing, really." Pride rang in his voice, despite the modest words. "Just part of the job."

The job. That was it. His family might own the property, but he worked. And not begrudgingly, like Ned did. Anyone could see his duties at the hotel mattered to him. And she had to admit that however awkward he seemed, Karl had proven himself better able to deny Ned's wishes than she had.

Lifting an eyebrow, she leaned back. "From what I saw of you this season, you're quite good at your job."

A smile twitched at the corner of his mouth. "I do my best."

Seemed he didn't get complimented much. Particularly without his father around to see how smoothly things went over the summer. Who else was in any sort of position to pat Karl on the back? A few of the senior department heads, perhaps?

"Though, the goal is to make my efforts invisible to the guests." A tinge of worry colored his voice.

"Oh, I'm sure they were." Her hand flew to her chest. "I was just paying special attention. I'd never been in a hotel before this summer, much less one as special as Twin Birch House. It opened my eyes to a whole new world."

Relaxing, he stretched his legs out and looked toward the lake. "Twin Birch House *is* special."

"Have you owned it long?"

"Decades. Our other properties are in the City. New York, that is."

She shook her head. "So much responsibility. And only, what, twenty-seven, twenty-eight?"

His chest puffed. "Twenty-five this past March."

"Only twenty-five? And running the whole operation by yourself, all season?" Like Irene, Karl seemed so much older than his years. Would she ever be so grounded?

"It was a bit of a test for me, if you want to know the truth."

She turned to face him. "And you passed with flying colors, wouldn't you say?"

"Not for me to judge." He took a drag from his cigarette, eyes back on the lake.

His cultivated indifference didn't fool her. "Well, I'm sure you did. And I've decided my next position will be in a hotel, without a doubt." Never mind the decision was made just this moment, it was made nonetheless.

"And the Gardners?"

She waved her hand with a smile. "Oh, my place with them was temporary, covering for their regular nanny."

"So, no more children?"

"Oh, I love children. Especially the sweet ones . . ." Her heart clenched at the memory of the Wainwrights. "But hotel work would also be . . . stimulating. Dealing with different guests all the time, solving new problems every day." Her excitement grew as the words flowed, for they were all true. "Running a place like this seems like half theatrical production, half military operation."

Karl chuckled. "Pretty well describes it. Your father a hotel man, too?"

"No. He was a clerk of some sort, I think. Passed away before I was old enough to understand what he did."

"I'm sorry."

"Long time ago." She refused to be sucked into memories of the ferry accident that stole her parents from her when she was six. "But I'm beginning to think the hotel business might be right up my alley."

"I can't imagine doing anything else."

She sat back. "Maybe even here . . . at Twin Birch House."

He shifted in his seat. "The hotel closes for the winter. Mr. Seward and his family take care of things until we open again in the spring."

"Naturally. Not much to do here in the snow, I'd imagine."

"That's right." He ground the last of his cigarette in the dirt and stood.

Her pulse quickened. She had to think fast or lose the moment. "So, what do you do all winter?"

"Work at one of our New York hotels, order supplies, and plan maintenance for this place. The wheels never stop turning."

She furrowed her brow and tugged at her chin. "But . . . Twin Birch House doesn't close for at least a few more weeks, right . . . ?"

His thumbs hooked into his vest pockets. "Mid to late October, depending on the foliage."

She sprang to her feet and clutched her hands together. "Perfect. If you'd let me work here until the end of the season, perhaps I can earn myself a spot at one of your city hotels, and return to Twin Birch in the spring."

Frowning, he kicked at the grass with the toe of his brown leather wingtips. "I can't—"

"And if it doesn't go well," she interrupted, "I'll leave whenever you tell me. No hard feelings."

He squinted at the cupola rising from the hotel roofline. "I make it a practice not to meddle in the department heads' purview. They become resentful." He peered down at her, his brow creased. "I'm sorry."

Her heart thudded in her throat as her one hope seemed to be setting sail. "Oh, I certainly understand."

His features eased as he turned to go.

"Perhaps . . . if Mrs. Juneau agreed?"

He stopped. "You're free to inquire." With a sober nod, he looked back over his shoulder. "I'll agree if the request comes from her."

Her stomach did a somersault as he walked away. "Thank you, Mr. Fiske. Thank you!"

Seemed she had a little more power than she'd imagined. Now all she had to do was convince Mrs. Juneau to give her a job . . . despite the fact she'd ignored the woman's advice all summer.

Chapter Thirty-Three

Vanessa stood before Mrs. Juneau's desk in the head housekeeper's small office behind the kitchens. Serenaded by the banging of skillets on burners, the squeak of metal carts rolling on linoleum, and the rumble of orders barked amongst the cook staff, she kept her head modestly bowed.

"You don't waste any time." Disapproval and amusement battled in Mrs. Juneau's voice.

Vanessa squinted up with a grimace. "You heard."

The older woman shot her a wry smile. "A public execution usually gets noticed." She put her hands together, making a steeple with her fingers. "The women's dormitory was abuzz. It's only a matter of time until young Mr. Fiske hears about it himself."

Vanessa's jaw tensed at the thought of girls she barely knew breathlessly recounting her ordeal on the train platform. "Nothing like fresh grist for the gossip mill."

"Indeed." Mrs. Juneau rose and leaned on her desk, her palms spread on her well-used blotter. "I'll take you on through the end of the season, but only because we Home girls must take care of our own."

Releasing her breath, Vanessa sprang to her feet. "Thank you, Mrs. Juneau, thank you." She dropped her eyes. "I'm sorry I disappointed you."

Mrs. Juneau pulled her crowded key ring up from her waist as she came out from behind her desk. "It's not me who was hurt by your poor choices." She stepped over to the metal cabinet in the corner. The way her fingers searched the keys reminded Vanessa of the Catholic nuns who used to visit the Home, counting their rosary beads.

"I know." She shifted her weight to one leg. "But I honestly don't understand why the other girls are so keen for me to fail."

Mrs. Juneau glanced over her shoulder looking a bit surprised. "Isn't it obvious?" She opened the cabinet and removed a black dress, white apron, and matching cap from the shelves. "If you rise, those with no hope of following feel left behind."

As Mrs. Juneau relocked the cabinet, Vanessa's thoughts flickered to the poor neighborhoods where most of the orphan girls came from. She could see how it might be easier to believe there was no chance of escape than to try getting out and failing.

Mrs. Juneau held the chambermaid uniform against her chest as she turned back toward Vanessa. "And for those born higher up the social ladder, if you don't stay in your place, it opens the possibility they could fall from theirs."

Vanessa bowed her head and rubbed her finger over the top of her ring. "I don't think I'm better than anyone." She tilted her face back up toward Mrs. Juneau. "I just feel like we're on different paths."

How many of those girls had met a fairy and were friends with water nymphs, for instance?

Mrs. Juneau narrowed her eyes but said nothing. After a moment, she gave a tight smile. "That's a lovely ring."

Pleased Mrs. Juneau noticed, Vanessa held her hand out, letting the sunlight from the small window illuminate the red stone. "My mother said it was my grandmother's. She promised it to me when I grew up." She pulled her hand back, her chest aching at the memory of her last day in their apartment. "I took it from my mother's jewelry box when the people came to take me and my sister away." Polishing the stone, she recalled the fights she'd gotten in protecting the ring from would-be thieves over the years. "Had to wear it on a leather string until it fit my finger."

"Nice to have a memento. I don't remember my parents."

"It's more than a memento." Vanessa's voice hardened. "It's proof. I'm not just a penniless orphan. I have a story. How else could I inherit a ruby ring?"

Mrs. Juneau glanced at the ring with a dented brow, then smiled again. "I think it's more precious as a reminder of your mother than all the gems in the world could be." She pressed the uniform into Vanessa's hands and waggled her left ring finger. "That's what this little fleck of diamond is for me."

Clutching her new uniform, Vanessa peered at Mrs. Juneau's ring. It was a thin gold band with a barely visible diamond embedded on top. The hope expressed in the humble jewel was touching. "How did you and your husband meet?"

Mrs. Juneau's hand clasped the locket around her neck. "Pierre was the iceman at my first position. Did deliveries for his father." Her smile widened as she opened the locket and gazed inside. "He had lots of brothers ahead of him and bigger ambitions than delivering ice. Eventually got work at Young's Hotel, and got me a job there, too." Mrs. Juneau's tone firmed as she lifted her eyes to Vanessa. "Been in the hotel business ever since."

"And Mr. Juneau?"

Her mentor's expression clouded as she stared at her husband's portrait again. "Lost him in a fire." Her mouth twisted. "In his father's icehouse, no less."

Only after hearing the sad conclusion did Vanessa realize how she'd clung to the idea that Mr. Juneau simply spent the summers elsewhere, that a warm reunion awaited Mrs. Juneau at the end of the season. "I'm so sorry."

"I was only twenty when I lost him, but no one's ever been able to fill his shoes."

"I'm sure you had many offers, though," Vanessa offered, trying to lighten the mood.

"Watch that honey tongue, my girl." Mrs. Juneau gave her a wry smile and snapped the locket shut. "You might catch more flies than you bargained for."

"Oh, I learned my lesson about flies." Bitter memories of Ned gave way to thoughts of Karl's stiff formality, which prompted a chuckle. "And I don't see Karl Fiske sprouting wings and little antennae."

Mrs. Juneau crossed her arms. "He wouldn't have anything to do with your sudden interest in hotel work, now would he?"

Vanessa's fingers dug into the folded uniform. "So now I'm some sort of gold digger? Just because I had the nerve to imagine Ned Cooper's intentions might be honorable?"

"I didn't say that." Mrs. Juneau rounded her desk and returned to her seat with a sigh. "Though you will need Mr. Fiske's personal support if you've any desire to come back next season."

Vanessa's mood blackened. "Because some of the guests won't like having me here."

"Some of our most important guests would be surprised, to say the least, given all that transpired."

She squeezed her new uniform. "But I've got a few weeks to win his support. Hopefully even get a job in one of his New York hotels."

"My, my. Aren't you the planner?"

"Never have been." Vanessa met Mrs. Juneau's eye. "But, acting on impulse all the time didn't work out so well. Time to try something new."

The woman's teasing expression grew serious again. "As I said, I've got no problem recommending we take you on until we close up, but I'm obligated to make sure Mr. Fiske knows the implications of bringing you back next season."

Her mentor's suggestion made Vanessa's stomach hurt, reminding her she still hadn't eaten. Would it never end? Always being a razor's edge from destitution? Dependent on the goodwill of so-called betters, who could withdraw their favor at any moment? A profound sorrow seeped from her bones. She stared down at the black dress in her arms. "I'm sorry I snapped at you. Perhaps I'm a little sensitive."

"Understandable."

Vanessa continued staring at the uniform. "Would you think me terrible if a part of what made me lose my senses over Ned was the prospect of never having to worry about my next meal again?" Raising her eyes, she awaited Mrs. Juneau's judgment.

The woman's face softened. "There's no arguing with that." Her hand returned to the locket at her neck. "A rich husband provides security that a mere job never could."

Relieved that her admission had not turned Mrs. Juneau against her, she allowed her attention to drift out the window. It was hard to imagine having feelings for anyone else after being so infatuated with Ned. And what did real love feel like, anyway? Was it less heart-stopping? More practical? Should she consider a more calculated approach to marriage? She pulled the folded uniform against her chest. Was it possible that's what the nymphs had been getting at? Just open her eyes—for a husband?

After she left Mrs. Juneau and went to retrieve her suitcase from the bushes, she continued to stew. Was it childish to think she'd fall for another man the way she went crazy for Ned?

Back at the dorm, she sat on her bunk, frowning as she toyed with her new chambermaid cap. Impractical or not, she'd rather be a spinster than marry a man she didn't love. To her surprise, thoughts of Avery Nolen sprang to mind. How she'd felt she was floating as he swept her around the dance floor. The warmth of his family outside the church that morning in July. And the splendor of his unguarded smile the day they'd met.

Interrupting her train of thought with a toss of her head, she placed the uniform on the bunk beside her. Despite her tender feelings for him, she mustn't forget Avery didn't show one jot of interest in her all summer. She rose and squared her jaw. The only thing she needed to be thinking about was doing a good enough job in the next few weeks to convince Karl Fiske he should give her a position in New York. It was her only hope for coming back to Twin Birch House in the spring. That's what she had to stay focused on.

Chapter Thirty-Four

Standing at the edge of the nymph's pond the next day, Vanessa let the paper sack she held fall back to her side. It was full of oatmeal raisin cookies the kitchen had made for the Labor Day picnic that afternoon. "If you can't eat them, what can I do to thank you?"

The nymphs giggled and splashed. A chubby girl with light tan skin and brown braids swam to the pond's edge. "So, we helped you?"

"Oh, yes! You told me to open my eyes. Exactly what I needed to do."

"And what did you see?" asked a woman the color of milk chocolate, her curls held back in a silver-threaded head scarf.

"Why, only the hotel owner's son." She bent her knees and squatted closer to the water. "Which resulted in a job at Twin Birch House. Who knows where it will all lead?"

The nymphs burst into gales of laughter. A brunette with a French accent winked. "Perhaps . . . to the hotel owner's son?"

Vanessa shook her head. "Not interested. I just want to work for him." Then she bit her lip, worried. "Why? Is that what you see?"

Again, they laughed. "We wouldn't know," a little blonde girl said with a pout. "We can only dream of living in your world."

Not exactly fortunetellers, the naiads. Vanessa lifted the paper sack and glanced around. "What should I do with them?"

Their eyes flickered to the passage behind her. "Why don't you share them with a friend?"

Sitting back onto the grass, Vanessa resolved to stay cheerful. "I'll most certainly do that the moment I make a few more."

"Vanessa?" Avery's voice sounded tentative . . . and hopeful.

She turned her head and there he was, standing at the passageway.

"Why, hello!" Vanessa scrambled to her feet as the nymphs melted into the pond.

He approached, his eyes sweeping the small clearing. "Wh . . . what are you doing here?"

"I found it yesterday." She glanced back at the lily pads. "Glad to see I'm not the only grown-up they like."

As he drew closer, his smile widened. "So . . . you've been through the passage."

"I have." Recalling the depth of her misery the day before, she sobered. "It appeared to me in my hour of need." She twisted her hands together. "If this was your private spot, I hope you don't mind the intrusion."

"Not at all. It's just . . . surprising. First the Wainwright children showed up, and now you." He pushed his glasses up his nose. "Before this summer, no one but my sister had ever been here with me."

She recalled the charming girl she'd met at church. "Hattie?"

He cocked his head with a crooked smile. "You remembered."

"Of course. She's delightful."

"Yes. Well, actually, I was referring to Bess."

"Your twin."

"That's right." Another smile flashed before his tone darkened. "But she stopped being able to find it a long time ago."

"So . . . we're the only ones who can see all this?" Vanessa swept her arm over the wonders of the glen.

"Can't say for sure. But I've never seen anyone else here." He hesitated a moment. "Bess and I call it the 'Enchanted Wood.'"

"You never brought Hattie?"

Shaking his head, he lowered his eyes and clutched the top of his leather bag. "By the time Hattie was old enough, she had too many friends she was sure to invite, and I'd gotten used to it being my private getaway." He glanced up. "Selfish, perhaps, but it's always been my nightmare that it would disappear for me one day, too. Or worse . . . get overrun with tourists."

"Are you sure?" Vanessa leaned forward with a raised brow. "We could make a killing selling tickets."

He pulled his satchel strap over his head. "Don't even joke about it, please."

Hands in the air, she grinned. "The secret's safe, I swear." Lowering her arms, she recalled how her spirits had been restored the day before. "It's my sanctuary now, too."

After settling on the bench, he spread his palms on his knees. "I thought you'd have left for Boston yesterday, with the others." The shift in him was surprising. Being in his private domain seemed to relax him now that he'd recovered from his initial shock.

"Change of plans. Seems I'll be staying on with the hotel for a bit."

Tugging his shirt cuffs, he smiled at the ground. "I'm glad to hear that."

It pleased her to imagine her presence affected him. "Yes. I'm delighted." She swallowed her smile as she smoothed down her apron. "Nursemaid to chambermaid in a snap of the fingers."

He coughed. "I have . . . employment news as well."

"Fabulous! What?"

"I'm going to be working for the Forest Service. Right in this area."

"So . . . not a doctor, like your father?"

His smile dimmed. "No."

Realizing her faux pas, she doubled the enthusiasm in her response. "Well, that's just wonderful. I'm so happy for you!"

"Thanks." He laid the satchel on the stone seat, glanced up at the willow behind the bench and ran his hand through his tousled hair. "So. Who have you met so far?"

"Well . . ." She clasped her hands together, relieved at the change in subject. "I met a fairy earlier this summer, but here in the Wood, just the water nymphs."

"Naiads?" He frowned. "In the pond?"

"Yes." Stifling the urge to run around like an excited child, she settled for twisting left and right, swishing her uniform skirt against her calves. "Don't you know them?"

"Not at all." He peered at the water. "Didn't even know they existed."

She stilled herself. "Seriously?"

He nodded as he pulled a thick notebook from his leather bag. "Never seen a fairy either." After sitting on the bench, he flipped pages until he stopped and pointed at one of the drawings. "These are the nymphs I see."

Settling next to him, she leaned over to get a better view. He smelled good. Nothing she could name. Just good.

"They're wood nymphs . . . in the trees." He showed her watercolor images of women and girls who seemed to be made of the trees themselves, their bodies intertwined with their trunks, their hair spreading out through the branches. Like the water nymphs, each was unique, and either inside her trunk, or leaning outside of it, but always attached in some way.

"These are beautiful, Avery."

He reddened. "Mainly I do flora and fauna. These are my private drawings. The ones from here." He pointed to the image of the longhaired nymph in the tree behind the bench. "That's Willow."

She touched the watercolor, then squinted up at the tree itself. "Well, I can't see her, or any of the nymphs you do." She let out a small laugh. "I guess there are different social circles, even here."

He smiled and leaned back on his hands. "So, what are fairies like? I've heard tales of them, but never a direct account."

She proceeded to tell him everything she could remember about the encounter as he peppered her with questions. It was a relief to share the event with someone; particularly knowing he wouldn't think she was crazy or making it up.

"What did the fairy say?" His eyes were wide, his face open and eager.

Her response stuck in her mouth. She didn't want to talk to Avery about Ned and the fairy's prophecy about a "man of sterling and gold." The statement that had led her to believe Ned was her match. It was too embarrassing. "Well . . ."

His brow creased and he sat back. "Forgive me if it was personal. I didn't mean to pry."

She reached out and laid her hand on his arm. "No. It's fine. She just . . . assured me that my future was bright. That I needn't worry."

His features softened. "That's excellent news."

With a nod, she withdrew her hand. "It was. And helped me with a difficult decision. Though now I'm not so sure I made the right one."

He pushed his glasses up his nose, apparently waiting for her to go on. She gave him a quick smile, hoping he'd understand she wasn't going to say more. As if reading her mind, he glanced back at the tree behind them and rubbed his hands together. "So. Willow tells me you brought cookies for the water nymphs."

She held up the sack, grateful for his deft change of subject. "Oatmeal raisin. But apparently they don't eat like we do."

"Guess I'll have to help out." He grinned. "They're my favorite."

As they munched cookies together, he flipped through the pages of his notebook, showing her the tiny lights he saw flickering in the center of the flower blossoms in the Enchanted Woods, and the forlorn, gray wood nymphs whose trees had died.

"Can you see the shimmers of the fairy's light? Hear tinkling laughter?"

He shook his head.

"The fairies are pickier than we are about who gets to see them," the naiads chimed in.

Vanessa told Avery what the water nymphs said. "Seems the enchanted world has its fancy class, just like ours," she added with a shrug.

"I wish I understood it better. Their world, I mean." He sighed and gazed over the glen. "I've asked so many questions, but I never seem to get a straight answer, or at least none I can understand."

"The water nymphs are just as cryptic, aren't you?" Vanessa put her hand on her hip as she scowled toward the pond.

The naiads replied with enigmatic smiles.

She turned back to Avery. "And it was like that with the fairy, too. She answered my questions in her way, but I really didn't learn anything of practical use."

He shrugged. "I finally decided I just needed to accept them." He swept his arm across the Wood. "Accept all of this, like I accept the phonograph. I don't fully understand how it works, but I still hear the music."

"Yes. Like a phonograph." Vanessa nodded with a smile. "That makes good sense." She rose from the bench, knelt by the pond, and stretched out her cupped palm.

"No!" cried Avery. "Don't touch the water."

She pulled her hand back with a glance over her shoulder. "Why not?"

"I'm not sure . . . but Willow's always warned me to stay away from the water."

Shocked, Vanessa turned back to her new friends. "Is that true? I shouldn't touch?"

A nymph shrugged, brown corkscrew curls bouncing at her waist. "What could be the harm in a drink of water?" A green-eyed redhead's expression was all wide-eyed innocence. "We're friends, aren't we?"

There was a hunger in the water nymphs' eyes that made her sit back on her heels. "Maybe later."

The naiads giggled, dipping in and out of sight. Feeling a little shaky, Vanessa returned to her seat next to Avery.

He set out his watercolors. "Willow warned me away from there when I was little. But none of the wood nymphs will tell me what would happen if I did. Could be nothing." He lifted a water jar from his satchel. "But I bring my own, just in case."

"Seems wise." The idea she couldn't completely trust the naiads stirred up the sting of Ned's betrayal. Vanessa's fingers curled around cool stone lip of the bench. Would she ever be able to rely on her instincts? Or would she end up burned by every flame that drew her?

Tossing her head, she chased her dark thoughts away, focusing instead on Avery's notebook. "Where did you learn to paint so well?"

"A little in high school, but mainly at Dartmouth, though I majored in botany. Fantasies of being the next John James Audubon." He glanced up. "You know his work?"

She shook her head. "Sorry."

"That's alright. Neither does my father."

There was pain in his voice, but she didn't want to make him uncomfortable by pursuing it. "So . . . who is this Audubon fellow?"

"A famous painter and naturalist." Avery's expression grew dreamy. "Traveled the country alone, painting what he saw. Created the most important catalogue of North American wildlife we have—particularly birds."

"Sounds a little lonely, traveling everywhere by himself."

Avery's shoulders hunched as he dipped his brush in the water jar, then moistened a block of red paint. "Sounds like heaven."

"Don't you like people?" She tried to imagine *wanting* to be alone.

He shot her a wry smile. "In small doses."

"So how'd you get so good at dancing?"

A wave of pink washed up from his collar to his cheeks. "Now you sound like Irene, exaggerating my skills."

"No exaggeration at all, I assure you." She raised the three middle fingers of one hand together. "Scout's honor." Her eye landed on his pocket watch and her smile vanished. "Oh my goodness, I didn't mean to stay so long!" She scrambled to her feet with a moan. "Wouldn't do to be late on my very first day!"

Chapter Thirty-Five

After Avery had packed up and left the Wood, Morniero floated down from his perch high atop Willow's boughs. Leaning against the curved sidearm of the stone bench, he crossed his ankles and folded his arms over his chest.

"Someone's grumpy," teased a blonde naiad with a giggle. "Do you need some sleep?"

"And miss your wit?" Morniero scowled at the nymph and her companions in the pond. "Never."

"Oh, don't be cross." She waved her arm over the water. "Join us anytime. We can assure you good dreams."

He shook his head with a frown as they splashed at him and giggled.

Moments later, Lachima flew in through the passage, her sapphire wings sparkling. As she transformed and fluffed her weightless mane of white hair, the naiads slipped under the pond's surface and disappeared.

Lachima flashed him a bright smile. "Hello, dear brother."

"Hello, dear sister. I'm glad to see you got my message."

"Yes, yes. From multiple sources." She glided over and sat on the bench, leaning against the opposite side arm. "So here I am. What's on your mind?"

"I wanted you to be the one to tell Willow about our agreement, and how you broke your word."

Lachima glanced up at the wood nymph, her smile fading. "What do you mean?"

"Don't be coy, now. I visited Vanessa's dreams and saw a most familiar figure in them. Someone who'd specifically promised not to reveal herself."

Willow leaned out of her trunk, the swirls on her skin standing out more markedly as she paled. "What is it? What do you need to tell me?"

"Oh, Willow." Sorrow marred Lachima's exquisite features. "I'm so sorry."

The nymph's rounded eyes flicked from Lachima to Morniero. "Tell me!"

"Please." Sounding desperate, Lachima turned to him. "You don't have to do this."

"The rules are for everyone's protection, no matter how difficult they are to follow."

Willow began to cry. "This is about Avery, isn't it?"

He turned to the wood nymph. "I promised to keep your secret from Mother, if Lachima promised not to reveal herself to the mortals." His shoulders slumped. "Secrecy is the only thing that keeps us safe. You both know this."

His sister stood and faced him, her voice trembling and fists clenched. "You worried I'd drive her mad, but Vanessa is fine. No one was harmed."

"This time." He gestured to the pond. "And now the naiads have opened the portal again."

A tiny fissure cracked Lachima's defiant attitude. "For who?"

He glared. "Who do you think?"

She hung her head. A rare gesture of contrition on Lachima's part.

"The problem is growing." He needed her to take this seriously.

Lachima stared over at the pond's still water, her silence betraying her genuine concern.

Sitting on the bench with his back to Willow, Morniero fixed his empty gaze on the ground beneath Lachima's feet, recalling their heyday. When mortals worshipped them, honored them. But that was long ago. "We're so weak without their devotions." He looked up at her. "If they were to turn on us again, do you think we could last?"

She sighed and sank onto the bench next to him. The angle of her head as she stared down at her long fingers confirmed her reluctant agreement with his fears.

Willow sniffled. "I'll let Avery go, I will." Her voice dropped to a whisper. "I know I've kept him too long."

Morniero shook his head. "Now that the naiads are misbehaving, too, there's not much point in me tattling to Mother." He sighed. "It won't be long until she comes on her own."

Chapter Thirty-Six

A few days later, Vanessa's heart was still racing as she leaned the hotel bicycle against the wall of the village post office, a box-like brick building. Flying down the road from Twin Birch House toward the center of Adamsville had been exhilarating. The uphill ride home would be a lot harder. The thought stilled her hands. Home? Was that what Twin Birch House had become?

She was still toying with the idea when she pulled the heavy door open. Inside the post office, a robust young woman with honey blonde waves confronted the sour-faced postmistress, her finger jabbing the counter for emphasis. "There's nothing unpatriotic or unfeminine about demanding our equal rights." Turning to leave, the girl bumped smack into Vanessa and dropped the package in her arms.

Together they stooped to pick it up but ended up knocking heads. "Owwwh." The blonde rubbed her head as she retrieved her parcel.

"I was just trying to help." Vanessa massaged her own lump.

The girl's big brown eyes crinkled as her frown twisted into a crooked smile. "I guess you won't make that mistake again."

Vanessa laughed. "Certainly not."

"But thanks all the same." The stranger pushed her way out the door, leaving Vanessa to approach the scowling postmistress alone.

On the way back, Vanessa overtook the blonde walking up the road. The bicycle's saddlebags were now filled with letters and parcels, making the incline as challenging as she had feared.

"Hello . . . again," she huffed, standing on the pedals to help move the uncooperative wheels.

The girl developed a lopsided grin. "You may as well walk with me." She shifted her package from under one arm to the other. "Beats a heart attack."

The bicycle was barely moving anyway, so Vanessa slid off. "And I'd hate my tombstone to read, 'She died doing the Twin Birch mail run.'"

The blonde nodded, adopting a serious expression. "Truly a senseless tragedy."

"Though I guess it's in poor taste to talk about tombstones right now," Vanessa added quickly, pushing the bike alongside her new companion. The tragedy of Gladys's beau and Irene's constant anxiety over hers had finally taught her to be more sensitive about the war.

The girl's jaw tightened as she stared at the road ahead. "We laugh when we can't cry anymore, right?"

Vanessa nodded and extended her hand. "I'm Vanessa Perkins."

"Bess Nolen." The girl's handshake was firm and businesslike.

"Oh! You must be Avery's sister!"

Bess turned, her face lighting up. "You know Avery?"

"Yes. We've been friends, of a sort, since June." Her mind flew to earlier that week when she and Avery shared cookies in the Enchanted Wood. Although they'd only been together less than an hour, she'd left feeling as though they'd known each other their whole lives.

Being so at ease with someone, and so fast, was new for her. It was different than with Ned, who made her feel bubbly all the time. The sensation with Avery was quieter. More comfortable. The difference between a friend and a lover, perhaps? It was times like this she wished she had more experience with the opposite sex.

She leaned toward Bess. "He says *you're* the one who deserves the credit for how well he dances."

"Wow." Bess turned her head, eyes wide. "Dancing and making friends? Are you sure we're talking about *my* brother, Avery?"

"You can't be serious," Vanessa replied with a laugh. "He's friends with Irene, and Gladys . . . and . . . well, I don't know who else. But he's quite charming, once you get to know him."

"He's a prince, but not many people get a chance to see it." Bess stopped in front of a simple, saltbox home with a chimney rising from the center of the peaked roof. "This is me."

"Have you just returned? Avery said you went to Washington after graduation."

"That's right." Bess squinted at the house. "Only been home a few days, but already feels like a year." She laughed and gave a wink over her shoulder. "Know what I mean?"

Vanessa cocked her head. "Not really."

Bess crinkled her brow a moment, then waved her hand. "Ignore me. Been out on my own too long."

How could anyone be less than thrilled to be home with their family? "Well," Vanessa pushed aside her confusion. "Lovely to meet you. Say hello to Avery for me."

"Pleasure." Bess waved over her head as she headed up the walk to the front door, and Vanessa returned to pushing her bike up the hill.

"Hey, Vanessa!"

She turned to see Bess retracing her steps along her walkway. "Why don't you come over for supper? I'm sure Mother would invite you."

Remembering Mrs. Nolen's kindness at the church earlier that summer, Vanessa smiled. "She already did, but I never got a chance to take her up on it. What time should I come?"

"How about six?"

"I'll be there . . . or, rather, here!"

Chapter Thirty-Seven

Avery snuck a glance at Vanessa carving her meat, then jabbed his fork into the roasted chicken leg on his own plate as though it might run away. Count on Bess to argue with their parents while they had a guest.

He'd been thrilled to discover Vanessa in the living room, talking with his father and sisters when he arrived home from work at his new job, but at this rate, his sister might drive her away before dessert. And it didn't help that Hattie hung on Bess's every word, like she was visiting royalty or something.

His twin's arms were crossed over her chest. "Ten days in jail was a small price to pay for women's rights."

"Who is this Inez Milholland you got yourself arrested over anyway?" His father also seemed to be taking out his frustration on the helpless chicken on his plate.

Bess glowered. "You see! This is why we need these kinds of protests! Inez Milholland drove herself to an early grave fighting for the cause, but people like you don't even know who she is!"

"She doesn't sound particularly sensible, dear." His mother lifted a forkful of lima beans. "Working herself to death?"

"Uuughhhh! She was a practicing lawyer, Mother! Can't get much more sensible than that." Bess threw her napkin on the lace tablecloth as she rose, then marched out of the room.

An awkward silence descended over the dining room table, broken only by the sound of forks scraping on plates and the clap of the back door slamming.

His little sister's eyes sparkled as she observed them all, her pink lips pressed together as she chewed. Hattie was enjoying the show so much; she could have been at the picture house.

"This chicken is delicious, Mrs. Nolen." Vanessa smiled as she took another bite, making Avery's heart soar in gratitude to her for changing the subject.

"So glad you like it, dear."

"It's that damn school that did this to her." His father stabbed at the roasted onions and potatoes on his plate. "Bryn Mawr. Nothing but radicals and socialists down there."

"Avery?" His mother patted her lips with her napkin in an overly delicate manner, a sure sign she was irritated with his father. "Has Bess gone to see the Sewards? She's been home four days already."

"I don't know." His stomach knotted, remembering how sad Irene was that Bess didn't tell her she wasn't coming home for the summer. "She's clearly not ready."

"She was practically engaged to the boy." His father nearly choked on his chicken. "Should at least show a little respect for the dead."

"Now isn't the time to discuss this." His mother smoothed the tablecloth on either side of her place setting. "I'm sorry I brought it up." She turned to Vanessa. "I do apologize."

"Oh, please don't apologize on my account, Mrs. Nolen. This is tame compared to the dinner table arguments I grew up with."

Hattie's eyes widened. "Really?"

"I was raised in the Boston Girls Home. Can't hear yourself think in a dining hall with a hundred other girls."

Lowering her fork, Hattie's voice trembled. "An orphanage? Like in *Oliver Twist*?"

"Conditions have improved since then, I'm sure . . ." Their mother threw a worried glance at their guest.

Vanessa waved her hand. "Doesn't matter. That chapter of my life is closed."

An orphan? It never occurred to him that someone as full of life as Vanessa could have grown up without a family. Avery's frustration drained away as he looked from his mother's graying head to his father's, and then at Hattie's heartbroken expression. He couldn't imagine losing any of them.

Chapter Thirty-Eight

Holding a plate of spice cake, Vanessa squeezed past Avery, who held the back screen door open with his elbow, a plate in each hand.

Dusk had fallen while they'd eaten supper, the sun near setting behind the mountains. Soon, it would be too cold to linger outside in the evening, and Vanessa sensed they were all clinging to summer as long as they could.

Avery's little sister followed close behind her, clutching a handful of forks in one hand, her own plate in the other. Glancing up from the bottom of the back porch steps, Vanessa caught Harriet giving Avery a peck on the cheek as she passed him. The love softening his features as he gazed down at his little sister was so unguarded and profound, it made Vanessa's chest ache. She hadn't realized how much she yearned for love like that until witnessing it firsthand all summer among the Wainwrights, Nolens, and a few other families at Twin Birch House.

Then Avery's expression clouded. She followed his gaze to Bess, who was sitting on a wrought iron garden bench—puffing on a cigarette. He strode down the porch stairs and a few steps across the back lawn to deliver a piece of cake to his twin. "So, now you smoke? And in front of Hattie?"

Bess glared at him as she took her plate. "Not you, too." She reached for the fork Harriet offered and slid over, making room for Vanessa next to her.

"I've seen her smoke plenty of times." Harriet dragged a nearby lawn chair over. "I'm not a child."

Avery pulled a chair over for himself with a sigh. "I know, Hattie, you're a full-grown woman of sixteen. It's Bess who's the child, going out of her way to get Mother and Father all wound up."

"How do you stand it?" Bess dropped her cigarette stub and ground it with her heel. "Their tiny, provincial mindsets?"

"Come on. Aren't you being a little harsh?"

Bess took a bite of cake. "Harsh? You mean like Father barely speaking to you just because you're not following in his footsteps?"

Vanessa swung her feet in little circles, realizing that her view of the Nolen's family life might have been a little romanticized. She felt compelled to interject, but kept her voice low. "Seems to me they just *care* about you."

Avery's smile made Vanessa glad she'd spoken up, and the chagrin on Bess's face was gratifying too. It was a relief to know his twin's griping wasn't as serious as it sounded.

"It doesn't matter." Bess talked with her mouth half full. "I'm only here for a few weeks. Promised I'd be back in DC by the beginning of October."

"So soon?" Harriet's dismay was heartbreaking.

To her credit, Bess shot the girl a sympathetic smile.

"What are you doing down there?" Vanessa asked before taking another bite of cake.

"I got a job in the lobbying arm of the NWP, working directly for Abby Scott Baker."

Bess's pride was obvious, even if Vanessa had no idea what she was talking about. "What's the NWP?"

"Oh, please!" Bess gave Vanessa's knee a light slap. "I can understand my crusty old father not knowing this stuff, but how can an independent young woman like you not know about the National Women's Party?"

Avery scowled. "Don't pick on her. I didn't know who they were either."

He was sticking up for her. Vanessa shot him a grateful smile, so shockingly moved she had to look away quickly. But she was genuinely interested in what Bess was saying. "What's the point?" she asked. "Won't women just vote the same as their husbands?"

Bess lowered her plate to her lap and took a deep breath. "Is that what you would do? Vote just like your husband?"

Vanessa imagined herself standing in a polling station, confronted with candidates and platforms she knew nothing about. Frankly, it was overwhelming. "Well . . . I expect my husband will be an intelligent and capable man." She avoided looking at Avery. "Why wouldn't someone like me rely on him to make those kinds of decisions?"

Bess laughed. "Are you a fortune hunter, Miss Perkins? Eyeing the Twin Birch House guests for 'intelligent, capable men' without wedding bands?"

The shock took her breath. What had Avery said about her? What did everyone know? Did the whole Nolen family think of her this way?

"Bess! That's enough." Avery's sharp tone let her know that at least *he* was not amused.

But if there were any hope of salvaging the situation, she'd have to hold her chin high. She'd done nothing wrong, or so she kept reminding herself. "No, no." She held her palm up to him. "Everyone else knows I humiliated myself with Ned Cooper this summer, why not her?"

"Oh, I'm so sorry." Bess tried to smother her laugh with her fist, but failed. "You mean, you really . . ."

The laughter put Vanessa more at ease. Bess hadn't been following up on a rumor. She'd been teasing, and accidentally hit too close to the mark.

"I did not . . . *pursue* him. But I chose not to deflect his attentions, either."

"There's nothing wrong with that!" Hattie sounded so offended it seemed she was the injured party. "Why wouldn't some fancy guest court you? You're beautiful . . . and sweet and-"

"Thank you." Vanessa reached over and clasped the girl's hand. "You're a darling."

"Better to laugh, than cry, right?" Bess's wicked grin was contagious.

"Indeed." Vanessa's voice brightened. "Besides . . ." She smoothed her skirt over her knees. "It led to my new job and, who knows, even romantic prospects that are somewhat more realistic."

Could she be more obvious? Again, she avoided looking at Avery. For goodness sakes, he had to think she was about to propose, right there in front of his sisters.

Hattie clapped her hands. "Who? Who?"

Bess shot a glance at her brother. "Someone from the hotel?" There was an edge in Bess's voice that, combined with Avery's concentration on his plate, made Vanessa's stomach clench. She waved her hands as she stared at the ground. "I shouldn't say. He's given no indication . . . He's just been quite . . . supportive of me."

Her mind flooded with Avery's kindness to her. Introducing his family after church, sharing the Enchanted Wood so generously . . . and just last weekend, showing such genuine concern after her breakup with Ned. She'd been hoping for some sign he shared her growing attraction. But fearing he was pulling away, she realized Avery's friendship was what mattered most. And despite herself, she wasn't completely over Ned yet.

"I can guess! Let me guess!" Hattie bounced in her seat. "Guest or staff?"

Vanessa's leg jiggled as her anxiety mounted along with Hattie's excitement, and Avery and Bess's increasingly heavy silence. "Now I've given the wrong impression. I seriously should not have said anything . . ."

Where was Hattie going with this? Evidently not to her brother. If his sister hadn't picked up on Vanessa's feelings, perhaps she'd succeeded in hiding her interest from Avery as well.

"Hardly any guests this late in the season . . . so I'm guessing staff." Hattie cupped her elbow in her palm, her other hand rubbing her chin. "But only 'somewhat more realistic'."

As Avery's sister carried on, clearly oblivious to everyone else's discomfort, Vanessa's leg stilled. She stared at remnants of the spice cake smeared on her plate. The girl wasn't going to give up until she had a name.

"I know! I know!" Hattie bounced on her seat as she clapped. "Karl Fiske! My friend Paulina's sister is a waitress up there and she wouldn't shut up about him all summer. Says he's running the place now, without his father or anyone."

"Karl Fiske?" The twins choked the name out in unison.

Vanessa recoiled. Even though she had no designs on Karl, their reaction hurt. It was like people's response to her and Ned all over again.

Bess turned her head away as Avery appeared to struggle for words. "Karl is a fine person." His voice was small and strangled. "We've known him for years."

"He certainly seems to be." The storm of emotion battering Vanessa's insides far outsized any possible slight on their part. Clearly it was much too soon for her to be considering romance again, with Avery or anyone else. "But I'm so sorry if anything I said encouraged speculation that direction." Placing her half-eaten cake on the wrought iron table next the glider, Vanessa forced a laugh. "Trust me, there isn't a bit of romantic interest between me and Mr. Fiske, on either side."

"Oh . . ." Hattie finally seemed to notice Vanessa's discomfort.

"But talking to him about Twin Birch House has sparked my interest in the hotel business. It's actually fascinating."

"Oh, indeed." Hattie's enthusiasm had a desperate ring. "All those meals and entertainments . . . and . . . and rooms to coordinate."

"It's getting dark so fast." Vanessa rose. "I best head back while there's still some light."

Avery sprang up. "I'll escort you."

"No, no. I'm fine. I promise." She simply couldn't keep up the fake smile for the entire walk back to the hotel.

The finality in her voice apparently kept him from offering again. "Well, thank you for coming."

Bess turned her face back toward Vanessa, her tone chipper. "We'll have to do it again soon."

"Yes, yes, of course." Vanessa rushed away, calling over her shoulder, "And please thank your mother for me!" Mercifully, her tears didn't spill until after she rounded the corner of the house.

Chapter Thirty-Nine

After Vanessa disappeared, Avery sank slowly back into his seat, fists on his knees as he stared at the ground. How had things gone so wrong so fast?

"I'm sorry. I never know when to stop." Bess sounded exhausted.

"You?" Hattie stood with her hands on her hips. "It was me who drove her away, blathering about Paulina's sister and Karl Fiske. How could you let me go on like that?" She ran into the house without waiting for an answer.

Avery watched the back door slam. Hattie's storms always blew over quickly. By the time they went back inside, she'd be helping their mother with the dishes, complaining about a strict teacher, or waxing on about a piece of music she'd heard at Paulina's house.

He turned back to Bess. "Even if there's nothing between Vanessa and Karl, I don't think I'm her type."

"Then she's a fool."

Dear—maddening—Bess. Always his fiercest defender. "One of us is, anyway."

He smiled and turned his head toward the street just as Vanessa rounded the bend, then disappeared once more.

Returning his attention to Bess, he cocked his head. "You and Karl?"

Bess snorted. "No. Just brought back a lot of memories all at once." She pushed her cake around with her fork. "Everything was so much simpler then, wasn't it? Whole summers with nothing to do but sail and picnic."

As the crickets furiously clicked their evening song, images of summers past spooled through Avery's mind. Sitting on a lakeside rock, sketching the sailboats in his notebook. Bess, Karl, and the other sailing buffs racing around yellow and orange striped buoys. Climbing Mt. Washington on his own. Visiting Willow and the other wood nymphs alone because Bess could no longer see the entrance to the Enchanted Wood. His summers hadn't changed as much as hers.

And he hoped the disastrous evening wouldn't stop Vanessa from going to the Wood. The hours they'd spent there on Labor Day were his happiest in years.

Leaning over, he put a hand on Bess's knee. "You need to go see Irene."

She covered her face with her hands. "I know, I know."

He got up and sat next to her on the bench, wrapping his arm around her. "I'll go with you, if it would make it easier."

Bess lay her head against his shoulder. "You're the best, Ave."

"I love you, too. But you still have to visit the Sewards."

<h1 style="text-align:center;font-style:italic">Chapter Forty</h1>

T he early September sun felt good on Vanessa's face as she waited for Irene to unlock the cottage door.

The last of the cottage guests had departed that weekend, and the grounds were particularly deserted thanks to the post-Labor Day exodus and a special trip to Boston the hotel organized for some of the remaining guests. They were off to see the Red Sox play the Chicago Cubs in the final games of the World Series.

"Nice to have some relief from all that baseball frenzy." The Series and Babe Ruth, Boston's talented and troublesome star, were an understandable diversion from newspaper accounts of the war abroad and anarchist bombings at home. But Vanessa still found them tedious.

"Don't let my brothers hear you speak that blasphemy." Irene raised an eyebrow as she picked up her bucket full of clean rags and walked inside.

"Oh, the boys are alright." Vanessa followed Irene into the entryway. "But doesn't the way some of the guests talk about the players being traitors and Bolsheviks grate on your nerves? They only talked of striking after the owners changed their deal at the last minute."

"I make a point of not eavesdropping on the guests' conversations. It can only come back to bite you." Irene directed her to the broom closet at the back of the kitchen. "Get your supplies from there. We'll start upstairs."

"Okay, boss." Vanessa tucked her hair into her kerchief, still in a sour mood from Friday night's dinner at the Nolens, even if it might have been a blessing. Best not to introduce romantic confusion into her friendship with Avery. Her fingers clenched around a mop handle as she yanked it out. She was still sick of people deciding who she was good enough for . . . and who she wasn't.

Lugging the tin of Murphy Oil Soap from the closet shelf, she remembered her march from the Nolens' back to Twin Birch House that night. Her heart had been pounding hard but returning to the grounds had calmed her. The solidity of the hotel's expanse, the warm light radiating from dozens of windows and the low hum of voices from the front porch had made her feel cocooned. Safer than she'd ever felt since losing her parents' protection. Within the resort's polished rooms, and on its manicured lawns, she'd found a new home worth fighting for.

Regardless of what anyone thought, she wasn't going to lose sight of her goal. Convincing Karl Fiske she was worth taking a risk on was still key to her new employment ambitions . . . and surely within her power. But she needed to make faster progress. With winter fast approaching, there wasn't a moment to spare.

Irene headed for the entryway. "You do the bathrooms. I'll do the bedrooms."

"Okay." Trudging up the stairs with her bucket and mop, Vanessa stewed over Irene's coolness toward her. After the spectacle on the train platform, the remaining dorm girls had pretty much shunned her. But she'd expected more from Irene. Her friend seemed perfectly happy taking over her responsibilities with Walter and Edna when Vanessa left them for the Gardners. Said she appreciated the extra money. Like Gladys, Irene didn't seem wild about Vanessa's relationship with Ned, but she had stayed friendly throughout the summer. Never seemed to judge.

As they headed in different directions at the top of the stairs, Vanessa continued to wonder. Could Irene have taken Mrs. Wainwright's side once her break with Vanessa was made public? To bask in the Wainwrights' glow was intoxicating, as she knew all too well. Perhaps Irene didn't want to leave that warm circle. She'd still be here when the Wainwrights returned next season, so it made sense if her loyalties remained with long-standing guests over some nursemaid from the Girls Home she'd only known a few months.

Vanessa lowered her bucket in the master bathroom. They were in "the Cedars," where Sarah Gardner's best friend had stayed with her family, though calling them cottages was ridiculous in Vanessa's opinion. They were two-story, four-bedroom houses, each with two full bathrooms. In fact, fully furnished middle-class homes but considered rustic by the standards of the Boston "Brahmin." Her stomach cramped imagining the satisfaction Ned's sister and her friend would get from seeing her clean its toilets now.

Confusion over Irene's behavior, disappointment in the Nolens, hurt over Ned and anger at herself—they all mixed to form a bitter brew that fueled her work. By the time she was done, the tiles glistened and fixtures gleamed. Tired, but satisfied Mrs. Juneau would approve, Vanessa was finally calm enough to approach Irene. Better to find out what was wrong than let her vivid imagination make a difficult situation even worse.

After depositing her cleaning supplies at the head of the stairs, she walked into the bedroom where Irene was busy covering furniture. She took a side of the white sheet in her friend's hands. Together they flung the cloth over the pinstriped mattress, releasing the scent of Borax and sunshine into the room. "Are you upset with me?"

"Not at all." Irene draped the dustcover behind the headboard with a frown. "Why would you think that?"

"It's just that you're so quiet . . . and barely even look at me."

"Oh? I didn't realize." Irene's hands fumbled as she pulled another sheet from the pile on the dresser.

Heart pounding in her throat, Vanessa straightened the cloth over the bedside table. "I just thought . . . perhaps you agree with Mrs. Wainwright . . ."

Irene sighed and appeared to choose her words carefully. "I agree that leaving her the way you did was unfortunate. But she didn't own you. You're free to work for whoever you want."

Vanessa's shoulders loosened. Irene was always so diplomatic and quiet around the guests. Who knew she had such an independent streak? "And Ned?"

"I feared he was using you." Irene hugged the folded sheet against her chest. "But you seemed so sure of yourself. And if anyone could marry up, it's you."

Pride tingled in her belly, but alarms sounded as well. "Why do you say that?"

"I don't know . . ." Irene cocked her head and raised her eyes to the ceiling. "You're light, like them. Not so close to the ground."

Vanessa's lips curled. "'Flighty' was what the warden at the Girls Home called it."

Irene shook her head. "That's not it. More like . . . sparkly." A dimple formed as she smiled. "Classy."

First Hattie, now Irene. Vanessa wasn't accustomed to compliments. The kindness and support dissolved a stone in her chest she hadn't realized was there. "Thank you."

"It's true."

Vanessa turned away, blinking back the tears welling in her eyes. "That's lovely to hear." Swiping her eyes, she refocused on her friend. "So, tell me. What *is* wrong, then?"

Irene sank into the wingback chair next to the bed. "I have no right to feel sorry for myself. Others have greater burdens than me . . ."

"Forget about everyone else for once. You're allowed to have feelings, too."

Irene turned her head, clutching a furniture drape in her lap. She took a deep breath. "It's just been . . . hard lately."

"Your mother? I gather she passed . . ."

"A year ago," Irene whispered with a nod.

Vanessa slid to her knees in front of Irene's chair. "No wonder you're blue. I still want to cry when I think of my mother, and she's been gone nearly fifteen years."

"But it's not just her. I'm losing everyone." Irene tried to smile, but failed miserably.

"Who else?"

Irene's lip shook. "My brother . . . Dewey. He was killed in France." Giving up, she bent over and sobbed into the cloth drape.

Vanessa sat back on her heels, knowing better than to say anything and embarrassed to have thought everything was about her. In time, Irene's sobs quieted to gentle sniffling. Standing up on her knees, Vanessa pushed a stray lock of hair behind Irene's ear. "And who are you losing now?"

Irene raised her bloodshot eyes. "Roy, for one."

"Your beau? The one who's overseas?"

She nodded. "He hardly writes anymore, and when he does, it's like there's nothing there. Like he doesn't even know who I am."

"Gladys said the same thing about Chester's letters." Vanessa instantly regretted bringing up Gladys's dead sweetheart. Unable to take back the words, she hurried on. "Don't they have to do that for the censors?"

"Of course he can't tell me where he is, or anything about the battlefield. But I'm talking about personal things." Irene plucked at the damp cloth in her lap. "In the beginning, he wrote about all sorts of details. Little things he was seeing. Funny things the other soldiers said. Sweet things . . . about missing me." Her faint smile evaporated. "But everything changed after Dewey got killed. Roy was there. Right beside him. They were best friends. We were like the three musketeers growing up. Always together." Her voice dropped to a whisper. "Ever since Dewey died, it's like someone else writes Roy's letters and he just signs them." She started crying afresh. "I miss him so much I can't breathe."

Vanessa rested her hand on Irene's knee, letting her cry. When her friend quieted again, she spoke as gently as she could. "Anyone else?"

Irene nodded and sighed. "Avery's sister, Bess."

"I met her."

"You did?"

"Yes. I ran into her at the post office this past Friday, then had supper at their house."

Irene's face pinched. "All summer I got just one postcard of the Lincoln Memorial from Bess. And haven't seen her since she's been home."

Vanessa had never had a lifelong friend to lose but could imagine Irene's pain. "Her mother did say something about her needing to visit . . ."

"I know why she's avoiding me, but still . . ."

It was a guilty relief to know she wasn't alone in finding friendship with Bess a complicated business. "Why?"

"They didn't tell you?"

"No."

Irene took a deep, shuddering breath and turned her eyes to the ceiling. "Bess and Dewey were sweethearts. I wouldn't be surprised if he secretly proposed before he left." Her voice caught as she lowered her head. "I think to Bess, we're all just painful reminders." A tear slid down her cheek. "And knowing Roy was there, that he saw it happen, must make it that more difficult for her to see me."

Vanessa bit her lip. "Oh, Irene."

"Bess may act strong, but she takes loss harder than most." Irene wiped her eyes with the damp sheet. "She started drifting away from me, from all of us, around the time my mother got sick . . . four years ago, now." She shook her head. "Last year, she was already back at school when Mama died . . . probably for the best."

Looking down at her hands, Vanessa spun her ring. "My sister died about a year after our parents drowned."

Blinking, Irene wiped her runny nose with the back of her hand. "That must have been horrible."

"I'm not telling you to make you feel sorry for me or anything. I just want you to know that I have some idea what it feels like. To lose a parent . . . and a sibling."

Irene squeezed her hand. "Aren't we the jolly pair?"

"Well, we should be." Vanessa scrambled to her feet. "We should dance and laugh . . . and tell the reaper he's taken enough from us. That he can't take one more soul!" She took Irene's other hand and pulled her up from the chair.

Irene laughed as she tripped over the drape that dropped from her lap. Vanessa raised their arms above their heads and twirled Irene in a circle with one hand. "Not one more soul!"

"That's right." Irene's voice quivered as she turned. "No more souls."

"Not one more!" She let go of Irene and spun across the room.

Irene spread her arms and threw her head back as she turned on her own. "Not one more! Not one more!"

"Not one more! Not one more!" chanted Vanessa.

Together they danced and screamed and cursed and laughed until their heads were light and their throats hoarse. After they'd calmed, they had to rush around to finish their work before Mrs. Juneau wondered what happened to them. But it was worth it.

Following Irene back toward the hotel, Vanessa put aside the unpleasant thoughts that were creeping back into her head. Sucking in a deep lungful of air and blowing it out again hard, she determined not to let anything interfere with her good mood. Something important happened in those unguarded moments with Irene, releasing her inhibitions and long-suppressed memories. Something worth holding on to.

She couldn't remember breathing so easily, her chest so free of tension and ache. Every girl at the orphanage had a sad story. By unspoken agreement, no one talked about her sorrows. Not seriously, anyway. Now she understood why. The silence kept them from focusing on the past. Looking forward, into the future, was the only way the group resisted self-pity and despair.

But keeping the pain bottled up had a price. Sharing her misery had released a bit of it. Left her stronger, not weaker, as she'd always feared. The experience also made her feel closer to Irene than she'd felt with . . . well, anyone, since losing Ruth.

Speeding up, she pulled alongside Irene on the wide, crushed granite path. She wanted to keep their new bond going. To confide more. Irene might even be an ally in her quest to return to the hotel in the spring.

Chapter Forty-One

"I hear Karl Fiske's been coming here for years." Vanessa swapped her heavy bucket to the other hand. "So, you must know him pretty well."

"Fairly well," Irene said with a shrug. "Used to spend more time together when we were kids. We all had more time for play back then."

"What's he like? What's he do for fun?"

Irene gave her a friendly nudge on the shoulder with her own. "Getting over Ned, are you?"

The warmth of Ned's lips on her neck and the charm of his dimpled smile flashed through Vanessa's mind. "Not as fast as I'd like . . . but that's not why I'm interested."

They neared the hotel's screened-in back porch, reserved for staff only. The chatting of the food prep workers drifted from the kitchen windows, accompanied by the staccato rap of their knives against wooden cutting boards.

"I need to get to know Mr. Fiske better. Help him consider me as favorably as possible."

Irene cocked her head. "But . . . not in a romantic way?"

"No!" She shook her hands by her sides. "Why is that the first thing everyone assumes? He's perfectly attractive and seems like a quality fellow, but I have no romantic interest whatsoever, I swear."

"Okay . . ."

"But I've most definitely fallen in love with Twin Birch House. I'm desperate to stay on somehow."

"Well. I certainly understand that. And nothing would make me happier." The warmth in Irene's smile made Vanessa want to hug her all over again.

"And for a couple of reasons, Mr. Fiske is the key to making it happen." Though she trusted Irene, she wasn't ready to explain that she believed her fate somehow involved the hotel owner's son because she was guided to him by the water nymphs that live in an Enchanted Wood, not a half mile up the mountain. She was still trying to make sense of the forest's mythical creatures herself, and wasn't anywhere near ready to discuss it with anyone . . . besides Avery, of course.

Irene considered for a moment. "There's only one thing that interests Karl as much as work." She grinned as she stooped to lift her bucket. "Take a gander at the trophy case in the lobby."

"Thank you! Thank you!" Vanessa threw her arms around her startled friend. "You're the only one who's believed in me."

The bear hug was so tight; Irene had to tilt her head to the sky to speak. "I think you're cockeyed." She broke free and put a hand on Vanessa's shoulder. "But I'm coming to think that's what makes me believe in you."

Vanessa's eyes misted as she grinned and stepped back to retrieve her own bucket. "Good enough for me."

Irene shook her head and chuckled as they made their way inside. As soon as they'd put their cleaning supplies away, Vanessa pulled the kerchief from her head and tossed her long braid loose. Her head was light, as though she and Irene had been drinking champagne all afternoon, rather than scrubbing and dusting. She skipped across the hallway to clock out, eager to change clothes, and investigate that trophy case.

Later that evening, Vanessa made her way to the hotel lobby wearing her freshest blouse and a subtle shade of lipstick from the dredges of one of Sarah Gardner's old tubes. The color set off her well-formed mouth without making her appear "painted." A technique she'd picked up from Ned's sister. She definitely wanted it to seem like she belonged in the "front of the house," mixing with the guests.

Large silver cups were on display in a glass-front case. Each trophy was etched with the winners of the hotel's various sporting competitions. Awards for the annual costume contest, talent show and carriage decorating competition were there as well. Off to the side, there was a plaque of past winners of the lady sailor division. It was not at all shocking to see Bess's name listed several times. Scanning the sailing regatta winners, she found Karl's name listed as the winner or second place finalist in his age-class every year from 1909 to 1913. So, he was a sailing buff. She sent silent thanks to Irene.

The question was, where would young Mr. Fiske be at that hour?

She surveyed the enormous lobby that formed the heart of the hotel. Potted ferns and writing desks, oriental carpets and reading lamps gave the room a homey feel, even though it was easily a hundred feet long. Balls cracked in the nearby billiard room, and the murmur of voices drifted in from a few lingering guests on the porch, enjoying aperitifs before supper. It was strange to see so few guests sprinkled on the clusters of chairs and sofas in the lounge. At the peak of the season, she'd seen it full of patrons, every seat taken. Nearly empty, it appeared a bit forlorn.

Then, as though summoned by magic, Karl Fiske walked down the main staircase, absorbed by a document in his hand.

"Hello there!" She bounced on her toes as she waved.

He appeared startled, but quickly composed his features and nodded. "Good evening, Miss Perkins."

"Do you have a moment?"

Frowning, he glanced around as though she might be speaking to someone else, then strolled over. "What can I do for you?"

"I just wanted to thank you again for giving me the opportunity to join the staff."

"It's Mrs. Juneau you have to thank."

"And I have, but you still had to approve." She swung her arm toward the trophy case. "And now I see you're a master sailor."

He stood a little taller as he glanced out the front door toward the lake. "Hardly a master, but I do enjoy the water."

"I don't believe I saw you sailing once the entire summer."

"You're right." His brow knitted. "I kept hoping to go, but every time I planned an outing, something came up that required my attention."

"But everything's calmed down now, with most of the guests gone." She swept an arc on the carpet with the toe of her shoe. "Surely you can squeeze some time in for a sail now."

With another glance out the front door, he nodded. "Right again. I should make some time before the good weather ends."

"It must be great fun."

"You've never been?" He sounded incredulous.

She shook her head, eyes wide. "No."

"You should try it. It's truly grand. And there are a number of lady sailors, too."

"But how would I learn . . . ?"

"The dock master gives lessons." His attention was diverted to Irene's father, who entered from the room behind the reception desk. "His name's Houkey. Tell him I sent you," he added before heading toward Mr. Seward.

After a few steps he stopped and turned back. "Pleasure seeing you again."

"Wonderful seeing you, too." She crossed her arms once his back was turned.

"*The dock master gives lessons.*" She'd been angling for an invitation.

Phooey!

Chapter Forty-Two

A week after the awkward supper with Vanessa, Avery dipped his brush in the water jar and swirled it in the turquoise square. He loved the simple act of coaxing paint from the blocks of color. Mixing hues to form a seemingly infinite array of new colors. The palette of the White Mountains' woods and valleys was deep and shadowy. Soothing and cool. But the palette for the Enchanted Wood was bold. Bright. He was working on a painting of the pond, hoping his increased attention to the water might lure the water nymphs into his sight. So far, they remained invisible . . . to him, at any rate.

"Have you tired of us?" teased Willow.

"You know I'd never tire of you." He smiled up at her as she leaned out of the tree trunk to get a better look at his easel.

"Perhaps you will," she said rather cryptically, glancing toward the passageway.

His brush stopped in mid-stroke at the sight of Vanessa emerging from the stone tunnel. His insides twisted. As beautiful as the wood nymphs were, none disturbed him like Vanessa did.

"And there is something we need to talk about." A tremor in Willow's voice hinted at sorrow he'd never perceived before.

He lowered his brush. "What is it, Willow? Is everything alright?"

She nodded. "Yes. I just need to speak to you . . . alone."

"Of course."

Her sad smile flickered, and he silently vowed not to let Vanessa's visits lead him to neglect the wood nymphs, especially Willow. She'd been his most faithful companion his entire childhood and deserved better. He followed Willow's gaze. At the mouth of the passage, Vanessa brushed stray leaves from her skirt, then glanced up at him and froze. He hadn't seen her since she'd fled his backyard and, evidently, she was still upset. He lifted the brush and waved, hoping to appear friendly and inviting. She seemed to brace herself before heading toward him. At least she didn't leave.

"Hello." Vanessa smiled as she got near, but he could see the tension in her face.

All the saliva in his mouth mysteriously disappeared. "Hello." He swished the paintbrush in the water jar.

"Before we talk about anything else, I want to apologize for my hasty departure the other night." She sat on the bench beside him and threw him a quick glance. "It was probably a bit confusing."

Hope stirred in his belly. Maybe they hadn't botched the evening as badly as it seemed. Leaving the paintbrush in the jar, he glanced back to see what Willow thought, but she had retreated inside the tree. Only her spine was visible in the bark running up the trunk.

His eyes returned to Vanessa. "I think it's we who owe the apology. Rare for us to entertain a guest we haven't known our whole lives." A brief chuckle escaped from high in his chest. "Seems we provided a rather unvarnished presentation of the Nolen family in its natural habitat."

"It's alright." Her laugh sounded genuine. "I'm still a bit weepy over Ned, I admit, and overreacted. But honesty is the best foundation to build a friendship upon, don't you agree?"

"Yes . . ." Why did the question feel like a trap? "Of course."

"Good." Something flashed in Vanessa's eyes he couldn't quite read, but she continued before he had a chance to contemplate its meaning. "Then . . . I'll admit I was embarrassed about Karl Fiske's name coming up in that way."

"Yes, I realize . . . and there was no—"

"Stop." Vanessa held her palm toward him. "It's fine." She smiled. "You have sisters, so you know young women think about young, unattached men with special interest, and I'm no exception."

So . . . she *was* attracted to Karl? He kept his eyes fixed on his partially completed watercolor.

"But after the . . ." Her voice caught. "Spectacle . . . I made of myself with Ned Cooper, the last thing I can tolerate is the idea that people think I'm chasing after Mr. Fiske."

He wanted to pull her onto his lap and hold her. To physically shield her from the cruelty of the world. His jaw tightened. "It was Cooper who was in the wrong this summer. Not you."

The gratitude in her eyes made him even angrier with Ned.

"I played my part." The resignation and responsibility in her voice doubled the respect he already had for her. "But that's all over now. And I have absolutely no romantic interest in Mr. Fiske, nor him in me."

Avery's mouth spread into a grin he couldn't contain. "I see."

"But I still need to overcome my . . . damaged reputation amongst the guests if there's any hope of him giving me a job in New York over the winter . . . and bringing me back here next season."

"You need to gain favor with Karl." He put his painting aside. "So he'll want to you stay on?"

"Exactly." She repositioned herself to face him on the bench. "I never had a brother, you see. I barely remember my father, and I was raised with a hundred other girls by five spinsters. You're the first man I've ever called a friend. The brother I never had. I want you to be honest with me, the way you are with Bess and Hattie."

He blinked. A brother? A friend? How could he fall so hard for a girl who didn't return a speck of his feelings? Sitting so close, inhaling her intoxicating scent. It was unbearable. He sprang to his feet and stepped toward the pond. "What do you mean? What do you want to know?"

"Tell me what sort of person he is. If there's any hope he'd . . . extend himself for someone like me."

He stared at the gaudy pink blossoms exploding amidst the emerald green lily pads as he considered Karl Fiske's character. "I . . . I'm not sure." He returned to the bench, trying to recall what he knew about Karl. "He and I were never close. He ran with my sister's crowd when we were younger."

"They both sailed, didn't they? I saw Bess's name on a lot of trophies at the hotel."

Nodding, he put a hand on his hip. "That's right. They were the sporty set."

"But is he a snob? Talking badly about the staff when we're not around?"

"No. I told you. He's a fine person."

Vanessa rose and began pacing in front of the bench. "Do you imagine he disapproved of Ned . . . and me?" Her cheeks grew pink.

"He certainly never said anything I know of. It's not his style to gossip." But would a man like Karl take a personal risk for a disgraced nursemaid turned chambermaid? One glance at Vanessa's open, hopeful face and Avery's chest tightened. How could anyone not help her?

"I'm working as hard as I can, and have an ally in Mrs. Juneau, but Mr. Fiske never sees my accomplishments, and he didn't even notice my embarrassing attempt to wrangle a sailing invitation from him. He has no reason to think I'm worth any special attention or effort." She flung her arms in the air. "I don't know what to do!"

"Well . . ." Avery's eyes followed her as she paced. He definitely wanted to help her return to Twin Birch House. No question about that. "What if you didn't do anything?"

She stopped and faced him, her eyes wide and wounded. "Just give up?"

"No. Not at all. But I get the feeling he's the sort of prey you don't stalk but rather wait for in a blind."

Her head tilted as her eyes narrowed. "A what?"

"A blind. It's where hunters hide themselves, waiting for timid game, like birds and deer." He smiled, warming to his metaphor. "Karl's the quiet, introverted type. It's possible your usual … enthusiasm … might make him nervous." The same could be said for him.

Her head tilted. "Ohhh." She resumed pacing. "I see what you mean. I can be rather animated. But wait." She stopped. "I'm still doing it."

Rejoining him on the bench, she placed her hands on her knees and closed her eyes. "I'll be still. Calm. Demure."

A few moments after she alighted, his stomach relaxed. "Yesss. That's it." His voice fell to a whisper. "You'd be amazed what kind of creatures come your way if you're still enough."

"This is good—"

He put his finger against her lips. "Shhhhhh. Just listen."

Smiling, she kept her eyes squeezed shut. He lowered his finger and they sat together in silence. He closed his eyes, too. The quiet was wonderful. Soothing. Little sound but the soft rustle of leaves . . . water trickling somewhere nearby, feeding the pond. A whippoorwill calling in the distance.

He hoped she could sense everything he loved about the wilderness. The mineral scent of the granite, the mustiness of the dying reeds at the edge of the pond, and the delicate jasmine from the fantastical flowers that grew only in the Enchanted Wood.

She touched his hand and his eyes flew open.

Her eyes were still closed. Sliding his fingers around hers, he basked in the pleasure of holding her hand and looking around the glittering wood. A brilliant white rabbit with sparkling fur nosed around the grass near the edge of the pond. Raising his free hand, he returned his finger to Vanessa's lips and tried not to think about kissing them. "Stay quiet and open your eyes," he whispered.

He moved his finger away as her lashes fluttered open. She spotted the bunny. Simple joy turned her face from lovely to magnificent. "When you're quiet and still, you see and hear what's there."

Her eyes glistened, her voice barely a whisper. "And he'll see me."

"He'd be a fool to miss you."

"Thank you so much." She squeezed his hand. "You're the best friend a girl could have!"

His stomach clenched. Best friend. Why couldn't that sound as nice as she meant it to be?

When the bunny they'd been watching hopped behind a rock and out of sight, Vanessa released Avery's hand and sat taller on the bench.

That should have done it.

After agonizing how she would behave the next time she saw Avery, she had come upon the brilliant plan to make it clear that she considered him like a brother. No risk of hurt feelings, no awkwardness. Best for everyone. And she was rather pleased with her acting. It was apparently quite convincing. In fact, the whole thing went better than she imagined it might, though her heart did twinge a bit at how easily he accepted her as a "sister."

"Your latest?" She leaned across Avery's lap and picked up his half-finished watercolor.

He pushed his glasses up his nose. "Guilty."

Slapping his arm, she held the stiff paper out in front of her. "False modesty is unbecoming. Didn't anyone teach you that?"

Crossing his arms, Avery made a show of his disapproval. "And didn't your teachers inform you that assaulting innocent men is unbecoming?"

"Not if they deserve it." She offered her sweetest smile. "But seriously, why not become an artist instead of a . . ." She lowered the watercolor to her lap. "What is it you're doing for the Forest Service? I don't believe you actually said."

"Inventorying plants." He tugged as his shirt cuffs, his lips tightening.

"That's a job?"

"My dream job." A smile cracked the line he'd made of his mouth. "I get to paint them, too. One day . . . James Audubon."

"The bird painter, right?"

"That's right." And there it was. The smile that turned her insides out. That reminded her that there was always a shining sun behind every storm cloud. All it took was a bit of genuine interest in him and what he cared about. Was it possible he didn't get that kind of attention at home?

"So, what, exactly, do you do all day?"

"Well." He swept his arm in an arc. "This whole area was made into a national forest in May. Now they need taxonomical keys, especially of trees, for possible use in the war effort." His words rushed out as his eyes lit up. "I get to describe, draw, and even name plants and cryptic species, like fungi and lichens."

"And you want to do that . . ."

"Yes! And I'm perfect for it. With the Forest Service so new, and so many fellows overseas, they're scooping up recent grads like me, and being a native son in these parts and everything, it's like they created the position just for me." His enthusiasm was contagious, despite the unappealing particulars of the job. It did sound rather marvelous for him, putting his unique blend of talents toward something of lasting importance.

She opened her mouth, then closed it again and smiled. "Then that's swell, Avery. Just swell. I'm glad you're happy."

"But . . ."

She shifted uncomfortably. "But nothing."

"Come on. Bess gets that tone, too. I can hear a silent 'but' like a cat hears a baby bird fall from its nest."

Glancing at him from the corner of her eye, she ventured into sister territory. "I just wonder if it's good for you to be alone so much."

His eyes flashed. "How many times do I have to say it? I like my solitude."

Despite his frustration, she was pleased to know a fire burned beneath his tranquil exterior. "Bess made it sound like you don't have many friends."

"People and I don't mix so well." His voice lowered. "That's what my father could never understand. Why the idea of being a doctor makes my skin crawl."

"But people like you. I know Irene does . . . and I do."

"I'm not the one complaining about not having enough friends." He glanced up at the willow tree behind them. "And I've got the nymphs."

"But only the wood nymphs." Her brow arched. "Not the ones in the water."

"That's alright." His smile twisted with a wicked grin. "My nymphs don't talk to you, and you're Miss Popularity."

His joking observation hit a soft spot. She bowed her head, thinking of Gladys, and several other girls she'd known over the years. "Only because I lose friends as quickly as I make them." Her laugh was short and tight. "Always restocking."

Sobering, he took her hand. "Well, then. You should know that it takes me so long to make friends, I don't let them go easily."

The tenderness she felt for him in that moment ripped a hole in her heart. It was probably best he thought of her like a sister. She couldn't have borne him discarding her like Ned did.

Chapter Forty-Three

After Vanessa left, Avery sat with his back against the curved arm of the stone bench, the portrait of Willow he was painting propped against his thighs. He dipped his brush in the smear of forest green he'd blended. "You're rather quiet today." Shooting Willow a quick smile, he added leaves to the bare boughs with rapid strokes of his brush. "Wasn't there something you wanted to talk about . . . when we were alone?"

Willow grimaced and intertwined her slender fingers. "You've grown up so much since we first met."

He laughed as he continued to paint. "That's true. How old were we when I followed Bess through that tunnel? Four? Five?"

"Four." Willow's smile was bittersweet. "We had to tell you the passage would close up if you didn't get back to your parents right away."

"That's right." He lowered his brush and grinned up at her. "We were building a fort out of loose rocks and sticks. Planning on spending the night."

"We'd never met children as determined as you before."

"Father was so mad we'd hidden so long. It was ages before he agreed to take us hiking again." He shook his head, chuckling at the memory.

"I thought we'd never see you again."

He resumed painting. "But I always come back."

She wrung her hands and bit her lip. "You do . . ."

"What is it, Willow?" He deposited his brush in the water jar and straightened his legs. "What did you want to talk about?"

She pressed her hands to her cheeks and angled her face toward the sky. "Things are changing."

An uneasy sensation awakened in his belly. "Things have been . . . different since Vanessa started coming here, I know."

Willow nodded. "You like her . . . very much."

"I do." He studied his knuckles. "You like her, too, don't you?"

"Yes . . ." Willow wrung her hands.

He swung his legs off the bench, put the painting aside and looked up at her. "I'd hoped that having her here would be a good thing. That you'd welcome her as much as I do."

She leaned over, draping her boughs around his shoulders. "I just . . . don't want to see you get hurt."

His discomfort flashed into anger, driving him to his feet. "I'm a grown man, Willow." He turned away and glared at the pond. "I don't need to be protected."

The sound of her cry made him spin around, regretting his anger already. She had withdrawn into her trunk, her eyes wide, and arms crisscrossed over her chest.

"I'm sorry." He stepped toward her, his palms up. "I didn't mean to lash out at you."

Sinking back onto the bench, he stared at the ground. "I'm only upset because you're right to worry." He leaned his elbows on his knees. "I'm crazy about her . . . and now that Ned's gone, I'd gotten the harebrained idea she just might start seeing me as more than a friend or . . ." His gut knotted. ". . . brother." He felt her gentle touch on his shoulder and breathed a sigh of relief. "I don't want to lose you, Willow." He turned toward her. "I can't imagine not having you here." He reached up and took her leafy hand in his. "Especially since it's quite likely I am going to get hurt."

They rested together in silence for a few moments, then she stroked his head with her other hand. "Don't worry, Avery." Her voice was choked with sorrow. "I'll do whatever I can to be here for you."

A crooked smile found its way to his lips. "Is that what you wanted to talk to me about? Warning me to be careful of Vanessa?"

She hesitated, then blinked a few times and nodded.

"Well, thank you." He reached up for her other hand.

This was the most intimate conversation they'd ever had. Perhaps now that he was grown, she would finally begin answering his questions.

"Is there anything, anything in the world I can do for you?" he asked. "You've been such a friend to me all these years, yet I know next to nothing about you."

But it wasn't to be. She merely withdrew her hands, shook her head, and gave him another one of her cryptic smiles. "There's nothing you can do for me, Avery, except to be happy."

"Well . . ." Resting against the arm of the bench again, he pulled the partially finished artwork back against his knees. "It would make me happy to finish this painting of you."

He reached for his brush. "And to figure out a way to help Vanessa return to Twin Birch House next season."

Chapter Forty-Four

Later that day, Vanessa scanned the front page of the newspaper lying on the village library's massive wooden desk.

"Flu Epidemic Reaches Boston Civilians!"

"Have you heard about this?" She pointed out the headline to the elderly librarian who was checking out her latest books for her.

The woman peered over her reading glasses to glance at the paper. "Terrible, terrible. They're calling it the Spanish Flu. Seems it hit Camp Devens hard."

Vanessa's heart clutched at the thought of Walter and Edna getting sick . . . and everyone else she knew back in Boston. "I hope it passes soon."

The librarian passed her the stack of books. "Times like this makes a person grateful to live out here in the country. Away from all that."

Walking from the library back to the hotel, Vanessa shivered as she approached the cemetery. Her thoughts lingered on the description she read of the flu mortalities already hitting the city. Faces with a bluish cast, coughing up blood, sudden deaths. Scores of soldiers already down, killed before they even shipped out. And the paper said flu was taking soldiers overseas as well. One more thing for poor Irene to worry about.

Her morbid thoughts were interrupted when she spotted Bess. Avery's sister was sitting on a stone bench near the back of the cemetery, her eyes downcast, a cigarette in her hand. The sight of a woman smoking had been shocking enough in the dark of the Nolens' backyard. It was even more so in broad daylight. Bess had clearly been influenced by the radicals she associated with in college.

Whatever her feelings about Bess's taboo-shattering conduct, it was the waves of sorrow billowing off the girl that wrenched Vanessa's gut. She simply couldn't pass her by. Raising the latch of the wrought iron gate, she let herself in. She'd never thought of herself as the nurturing type, more comfortable in the role of entertainer when tending young children. But she'd do her best. As she followed the cemetery path, her shoes rustled the first fallen leaves of the season.

"Hi, Bess."

Bess looked up, then turned her face away and swiped at her eyes. "Afternoon, Vanessa."

"Are you alright?"

Bess gave a curt nod. "Sure. Just dandy."

Vanessa turned toward the markers and headstones of the village's ancestors. They were mixed with newer tributes to their more recently fallen. Facing them, she had the sensation of floating above the ground, disconnected. Even in death, there was no home for her, no family to join.

"Is Dewey . . . here?"

Behind her, Bess's voice sounded distant. "Just a marker, for now."

How comforting it would be to have a place to visit one's dead. She didn't know where her parents were buried. And her sister? All they would ever say when she asked was that Ruth had "gone to heaven, to be with your mommy and daddy." When Vanessa had gotten older, she'd learned Home girls were disposed of in mass graves with the rest of Boston's paupers. "What little money the institution has is better spent on food for the girls who live," the warden had reminded her with a stern expression.

She lowered herself onto the bench beside Bess, then squared the stack of library books on her lap. Running her palm over the cover of Edith Wharton's *Summer*, she considered how trivial her recent problems truly were. Others' losses were counted in human lives. "I'm so sorry."

Plucking at her navy wool skirt, Bess shot her a sideways glance. "Did Avery tell you about me and Dewey?"

Vanessa shook her head. "Irene."

Bess nodded. "Irene. I have to go see her. See them."

"What's stopping you?"

After a moment of silence, Bess raised haunted eyes. "You know why I came home?"

"To see your family?"

Bess shook her head. "Because I'm a coward." Tears welled in her eyes as she took another drag from her cigarette.

"No, you're not." She turned away from Bess's misty eyes and gazed over the gravestones. "All those risks you and those other women take? Protesting in the street? Getting arrested?" She turned to face Bess again. "That's courageous."

"That's theater." Bess waved her hand. "It's exciting. Surrounded by your compatriots. Strength in numbers and all that. What's courageous is what happens in jail, when it's quiet and there's no one there to protect you. That's when the brave ones get stronger."

Vanessa gulped. "Was it terrible? Being locked up?"

Bess nodded, her eyes dull. "But that didn't stop the heroes." Her short laugh had a bitter edge. "When the guards mistreated us, they started a hunger strike. Even the old ones, like Dora Lewis." Her chin dropped to her chest. "I went along. Did what the others were doing, and we weren't in there more than two weeks. But in the dark of that cell . . . something changed in me."

"I . . . I'm sure you're just shaken. Who wouldn't be?"

"The truly brave aren't. I'm telling you." Bess's leg jiggled. "But I couldn't sleep, even after we got out. Got woozy just looking at a cop." Her voice lowered. "So, I ran home to Mommy and Daddy."

"Well, I don't blame you." Vanessa sat up taller. "If I'd had that option after my first two weeks in the Girls Home, believe me, I'd have taken it."

"That's different."

"The conditions may have been a little better, but when I was little, the Home was definitely a prison. No matter how scared I was, there was no getting out."

Bess stared at her few moments, then took another drag and tilted her face to the sky. "If I'm just 'shaken,' as you say, then how do you explain me being too chicken to go see Irene?"

Vanessa shrugged. "You tell me." If she'd known comforting Bess would be so combative, she might never have entered the cemetery. "Why *are* you afraid to visit her?"

Bess continued to stare at the sky, then crushed her cigarette butt and pulled another Lucky Strike from its green box in her handbag.

Not at all sure she wanted to hear Bess's confession, Vanessa stared at the gravestones, listening to the sound of Bess lighting up again. Smoking really was such a disgusting habit and smelled terrible. She had no idea why Bess chose to do it.

"I didn't love her brother anymore." Bess took another drag, then blew the smoke out in a long, tiny stream before sitting up straighter on the bench. "I mean, I loved him. I'll always love him. But we'd grown so far apart. From the day I went away to school, my world just kept changing. Teachers opening my eyes to what's actually going on out there . . . classmates who'd traveled and had ideas! But Dewey?" She shook her head. "He stayed exactly the same. Never left Adamsville. Hardly stepped off the Twin Birch House grounds. We barely had anything to talk about anymore . . . not that he noticed. Kept suggesting I drop out of school and come home, like it was some secret desire of mine I just wasn't acting on."

"Or perhaps . . . he did notice. And that's why he wanted you to come home." Vanessa ran her thumb along the feathered edges of the book pages, imagining how it would hurt to watch someone you loved outgrow you. "So things could go back to the way they were before you left."

Bess slowly cocked her head. "Possible." Her eyes narrowed as she took another drag.

Neither spoke for several moments. In the hush, the shouts of children playing Red Rover drifted from a nearby backyard.

"Were you and Dewey engaged?"

Biting her lip, Bess gave her head a quick shake. "I was home for the summer when he got his draft summons. He was going to ask me, but I already knew I couldn't say yes."

"What did you do?"

"Told him I thought it was bad luck for a couple to get engaged right before a soldier left for war. That I wanted my engagement party to be a happy occasion." Bess glanced over with a wry smile. "He got the hint and didn't ask. Said he'd have a lot to look forward to when he came home."

Staring at the dying grass, Vanessa sensed the lonely dead in their nearby graves. "And you don't want his family to find out your feelings had changed."

Bess nodded. "I know I'm making it worse by not going. But I just can't stand the thought of Dewey's father looking into my eyes, searching for the grief of a young fiancée." She picked at her cuticles. "I don't want to see Mr. Seward's face when he realizes it isn't there."

"I don't know about Mr. Seward." Vanessa faced Bess. "But I do think it's hurting Irene to have you stay away. Probably a lot more than it would hurt her to know you didn't want to marry her brother."

Bess shifted her eyes. "First Avery, now you."

A shiver went down Vanessa's spine, and she was overcome with the desire to leave. If nymphs and fairies lived in the woods, it was certainly possible the cemetery was home to more than dried up bones and moldering coffins. "Do you want me to come with you?"

With a quiet laugh, Bess rubbed her eyes with her palms. "And he offered the same thing."

Grief tugged at Vanessa's boots like quicksand, driving her to her feet. "We'll all go." She could hear her voice was overly bright. "Make it a party."

Bess stared at the ground, her shoulders hunched. After a moment, she dropped her cigarette and stood. "One crutch should be enough." Her boot heel twisted the butt into the dirt. "You're not bad, Vanessa, even if your thinking hasn't joined the twentieth century yet."

Vanessa put her hand on her hip and shook her head. "How does someone as sweet as Avery have a twin as sour as you?"

Bess threw an arm over Vanessa's shoulder. "My parents ask that same question every single day."

As they left together, the weight of Bess's arm unleashed a wave of emotion that cramped Vanessa's throat. The Nolen family had breached her defenses.

The two girls came to a stop at the corner of the Twin Birch House stables. Irene's house was a simple affair, with clapboard siding and a chimney on the side. The flowerbeds around the stone foundation were a bit neglected, even accounting for the expected end-of-season weariness. The groundkeeper's daughter seemed to have lost interest in flowers as the war dragged on.

"Are you sure?" Vanessa peered at the Sewards' faded green door. "I don't mind coming with you."

Bess nodded. "I need to do this alone." A loose tendril of her blonde hair lifted in a sudden breeze. She patted Vanessa's shoulder. "Just wish me luck."

"Good luck." Vanessa gave Avery's sister a one-armed hug, made awkward by the books she still carried.

Bess blew a couple of sharp breaths through her teeth and continued toward Irene's front door. A few moments after Bess's knock, the door swung open. Vanessa shrank back into the shadows of the stable as Irene and Bess stood staring at one another, frozen. Even from a distance, the force of their sorrow drove Vanessa's hand to cover her mouth.

Then Irene threw her arms around Bess. The two of them remained standing in the doorway, their shoulders shaking, faces buried in one another's hair. Pressing her back against the stable wall, Vanessa struggled for breath. That moment she'd had with Irene, dancing out their pain? It was just that. A moment. It took years to build the kind of relationship Irene and Bess shared.

Her eyes squeezed closed. After Ruth died, she'd blunted the agony with storybooks and fantasy worlds. As the years went on, her storytelling entertained the girls and made her popular, but also masked how she avoided getting close with anyone in particular. If no one was special, then no one special could be lost. Ironic that now, as death stalked both sides of the Atlantic with growing impunity, Vanessa regretted not having loved ones to potentially lose.

Chapter Forty-Five

The next day, Vanessa was the first to arrive on the dock. After leaving Bess with Irene, she'd gone to the Enchanted Wood in hopes of seeing Avery. He hadn't been there, but she'd found a note on her pillow when she returned to the dorm after supper.

Be at the docks tomorrow at 2:00, ready to sail. A.

So here she was, in her white dress with pinstripes, pressing her hat to her head to keep it from blowing away. Though charming, the wide-brimmed hat probably wasn't a good idea after all. But her attire was the least of her concerns as she contemplated the afternoon's aquatic adventure . . . and who, exactly, it would include.

The mystery was shortly solved when Avery arrived with Bess, her head bare, blonde braids pinned to the back of her head in a swirl. Striding down the dock in her calf-length linen skirt and matching drop-waist top, she could have been a model straight from the pages of *McCall's Magazine*.

"Why the long face?" Bess asked.

"A little nervous, I guess. I don't know how to swim."

"Don't worry, Karl's an excellent sailor."

Karl?

Realizing what was afoot, she wrinkled her nose at Avery, who appeared more sporty than usual, in linen pants and canvas shoes, the sleeves of his button-down shirt rolled up. "Wait in the blind, indeed."

He shrugged and pushed his glasses up his nose. "Anything to help."

Bess passed by her and continued over to the wizened boat master, his skin tanned and deeply lined from years in the sunshine. "Morning, Houkey! How are you?"

"Same as ever, Miss Nolen." The man's cornflower blue eyes crinkled in pleasure. "Been a while."

"Too long." Bess jerked her thumb toward Avery. "Took my brother to remind me. Talked Mr. Fiske into the outing, too, so we'll need two boats, if you don't mind."

"Coming right up."

As Houkey disappeared into the long, musty-smelling boat shed, Karl stepped onto the dock and Bess waved. "Ahoy!"

She couldn't shake the sense that Bess's cheeriness had a forced quality. Too bad she hadn't explained that she wasn't pursuing Karl Fiske romantically. Hopefully Avery had filled his sister in. Now that everyone had arrived, there was no chance to do it herself.

After being assigned to his boat, she stood in awkward silence as Karl strung the sail. He also looked quite sportive in brown wool pants and a white shirt with the sleeves rolled up, exposing a light dusting of blond hair on his muscular forearms. In contrast to the hush between herself and Karl, Bess, and Avery laughed and carried on as Bess prepared their boat for launch. Avery's twin clearly opened him up. It was heartwarming . . . and disconcerting . . . to see that side of him.

Karl's glances in the Nolens' direction suggested he felt as left out as she did. Conflicting emotions tangled in her chest. The shared exclusion pushed her and Karl together nicely. Perhaps Bess was doing it deliberately, helping the friendship along . . . or whatever it was Bess imagined she wanted from Karl. Yet the sensation of being an outsider amongst all of them, even Avery, still stung.

With a clap of his hands, Karl stood and faced her. "Ready, then?"

"Absolutely. Wonderful weather for sailing, isn't it?" Despite being late September, the day was warm and sunny, with a light breeze.

He frowned. "Wind's not so good."

"Oh."

He extended his hand with a weak smile. "Then again, the kind of blow I prefer might be a bit much for someone's first sail."

Clinging to Karl's palm, Vanessa stepped into the small wooden sailboat, not more than twelve feet long. It wobbled underfoot and she plopped onto her rear end onto one of the narrow benches in the shallow seating area. If Karl noticed her ungraceful landing, he gave no sign. Pushing the boat from the dock, he hopped in the back of the boat. Once he was aboard, she was slightly embarrassed by the tight squeeze. In the cramped space behind the mast, her knees were mere inches from his.

Doing her best to relax, she focused on the hotel as it receded behind them. It made quite the regal backdrop. While she admired the view, Karl kept his eyes focused on the water beyond her shoulder. He steered the boat with a long, wooden handle he slid back and forth with his left hand. The "tiller," he said it was called. With his right hand, he tightened and loosened the "sheet," a line threaded through the bottom frame of the sail.

"What age did you start racing sailboats?"

"Around ten."

"So young?"

He shrugged. "Children's division. Not too competitive."

After receiving clipped answers to several additional questions, her attempts at small talk petered out. How could she forget? Still and demure. Still and demure. With a smile, she lowered her hand to the cool water, letting her fingers trail. Silent now, she could hear the light, rhythmic knocking of small waves against the dinghy's hull. Sparkles of sunlight moved over the lake's greenish black surface, its shifting patterns mesmerizing.

Her gaze drifted toward Avery. He hadn't been at church that morning and she'd missed him. Uncomfortable, she'd reminded herself he was no doubt a man with numerous concerns and interests beyond running into a chambermaid who would be leaving town in a few weeks anyway.

"Are you enjoying yourself?" Karl focused on her for the first time.

Snapping her attention back to her host, she sat taller. The quiet business worked. She couldn't wait to tell Avery. "Oh, yes. I can see why you love it so much."

Karl's gaze returned to the expanse of lake before them. "Like flying must feel, don't you think?"

She closed her eyes and turned toward the front of the boat. The wind on her face made it easy to imagine skimming atop the water like a bird. "It is."

When she opened her eyes and faced him again, Karl's mood seemed improved. He made some adjustments to their course and the sailboat picked up speed, tipping to its side as they moved faster. She grabbed for the edge of the seat as her insides lurched. "Aaaahhh!"

Her distress had no apparent effect on him. "Look." He squinted at something ahead of them. "Do you see them?"

She twisted around and searched the lake and surroundings. Seeing nothing unusual, she held her hand to her brow and peered at the emerald mountainside beyond, peppered with tiny patches of orange, yellow, and tan foliage. "What?"

When she turned back toward Karl, his disappointment was unmistakable. "Nothing. Watch your head." With a sharp thrust of the tiller, the boat veered to the right. She barely ducked in time to avoid the boom as it swung across the hull and the sail puffed full of wind on the opposite side.

She scanned the water and shoreline some more. "Are they still there?"

"It's nothing. This . . . thing . . . that happens sometimes. Don't worry about it."

Her jaw tightened as she turned away, sickened that she'd failed his test. At least the boat had slowed and was sitting reasonably flat in the water again.

"Whooo-hoooo!" Bess shouted and waved as her boat approached.

Avery gave a small wave, then relaxed back on his elbows. Hard to believe he and the madwoman helming their boat were twins.

"Last one to Lover's Leap is an old fuddy-duddy!" shouted Bess.

Vanessa's stomach clenched at the sight of Karl's grin.

"You're on, Nolen!" This time, Karl gave Vanessa no warning when he swung the tiller. Only her wits kept her from being beaned by the lunging boom. Bile sprang into her throat as her side of the boat tipped backwards.

"Switch sides!" Karl barked like a crusty sea captain commanding his crew.

She clawed her way across the cockpit to sit on the rising edge of the boat, using every ounce of her weight to pull the craft back to level. A fruitless effort. Faster and faster they went, tacking back and forth across the length of the lake, Karl and Bess shouting at one another, stealing each other's wind.

Vanessa caught her hat as it lifted from her head, clutching the straw brim in her sweaty fist. She clung to alternating sides of the boat, silently saying her prayers as she stared at the crazed stranger who possessed the body of mild-mannered Karl Fiske. This was the guy who got his name on all those trophies.

Their boat passed a sharp outcropping of rock that was apparently the finish line moments ahead of Bess. Victorious, Karl thrust his arms in the air and howled. Laughing, Bess pulled near. "You're lucky I'm out of practice, Fiske!"

"Rematch going back? Downwind might be a little easier for you." His grin was downright wicked.

"No!" Vanessa blurted.

Everyone turned to her. She blinked up at Karl. "I'm sorry . . . Go ahead. I didn't mean to spoil the fun."

"I'll take a rain check." Bess lifted her hand to her brow and gave Karl a lazy salute. "Enjoy yourselves, kids."

The excitement drained from Karl's face and Vanessa winced. "Please don't let me stop you . . ."

"You're not." He pushed the tiller gently to the other side, maneuvering their craft in a semi-circle, heading back to the Twin Birch House dock. "I'm sorry I got carried away. Rude of me to forget you're not a sailor."

"It's certainly . . . exhilarating."

"I have missed it." He smiled briefly before his eyes slid back toward the hotel. "And promise a less 'exhilarating' return trip."

Facing forward, she hoped to hide her disappointment. Though she and Karl succeeded in making small talk about the hotel and its operations on the way back, it failed to deepen their friendship in any appreciable way. Once they were all back on the dock, the men helped Houkey get the boats out of the water before Karl said a hasty goodbye and headed back to his office. Avery and Bess apologized for having to run as well. Their mother was expecting them for supper and some neighbors were joining them.

Within moments, Vanessa was alone on the dock staring up at Twin Birch House. The cool breeze blowing over the lake raised goose bumps on her bare arms.

Chapter Forty-Six

Vanessa climbed the mountain wearing a light jacket from the hotel's lost and found. The nippy weather matched the chill in her spirit. A week had passed since the sailing debacle with no new opportunities to ingratiate herself with Karl. Hopes of convincing him to give her work in New York were rapidly fading.

After making her way through the passageway, she stood up and looked around. The Enchanted Wood had subtly changed to reflect the season. The tree leaves were intermingled with smatterings of red and yellow. The grass had deepened to a dark green, brushed with strands of gold.

Avery sat on the bench, painting. The sight lightened her mood more than she would have anticipated. "There you are." She plunked down next to him. "My very own Wizard of Oz, hiding behind his curtain."

He pushed his glasses up his nose. "Sorry the sail wasn't more of a success."

She sighed. "Who knew I haven't got a sailing bone in my body?" Pressing her hands to the cool stone on either side of her legs, she tilted her face up at his "But I appreciate you setting it up . . . more than you can imagine."

"My pleasure." He pressed the tip of his paintbrush against the lip of his jar, squeezing out the excess water.

"The whole idea that he'd ever bring me back next season is probably just wishful thinking." Swinging her feet, she sighed again. "But you were right, by the way."

"About what?"

"When I quieted down and relaxed, he warmed up."

"Bit of a traditionalist, that Karl." Looking satisfied, Avery leaned toward his painting, making a small refinement with his brush. "Except when it comes to Bess."

"You're right." Vanessa laughed as she pushed herself off the bench and wandered over to the pond. "He's like a different person with her."

Sinking to her knees, she closed her eyes and breathed deeply. The Wood's scent had turned to autumn aromas. Cinnamon and clove, with a hint of smoke. "But all my clever plans to improve my prospects aren't working out any better than being impulsive ever did."

"It's a complicated world. Now you know why I spend my free time here, with my paints."

She rolled her eyes at him over her shoulder. "That's hardly a solution"

He shrugged, continuing to paint. "If you say so."

Scooping up some dead leaves, she threw them at him, quite ineffectively. As they drifted back to the ground, she turned her attention back to the pond. The lily pads had fewer blossoms, their green platters edged with orange. The nymphs were nowhere in sight. She clutched her hands together and leaned toward the water. "Please come out. You were so helpful before, and I need your excellent advice again."

The naiads emerged but were markedly less jovial than usual. "I need . . . I need . . ." They mimicked Vanessa with pique in their tone she'd never heard before. "You want our help, but you're ashamed of us. Won't introduce us."

"I'm sorry." She sat back on her heels, genuinely confused. "Who do you want to meet?"

A little girl with dark ringlets smiled sweetly. "Where's Ned? We invited you both to come see us."

"Ned." She gripped her fingers so tight her knuckles turned white. "He's gone." The pain that had been gradually quieting resumed, pummeling her insides. "Returned to Boston with his family."

As one, the naiads roared with what sounded like frustration, then disappeared, leaving only ripples in the surface of the water to suggest they'd even been there. Stunned, Vanessa remained kneeling in silence for several moments, reliving the agony of her last encounter with Ned. The sickening realization that he'd never for a moment considered her a possible wife. Yet he'd seemed so hurt. As though it was she who had wronged him.

"Vanessa?" Avery's voice was soft with concern. "Everything alright?"

She nodded.

"Did I catch things right?" he asked. "They want to meet Cooper?"

Pushing herself to her feet, she walked back to the bench. "Apparently they wanted both of us to come see them."

"And didn't take the news he was gone very well, I take it."

Nodding again, Vanessa marveled at how comfortable she felt with Avery. Accepted and understood. She sat, her shoulders tensing in anticipation of testing that acceptance. "There was more of a reason for my involvement with Ned than you know."

"Uh-huh." He dabbed the tip of his brush in the tiny pool of paint he'd made atop the green color block, but she could tell from the tension in his movement that he was trying to disguise his interest.

"It was something the fairy said," she continued. "A prophecy, of sorts."

His brush stopped moving in mid-air. "What did the fairy say?" His voice was overly calm, like he was making an effort for it to sound that way.

Gazing downward, Vanessa twisted her ring. "She said . . . that my match is a man of true worth. A man of sterling and gold."

Vanessa turned her head, searching Avery's face for a hint of ridicule, but he merely seemed . . . disappointed. "That's why I was convinced Ned was my destiny. Why I was willing to take such risks."

He blinked. "I guess that makes sense." Turning away, he wiped his wet bristles with a rag. "Given his wealth and attentiveness."

"Exactly." Her breath escaped in a loud sigh. "I'm so glad you understand."

Continuing to wipe his brush, he kept his eyes on his work. "And what do you think now?"

She leaned back with a frown, her palms pressed against the cool stone. "I have no idea. Obviously I was wrong about Ned."

"Well . . . whatever the fairy said, I think you're brave." His eyes turned back to his painting—another blue butterfly. "And you deserve any prize you're after."

"Oh, Avery." Even though she was becoming more accustomed to hearing people say complimentary things to her, the extent of the pleasure was surprising. "You're making me blush."

He stood up and dumped the water from his paint jar, his eyes glued to the ground. "It's true. If I went after my goals with half your gusto, who knows where I'd be."

"You got yourself that dream job of yours, didn't you?"

"Inspired by you."

"What do you mean?"

He tucked the empty container in his leather bag and met her eyes. "You never thought Ned Cooper and his like were too good for you."

Clutching her elbows, she recalled the steel in his voice when he'd stopped her on the lawn after she'd fled from Ned in the woods. "I didn't think you . . . approved."

"I'm no fan of Cooper's, I won't lie about that."

If he didn't think Ned . . . or Karl, for that matter . . . were too good for her, could she have gotten everything else wrong about Avery, too? Getting flustered, she steered back to safer ground. "So, what's my relationship with Ned got to do with your dream job?"

His hands stilled as he stared down at his satchel. "It was never even discussed whether I'd follow in my father's footsteps to Dartmouth, just assumed. But I prayed all the medical schools would reject me." He gave a wry chuckle. "Unfortunately, with so many doctors serving overseas, their admission standards evidently plummeted." He faced her again. "That Forest Service application was the first time I took the risk of submitting myself for something I actually chose on my own . . . and cared about."

"And I inspired you?"

"That's right." His eyes warmed behind his glasses. "Your example helped me face the truth about what I really wanted and send it in." He slung his bag over his shoulder and headed for the passage.

Her chest felt too small to contain her swelling heart. "You're a gem, you truly are!"

He waved his hand over his head, bent over, and disappeared into the tunnel.

Once he was gone, she tucked her legs up and hugged her knees. So, Avery had always approved of her, and was likely even jealous. Despite the effort she'd put into thinking of him only as a friend or brother, the thought still made her smile.

Chapter Forty-Seven

The following morning, Vanessa sat next to Irene on a long wooden bench in the employee dining room.

"The season is nearly over." Karl addressed the assembled staff in solemn tones. "And I'd like to take this opportunity to thank you all for your service."

Clutching her waist and chewing the side of her thumb, Vanessa scanned the department heads arrayed behind Karl at the front of the room. Weak autumn sun shone through the windows, leaving half their grim faces in shadow.

"It was my maiden voyage at the Twin Birch House helm." Karl's smile was self-deprecating. "So, I especially appreciate everyone's patience . . . and the rescue efforts when I was in over my head." Light laughter eased the tension a bit. So many faces smiled up at Karl. He wasn't the same beleaguered young man she'd heard Ned pressuring in June about bringing a jazz band to the hotel. The summer had given his voice confidence and authority.

Though most of the remaining workers planned to depart for their winter jobs the next day, Vanessa was staying on the payroll until the last days of the season. After that, she had no idea what she would do, much less if there were any chance of returning in the spring.

"I know many of you intended to leave tomorrow, and I understand that the flu epidemic and the measures being taken to slow its spread have interfered with some of those arrangements, particularly those of you with plans to go all the way to Florida." He glanced back at Mrs. Juneau, who gave him a small nod in return. "So, I'm offering you continued lodging here at Twin Birch House. Though I'm not in a position to continue your salaries beyond your current contract, as long as travel continues to be restricted, you needn't worry about room and board. Are there any questions?"

Several hands rose. Karl gestured to one of the dining room waiters.

"Has the flu reached Adamsville?"

All eyes turned back to Karl, who clasped his hands behind his back. "Dr. Nolen has informed me that an unusual number of flu victims have been admitted to the hospital in the last few weeks, but so far, no one has died. We can only pray that this luck continues." He pointed to one of the few remaining chambermaids.

"Shouldn't we quarantine?" The big-boned girl searched the room for support. "I mean, how else can we keep it from getting here?"

A murmur of agreement and alarm rippled through the group.

Quarantine? Ever since she'd read the headline about the flu in the city, Vanessa had worried about the Wainwrights, some of the girls she knew from the Home, and a couple of younger ones still there. The staff had even taken to sharing copies of the Boston obituaries, looking for familiar names. But the idea of quarantine here at Twin Birch House made her consider for the first time the possibility of getting sick herself.

She grew lightheaded, overwhelmed by memories of holding Ruth in her arms, the little girl coughing and coughing. The thought of drowning in bloody phlegm tightened her chest. She could only breathe in sharp, tiny gasps.

"Are you alright?" Irene grabbed her hand.

Vanessa nodded, willing herself to think of something else—something happy. The Enchanted Wood . . . the water nymphs' laughter . . . Avery smiling at her from behind his easel.

Gradually, her breathing slowed and she focused on Karl. "...quarantine's a little extreme at this point." He turned and gestured back toward Mrs. Juneau. "But we do have gauze masks we recommend you use when dealing with any delivery people. We are also asking that the masks be worn by everyone working in the kitchen and by the wait staff."

Vanessa got up and helped Mrs. Juneau pass out the white rectangles with long strips of cotton twill sewn along the top and bottom edges for ties. Once they all had one and the staff was dismissed, she stared down at the mask. How much protection could its flimsy cloth really offer?

Later that evening, in Mrs. Juneau's private quarters, Vanessa leaned over the dresser toward the mirror to get a better view of a postcard stuck in its frame. A hand-colored photo of Florida's Royal Poinciana Hotel. Truly a tropical palace. "It looks heavenly."

Mrs. Juneau rose from the armchair in the corner and opened the dresser's top drawer. "I've got a whole collection here." Mrs. Juneau handed her a stack of postcards.

Sinking on the edge of the bed, she examined the images of swaying palms and crowded beaches. The pictures of elegant guests being ferried down wide walkways were particularly amazing. They sat in wicker chairs built onto the front of bicycles ridden by Black men in hotel uniforms. "This is where you spend your winters?"

After removing a needlepoint pillow and sitting back in her stuffed chair, Mrs. Juneau smiled. "Excellent life, wouldn't you say? White Mountains in the summer, Palm Beach in the winter?"

"And you all go together? You and the other department heads?"

"Only two of us. The headwaiter and his crew go to the Jekyll Island Club in Georgia. The chef and his team only go as far as Washington."

She ran a delicate finger over the fan of postcards in her hand. "Does anywhere feel like home?"

A wistful cast appeared in Mrs. Juneau's eye as she caressed her locket containing the picture of her dead husband. "This is home. I carry it with me." She gestured around the room. "Everywhere else is just where I stay."

But Vanessa wanted more than that. A real family. A real home.

"Now I've made you sad," said Mrs. Juneau. "There's no need, dear. I wouldn't trade the brief time I had with Pierre for anything." Her eyes grew misty, despite her smile. "And I feel like I have children everywhere I go. The girls who work for me up here and down in Florida almost always go off and get married, and some send me photographs of their babies." A chuckle rumbled from deep in her chest. "I have more honorary grandchildren than I could possibly count!"

Vanessa smiled and plucked at the bedspread's cotton flocking. "Do you think . . . the flu will come here?"

Mrs. Juneau's smile faded. "I don't know."

"So many died from consumption in the Home."

"In my day, too. The little ones, usually."

They sank into silence, lost in their tragic memories.

"They say this one started with soldiers. Strong young men." Vanessa couldn't understand how illness could be most deadly to those who were normally the hardiest.

"That's what I've read, too." Mrs. Juneau sighed. "First the war, now this. The world's turned topsy-turvy."

"I know there's nothing you can do. I just . . ." Vanessa waved her hand as she realized why she'd come. She was afraid and wanted her mother. Mrs. Juneau was the closest thing she had. With her head bowed, she slid off the bed and headed for the door. "Thank you for talking to me."

"You should consider coming, you know."

"Where?"

"To Palm Beach. With me."

"You'd give me work? At the hotel?"

"I watched you this summer, Vanessa. Even more since you've joined our staff. It's a rare bird who can walk and talk like a patron yet serve with humility."

She took a deep breath, her chest expanding. "Thank you. I'm . . . flattered."

"There are some interesting opportunities in hotel work beyond chambermaid and waitress for a girl like you."

"Oh, Mrs. Juneau. If we'd had this conversation a few months ago, I'd have jumped at the opportunity, without a doubt."

She rose and began to pace, praying she wasn't offending her staunchest supporter. "It's just . . . at the moment . . ." Her pacing came to a halt as she rubbed her ring, hearing the fairy's words again like a caress. *A man of true worth, of sterling and gold.* "I'm not sure where my destiny leads."

Mrs. Juneau smiled, her brow arched. "You've always struck me as someone who shaped her own destiny."

Looking down, she twirled her ring. Perhaps Mrs. Juneau was right. She had refused to rebuff Ned, left the Wainwrights in hopes of a brighter future and talked her way onto the Twin Birch House staff. But then, much of what she'd done that summer was inspired, if not motivated, by the words of the fairy and the water nymphs. Had she been making choices or following a predetermined path? How was she to know? "You see . . ." She raised her head, thinking of the fairy and the Enchanted Wood and the need for Karl Fiske to bring her to New York so she'd have the chance to return. "There are . . . elements . . . here that make it difficult to leave just yet."

"Aaah. Elements." The older woman folded her hands in her lap with a knowing smile. "Well, if remaining in Adamsville is your destiny, my dear, I do wish you the best of luck, and happiness as well."

Just as well Mrs. Juneau believed her to be referring to a suitor. Perhaps, in a way, she was, even if she didn't know his name. Overwhelmed by a surge of affection, she stepped across the room, bent over, and wrapped her arms around Mrs. Juneau's shoulders. "Thank you, for everything."

"Now, now, Miss Perkins." Mrs. Juneau's voice trembled a bit as she patted Vanessa's back. "I haven't done as much as all that."

Chapter Forty-Eight

In the evening's waning light, Lachima reclined with Morniero on the stone bench in what the humans currently called "the Enchanted Wood." Though no moon was ever visible on this side of the passage, the glow in the night sky matched the lunar cycle of the mortals' world. Six nights prior to the new moon, it would not normally be so dark. The untimely gloom was a sure sign of their mother's impending arrival. Known as Nyia, their mother was a primordial deity, one of the first to emerge from the Oneness when time began.

Refusing to appear concerned, Lachima ran her fingers through her mass of white hair. Her scalp tingled with all the new threads constantly being spun by her younger sister, Clona, while those recently cut by the eldest, Atroporta, came loose in her hands, crumbling to dust in her fingers. It hurt to be so far from her sisters. To experience them only through the ceaseless cycle of mortal births and deaths, marked by the perpetual renewal and loss of her white hair.

"Don't pretend you're not nervous." Morniero faced her, his back against the opposite arm of the bench. "I know you hate not knowing what might happen next." He waggled his bent knees, gently knocking the side of his ankle against her outstretched leg.

"But we both know what happens next, don't we?" They were failing at their mission to prove they could live secretly amongst the mortals, and she was as guilty as the nymphs. There would be consequences.

He shrugged, eyelids nearly closed. "I prefer to think we can't be sure."

Laughing eased her tension. Despite Morniero's teasing, it was a comfort to press her leg against his, to feel his presence. She cringed at the thought of admitting it to him, but she was glad he had chosen to accompany her to these new shores.

The sky continued to darken, soon dimming the stars. As the blackness descended, Lachima's limbs softened and heart slowed. Morniero's leg fell away from hers as they succumbed to their mother's gentle embrace. Their mother's love was infinite in all directions, unrestricted by even the faintest of light. Unbound, Lachima returned to night's womb, to the beginning, the origin.

Gradually, light reappeared. The nothingness slowly dissolved as the world resumed its normal shape. When she could bear it again, Lachima opened her eyes. Standing before them under a blanket of distant stars was their mother in her human form, her skin inky black, her flowing robes sprinkled with tiny flecks of light. Her hair, too, floated in a mass around her head, but her strands were as black as her skin, and were far more abundant than Lachima's. What all they represented, if anything, her mother would never say.

"Greetings, my children." The love pouring from her dark eyes was more profound than any Lachima had ever witnessed, yet only a fraction of what her mother could express in her natural, unbounded form.

"Greetings, Mother." She and Morniero spoke in unison, their voices equally relaxed as they sat up and made room for their mother on the bench between them.

Lachima trembled slightly as she leaned against her mother's side, a strong arm wrapping around her shoulder. The power her mother wielded was humbling, regardless of the fact she doted on all her children.

"So, tell me." Her mother's voice vibrated Lachima's chest like the beat of an enormous drum. "How is your experiment proceeding?"

Lachima and Morniero exchanged a glance before she spoke. "As expected." She straightened. "Mostly well, with minor exceptions."

Her brother sat up, too, but said nothing. His careful neutrality made Lachima want to kick his shins. At least he wasn't contradicting her.

Their mother caressed the backs of their heads and rose. "The others miss you." She turned to face them. "They grow impatient for your return . . . or to join you."

"Being amongst the humans is still helpful, Mother." Lachima thought of all the mortals she'd watched in the few centuries since coming to these lands. "We draw much sustenance merely being close."

"And the minor exceptions?" Her mother's eyebrow arched as she glanced at the lily pond.

Morniero leaned against the bench arm, bent his knee, and set his boot on the seat. "Nothing that has provoked hostility from the locals." He threw Lachima a pointed look. "Yet."

"Only a few humans are aware of us." Lachima twisted her hands together. "And there's been no problem with them."

"So, no further . . . incidents?" Again, her mother shifted her gaze toward the pond. A pointed reference to the disaster with naiads fifty years earlier.

"No." Lachima met her eyes, grateful it was the truth. "None since . . ." She waved vaguely at the pond. ". . . that. Perhaps we became a little . . . relaxed." Her fingers still tingled with the energy that had surged through her when talking with Vanessa, touching her shoulder. "But once we're able to distance ourselves from the few who have tempted us recently, I'm quite sure we'll be able to prove this can be done."

Her mother's gaze was merciless in its candor. "There is no escape from temptation."

Lachima summoned every ounce of her strength to rise and take her mother's hands. "We have not been perfect. It's true. But we're doing better all the time. Getting stronger."

Her mother's force drew her like the souls of a million mortals, making Lachima's voice shake as she resisted the urge to throw herself into the depths of her mother's shimmering robes. "W-we can live amongst them without interacting. I'm sure of it." The panic Lachima had been suppressing now threatened to choke her. "Please. Give us more time."

Her mother's eyes slid to Morniero. "Is this your wish as well?"

Lachima turned to her brother. The indecision on his face paralyzed her. If they were of divided opinion, their mother was nearly certain to make them return to the darkness with her. Away from the warmth of the sun. The scent of flowers. The sensation of a gentle breeze beneath her butterfly wings. It was a fate too horrible for Lachima to even contemplate.

Morniero draped his wrist over his bent knee and averted his eyes. "The experiment has always had risks." His cool demeanor returned. "But the rewards remain considerable."

Their mother laughed and Lachima's entire body resonated like a tuning fork with the sound. "So, you're in accord?"

Morniero's nod was barely perceptible.

With her hands on her hips, their mother laughed again. "You're also strong enough to withstand the pain of simply agreeing with your sister, my son. I promise."

Still smiling, she leaned over and kissed Lachima's forehead.

Morniero sprung from the bench with a bashful expression and came forward for his kiss.

"Take care of one another." Their mother's eyes grew darker as she squeezed their hands. "And the others. This arrangement only works if even the weakest amongst you can manage it."

They both nodded, and she was gone.

Relieved at their reprieve, Lachima closed her eyes, waiting for the hammer blow of longing that always accompanied her mother's departure to subside.

One more chance. They dared not fail.

Chapter Forty-Nine

Vanessa tied her apron strings behind her back as she hurried up the hotel's south wing stairs. A week had passed since Karl made his announcement about the flu. Despite the simmering anxiety amongst the remaining staff, she'd managed to forget all that for a few hours in the Enchanted Wood. Having so much fun with Avery, she'd lost track of time. By the time she found Irene in one of the wing's larger suites, she was out of breath. "I'm so sorry I'm late!"

Irene pulled rumpled sheets from a white, wrought iron bed. "Another 'hike' with Avery?" Irene balled the linens and turned with a grin, her eyebrow raised.

"That's right." Vanessa bit her lip and headed for the matching bed and began folding its white, cotton-flocked spread.

Avery had been attempting to paint the water nymphs based on her description, and she'd entertained them all with a story that kept getting sillier and sillier as it progressed due to his "help." At each plot twist, he speculated about what would happen next and she would incorporate his idea into the evolving storyline. She'd laughed so hard at one point that tears ran down her cheeks.

There'd been no declarations or kisses or anything like that. But something had shifted. Their friendship was growing easier, more fluid. And a few times, she'd even found herself wondering what it would be like to kiss him.

She batted two pillows together and laid them back on the bare mattress. Yes, there was potential for her relationship with Avery to take a romantic turn. But she wasn't ready to talk about it with Irene. As a friend of them both, Irene would be too enthusiastic, and she didn't want to disappoint her if things didn't progress any further.

"Hey, Vanessa." Irene's brother Nelson rapped on the doorjamb wearing a bellhop uniform. This late in the season, the regular bellhops were gone, so he and their two younger brothers rotated the duty. "Mrs. Juneau wants to see you."

Had her tardiness been noted? Vanessa held her hands together with a slight frown. "What is it?"

He shrugged. "Might have something to do with the new arrivals." Nelson was soft-spoken, though at eighteen, nearly the size of their father.

"New arrivals?" Irene blanched. "I thought we weren't taking anyone new until the flu passed."

He shrugged again and pointed at Vanessa. "She just told me to get you."

"All right, I'm coming. I'm coming."

Worry and excitement wrestled in Vanessa's belly. New arrivals sounded somehow hopeful. Yet what kind of emergency could require her immediate presence? She shot a quick glance at Irene, whose brow was knitted.

Turning away, she hurried after Nelson.

Mrs. Juneau waved Vanessa into her office. "Come in and shut the door."

She did as she was told. Karl Fiske stood by the window. Vanessa's stomach twisted. This was not good.

Mrs. Juneau rose and paced behind her chair. "We have a situation, Miss Perkins . . . and hope that you might be able to help."

"What is it?" She glanced toward Karl, but the way he blinked while giving her an encouraging smile was more concerning than a frown would have been.

"The Cooper and Gardner families have returned." Mrs. Juneau made the announcement like it was a hot coal she needed to spit from her mouth.

A familiar brew of dread and giddiness sloshed around Vanessa's insides. She pressed her lips together to prevent asking if Ned was with them. She shouldn't care. Whatever they'd had was over. Definitely over.

Karl cleared his throat. "They didn't feel safe in Boston and asked us to place them in a cottage until the epidemic has passed."

"Yet they took a train?"

Mrs. Juneau and Karl exchanged a glance. "Seems they arranged with Pullman for a private car to be added to the White Mountain Express."

So they were safe. Their kind were always safe, no matter what happened.

"The problem is . . ." Mrs. Juneau shifted from one foot to the other, making her keys jingle. "Some of the staff are reluctant to help them."

Karl clasped his hands behind his back and gazed out the window. "That's putting it mildly."

Fear bloomed in Vanessa's belly. Even though she couldn't picture the Coopers or Gardners actually getting sick, the idea that they might have brought the infection with them from Boston seemed quite possible. She gripped the sides of the chair. "And you want me to tend to them."

"Only if you're willing, Miss Perkins." Karl sounded miserable. "Naturally, we would continue your salary as long as they remain."

"There would be no physical contact." Mrs. Juneau's crisp authority was back. "All you would do is deliver their mail, clean linens, and meals. Everything is to be left on the porch. They'll be responsible for all their own housekeeping."

Her brow furrowed. "Mrs. Cooper and Mrs. Gardner will be doing their own cleaning?"

"Extraordinary times call for extraordinary measures." Karl's imitation of a recent guest—the pompous mayor of a small town—was flawless. He even kept a straight face while she and Mrs. Juneau stared at him with open mouths.

Simultaneously, all three burst into guffaws. The image of those fine ladies up to their elbows in soapsuds or picking up discarded garments from the floor would have been enough to start her giggling. But it was the release of pent-up anxiety that fueled her laughter and kept it going. She suspected the same was true for Karl and Mrs. Juneau, who never joked at a guest's expense. At least as far as she knew.

Even as she laughed, Vanessa realized this was exactly the sort of sign she'd been looking for. A reason to believe the fairy's prophecy. By the time everyone's slightly hysterical chortling had quieted down, she knew what she would do.

Chapter Fifty

That evening, Vanessa made the first meal delivery to "the Timbers" cottage, where the seven new arrivals were staying: Sarah Gardner, her husband, Cecile and Arthur, the elder Coopers . . . and Ned.

Mrs. Juneau had decided it was most efficient to send baskets with picnic meals, rather than attempt any kind of plate service. Nothing could be taken out of the cottage, so bread, fruit, and cheese were wrapped in cloth. Warm meat and vegetables were placed in casserole dishes. Vanessa used a wheelbarrow to get the load across the lawn, her heartbeat thundering in her ears. After she'd unloaded the baskets onto the porch, she rapped on the door and turned to leave.

An urgent tapping on the front window stopped her. Her heart lurched into her throat. Half of her prayed it was Ned, the other half prayed it wasn't. She faced the window slowly, glad she'd checked her hair before coming. It was him. Her palms grew damp and her knees softened. Ned was as handsome as ever. His lips reminded her of how they felt on her neck . . . how his hand had felt as it moved from her shin to her knee . . .

No. That was over. Done.

She clenched her fists and nodded in what she hoped was a cool and aloof manner, then turned to leave once more. The tapping on the window intensified as she reached the steps. Relenting, she turned back to see Ned holding up a finger, mouthing, "One minute."

He disappeared and she folded her arms, staring up at the moths hurling themselves against the lanterns hanging on either side of the door. As much as her pride tugged at her to leave, a ridiculous, irrational hope that the fairy's prophecy was true forced her to stay.

A handwritten note pressed against the windowpane.

I was wrong. Please forgive me.

The simple message set a flock of hummingbirds loose in her chest. Never before had she appreciated the power of a genuine apology. A moment later, the sign slid away and Ned's face reappeared, looking adorably contrite. Though he was a long way from proving himself a "man of worth," his acknowledgment did wonders to restore her lost dignity.

She nodded, her lips pressed firmly together, then turned on her heel. Smiling broadly once her back was turned, Vanessa pushed the wheelbarrow back toward the hotel, using every ounce of self-control she possessed not to skip.

❧❧❧❧❧

The next morning, Vanessa plopped onto the stone bench by the pond in the Enchanted Wood and swung her feet. "Guess who's back?"

Uncharacteristically quiet, the naiads glanced at one another for several tense moments. Then, by some sort of unspoken agreement, something shifted, and their usual giddy enthusiasm resumed. "Ned Cooper!" Before long, they were all young girls, splashing and twittering. "We like Ned Cooper."

"I know you do." She kicked at the carpet of fallen leaves between her and the pond. "And he apologized."

"He's sorry! He's sorry!" The naiads seemed as happy as she'd been, dipping in and out of the water.

Their exuberance tempered her own. She planted her feet and crossed her arms. "He's still got a lot of work to do if he wants to get back in my good graces, but it's a start."

"A good start." A plump nymph with ringlets showed her dimples. "Bring him soon. We want to meet him."

Vanessa's head tilted down and she twisted her ring. Yes, she could imagine forgiving Ned over time if he proved himself sincere. But did she want to bring him to the Wood? At this point, even the idea made her feel insecure. Exposed. "I would, but he's quarantined because of the Spanish Flu."

They cocked their heads. "The Spanish Flu?"

"It's a horrible disease that's killing people in Boston and spreading fast." Saying it aloud was worse than thinking about it. "We're all terribly frightened." She stared down at the dead leaves around her feet. Spectacular, but dead nonetheless. "I wish I could ask the fairy what it means for us."

A freckled redhead twirled a lock of hair with her finger. "She doesn't know when your thread will be cut."

At last, a bit more information. Her thread being cut sounded like a reference to the mythological Fates, who determined the beginning, end, and contents of one's life. "No?" Vanessa kept her voice steady, almost uninterested. "What does she know, then?"

"Not as much as she'd like."

Vanessa couldn't tell whose ignorance amused the naiads more, the fairy's or her own.

A black-haired nymph with almond eyes tilted her head against the redhead's. "But she might tell you more. You enticed her to visit you once, after all."

"Is that unusual? I thought plenty of people saw fairies around here."

"Mainly children and old people."

Of course. She hadn't believed Walter about the fairies, had she? "In other words, anyone who can be easily dismissed."

The nymphs nodded and swam closer. "But the veil between you and us is thin." They laughed. "She couldn't resist."

Even as her vanity was stroked at the notion she was so special, an unpleasant pinch developed in her chest. "Resist? Did the fairy do something wrong by talking to me?"

They shrugged and giggled. "We shall see."

Swiveling her eyes from left to right, trying to catch edges of light, Vanessa couldn't hide the frustration in her voice. "Is she here now?"

"No. Her kind come and go as they please." The water began to roil and the nymphs' voices deepened. "Yet we're trapped here . . . forever and ever."

Vanessa's fingers tightened on the edge of the bench. The naiads had never told her anything about their world. Since first encountering them, she had peppered them with questions. But they always answered in such riddles that she'd soon given up, just as Avery said he had.

"How long have you been here?" She kept her voice low and held perfectly still.

"We forget." They spoke in unison.

Forget or refused to say, it was impossible to tell.

"Oh," she said casually. "A very long time, then."

They nodded, and the sorrow on their faces softened her irritation with their opaque replies. "It must have been lovely where you came from for you to miss it so much."

As one, the naiads sank below the surface, which became smooth and still. She waited, but they did not return.

"I take it our conversation is over." With a sigh of frustration, Vanessa took a deep breath of the crisp morning air. The scent of cinnamon and clove had strengthened as September gave way to early October. Though still unnaturally colorful, the Enchanted Wood's palette had shifted into orange, gold, red, and brown. Even outside the Wood's magic, the forest was aflame.

Now she knew what Irene was talking about when she said the hotel normally got a fresh wave of guests that peaked in mid-October, there to see the best of the fall foliage.

Nonetheless, with neither the nymphs nor Avery for company, the gorgeous location began to feel a bit lonely. Since starting his job, Avery had begun spending Sundays with his family after church, leaving Saturday his only day in the Wood.

Selecting three or four of the prettiest leaves from the ground, Vanessa tilted them at different angles to see how they sparkled and glittered in the Wood's warm light. She stuffed them in her coat pocket, determined to take them to him. Then he'd have something to paint when he was unable to come all the way up to the Wood. In fact, Vanessa realized with a smile, she looked forward to seeing the entire Nolen family.

Making her way down the mountain, Vanessa spotted Avery's familiar head of shaggy, brown hair as he came up the path. She shook her head with an affectionate sigh. Most young men seemed to take enormous care with their hair. Parting it to show crisp white lines of scalp, greasing it to lie flat on the sides. But not Avery. He didn't seem to even notice those sorts of things.

Now that Ned was back, the difference in how they each affected her was clear. Even now, Ned made her nerves jangle, stirred excitement in her belly. With Avery, she felt more of a deep, rumbling affection.

Were either of those what real love felt like? How was anyone to know?

She stopped and stepped up on a rock at the side of the path, waiting for Avery to reach her. With his head bent and attention on the craggy ground before him, he hadn't seen her. As he drew closer, it was clear something was off. His shoulders had an unusual slump; his step was heavy.

"Fancy meeting you here, Mr. Nolen!" She spoke brightly, wanting him to look up at her and smile. Reassure her that everything was all right.

He did raise his eyes, but his expression offered nothing to quiet her fears. "Back to formality, are we?"

She hopped off the rock and headed down the path toward him, but he thrust his hand forward. "No! Stay back."

"Why?" She halted her momentum with a palm against a tree trunk. "What's wrong?"

"It's my mother." He turned his head, his voice choked. "She's sick."

Her hands flew to her mouth. "The flu?"

He nodded.

"Oh, Avery. I'm so sorry. Is there anything I can do?"

Shaking his head, he ran his hands through his hair. "Bess and Hattie are with her now. Father's at the hospital." He dropped his hands. "Any illness at the hotel?"

"Not that I know of."

"Thank God." His expression had a focus and intensity she'd never seen before. "Promise me you'll protect yourself."

She nodded, her fingertips growing cold. "I brought you something." When she pulled the enchanted leaves from her pocket, her heart sank. Though still pretty, they were now just ordinary leaves. "They changed."

His smile was bittersweet. "I did the same thing when I was little. Tried to bring my mother a bouquet from the Wood. But as soon as I left the passage, they turned into plain old wildflowers."

Letting the leaves fall to the ground, Vanessa stuffed her hands into her pockets.

"Thanks for thinking of me, though." The flatness in his tone was difficult to hear.

"The Wood wasn't the same without you," she replied.

He blushed and pushed his glasses up his nose. "I've sort of gotten used to you being there, too."

Hugging herself against the nip in the air, Vanessa swung a foot across the piles of dead leaves blanketing the path. He was going to find out Ned had returned one way or another. Best not confuse matters by acting like she didn't want him to know of his return. "Did you hear the Coopers came back?"

As she anticipated, his tone hardened. "The Coopers?"

"And the Gardners. They're all self-quarantined in the Timbers cottage."

His eyes widened in alarm. "They're sick?"

"Not a one." Again, she was struck with the advantages the wealthy enjoyed. "They're here to make sure they stay that way. I'm their lifeline, delivering meals three times a day."

Jamming his hands in his coat pockets, his expression darkened. "And Ned's with them."

She nodded, unsure what to say. Was he concerned about her wounded pride and wanted to know Ned was contrite, starting to make amends? Or was Avery more worried about the return of a rival and preferred to know she had no intention of falling under Ned's spell again?

Given the circumstances, sidestepping seemed wisest. "That's right, but what matters now is your mother. Are you sure there's nothing I can do?"

He shook his head and moved off the path into the woods, giving her a wide berth. "I'm seeing if they can help." He gestured up the hill with a jerk of his chin.

Visiting the Enchanted Wood the day of her grand humiliation on the train platform had made her feel much better. But she couldn't think of anything the nymphs had done to directly assist her. It was more like . . . they'd given her confidence when she'd needed a boost. "I hope they can help. I really do."

"Thanks."

Keeping a wide berth, she moved downhill, then turned back to face him.

Strain exaggerated the angles on his face. "You take care, Vanessa."

She waved, then watched him rejoin the path and trudge uphill.

"You, too, Avery," she whispered to herself, long after he could possibly hear.

Chapter Fifty-One

Ned Cooper was back? Avery sprang up from the stone bench. He couldn't dwell on that now. His angry marching took him in tight circles around the glen. He needed to think about his mother—the reason he'd come.

Snippets of harp music drifted in and out at the edge of his perception. The various wood nymphs were leaning from their trees, swaying to the tune they seemed to hear without difficulty. They knew he was there. They'd address him when they were ready.

He returned to his seat, determined to wait . . . and resist dark thoughts of Vanessa seeing Ned multiple times every day.

"I feel your heart hurting." The soft boughs that made up Willow's hair dangled over his shoulders as she whispered in his ear.

"It is."

"Tell me."

"It's . . . my mother."

Still too agitated to remain sitting, he rose again and walked to the end of the bench, gripping the stone arm with both hands. "She's sick."

"I'm so sorry to hear that." Her mournful tone forced him to pull his spectacles off and rub his eyes before any tears could spill.

"With the Spanish Flu." His voice caught. "It's quite serious. And . . . and I was hoping you could help."

Willow wrung her leafy hands. "Oh, Avery. It doesn't work like that."

A jagged ball of anger formed in his belly as he put his glasses back on. "But you're magic. There must be something you can do."

"We may seem that way to you. But then, you all seem magic to us."

"Humans?" He snorted. "We're not magic at all."

She laughed softly and was joined by several others who had begun to listen to their conversation. "You can come and go at will, can't you?"

"Well . . . yes."

"And you do so much living in your little, tiny lifespans," added a nearby fir nymph.

From across the pond, a maple tree nymph drawled, "And you make things with your hands from ideas you have in your minds."

Willow spread her boughs. "You see. We could go on and on. But we don't have the kind of magic that can make things happen in the human world."

"Could the fairies help?" He was grasping at straws, but it was all he had.

"It's not the sort of thing they do either." She glanced anxiously at the other nymphs, then back at him. "Besides . . . you've never seen one, have you?"

His grip tightened on the curved stone as he stared over at the seemingly empty pond. "Not for lack of trying."

Willow reached over and swept a few of her boughs across the front of his chest. "All we can do to help is tell you what we see in your heart, which sometimes you can't see for yourself."

He clenched his jaw and hung his head. "So . . . what do you see in my heart?"

"That you need to go be with your mother." The maple nymph's voice was as sweet as the syrup in her host tree.

"I've been there." His fists balled. "I can't help her."

Willow clasped her hands over her chest. "Perhaps you don't recognize what you give her."

He pushed away from the bench, needing to take action of some kind. The alternative was a despair he wouldn't permit himself. "If there's nothing you can do to help, I've got to go."

Receiving no reply beyond the wood nymphs' sympathetic expressions, he turned and strode toward the rocky exit.

"Goodbye, Avery!" Something in Willow's tone made him stop. "I wish you all that your heart desires." Her blessing sounded more sad than hopeful.

He turned back, grateful for her quiet companionship for so many years. "Thank you, Willow. I wish the same for you."

His throat ached as he made his way through the passage. The creatures of the Enchanted Wood weren't to blame for what was happening to his mother, or for Ned Cooper's return. But he almost wished they were. Then he'd have somewhere to direct the rage building in his chest.

He straightened his back after emerging from the stone passage and looked around the ordinary White Mountain woodland. It was the first time he could remember leaving the Wood feeling worse than when he arrived. Alone outside the passageway, his anguish deepened when he realized that after all their years together, he still had no idea what lay in Willow's heart.

Chapter Fifty-Two

Vanessa lowered the wheelbarrow handles in front of the Timbers cottage. Ned stood at the parlor window. She returned his brief nod, then unloaded the supper casseroles by the door with her head turned. Gnawing her lip prevented the betrayal of a grin. When she was finished, she glanced back. He was still there . . . gesturing for her to come closer. Refusing to talk to him during the day's earlier deliveries had been a test of his commitment. This being his third try, she wiped her hands on her apron and walked over to the window.

"Good evening." His voice was only slightly muffled by the glass that separated them.

Her hand rose reflexively to make sure her hair was still tucked into its bun. "Good evening."

"I don't know how you do it."

"Do what?"

"Make a hotel uniform seem like an empress's gown."

She could hear it now. The emptiness in his flattery. She had been too dazzled to notice it during the summer. With arms crossed, she frowned. "Your honeyed tongue doesn't fool me anymore, Ned Cooper."

He blinked a moment, then grew serious. "I meant it when I said I'm sorry."

"As you should be." She bit the inside of her mouth. He had no right to see how the memory of her humiliation still pained her.

After a quick glance over his shoulder, he leaned closer to the windowpane. "I don't know what to make of you, and obviously . . . misjudged."

"What could be mysterious about me? A simple nursemaid from the Girls Home." She held her skirt out. "Correction. Simple chambermaid from the Girls Home."

An impish grin lifted the corners of his mouth. "Now, now, Miss Perkins. You know that doesn't begin to describe you."

She had to look away to keep from smiling herself. When she turned back, she was surprised to see the seriousness of his expression. He pressed his palm to the glass. "Remember, we promised each other honesty."

Honesty. That was all he'd offered, and despite her dashed hopes and his embarrassing assumptions about her propriety, he'd never lied to her. She lifted her chin. "You're right. I do think I'm more than a simple nanny or chambermaid." Her head dipped as she ran her thumb over the stone in her ring. "I just don't know exactly what else I am."

"Fair enough." He was smiling again. "And I can honestly say that I'm a lucky bastard born with a silver spoon in my mouth and it's made me a spoiled brat."

Disarmed by his harsh assessment, she laughed. "Hazard of wealth, I suppose."

His eyes slid to hers, more vulnerable than she'd ever seen them. "But it's my wealth you were after, wasn't it?"

Her breath caught as they locked eyes. He was partially right, of course. "Hardly the only thing." Picturing herself in his place, chased after by fortune hunters, she imagined drawbacks to being wealthy she'd never considered. "But I'd be lying to say your money didn't hurt."

The corners of his mouth twitched. "More honesty. I appreciate that."

"But you know it was far more than that." A hitch caught in her voice. "I loved you."

He nodded, head bowed. "And you got to me more than I realized." Crossing his arms, he frowned at his feet. "I started missing you the moment you ran off."

They stood in awkward silence. Everything had shifted. They were in uncharted territory together.

She peered around the empty room behind him. "How is everyone? Cecile and Albert are well?"

"We're at each other's throats and it hasn't even been two days." With a glance over his shoulder, he loosened his arms and leaned a hand against the wall. "I'd give anything to be out there with the rest of the world, flu be damned."

"So none of you are sick?"

His knuckles rapped on the window frame. "So far, so good. Besides, we're stocked to the gills with supplies, should anyone so much as sniffle. Sarah's spreading Vicks VapoRub on the children as a precautionary measure, so the whole house stinks of menthol."

"You have Vicks? They're saying that really helps."

He snorted. "Must have a case of it."

She thought of Avery's face when he told her about his mother being sick. "Can you spare a jar? Avery Nolen's mother has the flu and it might help."

"Sorry to hear that." His face clouded and he lowered his voice. "But we're not supposed to send anything out of the house." He gestured to her and the casseroles on the doormat. "That's what all this rigamarole is about."

"But none of you are sick. Just . . . don't touch it with your hands and put it outside the door."

The corner of his mouth curled upward. "I'm game if you are, my little rebel." Something caught his attention and he glanced over his shoulder. "They're in the hallway. I'll put it out when they're gone."

Before she had a chance to get away, the front door opened and Ned's mother and sister stepped onto the porch. Vanessa flattened herself against the wall, parting her lips slightly to silence her breathing.

If they saw her, she'd be dismissed. She was sure of it. They'd gone to a lot of trouble to keep their family away from other people. Finding themselves just feet away from a maskless chambermaid would defeat the entire purpose.

Fortunately, there was a screen door that opened out. It provided a bit of protection, though she was clearly visible if either one looked in her direction.

Her eyes darted nervously to the wheelbarrow, its handles in plain view from the front porch.

Mrs. Cooper stood with her back to her, holding the screen door open, while Ned's sister picked up a casserole dish and returned inside. His mother bent down to pick up another, then retreated inside as well. The screen door slammed behind her.

Finally allowing herself a deep breath, Vanessa ran down the steps and grabbed the wheelbarrow. After pushing it around the corner of the house, she hid behind the bushes just in time. Ned's mother and sister returned for the last of the casseroles, then went back inside. The screen door closed, followed by the soft click of the front door latching.

It was quiet for a while, then the door creaked open a third time. She poked her head up and saw Ned place a small jar on the doormat, his hand wrapped in a dishtowel. He scanned the shrubbery and finally caught sight of her waving through the bushes at the end of the porch. To her chagrin, his smiling face was as appealing as ever. He blew her a kiss. She rolled her eyes . . . and blew him one back.

Once he'd disappeared inside again, she chuckled quietly as she collected the precious green jar. She'd never trust her heart to him again, but he still knew how to make her laugh.

Chapter Fifty-Three

A very." His eyes fluttered open as Bess rocked his shoulder. "Avery, wake up." Her voice was anxious, her eyes trained on their mother in the bed. He sat up in the horsehair armchair that had been in his parents' bedroom his whole life. This was the first time he recalled sitting in it by himself, rather than cuddled as a small boy on his mother's lap.

"What happened?" He adjusted his mask and grabbed the washcloth from the bowl of water at the bedside, then wiped his mother's scorching brow. Her skin was blue and her breathing labored. She seemed much worse in the morning light than she had the night before.

"Nothing." Bess picked at her cuticles, her gaze dull and voice slightly muffled by the mask. "I just couldn't be alone with her another minute."

Hattie appeared in the doorway in bare feet, her eyes round in alarm above her mask. She pulled her thin cardigan tight around her muslin nightdress. "Why is she so blue?"

Bess stood by Avery's side, her shoulder touching his. "The bad ones at the hospital look like this, too." Her voice was flat, lifeless.

"Where's Father?" He squeezed the cloth in the water bowl. "He should be here."

Hattie took slow, cautious steps into the room.

"There are so many patients." Bess sighed and sat on the edge of the mattress. "Every bed filled and then some."

After lowering herself gently onto the opposite side of the bed, Hattie took hold of their mother's limp hand. "Everything's all right, Mother. You'll be feeling better soon."

The hopefulness in Hattie's voice sliced Avery's heart open. He'd read the newspaper accounts and his father had also made it clear. There was nothing more to be done for his mother than he and Bess were already doing. But his soul rebelled against the invisible plague, searching for a solution. Or barring that, someone to blame.

"It's been too long. He should have come back." Avery wiped his mother's burning hand with the compress, then held her palm against his. "Why hasn't he come?"

Bess took their mother's hand after he released it. "Father's needed more there."

He balled up the wet cloth and pressed it into his sister's hand. "He's needed here."

Avery pumped the bicycle pedals as hard as he could, willing the wheels to carry him faster. His thighs burned and the cool air swept away the last remnants of sleep.

When he arrived at the hospital grounds, he dropped the bike on the grass and sprinted up the stone stairs to the main entrance. Clusters of people in gauze masks gathered on the lawn. Their faces were drawn. Black circles drooped beneath their eyes. Families.

After flinging the door open, he tied his mask on and stopped a nurse passing with a mug of coffee. "Have you seen my father?"

"Hasn't left the patient ward all night." She held the mug out to him. "Can you take that to him? I've got to get more sheets."

Taking comfort from the mug's warmth, Avery nodded. The smell of the coffee reminded him how little he'd eaten the previous two days. It was already Monday and his last real meal had been the bacon and eggs his mother made him on Saturday morning.

Possibly the last meal she'd ever prepare.

The thought chased away what little appetite the coffee had aroused. Hurrying through the hallways, he held the mug out in front of him. Focusing on not spilling any allowed him to ignore the sounds of sickness and dying bouncing off the corridor walls. Once he got to the general patient ward, he stood in the doorway, stunned.

Bess was right. Every single bed was occupied, some with two patients. Nurses and volunteers scurried from bed to bed, holding bowls for the bloody phlegm being coughed up, or pressing glasses of water to chapped lips, trying to get liquid down constricted throats. The stench of blood and piss brought a surge of vomit to his throat, but he turned to face the wall and willed it back down. He refused to add to their workload.

After he was more composed, he turned back to scan the room for his father. He almost didn't recognize him. Normally loud and overbearing, his father tended to command a room. He'd expected to find him marching up and down at the foot of the beds, barking orders to a bevy of nurses. Instead, he'd found a hunched over, diminished version of the lion he knew. An old man shuffling from one bedside to the next. The nurses had to lean in to catch what he was saying, and sometimes, it appeared he would merely hold the patient's hand and purse his lips, staring off into space.

He hurried over. "Father."

His father turned his bloodshot eyes toward him and blinked, almost as if he didn't recognize his own son. "Avery?"

"Here's some coffee." Holding the mug out with one hand, he gripped his father's elbow with the other. "Why don't you sit down a moment and drink it."

Looking up and down the row of beds, his father shook his head. "Too many. No time for that . . ."

Panic flapped and clawed in Avery's belly. He felt ten years old, living a child's nightmare. His parents were missing and he was lost, with no idea what to do. "It's all right, Father. The nurses will take care of the patients for a little while."

"Yes, Dr. Nolen." Nurse Hutchins was also a shadow of the woman he'd worked with during the summer. "We can handle things for a few minutes, while you take a break."

After another mournful scan of the room, his father allowed himself to be guided into a chair, where he closed his eyes as he sipped the coffee.

Standing over his father, Avery thanked God the exhausted man hadn't fallen ill. It was truly a mysterious disease, wiping out entire families, while sparing others completely. His father had told the family most people ultimately survived, but staggeringly high numbers were dying—particularly the young and otherwise healthy.

His father's eyes closed as his chin dropped.

"Nurse Hutchins!" Avery grabbed the mug from his father's hand.

In an instant she was at his side, shaking her head. "It's about time he got some sleep."

He gripped his father's shoulder to keep him from falling over.

"We've been trying to get him to lie down, but he's refused. Let's get him to the sofa in his office." Stooping over, she took his father's wrist and lifted his arm around the back of her neck. "You take the other side."

They dragged his sleeping father between them down the hall. When their awkward trio arrived at his father's office, they discovered two volunteer women with long aprons over their wool dresses asleep on the sofa, their heads at opposite ends. Nurse Hutchins left Avery shouldering his father to shake one by the shoulder. "Ladies, I'm afraid we need the bunk." Blinking and bleary-eyed, the women slowly rose. Seeing his father's head lolling against Avery's shoulder, they sped up vacating the leather sofa with little cries of alarm and apology.

Once his father was transferred to the couch and snoring gently, Avery's heart slowed, but his worry remained. His father was clearly pushing himself to his limit. He didn't need medical school to know this was a dangerous thing to do while treating such a deadly illness. He couldn't lose both parents.

Nurse Hutchins was already heading out the door.

"It's my mother," he blurted. "I think she's dying."

The nurse stopped, her face crumpling. "Not Catherine . . ."

He nodded, fighting his tears. "What can we do?"

"Keep her hydrated and propped up, to help her breathe. Clear her mouth out whenever she spits up . . . and pray." Clutching the doorjamb for a moment, Nurse Hutchins composed herself, then disappeared.

Avery turned back to his father. Dark circles stood out under his ashen skin. The scenario he'd envisioned—his mother smiling in grateful relief at his father's arrival . . . everyone knowing that everything would be all right . . . It wasn't going to happen.

Leaning his hand on his father's desk, Avery stared at the books, diplomas, and the stacks of medical records. What responsibility the depleted man on the sofa carried every day. Though Avery had vaguely imagined having to take care of his parents in some distant future, nothing had prepared him for the moment arriving before his twenty-second birthday.

With a deep breath, he straightened his spine, pushed off the desk, and left the room. He was needed at home.

Chapter Fifty-Four

Hours later, Avery pulled a gauze mask from his pocket as he crossed the entryway to answer the front door. The knocking sounded urgent. His throat clamped. At this point, no urgent news could be good news. He cracked the door open and frowned, confused to find Vanessa at the bottom of the porch steps. Then his stomach knotted. "What are you doing here? You're supposed to stay at the hotel."

With feet planted and hands behind her back, she twisted side to side, swirling her black skirt around her legs. "I brought you something."

Despite the mask covering most of her face, her expression was so optimistic, his insides softened. Centuries had passed since he'd seen happy eyes, or so it seemed. "What is it?"

Her arm swung out from behind and she presented a jar of Vicks VapoRub on her flattened palm. Like it was the Hope Diamond. And at this moment, it was more valuable to him than that enormous gem could be. "Where did you get that?"

"Ned's family brought a case with them."

A shadow descended on his heart again. "You've been seeing him?"

Her face fell. "He's not as bad as you think. He's apologized for what happened and is trying to make up."

"I'm sure he is."

Her shoulders stiffened. "And I thought you might appreciate this."

"I'm sorry." He rubbed his eyes under his glasses. "It's just been . . ."

"How's your mother?"

The pain couldn't be worse if he'd swallowed a burning ember. "Not good," he croaked. "And Hattie's feeling poorly, as well."

"I'm so sorry, Avery." He could hear tears in her voice and looked up. "I hope this helps." She stepped forward and placed the Vicks at the top of the steps, then turned and retreated down the walkway. "Please let me know if there's anything else I can do."

"I will. And thank you."

She turned back and stood motionless as they stared at one another. As much as they both wanted him to ask her for something that could actually help, there truly was nothing she could do.

"Well . . . see you later." She offered a peppy salute, then turned and strode to the sidewalk and back toward the hotel.

Unable to resist watching her, he waited until she was no longer in sight to close the door and return to his mother's sickroom.

❧❧❧❧

As dawn's long fingers snuck around the bedroom shades, Avery and Bess sat on either side of his mother's bed. The distinctive smell of the Vicks filled the room. Eucalyptus and mint were his best guess. His mother's feet were now completely black and her face the shade of blueberries. Her nightgown was stained with blood, but they didn't have the heart to change her into a fresh one. Every move seemed to agonize her. The end was near, and all they could do was sit by and hold her hands.

As his mother breathed in long, shuddering rasps, he looked over at Bess. His sister's eyes were puffy and vacant as she stared at their mother's face. Wavy blonde strands had fallen from her bun, and she hadn't bothered to put them back up. He rarely saw her with her hair down anymore. It made her appear younger . . . unusually defenseless.

A wave of tenderness swept over him. Normally so ferocious and strong, Bess had terrified him when they were growing up, though she never laid a hand on him. She was simply aligned with their father, expecting Avery to somehow be bigger in the world. To be more like them.

The gasping breath stopped, replaced by a wet, choking sound. He sprang to his feet and grabbed his mother's hand. Her eyes opened wider, her lips moving open and closed. And then there was no more movement. No more sound.

Glancing back at Bess, Avery longed to meet her eyes. To feel their bond and know he wasn't alone in hell. But she was frozen, tears falling silently down her face as she stared at their mother's motionless face. He leaned over and slid his mother's eyes closed with his palm. The pain carving up the inside of his chest threatened to either kill him or drive him insane. He needed to move, needed to *do* something. "I'll go check on Hattie."

Bess didn't reply.

Staggering into the hallway on wooden legs, he made his way toward their little sister. He and Bess had alternated between the two sick rooms all night, leaving him nearly delirious with fatigue, and now, grief.

The room Bess and Hattie shared was dim, painted a deep orange hue from the faint morning sun penetrating the drawn shade. He was grateful that Hattie was too feverish to understand anything he said, sparing him from delivering the bad news about their mother. For a little while, at least.

He walked to the dresser, where he lifted the compress from the bowl of water and squeezed it out before moving to the side of her bed. Tears blurred his vision as he reached the wet cloth toward Hattie's forehead. Strands of dark hair clung to the sides of her face, framing her open eyes. Her lips were pulled back in a grimace.

She, too, was dead.

The howl that ripped from his lungs expressed only a fraction of his agony. His senses had been so overwhelmed by the thought of losing his mother, he hadn't been able to acknowledge the danger Hattie was in, even as he tipped warm broth across her chapped lips and packed rolls of chipped ice around her neck. His legs went wobbly and he slid to the floor, the useless compress dropping from his fingers. With arms crossed over his knees, he bent his head and sobbed until his throat was hoarse and sleep eventually overtook him.

Hours later, he found Bess still glued to the chair in their mother's room.

Chapter Fifty-Five

After posting her latest letter to Gladys, Vanessa tilted her head back to see the explosion of yellow, red, orange, and gold foliage overhead as she pumped the bicycle pedals up the hill, a tiny packet of hotel mail in the bike's saddlebags. The climb was easier now, compared to the day she'd met Bess on her way back from the post office. Her legs had gotten stronger with practice.

She glanced over at the Nolen house as she rode by. Bundled in heavy coats, the twins sat in matching rockers on the front porch. Vanessa braked and waved. Neither waved back. Bess blew a puff of smoke into the crisp fall air. Anxiety growing in her belly, Vanessa leaned the bike against their front fence and walked toward the house. "Avery? Bess?"

Neither one moved. They just watched as she drew closer. Then she knew. Their mother was dead.

Vanessa's steps slowed as she neared the porch. Stopping a few yards from the low stairs, she pulled her mask from her pocket and tied it on. The flimsy items had seemed rather a nuisance when Mrs. Juneau handed them out to everyone. But now it seemed disrespectful not to wear one.

A heartrending wail erupted somewhere inside the house. Their father.

"I'm so, so sorry."

Avery's eyes were rimmed in red. "Ha—" He coughed, cleared his throat and tried again. "Hattie, too."

A loud buzz rang in Vanessa's ears. Unable to do more, or to face the fear she'd seen in Avery's face, she had convinced herself the Vicks would cure his mother. That she had saved the day and everything was going to be fine. She'd buried his comment about Hattie feeling poorly even deeper than any lingering concern about his mother.

But now the comfort of denial was stripped away. It was all terribly real. People she knew were dead. Not just people. Dear Mrs. Nolen, with her soft hands and worried eyes. And Hattie! Bursting with life and the picture of health. It was impossible to believe.

But they were dead, regardless of what she believed. The gauze masks, the quarantines, the hotel staff not being able to leave. All the fuss wasn't a game. It was an attempt to keep people alive. They all might die.

Numb, Vanessa was only vaguely aware of her lips moving, words flowing off her own tongue. "Is there . . . anything I can do?"

For several excruciating moments, the twins merely stared, their eyes vacant. She desperately wanted to hug them, comfort them somehow, but in their horrible new world, that simple gesture risked spreading the tragedy further. "I-I'm so sorry." The sentiment was so inadequate for the situation. But she had no other words to offer and turned to go.

"Can you . . . tell Karl?" Bess's voice was weak and shaky. "The hotel people should know."

"Yes, yes of course. Any other messages?"

"Public gatherings are discouraged." Avery's voice sounded as tired as his sister's. "So, no funeral date yet."

"The undertaker is scheduling one per day," Bess added. "He'll let us know when it's our turn."

Vanessa's fists clenched. "When will this end?" Guilt assaulted her instantly. Who was she to complain in light of their loss?

The sobbing inside quieted. The twins exchanged a glance. Bess crushed her cigarette butt with her heel and they rose together.

"Thank you for coming by." Avery's strained smile was worse than his blank expression had been.

Bess pushed the front door open, then turned back. "And for the Vicks."

Vanessa nodded, her throat too tight to speak. She remained frozen as Avery followed his sister inside.

Right before the door closed, he glanced over his shoulder and their eyes met. It was how she imagined a man entering the Sahara might look back at the last oasis. In that instant, a wave of affection swelled so powerfully in her chest it took her breath away.

Vanessa braked the bicycle, its wheels crunching on the gravel near the staff entrance at the rear of the hotel. An earlier rain had left the late afternoon air crisp and the birds quiet.

Her mind still on the Nolens' terrible news, she took the mail from the saddlebag and discovered Irene's father sitting at a long picnic table outside the staff kitchen. He clutched a coffee mug, his puffy red eyes staring into space.

"Mr. Seward! What's wrong?"

His eyes moved slowly toward her. "My boys."

Her hand lifted a few inches, instinctively reaching for something to hold onto, some support. "They're sick?"

He nodded as her hand dropped back to her side.

"All of 'em." Grief cracked and pitted his already gravelly voice.

It beggared imagination. How could one family be so afflicted? "Where's Irene?"

"Tending them."

Her breath came in sharp bursts as she gripped the mail tighter. "All alone?"

He hung his head.

She tried to be sympathetic. The man had lost his wife and oldest son in the past year. But all she could think was that Irene had lost her mother and brother, yet she was in there, taking care of those that were left.

At the rear side of the Sewards' house, the sporadic plink of water dripping from the porch roof sounded ominous as Vanessa approached. The depth of Karl's moan when she'd shared the news about Mrs. Nolen and Harriet, and the speed with which he had left for the Nolens' house had left her shaken. No question, Karl Fiske was as fine and decent a person as Avery claimed.

She stood on her toes and looked through the kitchen window framed by curtains of orange and yellow calico. Irene was there. At the sink, her head bowed and eyes closed.

Knocking on the back door, Vanessa remembered dancing with Irene's three remaining brothers earlier that summer. Seventeen-year-old Frank, the middle brother, was the jokester of the three and almost the size of Nelson, while Denis, fifteen, chased his older brothers around like a goofy puppy. It was nearly impossible to imagine any one of them lying still, much less on a sickbed.

Irene trudged over, her weary face appearing in the glass pane at the top of the door. "You shouldn't be here."

"I don't care. You need help."

"I'm alright. I can handle it." Irene's jaw was set. The ferocity in her eyes brooked no argument.

"Please. There's got to be something I can do." Why did it sound like she was asking Irene for a favor, rather than riding to her friend's rescue?

Irene's voice softened. "Just help Pa. He'll be sleeping in a staff room at the hotel for a while."

"I'll do that. I swear."

"You're a good kid."

"Kid? You're only a few months older than me."

Irene laid her palm against the windowpane with a gentle smile.

Vanessa pressed hers against the glass to match. "You don't have to do this alone."

"You're helping me by looking after Pa."

There was no way she could tell Irene about Avery's mother and Hattie. Not now. Instead, she nodded, mute. Irene walked away, disappearing down a hallway off the kitchen. Abandoned on the back step, Vanessa turned slowly to face the woods behind the Sewards' house. Oh, how she wanted to run straight for the Enchanted Wood, where everything was beautiful and safe.

After several moments, she walked around the corner of the house. In the distance, the gaslight beside the staff kitchen door formed a beacon in the afternoon shadows. At the edge of its pool of light, Mr. Seward still sat clutching his mug. Unable to keep the people he loved from dying.

Reluctantly, Vanessa put one foot in front of another and made her way toward him.

Chapter Fifty-Six

Not much dance left in her step." Morniero glanced at Lachima as Vanessa plodded below them on her way back to the hotel. "She could use a lakeside waltz."

Their backs were against an oak tree's thick trunk, their shoulders touching and legs extended along the branches that served as their seats.

"Been visiting her dreams, have you?" Lachima's tone was teasing, but there was sadness in it, too.

"They're quite textured." He rubbed his chin. "Not surprising she's a story-teller."

Lachima sighed. "At least she's not having nightmares."

He turned to face her, serious for once. "If it pains you so, why do you make them suffer?" Reaching over, he ran his fingers through a lock of her floating hair, the strands soft and cool against his skin. "It's you who determines their fates between birth and death, is it not?"

She pulled her legs up and wrapped her arms around them, her chin resting atop her knees. "You know it's more complicated than that."

"Of course." Turning on his branch, he allowed his boots to dangle. "But is there really nothing you can do to avert these wars and plagues the humans continually face?"

"Their woes are as vital as their joys." She ran her fingers over the silky flow of her dress. "Together, they are the warp and weave of the fabric of their lives."

Morniero's snort was soft but pointed. "They might appreciate a bit less warp, even if it made the fabric less fine."

"I don't have nearly the influence I used to." Despite his effort to keep a light tone, Lachima remained serious. "And it's never been me alone who determined their fate. It's more like . . . a duet."

Morniero sobered. "I've always wondered how it worked." He stared into the evening sky. In all the millennia since they'd been born, they'd never spoken so directly of their differing powers. All their mother's children simply acknowledged one another's presence in the world. Intuited the role each played for the humans, whose lives were so entwined with their own. He threw her a shy glance. "I believe you three control my life, too."

Lachima looked down at her hands. "Yes. Fate applies to man and god alike."

A wave of anxiety swept through him. It was an emotion he normally only experienced while inside a human's dream, and it was quite unpleasant. "There's no need to say, if it's too much, I mean."

"That's alright. I don't mind telling you." Lachima gazed into the distance. "Clona plays the opening bars, the circumstances of each individual's birth. With her melody already playing, I pick up the tune, directing it one way or another. But then you each start singing along, adding strains of your own."

Her voice grew more lyrical as she continued her metaphor. "The choices you make inspire the opportunities and challenges I present next. Determine how dramatic or quiet your song turns out to be. We write your fate together."

"So." He raised an eyebrow at her. "Sounds like my work in humans' dreams might have more influence than you've let on."

Lachima smiled sweetly. "I'll admit that, on occasion, a dream will inspire a human to change the melody of our song, or shift it into a different key." Resting her cheek on her knees, her smile faded as she looked toward him. "But no one knows when Atroporta will cut your thread and stop the music."

He looked back up at the stars, considering what life would be like knowing when it would end. "Probably for the best."

"Agreed." She sat up, pressing her back against the trunk once more. "But don't overestimate your importance, Morniero." Her cheek dimpled as she winked. "You might get more involved than you'd care to be."

Chapter Fifty-Seven

Looking around the small cemetery, Vanessa could identify at least four new graves. Two days had passed since Avery's mother and sister died. The speed of the burial was no doubt a testimony to the affection Adamsville's small community had for them both. An umbrella kept the drizzle off her head, but the bench where she had listened to Bess's secret was too wet to sit on. She was already nostalgic for those comparatively carefree days just weeks earlier. Back when an ocean separated them from danger, or so they thought.

The remaining Nolen family stood at the edge of two newly dug holes. An attendant positioned a black umbrella over Reverend Tiller and his Bible. Avery held one over Bess, while his father handled his own. How Vanessa wished she had a magic wand to wave and erase their tragedies, lift their pain away.

A quick survey revealed a few other lone mourners, an occasional couple. Mr. Seward representing his family. Karl Fiske for the hotel. Not a gathering, technically. But a paying of respects. In normal times, she imagined every able-bodied resident of Adamsville would be in attendance.

Shivering, she couldn't help thinking of the funerals she had missed. Her parents'. Their bodies never recovered from the Charles River. Ruth's. Her body taken from the Home while Vanessa slept, buried in a mass grave God knows where.

Her eyes closed as she strained to hear the minister's words.

"Our days on this earth are numbered . . ." Snippets reached her ears. "Joys and struggles . . . in the end . . . called death . . . look back and see . . ."

For a moment, she allowed herself to imagine he was saying them for *her* family. To bring a bit of solace for *her* losses, too. The wind picked up, rustling the birch leaves overhead, and the rest of the minister's words were lost.

After a few moments, Bess cried out and Avery caught her in his arms, letting his umbrella fall. Vanessa blinked back tears as their father moved his umbrella to cover them both. Avery comforted his sobbing sister while Reverend Tiller finished up.

The ceremony concluded, Dr. Nolen patted Avery's shoulder, kissed Bess on the forehead, then headed out of the cemetery and on toward town—away from their house. To the hospital, most likely. Always the hospital.

Gradually, the other mourners let themselves out through the gate, spacing their exits so that they would not get too close to one another. Soon, only Avery and Bess remained at the graveside, once more huddled together beneath his recovered umbrella.

Two men in canvas greatcoats and heavy boots stood at a discreet distance, leaning on their shovels as they cupped hand-rolled cigarettes under their palms, protecting the butts from the rain. She wanted to rush at them, shoo them away. As if postponing the burial would buy Mrs. Nolen and Hattie more time.

Later that evening, Ned shook his head on the other side of the windowpane as Vanessa deposited the last of their supper onto the mat. Lamplight behind him bathed the porch in a soft glow. "You've been working too hard. You need a break."

She jerked upright. "How can you talk about my workload when I just told you about the funeral for Avery and Bess's mother and . . ." Her voice caught. ". . . and little sister?"

Ned ran his hands over his head. "Forgive me. I don't mean to sound callous. It's just that . . . I didn't know either one of them . . . and I'm going a bit stir crazy in here."

"Well, maybe you should drink some more champagne. Get your mind off your troubles." She spun around and headed for the steps.

"Oh, come on, Vanessa!"

She turned and caught him glancing over his shoulder before turning back toward her.

"Don't listen to me." His saucy attitude was gone.

"Don't listen to you?" She steadied herself against one of the porch posts flanking the stairs.

"I told you." His tone was flat and dull. "I'm a spoiled brat who thinks of no one but himself."

"Your words, not mine."

"That's why I need you." His voice dropped further. "To make me a better man."

She frowned and crossed her arms. Every time she thought she had him figured out, he said something unexpected and she wasn't so sure anymore.

"We're birds of a feather, you and I." He gestured for her to return to the window. "Please."

It wasn't his fault the flu was killing people. And that's what was actually upsetting her. Not Ned's misguided efforts to be supportive. With a sigh, she walked back over. He lowered his head near the glass. "Can you keep a secret?"

She thought of the Enchanted Wood and the nymphs who wanted so badly to meet him. "Seems to be my specialty."

"I've been taking walks . . . at night."

Her full attention switched back to Ned. "Going out?"

He nodded with a sheepish look. "By myself, just roaming the woods. No danger to anyone."

"Well . . . I don't suppose there's any harm in that . . ."

"Exactly. I knew you'd see it my way." He ran his finger down the pane, his eyes dancing. "We're not like other people. We play by different rules."

It's what she wanted to hear, wasn't it? That there were options beyond the course set for her by the Girls Home and the uniforms she seemed destined to wear? And that the flu, despite its power, could not reach her?

She glanced toward the front door. "They're going to come for the food any minute now."

"So meet me tonight."

Her head snapped up. "What? No!"

"I don't mean getting close. We'll maintain a healthy distance. Just come. We'll keep each other company. Get our minds off all this death."

"You're crazy. I've got to get back to work." She dashed across the porch, not wanting him to see how appealing his suggestion was.

The autumn had become so bleak that summer memories of kissing Ned by the pond had begun reappearing in her dreams. Recapturing even a fraction of those carefree moments would be a welcome respite from the misery surrounding her in the waking hours.

Chapter Fifty-Eight

Two days after the Nolen funeral, Vanessa headed to the Sewards' house. Mr. Seward had told her the boys were on the mend, and she just wanted to be around some happiness for a change. Their recovery would certainly be cheering everyone up.

Across the lawn, Irene's father left their yard, walking toward the stables. His gait was stiff, like he was sleepwalking or something. He didn't look right. The groundskeeper normally walked like a giant, swinging his arms and legs through the air before him.

Vanessa picked up the front of her skirt and ran toward the Seward's house.

"Irene!" She banged on the back door, then stood on the bench against the wall to peer through the kitchen window. "Irene!"

There was no answer. She pulled her mask from her pocket and tied it on, then opened the door. Quarantine be damned. "Irene!"

Still nothing. Closing the door behind her, she scanned the room. Dirty breakfast dishes were in the sink, the smell of bacon lingered from the heavy skillet still on the stove. A quick glance down the hallway off the kitchen revealed Irene's open bedroom door.

Vanessa walked softly down the hall to the doorway. Irene's brunette waves fanned the pillow on an iron-frame bed beneath the window, her back to the door. "Irene?"

No response.

Vanessa entered the small room, furnished with only the bed and a pine dresser draped with a lace runner. She sank onto the edge of the narrow mattress. Irene's eyes were open, staring at the wall.

She placed her hand on her friend's hip. "What happened?"

After a long moment, Irene blinked. "Nelson's dead." Her voice was flat, dull. Dead like her brother.

Vanessa hung her head. "Oh, Irene." Her eyes misted. "I thought they were doing better."

"I thought they were."

"Frank and Denis?"

"Still weak, but improving. They don't know yet." Irene pulled into a fetal ball. "Pa found him." Her voice was soft and raspy. "He finally thought it was safe to come back. That no one else would be taken."

Silence yawned as Vanessa struggled with the enormity of the Sewards' tragedy. "What can I do?"

No answer.

After several minutes, she rose from the bed and headed for the door.

"Tell Karl."

Vanessa stopped and turned.

"He'll know what to do." Irene crossed her arms and clutched her shoulders. "And check on Pa."

"But, Irene. What about you?"

"I'll be fine. I just need . . . a minute." Her voice was muffled by the wall. "Please. Go."

Chapter Fifty-Nine

Avery rubbed the stubble on his chin on the way to answer the door. He was on leave from work, and avoiding people more than ever, so it hardly seemed worth the effort to shave. When he opened the door to find Vanessa standing at the bottom of the steps, he regretted the decision. She was wearing that damned mask again. What he'd give to see those lips.

"Hello." She was clearly miserable.

"Hello," he replied

"How are you doing?"

The concern in her voice made him rub his chin again. Apparently he looked even worse than he felt. He hadn't slept well since the double funeral. Bess, on the other hand, had barely gotten out of bed. He wouldn't know about his father, who hadn't left his work at the hospital in three days. "Okay. How are you?"

Vanessa's eyes wrinkled, suggesting at least a weak smile under the mask somewhere. "Getting by." She twisted her fingers together. "I've got some bad news."

Avery's hand moved to the doorjamb. He couldn't help sorting people into categories in preparation for her announcement. A ruthless accounting of who mattered to him most. Beyond his immediate family, Irene topped the list, and he knew she'd been tending her sick brothers.

His fingers tightened on the wood. "What is it?"

Tears filmed her eyes. "Nelson died."

"Cripes." Three years younger than Avery, but far bigger and stronger, Irene's youngest brother seemed as indestructible as a man could be. He'd even been a match for his older brother by the time Dewey shipped out.

"The funeral is supposed to be Monday afternoon."

"We'll be there." He could only think of Irene. Was there no mercy in this world?

Vanessa turned to go, then hesitated. "Is there anything you need? Anything I can bring?"

There was that flash again. The resemblance between Vanessa and Hattie. His fists clenched as a sledgehammer of pain slammed his chest. "Just . . . take care of yourself."

Her laughter had a hysterical edge. "How? This flu comes on so fast, any of us could have it already and have no idea."

Hearing her so frightened was worse than acknowledging his own fear of falling ill. "Well, be careful anyway."

Taking a step forward, she lowered her voice. "Did the nymphs say there was anything they could do? Anything at all?"

He shook his head, remembering the last time he'd been to the Enchanted Wood. Only a week had passed, but that visit took place in another lifetime. "Nothing." A bitter laugh burst through his teeth. "For all their beauty, seems they're less magic than we are. Or so they say."

Gazing down, she swished her toe in an arc on the walk. "I'm sure the wood nymphs would have helped if they could."

"I know." He closed his eyes and leaned his head against the door frame. The nymphs were like exotic flowers. It had been folly to hope for assistance from them.

Her foot stilled. "Have you been back there, since . . . everything?"

With a sharp shake of his head, he straightened and opened his eyes. "Can't leave Bess." And, in truth, he wasn't much interested in returning to the Wood without the expectation of meeting Vanessa there, too. "Thank you for bringing the news . . . and for all your help."

She dipped her head. "I'm afraid I'm not actually helping anyone."

His throat clamped. "Just seeing you is more helpful than you know."

The gratitude in her eyes . . . the way her hidden smile made them crinkle above her mask. It was almost more than he could bear. Stepping back, he prepared to close the door. "Take care of yourself," he said for the second time.

"You, too." She turned and headed back down the walkway.

Once she was gone, he rubbed his hands over his face and forced himself to focus on issues he could actually do something about. Turning back toward the stairs, he decided to shower and shave before rousing Bess. They might only be able to talk through the Sewards' front door, but she was going with him to pay their respects—whether she liked it or not.

Chapter Sixty

As Vanessa wandered away from Avery's house, she spotted a sparkle of blue in the bushes along the side of the road. Drawing closer, she realized it was the enormous sapphire butterfly that had led her and the children to Avery back in June, or at least one just like it.

The azure creature took off and landed on the wrought iron fencing that bordered the cemetery. When Vanessa reached the fence, she gripped the bars with both hands and looked over the tombstones. In addition to the soft dirt mounds that marked the Nolen graves, several new ones had appeared. There was no denying it. Sooner, or later, everyone was going to die. They would all end up like Mrs. Nolen and Harriet. Lying in the frigid ground, alone. Her fingers tightened on the cold iron. The only question was when death would arrive.

The butterfly flew over and landed on Hattie's grave.

Tears welled in Vanessa's eyes as its wings pulsed gently above the brown dirt. Dear Hattie. The girl had originally made her think of Ruth. But now, she recognized herself in Avery's auburn-haired sister. The idea that the spirited girl now lay in a coffin, deep within the ground, made Vanessa clutch her throat. Any one of them could fall sick tomorrow. And what living had she done?

She thought of Avery, his solitude, his satchel of beautiful watercolors that almost no one ever saw. Then of Bess, who struggled and fought and got arrested for what she believed in. Yes! Bess lived. She made mistakes, paid a price. But she lived.

The butterfly on Hattie's grave made her think of the Enchanted Wood. How she and Ned had been right in the middle of it when they cuddled on the rock by the pond, unaware of the alternate world surrounding them. Panic squeezed her lungs, making it hard to breathe. She needed to live.

She turned and fled the cemetery, running all the way up the hill to Twin Birch House.

A few hours later, Vanessa hurried to unload the supper dishes onto the Timbers cottage mat. She'd thought of nothing but this moment since fleeing the graveyard. She kept an eye out for movement at the window as she worked, the simple task reinforcing her resolve. Ned finally arrived as she placed the last pot down. She strode over to face him through the glass. "Yes."

His eyebrows rose. "Yes?"

"There's something special you need to see."

"An adventure." He leaned forward with a grin. "I knew you wouldn't let me down."

"Meet me at midnight, by those mossy boulders near the pond."

"I remember them well." He ran his hand over his slicked hair. "Why the change of heart?"

"Life's too short."

Ned nodded, a smile tugging at his perfect lips. "Indeed it is."

Chapter Sixty-One

S hortly after midnight, Vanessa arrived at the boulders. All evening, she'd worried Ned wouldn't be able to perceive the passage, or would be so overwhelmed by the strange new rocks that he'd refuse to venture inside.

Her first concern was addressed immediately. He was already there, hands on his hips and brow creased as he stared at the unfamiliar stones. "This isn't quite how I remember things."

She nodded. "There've been some changes." Pulling her mask over her face, she pointed to the passage entry. "It's a different way to get to the pond."

Scratching his head, he turned around slowly. "Strange."

"Don't worry. I've been through here plenty of times already. You won't believe what's on the other side." Bending over, she headed into the tunnel, sure Ned would follow. He might think the whole thing odd, but she couldn't imagine him resisting his curiosity. Or letting fear keep him from a possible amusement.

"Hey. Wait for me."

She smiled and continued the awkward, crouched journey. After emerging from the passageway, she stretched upright in the Enchanted Wood. A few moments later, Ned stood up beside her and gestured to her mask. "You can take that thing off, by the way." His deep voice still softened her knees. "I'm willing to take my chances."

Neither were sick, and the mask was awful to wear. And that's why she'd brought him, wasn't it? To dare living, rather than cowering in the face of death? Plus, she reminded herself as she reached up to untie the strings, it would remind her to keep a safe distance from him.

"There's that pretty face."

She couldn't help smiling. "Are you physically capable of not flirting?"

"Never cared to find out." Ned winked, then swiveled his head, squinting. "So, this is our pond?"

He switched on the flashlight he'd brought from the cottage. The devices had become fairly common, but she still found them a bit magical, the way they made light without any sort of wire or flame.

"Yes and no. We call it the Enchanted Wood." She smoothed her skirt and scanned the glen. The diffused moonlight washed out the bold colors of the leaves, but the delicate sparkle on every edge gave the Wood a different kind of haunting beauty. The naiads giggled, their constant movement making soft splashing sounds.

Ned's light swept over the trees, bushes, and pond, making everything twinkle as though covered in the lightest of snowfall. She glanced over, hoping to see his eyes widen in wonder. "What do you think?"

Taking a few steps forward, he continued scrutinizing the clearing. "It's a little different, I suppose."

Her breath rushed out in a swoosh. "It is. You see it, don't you?" Powerful memories she'd fought hard to resist now slipped past the barriers she'd constructed. Ned's confusion and hurt at her refusal their last night together. The fairy's promise of a man of sterling and gold. The feel of his fingers sliding up the inside of her leg . . .

"I see . . . something . . ." Moving closer to the pond, Ned's beam raked the nymphs, who dove under the surface in unison.

A light tinkling sound prompted her to reach out to put a hand on his sleeve before remembering herself and stepping back. "Can you hear it?"

He stopped and held still. "Someone's here . . ."

Grinning, Vanessa clasped her hands together. "That's the fairies!"

She circled him at a distance to the opposite side of the pond. He'd successfully entered the Enchanted Wood and there was a good chance her fairy was nearby. Surely, the creature would reveal herself, or give some sign if Ned was actually her intended match.

The pond water was still and undisturbed. Vanessa frowned. "I think the flashlight scared the nymphs away."

Ned directed the beam across the water, then moved it up to Vanessa's face, blinding her. "Fairies and nymphs?"

Holding her palm up to block the light, her voice faltered. "Yes . . ."

"Vanessa . . ."

Her gut knotted. "You said you see it. The difference here."

Sweeping the flashlight around the Wood again, Ned put a hand on his hip. "I see a lot of dew, or something. It's making the leaves sparkle. It's kind of closed-in here, probably trapping the mountain fog."

"But you hear them . . ."

He clicked his light off. "Faraway voices, maybe. Hotel staff, carried on the wind, most likely."

The humiliation of the train platform came rushing back, making her dizzy. She couldn't bear to appear delusional a second time. "Come back, sillies." Her voice rose along with her panic. Why were they doing this? She fell to her knees at the water's edge, keeping her voice light despite the sinking of her heart. "You wanted to meet him."

The nymphs reemerged, swaying in the diffuse moonlight, playing with their long hair. "You brought him." They seemed strangely tentative, almost nervous. "We have to be strong."

"I had no idea you were so shy. Just say hello." Vanessa forced a laugh. "He doesn't bite."

Their eyes drifted to Ned, their voices unusually husky. "But he's so hungry."

"He was able to see the passage and come through." Vanessa glanced up at Ned, reluctant to speak of the fairy and her prophecy before he could even see the nymphs. "It's just possible he's you-know-who."

But she didn't even want Ned anymore, did she? What had seemed so clear when she'd recovered her spirits here in the Wood, laughing with Avery, was now confusing. Murky. What could it mean that everything felt so normal and straightforward with Avery, yet so complicated and emotional with Ned?

"Who are you talking to?" There was an edge of panic in Ned's voice.

"The water nymphs." She offered another forced laugh. "They're concerned you're hungry. You must assure them you've had supper." Returning her attention to the naiads, she clasped her hands in front of her chest. "Please!"

"We didn't think you were bringing him." They began to drift about, nothing like the exuberant dipping and splashing they normally did. Something had changed. But now Vanessa cared less about entertaining Ned and more about making sure he didn't think she'd lost her mind. "Well, I did bring him. So don't disappear when he turns on the light." She couldn't hide the frustration in her voice. "That's all I ask."

Ned backed away, his voice shaky. "You're talking to *yourself*, Vanessa."

The nymphs swept their fingers over the water's surface, their eyes fixed on Ned. "It's up to him to see what he sees."

The tension in Vanessa's chest loosened. "Thank you." Pushing herself to her feet, she faced him and pointed down to the pond. "I know it seems that way, but I'm not, I promise. Just shine the light on the water again. One more time."

"There's nothing there."

"Then what's the harm of looking?"

"And then we'll go?" Irritation overwhelmed the concern she'd first heard in his voice.

"Yes."

Vanessa held her breath as Ned walked back to the edge of the pond and switched the flashlight back on.

"Don't let him touch the water."

Vanessa sucked in her breath and turned toward the familiar voice.

The fairy drifted a few feet away, her hands clasped and brow furrowed. This time a magnificent male also floated at her side, his snow-white hair slicked back.

"We can't stop him." The male's voice sounded like mountain water rushing over granite. "Use whatever influence you have." Moonlight reflected off a silvery cape draped over his shoulder. It was fastened at the neck by a silver filigree clasp, a brilliant emerald at its center.

"My God!" Ned stared at the water, either not seeing or not caring about the fairies. His beam was directed straight down, scanning the bottom of the pond.

"What?" Vanessa turned back toward Ned, still struggling to breathe. "What do you see?"

He kept staring at the water. "Amazing."

"So you see them?" Stepping forward, Vanessa followed his beam as it danced over rocks and pebbles she could now see lining the bottom of the pond. The flashlight was evidently strong enough to reveal what the diffused daylight of the Wood never did. "The nymphs?"

He dropped to one knee and reached his hand toward the surface.

"Don't touch!" She stretched her arm out over the water. "It's dangerous."

He looked up at her, his voice cold and hard. "All right, Vanessa. Whatever you say." Snapping the light off, he stood up. "But it's getting late. We should get back."

The fairies were either gone or invisible to him.

"But did you see them?"

He tucked the flashlight in his coat pocket. "Yes. I saw them."

The ache spreading in her chest called forth every disappointment she'd ever endured. What did the fairies and nymphs gain by raising her hopes, then dashing them? By revealing a magical world to her, and to Avery for that matter, but withholding all magic from their real lives? Her steps were mechanical as she followed Ned back toward the stone passage, ignoring the sound of the naiads splashing and giggling again.

"It's best he never comes back here." The fairy's voice trilled behind her.

Vanessa spun to face the glittering pair. "I don't understand your riddles . . . and your warnings . . . and why you all keep playing with me so . . . cruelly."

"The nymphs do not wish anyone harm." The fairy waved her hand toward the pond. "They simply get overwhelmed by their . . . hunger."

"But they have no power of their own." There was pity in the male fairy's voice. "They can only use what they find in a human's heart to satisfy their needs."

But was his sympathy for the nymphs or the humans? Unable to tell, she rubbed her arms. The naiads were dangerous. Never her friends. Looking around at the deceptive beauty of the Enchanted Wood, she could only manage tiny gasps of air. "I wish I'd never seen this place."

"That may be, but no one here speaks anything but truth." The male fairy's expression was as kind as his face was handsome, and for a moment, he seemed familiar. Like she knew him from somewhere.

"Be well." The female laid her hand on Vanessa's heart. A flood of tingling warmth engulfed her chest, overwhelming the pain and tension she held there. Closing her eyes, Vanessa relaxed into the sense of well-being that surged through her limbs, up her neck and into her head.

When her eyelids fluttered open again, the fairies were gone. Dazed and floaty, she turned toward the stone tunnel, but Ned was no longer in sight.

"Goodbye, Vanessa!" The naiads spoke in myriad voices. "Good luck with your man of sterling and gold!"

Coming back to her senses, she fled to the passage, their laughter nipping at her heels.

Chapter Sixty-Two

"N ed!" Vanessa called out, just catching sight of him in the moonlight ahead. He didn't respond, so she hurried down the mountain path quicker. "Ned, wait!"

With every passing minute, the warmth from the fairy's touch cooled. Finally, he stopped and turned around. "That was quite something." Leaning against a tree, he pulled a bottle of Canadian Club from inside his coat and uncorked the top.

Her jaw clenched. Imported whisky had been banned for a year, but those laws evidently didn't apply to the likes of Ned Cooper . . . or, like so many other rich people, the family's cellar was sufficiently stocked to make the impending Prohibition meaningless. The last of the fairy's warmth disappeared. "It was a mistake to take you there."

He tilted his head back and took a long swig. "A bit late for regrets."

"It's dangerous, Ned. There's something dark there I never saw before." Vanessa's stomach roiled as the nymph's giggles and the male fairy's words rang in her ears . . . "*No one here speaks anything but truth.*"

"Whether you saw the nymphs or not, they're a threat of some sort." She twisted her hands. "A serious one. You should never go back there."

Ned held the bottle out, offering her a drink. "I'm a free man, Vanessa. I'll do as I please."

She crossed her arms, ignoring his gesture. "Like worm your way back into my good graces?"

The wince was quick, but she caught it before he stared at the ground, spreading his feet. "I've always been honest with you, this summer, and since I've been back." He raised his eyes. "But nothing can ever come of this." He swept his hand in a circle encompassing them both. "You must know that."

Of course she knew, but it was still hard to hear spoken aloud. "So that talk of us being birds of a feather, people who play by different rules . . . that was all just to get me to entertain you, to ease your boredom."

He tossed the empty bottle into the ferns. "I do love your passion." He was back in control, his slightly aloof, amused demeanor firmly in place. "But the little talk you just had with your imaginary friends simply confirms my point."

Shaking her head, she leaned against the tree trunk inches from her shoulder. "They're not imaginary." Her voice was hardly more than a whisper. "Avery sees them, too."

Ned's laugh was quick and harsh. "I suggest you both keep that to yourselves."

Her eyes narrowed. She'd known Ned to be careless and self-centered, but never so ugly.

"And, in the spirit of honesty . . ." He rubbed his palm over his hair. "You should know I'm asking Cricket Holmes to marry me once this whole flu nightmare passes." His tone grew soft. "I'm quite sure she'll accept."

Her fingers dug into the rough tree bark. She knew who Cricket Holmes was. Boston royalty . . . and pretty. A perfect wife for the heir to the Cooper fortune. Fairies and nymphs were far more real than her chances of marrying a man like Ned. She no longer wanted to, but the presumption she wasn't worthy to wear his ring shriveled her last remnants of affection for him.

"I'm truly sorry if you regret the time we've had together. I certainly don't." He turned and took a few steps away, then stopped and turned. "And as a sign of my genuine friendship, soon I'm going to give you a real ruby to replace that costume piece you wear."

Vanessa's entire body trembled as she stared down at her ring, bloodred against her pale white skin.

Chapter Sixty-Three

The hallway was dark as Vanessa felt her way along, tiptoeing past the staff kitchen doorway. The shaking had finally abated enough for her to stumble out of the forest, swallowing a fury that tasted of moldy bread.

"Vanessa."

She yelped before covering her mouth. It was Mrs. Juneau, from somewhere inside the darkened room.

"Join me." It was not a request.

Pulling her mask from her pocket, Vanessa stepped into the kitchen, dimly lit by the half-moon framed in the high window, and tied it on.

"It's got to end, you know." Mrs. Juneau's back remained turned.

"Even the plague did, eventually." Vanessa could hear the hysteria under her own short laugh.

"That's not what I'm talking about."

Vanessa sighed and sank into a chair across from Mrs. Juneau's seat. "It never started again, if it's Ned Cooper you mean."

The kettle began to grumble as the water heated.

"Good."

Twisting her ring, Vanessa squeezed her eyes shut. "You know my stone isn't a ruby, don't you?"

Mrs. Juneau turned around, compassion in her voice. "Yes."

"But you didn't say anything."

The older woman folded her hands together. "If you needed that story to make yourself feel special, who am I to take that away from you?" She turned back toward the lightly whistling kettle. "The world doesn't need *my* help snatching dreams from young girls' hearts."

The room gradually lightened as Vanessa's eyes adjusted to the dark. "I've been such a fool."

Boiling water sizzled and hissed as Mrs. Juneau poured a fresh mug of tea. "We all make mistakes. All that matters is whether we learn from them."

Vanessa propped her elbows on the red-and-white-checked tablecloth, cupping her cheeks in her hands. "I guess I'm not the first girl to sit in this kitchen with you in the middle of the night."

Mrs. Juneau placed the hot tea in front of her. "Times change. Girls . . . not as much."

Vanessa clasped her cold fingers around the warm mug, lowered her mask, and inhaled the scent of chamomile for a welcome moment.

"Despite your warning, I reached for the stars." Vanessa's chest tightened as she raised her eyes to Mrs. Juneau's kindly face. "And let my toes lose touch with the ground."

When Vanessa delivered breakfast the next morning, her heart jumped into her throat at the sight of Ned's father in the window. He rapped against the pane with his wedding band, a frown hooding his eyes under heavy brows. She wiped her damp palms against her skirt and walked over.

"Where is he?" Mr. Cooper demanded. "Where's my son?"

Dread mushroomed in her belly. "I . . . I don't know, sir."

He shook his finger at her. "Don't you lie, girl. This is serious."

"I have no idea, Mr. Cooper, I swear!"

The man glanced away, revealing genuine concern behind his bluster.

"Are you sure he's not in the house?" Vanessa peered around him, scanning the room beyond.

"If he was, I damn well wouldn't be asking you, now would I?"

Had something happened to Ned on his way home? "Wh—what do you want me to do?"

"I know you two were thick as thieves. You think we didn't know he was always in here talking to you?"

"I . . . I don't know where he is."

"You lured him out. I know you did!"

Vanessa backed up. "Mr. Cooper!"

He waved his hand in disgust. "Go tell Karl Fiske to get a search party together. I want my boy found."

Vanessa raced across the lawn to find Karl, her stomach knotting at the thought of where Ned might have gone after they parted.

Chapter Sixty-Four

Breathless, she knocked on Karl's office door. "Mr. Fiske? It's Miss Perkins!"

There was no answer and she knocked again. "Mr. Fiske, it's an emergency."

When there was still no response, she opened the door and stuck her head in. "Mr. Fiske?"

He was sitting in his chair, his torso sprawled across the desk. She rushed over. A pool of saliva stained the blotter and his eyes were closed. She shook his shoulder. "Mr. Fiske! Wake up!"

He lifted his head and coughed as he sat up, looking around in a daze. "What happened?"

"You fell asleep on your desk. We need to get you to bed."

Waving his hand, he seemed to have trouble focusing. "I think . . . I might have . . ."

"Shhh. Come on, let me help you." Bending down, Vanessa grabbed his hand and slung his arm around her neck. She stood up, dragging him to his feet. "Let's go. One step at a time."

Once they reached the hallway, she called out as loud as she could, "Mrs. Juneau!"

In a moment, Mrs. Juneau appeared at her office door. "Oh, no." Stopping at the kitchen door, Mrs. Juneau leaned in. "Mabel, get some wet towels and a pot of tea going. Mr. Fiske is ill."

Together, Vanessa and Mrs. Juneau got Karl to the first floor and into his bedroom. They wrestled him out of his coat, vest, and pants, all modesty forgotten in the crisis of the moment. Once he lay down, beads of sweat sprang up on his forehead and another coughing fit overtook him.

Mrs. Reynolds arrived with the towels and tea, her face was so full of sharp angles it seemed made of the local granite. Mrs. Juneau wiped the damp from Karl's face and neck, then tucked the covers under his chin. He'd fallen asleep again.

Vanessa stood back with her hands clasped in front of her and cleared her throat. "I have more bad news."

"What is it?" Mrs. Juneau slid her fingers beneath her glasses and rubbed her eyes as she sank onto the edge of Karl's bed.

"Ned Cooper's gone missing and his father demanded we get a search party going."

Mrs. Juneau swiveled her head toward the cook. "That will be all for now, Mabel. I'll let you know if we need anything."

Mrs. Reynolds's eyes swept to Vanessa, then she bustled from the room making tsking noises under her breath.

"Do you have any idea where he might be?" Mrs. Juneau asked the moment the cook disappeared.

"I swear, I don't!" Vanessa raised her hands. "We met briefly in the woods and went our separate ways. I came directly back . . . and talked with you in the kitchen. I assumed he went back to his cottage. Where else would he go?"

The lie in her question stabbed at her heart. Of course she knew where else he might go. But there was only one other person she could share that fear with, and it wasn't Mrs. Juneau.

With a sigh, the older woman stood and put her hands on her hips. "Go tell Mr. Seward. He'll gather the men . . . the precious few we've got left."

Vanessa headed for the door.

"And be sure to get Avery Nolen to join in," Mrs. Juneau called after her. "He knows the woods around here better than anyone."

Chapter Sixty-Five

A very smiled to find Vanessa at his door yet again. Her visits made the ringing doorbell less painful. He stepped onto the porch, pulling his own mask on to match hers. "I'm glad to see you."

"You too." She backed down the steps. "But I'm afraid something terrible's happened."

His chin sunk to his chest as he heaved a sigh. "Who?"

Her eyes flickered up. "Not the flu." She looked sheepish . . . and worse, frightened. "It's Ned."

It wasn't such a surprise. Avery had known Ned's return spelled trouble of one sort or another. So why did it feel like he'd just been clobbered with a baseball bat? He crossed his arms, tucking his hands beneath his armpits. "What about him?"

"I . . . I took him to the Enchanted Wood." Vanessa twisted her hands. "To meet the nymphs."

Breathing slowly through his teeth, he did his best to react normally. Like the idea of Ned Cooper in the Enchanted Wood didn't bother him in the least. "And . . . that's the terrible thing?"

As Vanessa bobbed her head up and down, her lower lip trembled. Her distress overwhelmed his lingering resentment. "What happened?"

"I don't know, but something bad. We went last night."

The image of Cooper ogling the wood nymphs made him physically ill. He uncrossed his arms, took a step forward, and leaned against the porch railing. "So what happened?" It was a struggle to keep his voice steady.

"Well, once we were there, Ned started acting strange. Like I was crazy for seeing and hearing things. But I think he saw something, too, but didn't want to talk to me about it." She ran her hands over the sides of her head and began to pace. "The fairy appeared, two of them, actually. They said he needed to stay away from the pond. That it was dangerous." Her words flowed faster and faster. "I tried to tell him, after we left. Make him understand. But he said whatever he could to get rid of me. And it worked." She let out a bitter laugh. "He made quite sure I'd leave him alone."

Despite his jealousy, Avery's fists balled at the thought of Ned mistreating Vanessa. The spoiled, selfish fool.

"And now he's missing." She came to a halt, clearly on the verge of tears.

"Missing?"

"He wasn't in the house this morning. Mr. Seward's organizing a search party. But, Avery, I have a bad feeling he went back to the Enchanted Wood. Why else wouldn't he go home?"

"Possibly went to visit another . . . friend?"

She flinched and he felt like a heel.

"Anything's possible." Her chin jutted forward. "Mrs. Juneau said to include you in the search party since you know the woods best."

His teeth ground. There was no decent way to get out of looking for the bastard. "Let me get my coat and tell Bess I'm going out."

"How's she doing?"

"Starting to boss me around again."

Vanessa attempted a smile. "Feeling better then."

He shifted his eyes toward the street, his grief still so raw he couldn't image himself or his family feeling better again. "I know some old timers we should round up, too. There's a lot of territory to cover if he's not in the Enchanted Wood."

"We've searched the grounds thoroughly and found no sign of young Mr. Cooper." Mr. Seward addressed a group of six or seven men and boys. Avery recognized most from the hotel staff and the neighboring farms. A number carried rifles and each stood apart from the others, spreading them across the Sewards' yard. Maybe half wore masks.

"However," the groundskeeper continued, "Ned Cooper's nephew has apparently admitted that our missing young man left the cottage with a pillowcase in the middle of the night, talking of bringing back treasure."

The search party members exchanged glances, as did Clarence Robie and Henry Verville, the snowy-haired pair Avery had recruited from the village. They'd both been timber men in their youths, and he still encountered them out in the woods from time to time.

He looked over at Vanessa, who stared at him pointedly. As much as he wished she were wrong, it was hard not to agree with her theory on Ned's whereabouts.

"Based on the nephew's report, it seems safe to assume that Mr. Cooper was likely under the influence of alcohol, and if all goes well, we'll find him passed out somewhere nearby."

"You thinkin' what I'm thinkin'?" Avery heard Mr. Verville whisper to Mr. Robie, who nodded.

As Mr. Seward began giving out search quadrants to the various teams, Mr. Verville stepped forward. "Me and Henry will take north of Kittredge Creek."

Exactly where the Enchanted Wood was located.

Mr. Seward nodded. "Thanks for helping out."

Avery strode over to stand next to Mr. Verville. "I'll join them."

On the groundskeeper's nod, Mr. Robie swept his hat off and spoke in a low voice. "And sorry about your boys."

Mr. Seward's lips tightened beneath his bushy mustache and his face reddened. He nodded crisply and patted Mr. Robie's shoulder before the two old-timers headed across the yard. Avery glanced back at Vanessa, the weight of an anvil pressing his chest. Her eyes were round, hands clutched at her waist. With lips tight, he gave her a quick wave, then hurried after the old men, who were already marching into the woods.

Every instinct told him he would not like what they would find.

Chapter Sixty-Six

As Avery followed Mr. Robie and Mr. Verville up the mountain path, it occurred to him that every tree, bush, and rock was as familiar as his bedroom furniture . . . and that neither of the old men were doing much searching along the way. Rather, they seemed to be heading somewhere. With every step, he grew more certain of exactly where they were going.

They left the path just where he expected and soon arrived at the mossy boulders he knew so well. Then his feet stopped beneath him.

It was gone.

Normally a wall of stone sloped at least twenty-five feet down the hill and rose well above his head, forming a partial barrier around the Enchanted Wood. Now there was nothing but a small outcropping of granite that could easily be scaled or walked around. There was no sign of the passage at all. The moment that had come to Bess so long ago had finally arrived for him.

Avery leaned on a nearby oak tree, recalling his final departure from the Wood. He'd been angry, frustrated that the nymphs had no advice, no words of wisdom. They just sent him home to his mother's bedside. Tears welled in his eyes. In his heart, he'd known that Willow's goodbye was her last. That something profound had changed between them.

But the events at home had been too overwhelming for him to think about the Wood. Since his final departure, he'd rarely considered Willow, or any of the wood nymphs who'd been his companions for all those years. Nonetheless, the Enchanted Wood's absence left him exposed. No refuge remained to shield his heart from the full force of his father's disappointment in him, from his grief at the loss of his mother and sister . . . and his heartbreak at Vanessa's indifference. The Wood had been his solace, the one place he was always welcome, where he always had sympathetic company.

The other two headed right over the boulders. They knew this place. He was sure of it. Pushing away from the oak, he staggered after them.

Once he'd scrambled over the rocks, he stood in a patch of woods that was at once familiar and completely different. The pond was where it always was. But there were no lily pads. A long, flat stone sat by the edge of the pond, but it was not carved. It had no arms or decoration. And a tree reached for the sky behind the flat rock. But it wasn't a willow. Just a plain old yellow birch.

His knees gave way and he sank onto the rock he'd just climbed over. Willow was gone. He stared around at all the trees. The ordinary trees. Their bark solid and unmoving. No nymph swayed beneath their rough exteriors or leaned out to greet him with waving arms that ended in leafy twigs. And the sound. Nothing but leaves rustling and birds calling in the distance. No hint of laughter, or tinkling voices. Whether they were dead, or merely hidden from his view, the effect was the same. His best friends, his most reliable allies, were gone. His eyes misted as the wound already ripped in his heart tore a few more inches.

His companions walked to the edge of the pond. A matched pair, they put their hands on their waists as they contemplated what they saw. "Yep," he heard Mr. Verville mutter, "just like Ezra."

Avery lifted his glasses and swiped his eyes with his sleeve, pushed himself off the rock, and propelled himself over to the other men. He had to see for himself, though he was nearly certain what they had found. Once he arrived at the water's edge, his insides seized.

Sure enough, Ned Cooper's gray face floated inches below the pond's clear surface. Dark hair waved around his gently bobbing head. His eyes were open and lips pulled back in a macabre smile. Stranger than that, though, was that his naked body was snarled in a tangled web of roots and vines. They circled his torso and limbs, entwined his ankles, and wove around his wrists. Clutched in his left hand, a pillowcase with the Twin Birch House monogram billowed and swayed in the water.

Avery averted his eyes from the corpse, desperate for a distraction. "Who's Ezra?"

"A fella we used to run with, back when we were kids." Mr. Robie pulled his hat off.

Mr. Verville swept his arm around. "Called this place the Fairy Glen."

"After Ezra's pa was killed at Gettysburg, their family was goin' hungry." Mr. Robie rubbed the back of his neck. "His ma needed more help than Ezra wanted to give."

"He was never one for hard work." Mr. Verville shook his head of white hair.

"Then one night his little brother caught him sneaking out of the house in the middle of the night with a sack, promising to bring him back some treasure if he kept his mouth shut."

"It was us who found him in this here pond the next day."

Avery stared at the water. The water nymphs. It had to have something to do with them. There's no way it didn't.

Mr. Rosie nodded. "All bound up, just like this poor fella."

Mr. Verville pointed to the pile of Cooper's clothes. "An' just like Ezra, seems this fella went swimmin' of his own free will."

Avery was grateful not to be in charge. "What should we do?"

"Well." Mr. Rosie scratched the back of his head. "Folks find him like this, bound to generate a lot of talk."

"Whole place would be a curiosity," added Mr. Verville, with a quick glance in Avery's direction.

"A magnet," Avery agreed. He had a distinct sense the men shared his reluctance to have the area become a destination spot.

"But if he was dressed . . ." Mr. Rosie put his hands back on his hips.

"Without them vines . . ." Mr. Verville added.

Avery grasped where they were going. "I'm sure the Cooper family would prefer a simple explanation," he offered.

It was decided. Working quickly and with a minimum of discussion, the three men rolled up their sleeves and untangled the body from the vines' ropey grip. Wrestling the stiff corpse back into the dry clothing was not easy, and he was thankful the old men were there . . . and stronger than they appeared.

Between them, they managed the task, then lowered Cooper back into the water to wet his clothes before lying him on the ground beside the pond. While the older men rolled down their sleeves and pulled their coats back on, Avery stared around the glen once more, tears welling in his eyes.

Mr. Verville put a hand on his shoulder. "When I was a child, I spake as a child, I understood as a child, I thought as a child: but when I became a man, I put away childish things."

The old man's hazel eyes were full of compassion and Avery was sure the old man knew why he was so sad. He glanced over at Mr. Robie, who was looking at him with the same sympathetic expression. Seemed they all knew the pain of losing the Wood.

"Corinthians 13:11," Avery whispered.

Mr. Verville nodded and Avery understood. It was time for him to put away childish things.

"I'll stay. Make sure no critters mess with him." Mr. Robie settled onto the granite slab that used to be an ornate stone bench.

After giving Avery's shoulder a quick pat, Mr. Verville headed back the way they came. Avery took one last glance at Mr. Robie's expressionless face and Ned Cooper's corpse, then followed.

Hours later, Avery and three boys from the Twin Birch Farm lowered the stretcher handles to the wooden floorboards of the Timbers' front porch. Relieved of the heavy load, he stood up and arched his back. It was almost sundown, and his stomach was as empty as his muscles were sore.

The acting police chief stood at the window talking to Ned's stricken father through the glass. The old man had come out of retirement to take over the decimated force when the current chief and three of its four officers joined the Army.

"Between the empty bottle of Canadian Club and the discovery of your son's body in the pond, it looks like a pretty clear case of accidental drowning, Mr. Cooper." The chief rubbed the sides of his generous belly. "But we can open an investigation if you are in any way dissatisfied with this explanation." The chief's hand rose to his neck. "Though, I must warn you . . . with resources as challenged as they are due to the war, and matters made even more difficult by this blasted influenza, I can't make any promises about how much time such an investigation might take . . ."

"No, no, Chief. I'm sure that's what happened." Ned's father's voice dripped with disappointment and disgust with his son.

A twinge of sympathy for his rival pinched Avery's gut.

"No need to trouble you and your men any further." The powerful man's tone had an air of finality.

"Good decision, sir," said the chief. "To do more would no doubt be fruitless, and simply prolong the suffering for you and your family."

Mr. Cooper pursed his lips, clearly unmoved by the chief's self-serving words of comfort. "Will you be sending the undertaker?"

"He's already been summoned." The chief pressed his hat back on his head. "Though, like everyone else, he's pretty overwhelmed."

"We won't be needing a burial. Just a coffin. We're returning to Boston in the morning." Mr. Cooper tucked his chin. "Seems the grim reaper doesn't need the flu to do his dirty work."

The chief bowed his head. "I understand. And if I haven't already said it, please know we're all sorry for your loss."

He turned and crossed over to Avery and the other young men lingering on the steps, awaiting instruction. "Thanks for your help, boys. The hotel has invited you to stay for supper, so go on over."

Avery stared down at the corpse. He'd been so caught up in the loss of the Wood and the logistics of getting the body down the mountain that he'd been blocking the true horror of the situation. He never liked the guy, but that didn't mean he wished Ned Cooper dead. Much less murdered. A fate Willow had protected him from. Another gift he'd never thanked her for.

Despite the rigors of the day, Avery lost his appetite. He willed his stiff legs to carry him down the porch steps and over to Mrs. Juneau, who stood with hands clasped, her face pale. He could depend on her to deliver his goodbye to Vanessa.

Tonight, he needed to be alone. To mourn his own losses.

Chapter Sixty-Seven

Sitting on the stone bench, Lachima stared at the dead leaves covering the patch of ground between the passageway and the pond. Morniero sat beside her, silent and brooding, while Willow hovered over her shoulder, leafy fingers knotted over her chest. She wasn't alone, but the company of her brother and the wood nymph provided no comfort.

All she'd wanted was to speed things up. Move Vanessa past the sorrows of her childhood. Intervening always had unintended consequences. Every time. And Atroporta's decisions were final. Once she cut a mortal's life thread, there was no restoring it.

"You were right." Lachima shook her head. "I never should have spoken to Vanessa."

"Ezra was poor. An easy target." Morniero kicked at the leaves. "Ned should have resisted the bait."

Lachima bowed her head. As Ned's thread twisted toward the moment of shining his flashlight into the nymph's pond, she hadn't seen the true depth of his dissatisfaction. His desire to be free of his father's money . . . and the control it gave him over Ned's life. But the naiads had seen it. Taken advantage of it.

Turning to her brother, Lachima straightened her back. "This wasn't how I hoped things would go, but we're back where we needed to be." Her voice quaked. "Hidden from those with the power to harm us."

"Thank you for letting me say goodbye." Willow's grief was only made more poignant by her gratitude.

Lachima laid her hand on the wood nymph's shoulder, wishing the comfort she and humans provided one another extended to creatures beyond the mortal world. Willow wiped the sap from beneath her eyes, her smile crooked. Removing her hand from Willow's shoulder, Lachima turned back to face the blanket of dry, curling leaves at her feet.

She and Morniero were in this together. He'd taken the risk to join her here, far from their only remaining comfort—their family's embrace. It was past time she treat him as the partner he'd proven to be.

"So." She tilted her face toward his. "Any thoughts on what we should do about the naiads?"

Chapter Sixty-Eight

The clip-clop of horses' hooves descending Twin Birch's driveway marked the police chief's departure from the Timbers cottage, and Vanessa was sent up with supper. Tears blurred her eyes. Ned's body had been found in a pond. That's what Mrs. Juneau had announced to the staff. Drowned.

She'd also told her Avery went home. That he would visit tomorrow.

Even without Avery to confirm it, Vanessa knew. There was only one pond Ned would have gone to after leaving her. One pond so dangerous that even touching the water was to be avoided. No wonder Avery left the grounds as soon as he could. His irreplaceable retreat had been desecrated . . . and it was her fault. She'd been a pox on both their lives.

After arriving at the base of the Timbers' porch, she lowered the wheelbarrow handles and picked up the first dish. Though her love for Ned had been thoroughly extinguished, now that his life had been cut short, she found herself recalling her fondest memories of him. Their first conversation at the pony corral. Reading books together on the bench in the lares' garden. The taste of his kisses mingled with the smell of lilacs. He'd been so vibrant. His life so full of promise. Tears spilled past her lashes. How could he be dead?

Something moved down the porch. "Oh!" She almost dropped the platter of roasted turkey on the mat.

Ned's father was sitting in one of the cane rockers on the porch. "Sorry to startle you." He was wrapped in a cashmere coat, a black derby on his head.

She set the tray down, then rubbed the tears from her cheeks and swiped her dripping nose with her sleeve. "I just wasn't expecting you out here, Mr. Cooper. That's all." Groping in her pocket for her mask, she backed away.

"It's harder to be stuck inside day and night than you might think." He gestured down the porch. "And somebody's got to stay with him until the coffin arrives."

Vanessa's eyes followed his finger to Ned's blanket-covered corpse, lying under the window where they used to talk. She covered her mouth with both hands.

"That's my son." Mr. Cooper's voice cracked.

Vanessa nodded, mute, as he took out a handkerchief and blew his nose. Seeing the body made Ned's death unavoidably real. It took all her strength not to go over and lift the sheet. How she wished she would find out the person under there was a stranger. That it had all been a big mistake. That Ned had gone to some bar after leaving her. Or had snuck into some local girl's bedroom and fallen asleep. She didn't care, just as long as he wasn't dead. But she knew it was all a fantasy. That Ned's body really was under that cloth—because she'd taken him to meet the naiads.

"I'm . . . I'm sorry." She hurried back to the wheelbarrow for the next load, concentrating on the work to avoid looking at either the grieving father or the draped corpse.

"I also wanted to speak with you." Mr. Cooper's voice was stronger now.

"Me?" She lowered the pot of vegetable stew to the porch floor, her stomach tensing.

"My son was a drunk, Miss Perkins."

"Excuse me?"

"He was a womanizer and ne'er-do-well with too much money. Despite all that, the one thing he never did was take leave of his senses."

"Yes, sir." Why was he saying all this?

Mr. Cooper reached into his coat and pulled out a narrow leather folder and pen. "I'd like to ensure that whatever . . . unusual . . . behavior you might have seen Ned exhibit before his untimely death, you keep it to yourself."

The blood rushed to her head as he flipped the checkbook open. Fury burned away her tears. "There's no need for that."

"Oh, I think there is. You're not the first to chase my son's wallet. I'd like you to feel your efforts were a success, so you find no reason to make up any losses, so to speak."

"I wasn't after some payoff from Ned. I wanted to marry him."

"Marry him?" He spit the words out like they were bits of rotten fish on a spoonful of lemon sorbet.

She drew herself up. "Yes. And there was a time when he did nothing to discourage my illusions."

His tone darkened. "Are you with child, girl?"

"No!" She clutched her hands together, stretching the skin across her knuckles as she focused on the porch floorboards. "I learned, of course, that our marriage was as unimaginable to Ned as it is to you. But I was crazy about him this summer . . . maybe too crazy." She raised her head to meet his eyes. "I want nothing from you, Mr. Cooper, especially your hush money."

She started to leave, then turned back. "And unlike you, it wouldn't have occurred to me to run him down the way you just did, regardless of what I thought or how much he hurt me."

He was still staring at her, open-mouthed, when she turned and marched down the stairs. Picking up the wheelbarrow handles, she headed back to the hotel, a pumpkin pie bouncing at the bottom of the cart.

No wonder Ned was so cynical. Maybe being raised in some families was worse than having no family at all. Vanessa's steps slowed along with her breath. If the Coopers and Gardners were leaving, she'd be out of a job tomorrow. Might as well spend the evening with people who deserved something sweet.

Abandoning the wheelbarrow, she picked up the pie and marched across the grass toward the Sewards' house.

Chapter Sixty-Nine

Avery took the long way home in a failed attempt to clear his head, then dragged himself up the front walk, every muscle in his body stiff and sore.

"Any luck?" Bess took a drag from her cigarette. She was buried in his old pea coat, sitting on the porch in the dark.

"You should smoke in the back, at least. Give the neighbors less to gossip about."

"I don't give a hoot what the neighbors think." Bess conjured a bright, fake smile he'd come to know well.

Sinking into the wooden chair behind her, he gazed out toward the road. "I'd hardly describe finding Cooper as lucky."

Her voice fell. "Tell me."

"Drowned."

She barked out a bitter laugh. "Creative alternative to bullets or the flu."

"Yeah." He sighed and dropped his face into his hands.

"Aave. What's wrong?"

"Tough day, that's all."

For a moment, all he heard was the sizzle of her cigarette.

"The lake?"

Ned Cooper's dead face reappeared before his eyes. "The pond."

"*The* pond?"

"Yep." His voice cracked.

"Spill, Aave."

The tenderness in her voice was what broke him. If she'd been her usual hellcat, he could have kept hold of himself. The downside of being a twin. "It's gone."

He heard Bess get up, then felt her hand on his shoulder. "The Enchanted Wood?"

Silent tears leaked from his eyes as he nodded.

"Oh, Aavey, Aavey. I'm so sorry."

"It's like it never existed."

"I'm glad you had it as long as you did." She caressed the back of his head.

He stared back at the road. "Vanessa could see it. And things I didn't even know were there."

Bess's hand stopped moving. "You took *her* there?"

"She found it on her own. Nothing to do with me. Then she took Cooper, and the rest is history."

Bess lowered herself into the porch chair next to his. "You think she had something to do with . . . what happened to Ned?"

"No!" His hands balled into fists. "Not intentionally, anyway."

She stared up at him a moment, then sat back, her gaze moving to the front gate. "If you say so."

He ran his hands through his hair as he rose. "I do."

"I like her, too." She took another drag. "But the girl's been nothing but bad news for you . . . and Ned."

His body tensed and his blood pounded in his ears. "Don't, Bess. Just don't."

He slammed the door on his way in, not sure who he was angriest with—Vanessa for disappointing his hopes, his sister for speaking against her, or himself, for falling in love with the light-footed girl with sapphire eyes when he should have known better.

Chapter Seventy

The next morning, Vanessa's breath came out in white puffs as she hiked the path up the mountainside. Her work at Twin Birch House was finished. Mrs. Juneau confirmed it at breakfast. Like the other workers whose employment had ended, she was welcome to room and board until the travel restrictions eased, but there'd be no more pay.

She arrived at what used to be the entryway to the Enchanted Wood and stopped cold. It was gone. Completely transformed. A sodden cloak of sorrow pressed her shoulders as she made her way around the sloping rocks, stepping over them when they got low enough to scale. The wood and pond were still beautiful, but the magic was gone. It was the end of a dream.

Hardly a surprise. She'd told the fairies she wished she'd never seen it, after all. Sinking onto the flat rock that sat where the carved stone bench had been, she stared into the murky pond water, now choked with loose vines and thick roots. Closing her eyes, she tried to ignore thoughts of Ned's drowned body floating there. What it must have looked like.

The hard granite chilled her bottom through her coat and skirt. She pulled her knees up, wrapped her arms around them and stared into the cloudy water, mourning them all. Poor, dead Ned, who might have been a better man if he'd had a better father. Nelson, and Hattie, and Mrs. Nolen. She grieved on behalf of Irene . . . and Mr. Seward, who lost more family than anyone should. And Mrs. Juneau, who passed every year without her beloved Pierre. For Bess and Avery . . . and for herself. A stupid, flighty twit who made the same mistakes over and over again.

After her bleak tour of all those who had suffered so much, she got up and took a few wooden steps to the edge of the pond. Closing her eyes, she sank to her knees amongst the dead leaves as she imagined the nymphs laughing and playing in the sea of lily pads. They'd just been using her . . . to feed their hunger. Shame burned her cheeks. There had been warnings. Signs their motives were selfish.

But had she been so different? Driven by her past hunger . . . and fear of it returning. Thinking only of her future with Ned, while Gladys worried herself sick. Going to the Gardners, when the Wainwrights deserved better. Trying to stuff herself with "life" by taking Ned to the Wood, already knowing his charisma was as enticing and dangerous as the gingerbread house that lured Hansel and Gretel into the clutches of the witch.

And Ned had been driven by hunger, too, hadn't he? Hunger for riches. For it was treasure he saw in the pond. Wealth he could carry in a pillowcase. Despite everything he already had, he'd needed more. And needed it all for himself, refusing to share what he'd seen with her.

Everything but one promised ruby, that is.

Her own folly had no doubt closed the Wood to her. All she could hope was that it hadn't cost Avery his sanctuary as well.

Nelson's funeral that afternoon was as agonizing as Mrs. Nolen and Hattie's had been. Irene stood alone with her defeated father, the two remaining boys still too weak to leave the house. The weariness in Reverend Tiller's voice made it sound like he was losing faith in the words he'd read too many times over the graves of those too young to go.

Worse though, Avery never showed up. Bess and Dr. Nolen had made a quick appearance, arriving together, straight from the hospital. As soon as the ceremony ended, they had said their condolences and hurried back down the road.

If they'd noticed or found it odd that Avery wasn't there, they gave no indication. Maybe they thought he'd been there earlier. Their apparent lack of concern was somewhat comforting, but something still didn't sit right. She hadn't seen him since he'd departed from the Sewards' yard with the two old men. Only a day had passed, but it seemed like much longer. And he hadn't come by in the morning either, like Mrs. Juneau had said he would.

After squeezing Irene's hand and Mr. Seward's arm, she left the graveyard and crossed the street. The Nolens' walkway was visible from the cemetery gate and she hurried for it.

The headline of the newspaper on the front porch read,

"Allied Forces Gaining Ground!"

Thank God. Maybe there was an end in sight to the carnage overseas.

No one answered the bell, so she knocked. Still no answer. It made no sense. If he'd been at the hospital, he would have come with his sister and father. It was quite possible he'd lost the Wood, too, and even blamed her. But however upset he might be with her, he'd never skip Nelson's burial just to avoid her. He was a far bigger man than that. So why wasn't he there?

She sat on the top step and gripped the edge of the porch, the rough plank digging into her palms as she scanned the empty yard and road beyond. Closing her eyes, she pretended he was there, sitting next to her. Like he'd sat with her so many times on the stone bench. She could almost feel his finger against her lips. "*Shhhhhh. Just listen.*" That's what he'd said. A tear slipped down her cheek as she quieted her thoughts and listened.

The rapid clicking of a squirrel's claws on a nearby tree as it wound its way up the trunk. Horse hooves on the hard-packed dirt road somewhere around the bend, out of sight. The caw of a crow up in the trees in the next yard over. A cough.

Her eyes flew open. Another cough. She sprang to her feet and hurried to the middle of the walkway. Clamping her hat to her head, she turned and looked up toward the second-floor windows. More coughing . . . from inside the house. "Avery!"

She flew up the porch steps and opened the unlocked door. "Avery?" The front parlor to the right and dining room to the left were deserted. She ran up the stairs, following the sound of coughing. It was coming from the room at the end of the hall, with its door open.

Rushing in, she found him lying in his bed. His face was the color of a pink rose, his sheet soaked in sweat. "Avery, you're sick." She hurried to his side. Even flushed with fever, he was handsome in a way she'd never seen before. And his bare shoulders were so much more muscled than she would have imagined.

He grimaced up at her. "Get back." Rolling on his side, he succumbed to another coughing fit.

Glancing around the room, she felt for a moment like she was back in the Wood. The walls were covered with his watercolors of the wood nymphs, the pond, the flowers. He had them arranged by season, so she got to see how it looked in winter, when everything was silver and white.

She tore her eyes from the paintings and ran downstairs to the kitchen, flinging cabinets and drawers open until she had a pot to fill with water and clean dishtowels to wipe his face with. She grabbed an ice pick from the drawer and pulled the ice from the icebox. "You will not die, Avery. You will not die." Directing all her fear into the pick, she slashed and chipped at the ice until she had enough to fill a dishtowel.

Back upstairs, she ignored Avery's protestations as she slipped the bundle of ice behind his neck, then began wiping his face, chest, shoulders, and arms with cool water she'd brought from the kitchen. He was too weak to put up any meaningful resistance. "I was fine last night . . ." He licked his lips and took a breath. "But woke up this way."

"We need to get you to the hospital."

"There's nothing . . . they can do."

Squeezing excess water into the pot, she shook her head. "Your family's there. It's where you need to be."

Chapter Seventy-One

Vanessa hated leaving Avery, but there was no way to get him to the hospital without help. Her side had a stitch from running all the way from the Nolens' house as she bounded up the institution's steps. Inside the heavy front door, she grabbed the arm of a nurse rushing by, her arms full of folded sheets. "Please, I need your help!"

The frazzled-looking woman turned to Vanessa without a word.

"Dr. Nolen's son is sick. I need help getting him here."

"Avery?" The woman's exhausted face fell.

Irritation constricted her throat. "Yes. Who can help me bring him here?"

"Mrs. Donnally's been taking the wagon . . ."

"Excellent. Where can I find her?"

The nurse shrugged vaguely. "She's been sleeping in Dr. Nolen's office . . ."

"Where is that?"

"Last door on the right." The woman pointed her finger, then turned and hurried off in the direction she was originally heading. Vanessa rushed down the corridor.

A stocky redhead lay sleeping on the sofa in Dr. Nolen's office. "Mrs. Donnally?"

Rolling over, the middle-aged woman blinked her eyes in sleepy confusion. "Yes?"

"We need to bring Avery Nolen in. He's sick."

With a heavy sigh, Mrs. Donnally swung her feet to the ground. "Alright, dearie, let's go."

As Vanessa followed the exhausted wagon driver down the hallway, she glanced inside a patient's room and bit her lip. Two cots were crammed in next to the two beds, and all four contained young people, in their late teens to mid-twenties. A boy with thick blond hair was the color of a blueberry milkshake.

"Vanessa?" Avery's sister stood in the doorway of another room. It looked like Bess had lost ten pounds since she'd last seen her. She was wearing a kitchen apron over her clothes, which only partially protected them from the blood spattered across her front, and there were black circles under her eyes. "What are you doing here?"

"It's Avery."

Bess's face drained of what little color it had and her head shook back and forth. "No. No. No."

"We're bringing him here right now."

Bess reached behind her back and began fumbling with her apron strings, still shaking her head. "No, no, no, no."

"You stay here." Vanessa backed away. "Mrs. Donnally and I can do it."

Before Bess could respond, Vanessa turned and ran after the quickly striding woman, who pushed through the hospital's back door, flooding the hallway with sunlight.

"Is he upstairs?" Mrs. Donnally halted the horses in front of the Nolens' gate.

Vanessa nodded.

"Then we'll have to walk him down. Stretcher's too hard to keep flat on the way down the stairs."

"Whatever you say." Vanessa jumped down from the wagon bench. The woman's authority made her insides relax, even if the only problem she solved was the mechanics of getting Avery to the hospital. She didn't want to think of the horrors she'd seen there.

Vanessa led Mrs. Donnally into Avery's bedroom, trapping a whimper of relief in the back of her throat. He was flushed with fever . . . but still alive.

"Hello there, Mr. Nolen," boomed Mrs. Donnally behind her. "Let's get you over to the party, shall we?"

His eyes fluttered open, his voice weak. "I don't want to go." He tried to scoot himself up on his elbows but collapsed onto his back.

"There, there. Aren't you the kitten?" Mrs. Donnally cooed as she threw back the covers without ceremony. His plaid-flannel pajama bottoms were soaked with sweat, clinging to his legs. She leaned over and grabbed him under his arms, lifting him to a sitting position. "Git over here, lass," she called over her shoulder. "Can't do this by myself."

Clamping her jaw shut, Vanessa hurried over and lifted Avery's feet over the edge of the bed.

"I'm cold," he murmured, hunching his bare shoulders.

Vanessa tugged open dresser drawers and rifled through them until she found his flannel pajama top. She and Mrs. Donnally wrestled him into it, then pulled thick socks and boots onto his feet. Once they got him standing up, they draped his blanket around him and folded his arms around each of their necks.

"All righty. Time to get you down those stairs, sure."

On the way out, Vanessa took his wool coat from the hook by the door and wrapped it on top of the blanket already over his shoulders. Getting him into the back of the wagon was no easy task, as the bed was a good four feet off the ground. After awkwardly pushing and folding his body onto the rough wooden planks, Vanessa climbed up with him. Enfolding him in her arms, she held his head against her chest while Mrs. Donnally closed the rear gate and mounted the driver's seat.

Avery mumbled into Vanessa's jacket. "My father . . ."

"Will want you nearby so he can tend to you."

Looking down at his dark lashes against his feverish cheeks, Vanessa realized they'd forgotten his spectacles in his bedroom. His naked face looked so open and unprotected. She called up to Mrs. Donnally, "His glasses! We forgot his glasses!"

"He needs to get out of this cold. You can fetch them for him later." She clicked at the horses to get them going.

Vanessa stroked Avery's damp hair away from his face. "I'll come back and get them for you. I promise."

"You're my angel." He gazed up at her with a smile that would have seemed drunken in different circumstances.

As his eyes drifted closed, Vanessa's heart did a somersault in her chest.

Vanessa and Mrs. Donnally pushed their way in the hospital's back door, Avery's wobbly legs barely shuffling between them.

"Bed for Avery Nolen!" Mrs. Donnally shouted as they entered the hallway.

"In here!" Bess stepped from a patient's room and gestured them in. There was barely enough space to walk between the room's two beds and the cot set up between them. The man in the other bed and the two children on the cot were either sleeping or watched through half-closed, glassy eyes. Vanessa didn't want to think about what happened to the bed's former occupant as she and Mrs. Donnally got Avery stretched out on the fresh sheets. With all the coming and going of patients, the hospital ran a lot like a hotel.

Vanessa gripped Mrs. Donnally's arm. "Thank you."

"Pleasure, pet." She smoothed her crumpled skirt. "You just take good care of him."

"We will," said Bess before Vanessa could reply.

Avery's eyes were shut again, his breathing labored.

"It was that stupid search party that did this to him." Bess tucked the covers around her brother in sharp, jerky movements. "Traipsing around in the cold for hours."

Vanessa hung her head. The search party she'd dragged him into.

"Tell my father he's here." Bess's order was clipped, her mouth tight.

Glad to get away from Bess's fury, Vanessa hurried back into the hallway. Disoriented, she went down a few wrong hallways before she found Dr. Nolen's office again. This time it was Avery's father stretched out on the sofa. How was it possible they'd been running themselves ragged down here and no one knew about it at the hotel?

"Catherine," Dr. Nolen cried in his sleep. "Catherine!"

Vanessa frowned. What blows he's been dealt, and now more bad news. Calm again, he rolled onto his side. Standing at the arm of the ancient leather couch, she considered his profile, imaging what Avery would look like as he aged. They had the same nose.

Giving the doctor a few more moments of peace, she focused on the colorful illustrations on the walls. They revealed the inside of the human body—the skeleton, digestive track, and nervous system. Both father and son surrounded themselves with beautiful images reflecting their passions. She reluctantly turned to the sleeping doctor again. "Dr. Nolen." She shook his shoulder gently. "Dr. Nolen."

He sat up with a start. "Huh!"

"I'm sorry." She backed away. "I didn't mean to startle you."

He groped for his spectacles on the low end table. "What is it? Why'd you wake me?"

"It's Avery. He's got the flu."

Dr. Avery's hand froze in the middle of wiping his glasses with his handkerchief. In a moment, he resumed rubbing. "He's here?"

She nodded. "Mrs. Donnally and I brought him."

"He told us you hike with him."

Not exactly. "We both . . . enjoy the woods."

He put the glasses on and peered up at her, his salt-and-pepper hair rumpled. "You've been a good friend to him."

The image of the stripped-down, ordinary clearing where the Enchanted Wood used to be flashed before her eyes. "I'm not so sure about that."

Dr. Nolen shook his head as he rose with a grunt. "I'm sure. The boy's always been particular about the company he keeps." He staggered toward the door. "Spends too much time out there, all alone."

Chapter Seventy-Two

The following afternoon, the staff kitchen smelled of chicken soup and fresh baked bread. "Working your magic again, Mrs. Reynolds?" Vanessa sniffed the air from the doorway. "No one could make food that smelled this good without supernatural help."

Scowling, the craggy-faced cook turned from the stove and gestured for her to sit down. "You don't need to flatter me into feeding you, girl."

When had she last eaten, anyway? She'd been taking turns with Bess at Avery's side all night and well into the morning. His twin was still giving Vanessa the cold shoulder but had grudgingly begun to accept her help. When a new influx of patients showed up, Bess even left her alone with him for over an hour when she'd gone to help the nurses craft more makeshift beds.

Vanessa tossed a pile of newsprint flyers on the table where Mrs. Juneau and Irene hunched over soup bowls. "These are from Reverend Tiller, since church services have been canceled."

Irene pulled one of the sheets toward her and scanned its contents. "His last few sermons."

"Times like these test the faithful, yet attract new converts," said Mrs. Reynolds with a shake of her head.

"No doubt." Vanessa settled into a chair across from Mrs. Juneau and Irene. "How's Mr. Fiske doing?"

"The same." Mrs. Juneau's brow wrinkled. "Where were you last night? We were worried."

The cook pulled on her mask and crossed the kitchen with a bowl of soup and a roll. Vanessa sat back for the woman to place the meal in front of her. "Avery's been struck by the flu."

Irene's spoon stopped halfway to her mouth. "Avery, too?"

She nodded. "I helped get him to the hospital, then stayed there through the night." Fear for Avery and the idea that someone had missed her and worried brought a lump to Vanessa's throat. "Sorry I didn't get word to you."

Irene's face slackened and she lowered the spoon, her dull eyes focused on the center of the table.

"Thank God Denis and Frank are on the mend." Mrs. Juneau fixed her gaze on Irene, her tone pointed.

Irene managed a hint of a smile. "Yes."

"So, let's not give up hope on anyone, shall we?"

Nodding mutely, Irene made another attempt at getting some soup in her mouth.

Chasing thoughts of Nelson from her mind, Vanessa turned to Mrs. Juneau. "The hospital is desperately shorthanded. It's overflowing with folks from all over the county and the staff are dead on their feet. I'm going to stay there a bit longer . . . and thought maybe the hotel could help."

Mrs. Juneau set down her mug with a frown. "What else do they need?"

"Just about everything. Sheets, towels, food, coffee."

"Irene, tell your father to bring the wagon around. Mabel, pull whatever we can spare from the pantry. I'll get the linens." She rose. "Why on earth didn't Dr. Nolen send word?"

"He's not exactly himself . . ."

The doctor had stopped by Avery's bed every few hours, but there was nothing he could do that the nurses and volunteers couldn't do just as well. All that could be done for the flu victims was to try to keep their temperature down and liquids in them.

Other than that, it seemed only God knew which ones would pull through and which would turn blue and drown in their own fluids.

Vanessa clung to the wooden seat as Irene clicked at the team of horses pulling the wagon down the hotel drive. "How's your father holding up?"

Her friend shrugged. "Eating again. That's something."

"I wish you had let me help . . . with your brothers."

"You tended to Pa. That was plenty."

"I hardly did anything. Brought him coffee, what little news there was. You did the hard work." Vanessa shuddered. "One day in the hospital and I'm ready to curl into a little ball."

"I like taking care of people." Irene guided the horses onto the road at the end of the drive. She threw a nervous glance at Vanessa. "Even applied to nursing school in Boston, but you can't tell anyone."

"Nursing school? But, what about your fiancé? Aren't you getting married when Roy gets back?"

Irene's jaw tightened. "There's no guarantee he's coming back. I have to accept that."

"Oh, Irene!" She reached over and squeezed her friend's arm. "He'll be back. You have to believe that."

"I can believe anything I want. But nobody knows when this horrible war will end, or if he's even alive right this very minute. I've got to be prepared for anything."

Vanessa couldn't fathom leaving a family behind by choice. "What about your father? Your brothers . . ."

"If Roy doesn't come home, I couldn't stay here." Irene glanced around at the farms and village homes on the outskirts of Adamsville. "There isn't a single place I can look that doesn't remind me of him. Of something we did together."

"Oh . . ." Vanessa's mind drifted to Avery as they passed his house. How would it feel to see its clapboard sides and charming front path, knowing he was dead? And he was only a friend, not a fiancé. She glanced at Irene's stoic profile, then shot her hand out to grab her friend's arm. "Wait! I almost forgot. I need to get Avery's glasses for him."

Running up the Nolens' walkway a few moments later, Vanessa clenched her jaw. Avery would get better and need them again. He would.

Chapter Seventy-Three

After looking in on Avery, whose condition was unchanged, Vanessa took a hard look around. As anticipated, the supply delivery had delighted the overwhelmed staff and volunteers. Irene was already helping tend patients, but the thought of all those bodily fluids made Vanessa's stomach lurch. There had to be something else she could do to help.

It was clear the chaos at the hospital was partly due to overcrowding and exhaustion. But part of it was caused by inefficiencies that Twin Birch House would never tolerate. The kitchen had a terrible layout, with incoming traffic constantly bumping into outgoing. The laundress was forced to twist the water from wet sheets by hand due to an inadequate wringer. Patients requiring frequent monitoring were in distant rooms from the nurses' station, while people who could be left alone for longer were housed closer. She could just imagine Mrs. Juneau and Karl shaking their heads and clucking their tongues. Unfortunately, most of the problems were beyond her ability to fix.

Discouraged, Vanessa headed back toward Avery's room to check on him again. As she passed the supply room, she glanced in to see a petite nurse on her toes, reaching into the back of a cabinet. She was bathing thermometers in alcohol, then restocking a canister sitting behind some bulky surgical equipment.

Vanessa stopped. Thermometers were used all the time. Why were they in the back of the cabinet? Mrs. Juneau wouldn't have approved such a poor arrangement at the hotel. Once the nurse left, Vanessa slipped in and hurriedly reorganized the offending shelves, finishing just as the supply room door opened. She stood back with crossed fingers when Nurse Hutchins entered, bags under her eyes.

The nurse headed straight for the cabinet, opened the door, and reached in. "Oh!" In apparent surprise and confusion, her arm knocked against the container of thermometers now conveniently placed at the front of the shelf.

Vanessa's hands flew to her mouth as the thermometers exploded on the linoleum floor. Nurse Hutchins jumped back with a yelp and they both stared down at droplets of mercury skittering around amidst shards of glass.

"I am so, so sorry."

The woman raised her red-rimmed eyes. "You did this?"

"I . . . I thought it might be easier for you. Better than always having to reach past the stuff you don't use as much."

And now you see why they were placed at the back of the cabinet." Nurse Hutchins's voice trembled.

Vanessa nodded, misery swelling in her throat. "I didn't think about that."

"You'd best get out of here." The nurse's shoulders slumped as she waved her hand. "That mercury is toxic . . . I've got to get it cleaned up . . . and re-sort the shelves."

"Can I help?"

"No. Please." Nurse Hutchins gestured with her hand. "Just leave."

Vanessa teetered away from the supply room, her shoulder bumping along the wall. What an idiot. Her nails dug into her palms as the words of the Home's matron rang in her ears. *"Silly, flighty girl. Get your head out of the clouds and make yourself useful."*

"Miss Perkins!" It was a dark-haired nurse she'd met the night before, the one with a large mole on her cheek.

Vanessa stepped through the open door of the general ward. The exhausted nurse stood at the bedside of a towheaded farm boy of nineteen or twenty. "Can you take over for a minute?"

With a nod, Vanessa walked to the other side of the bed. If this was the only way she could be of actual assistance, so be it. Just as she arrived, the boy coughed up greenish mucous into a nearly full kidney dish the nurse held under his chin. Vomit surged up the back of Vanessa's throat. The woman moved the dish gingerly toward her. "Hold this until I get back with fresh ones."

Terrified the container would spill its disgusting contents, Vanessa forced herself to take the bowl from the nurse's hands. Grimacing, she turned her head away as the woman rushed from the room. The young man lay back, his breathing little more than rattles and gurgling. She squinted at the wall, trying to keep the bowl below her line of sight.

From the corner of her eye, she noticed the boy's face turn darker and darker blue. He was getting worse. The patient's eyes widened, and pink foam erupted from his mouth and out his nose. "Nurse!" Vanessa screamed when his arms began waving in front of him, like he was literally grasping at the air. "Nurse! Come back!"

"It's alright, I'm here." Irene left the bedside of a delirious young woman with messy dark braids. When she arrived at the opposite side of the bed, Irene took the young man's hand and stared into his face. Vanessa could practically see the compassion flowing from her friend's eyes. How did she do it? Remain so calm? It took every bit of willpower she could muster to stay by the young man's side, rubbing his shoulder as he gradually weakened. "Thank you," Vanessa whispered across the boy's blood-spattered nightshirt.

"It won't be long now." Irene's voice was impossibly gentle. She could be a nun.

Soon, he was lying flat, staring at the ceiling, rivulets of bloody foam puffing from his lips with each labored breath. A few moments later, he breathed his last. When it was clear he was gone, Irene closed her eyes and bowed her head.

Vanessa put the dish aside and imitated her. After a few moments, Irene ran her palm down the boy's face, closing his eyelids. "That was Joe Ross." Irene's voice flattened. "One of Frank's classmates."

The emptiness in her friend's voice opened an abyss in Vanessa's chest. "I've got to check on Avery."

She ran from the room, leaving Irene alone to stare down at the corpse of yet another young man.

Vanessa was breathless when she skidded into Avery's room. Bess was there, wiping his forehead with a damp cloth. The blonde's head snapped up, fear in her eyes. "What is it?"

Avery was still pink and sweaty, not blue. As long as he didn't turn blue. That's all that was important. "I just . . . needed to see him. Make sure he was alright."

"He's *not* alright."

"I just mean . . . he's not . . ."

"Dammit, I know what you mean."

Vanessa stood frozen in the doorway, staring at the twins.

Bess stared down at Avery. "He was an innocent until he met you." She swiped away a tear and let out a bitter laugh. "I stopped seeing the Enchanted Wood when we were still kids. But not him. He still had the soul of a child." She picked his hand up between hers. "But that's all gone now. First Mother and Hattie, then the Wood . . ."

Vanessa's shoulders slumped. Why was Avery being punished? He'd done nothing wrong. Nothing to deserve being banished from the Wood. "I'm so sorry."

"It meant everything to him."

Turning on her heel, Vanessa ran down the hallway. Even as she grieved for what was lost to Avery, she feared losing him. He would forever connect her with the loss of that magical world. God may have taken his mother and sister, but it was she who was responsible for the disappearance of the one place where the pain of those losses could be forgotten.

She pushed the hospital's front doors open, ran down the steps, and fled across the lawn.

Chapter Seventy-Four

As Vanessa reached the edge of the hospital property, an owl hooted in the dusk from somewhere nearby. She stopped and wiped her runny nose with the back of her hand, looking around. She had the distinct impression the bird was talking to *her*. It hooted again. Scanning the trees, she searched, but found nothing. On the verge of giving up, she spotted it. Brown-and-white striped, its eyes were framed in big, dark circles. Round like Avery's glasses.

Avery.

Vanessa pictured him heading off with the search party. Holding Bess up in the cemetery. Leading her and the Wainwright children out of the woods. If their positions were reversed, he would never abandon her.

Her thoughts went to Irene, standing alone beside that dead boy. Irene, who had lost two brothers. And her mother. Yet she wasn't running away.

"Why didn't you tell me about Karl?"

Vanessa turned to find Bess striding across the lawn, pulling her coat on.

"What?"

Tears glistened in Bess's eyes. "No one told me he was sick." Her face was pale. "I had to hear it from Mrs. Donnally."

It all made sense now. The way Bess pulled away when Hattie guessed Karl Fiske was the object of Vanessa's affection. Their matching intensity during the sailing race. Bess was in love with Karl.

"I'm sorry . . . I was so caught up with Avery . . ." Vanessa thought back, horrified to realize it had been over two days since Ned went missing and Karl fell ill. Avery had been at the hotel that day as part of the search party, so she would have assumed he heard about Karl and had told Bess. But it appeared everyone else had been as caught up in the chaos around finding Ned as she had been. It must never have come up.

Vanessa gripped Bess's arm, desperate to make up for the oversight. "Mrs. Juneau is tending him personally, and she told me this morning that he's gotten no worse."

Bess squinted in the direction of the lake. The hotel was just visible through the trees lining the hospital grounds. "Keep an eye on my brother. I'll be back soon."

"I'm truly sorry. I didn't know about you . . . and Karl."

Bess yanked her arm away. "He's just a friend. A dear, dear friend."

"I'm still sorry I didn't mention it." The wounded look in Bess's eyes pierced her heart. "I'll do my best for Avery while you're gone, I promise."

Bess pulled in her breath, like she wanted to say something else, but instead she pursed her lips and hurried toward the road.

Vanessa's fists slowly clenched. She might not have anything to offer, but at least she wouldn't leave him. Or the others. She wouldn't. Firming her jaw, Vanessa strode back into the hospital.

Chapter Seventy-Five

Sitting next to Avery, Vanessa looked down at the two children lying head-to-toe on a cot next to his bed. A little girl who appeared to be about eight, and a slightly younger boy. Vanessa's heart pinched thinking of Walter and Edna. Two even smaller girls sat on the edge of the cot playing a listless game of pat-a-cake. Their faces were almost entirely covered by the gauze masks tied to their little heads. Vanessa looked up at the scrawny woman tending to the man wheezing in the bed next to Avery's. "Are they all yours?"

The tired mother nodded. "Didn't want to bring 'em here. But we got no money for house calls."

"If it's any comfort, this is Dr. Nolen's son."

The woman's eyebrows rose as she knelt to wipe sweat from the foreheads of the children on the cot.

"I only say that so you know your family's getting the best care anyone knows to give."

The mother sat up, her collarbones visible through her worn cotton blouse. "Can't say I'm glad to see the doctor's kin's struck down, but it's good to hear there ain't no better place for Elton and the kids to be."

Vanessa dredged up all the confidence she could muster. "There isn't."

After wiping Avery's brow, she squeezed the washcloth in the water basin again. Did the compresses even help? Her lips pressed together. Or was all the wiping just busy work to make caregivers feel like they were doing something?

The drone of the little girls' clapping was sad . . . and increasingly irritating. Vanessa smiled down at them. "Would you girls like to hear a story?"

They dropped their hands, abandoning their game without hesitation. "Yes, ma'am." Their mother shot her a look of pure gratitude.

"Once upon a time . . ." Vanessa wrung out her washcloth. Even the feverish children's eyes moved toward her. "A wicked witch walked around her glittering mansion, admiring all the gold and jewels she'd stolen. But something was bothering her. No matter how rich she got using her black magic, she never got any happier. 'What's wrong?' she asked the magic mirror on her wall."

Avery groaned in his sleep. Vanessa fell silent as he rolled his head on the pillow. When he settled again, she let her breath out and resumed her story. "'You're not happy because you're lonely,' said the mirror, which always spoke the truth. 'Ahhh,' said the witch. 'You're right. I must fill my home with children. Then I won't be lonely anymore.' So the witch went out into the countryside and started kidnapping children from villages throughout the land."

The youngest child leaned into her mother's legs, eyes widening.

This was a new version of an old story, so Vanessa wasn't exactly sure herself how it was going to end. "Soon, her mansion was filled with little boys and girls," she continued. "But that didn't help matters at all. Instead of making the witch happy, the children just cried all the time, begging her to let them go home."

The woman's husband turned his head to listen, his eyelids fluttering with the effort of keeping them open. Vanessa embellished the storyline with several twists to make it last as long as she could, but eventually brought the story to a conclusion. "Realizing the error of her ways, the witch returned the children to their families and vowed that from that day forward, she would only use her magic for healing. She turned her mansion into a hospital, and soon villagers far and wide went there to get better whenever they were hurt or sick. And before long, the witch was completely forgiven and beloved by all, never to be lonely again."

Light applause broke out behind her. Startled, she turned to find Dr. Nolen, a volunteer, and Nurse Hutchins standing in the doorway, smiles brightening their exhausted faces.

"Oh! I didn't see you there."

"Just what we've needed around here." Dr. Nolen entered. "A little distraction from all the misery."

Nurse Hutchins nodded at Vanessa with an arched eyebrow, then she and the volunteer disappeared. Vanessa dipped her head to hide her smile. She'd finally managed to do something useful.

"How's he doing?" Avery's father laid his palm on his son's forehead.

"No better. But at least no worse."

The tenderness exuding from Dr. Nolen's face as he lifted Avery's hand and pressed it to his cheek brought a lump to Vanessa's throat. After resting his son's hand back on the blanket, he pulled a handkerchief from his pocket, wiped his eyes, and blew his nose. When Avery's father passed by on his way to visit the room's other patients, he squeezed her shoulder. "Thank you for being here . . . with him."

She nodded, blinking back tears.

As Dr. Nolen tended to the tired woman's sick husband and the children, Vanessa's gaze returned to Avery. No wonder he was such a good man. He had a good father.

Chapter Seventy-Six

A very opened his eyes to find sunlight streaming in a window, broken up by the horizontal blinds. He raised his head, winced at the shooting pain in his throat and dropped his head back on the pillow, his head turned away from the window's glare.

A thin woman was asleep in a chair by the wall, two little girls curled on her lap. A man whose breath sounded like a baby rattle was in the bed next to his, and two droopy-eyed children lay motionless on a cot between them. He was in the hospital.

The last thing he remembered was falling into bed the night after finding Ned Cooper's body. He closed his eyes, remembering the weight of the corpse as they loaded it onto the stretcher. Hauling it up the Timbers cottage porch. His mother and sister's coffins being lowered into their graves. And Vanessa's worried face as she watched him head up the mountain to find Ned.

Vanessa . . .

Something pressed on his legs. He raised his head and opened his eyes to the glorious sight of her auburn bun lying loose and messy on his blanket. She sat in a chair, her upper body draped across the foot of his bed, her head resting atop folded arms.

Snatches of the past several days flashed through his mind. Vanessa in his bedroom, looking at the paintings on his wall. His head in her lap, looking up at a beauty mark under her chin. Her anxious face near his, coaxing him to open his mouth for a soupspoon she held to his lips. No way to tell which parts happened and which parts were a dream.

"Oh, son."

Avery's gaze moved from Vanessa's hair to his father, standing in the doorway. The man's clothes hung on his frame. The circles under his eyes looked like bruises. When did he get so old?

"Good morning." Avery barely recognized his own scratchy voice.

His father was at his bedside in three long strides. "Thank the Lord, you made it."

The trembling in his father's voice and the watery film over his eyes made Avery's throat cramp. He did his best to smile. Anything to relax his father's face. "Appears so."

"You're not out of the woods yet, though." His concerned father dissolved, replaced by the professional Dr. Nolen. But Avery would always remember the relief in the father's eyes. For better or worse, his father loved him. "You need to keep resting. Drink plenty of water, get your strength back so you don't relapse."

"Yes, Father." Avery nodded, his newfound understanding pushing a grin to his cracked lips. He gestured to Vanessa with a limp finger. "Pretty sure it was Vanessa who found me."

His father nodded, his expression softening as he glanced at down at her. "An iron butterfly, that one."

Avery squinted up with a half-smile. His father didn't make a habit of speaking in metaphor. "Good description."

"Barely left your side." His father looked pointedly at him from under his bushy eyebrows as he stroked his mustache.

"Avery?" Vanessa sat up, wiping her mouth and smoothing her hair back in place. A crease in her cheek from sleeping on her cuff returned the lump to Avery's throat. "You're awake!"

The joy in her voice was more precious than a fistful of diamonds. "Thanks to you."

His father coughed and backed away. "I'll check in on you later." He raised his finger. "Now don't forget what I said about relapse." His father gave the patients sharing his room a quick examination, then left.

When his father was gone, Vanessa moved closer, her face clouding. "I'm so, so sorry."

"For saving my life?"

She lowered her eyes. "About the Enchanted Wood."

It came back in a rush. The pond. The bench. The tree. Ordinary. Drained of their magic. His stomach ached, like he'd been kicked in the gut. "It was . . . everything to me."

Vanessa's chin jerked as though he'd slapped her. "It's all my fault." Her voice was a sorrowful whisper. The pain of swallowing silenced him. He rolled his head, saw a glass of water on the bedside table and reached for it. "Here, let me help!" Vanessa grabbed the glass and handed it to him. The cool liquid on his throat was an elixir, restoring him.

When he passed the glass back, she put it aside and stood there, motionless. She'd changed. When they first met, she was in constant motion. She didn't walk, she danced. She didn't sit, she perched. It had delighted and overwhelmed him. But now, there was a stillness in her. Had she calmed, or did something inside of her die?

His thoughts returned to the Wood. He missed it, certainly. But there was a new sensation arising in his chest, dissolving the pain. He raised his eyes. "But you know what?"

"What?" She kept her gaze fixed on the center of his bed.

"Now, there's something I care about even more than the nymphs and the Wood."

"And what's that?" Hope flickered in her voice.

"You, Vanessa. You."

Her eyes moved back to his face. "Me?"

"Yes. Ever since you started going there, something changed." As the words came, his understanding firmed. "I wasn't going there for the Wood anymore. I was going to see you."

She blinked several times.

"And I think . . ." The words kept tumbling from his mouth, like a dam bursting on a mountain creek. "I think it's a *good* thing the Wood is gone."

"You do?" Relief and confusion waltzed in her expression.

He nodded as he pushed himself higher on his pillow, remembering Mr. Robie quoting Corinthians. "I think I was in danger there. Of losing myself, like Ned."

Vanessa lowered her eyes and twisted her ring. "I've been thinking about the Wood a lot since it disappeared." Tilting her face toward the window, she frowned. "I've wondered if you couldn't see the naiads because your heart didn't have a hole to fill, like Ned's. Like mine." She faced him again. "You saw the wood nymphs. Prisoners of their trees. And imitated them, in a way, didn't you? Isolating yourself in the Wood, getting a job that keeps you in the forest all day."

Yes. It made sense. Why hadn't he seen it before?

"I realize now, despite all their giggling, the naiads aren't very happy." Though still startlingly blue, her eyes had gained a certain . . . depth, since he'd first met her.

"The wood nymphs either," he mused. "Nothing ever changes for them, does it?"

"That's right." Vanessa sat on the edge of his bed. "They live in a beautiful place, where nothing can ever go wrong . . . but it's not real life, is it?"

"It's true." Irene was at the doorway. "You're awake."

Vanessa slid off the bed as the excited brunette rushed over and pulled Avery into a bear hug. "Don't you ever give us a scare like that again, Avery Nolen. You hear me?"

He laughed, not caring how her grip hurt his tender muscles. "I'll do my best." Then he bent his head against Irene's shoulder, not wanting anyone to see the tears that welled in his eyes as he realized how well-loved he was. Despite all the time he'd spent trying to get away from everyone. "Where's Bess?" He was definitely getting mushy if he wanted to see *her*.

"She went up to the hotel to see Karl." Vanessa sounded worried.

"He's sick, too?" His head fell back on the pillow. Bess couldn't lose Karl . . . not so soon after Mother and Hattie.

His eyes slid to Irene, who seemed more angelic with every blow death dealt her. He didn't think Bess could bear more grief with the same stoicism.

"I've got to get back up there with the wagon." Irene released him from her hug. "I'll let her know you're on the mend. Hopefully she'll return with good news about Karl, too."

"And I'll go get you some soup and tea." Vanessa gripped the foot of his iron bed frame. "You need to build your strength back."

The intimacy of their conversation about the Enchanted Wood was gone. His stomach twisted, realizing he'd essentially declared himself to her. Avery frowned as the girls left the room. Vanessa had not said anything about returning his feelings.

Chapter Seventy-Seven

S oon after she returned to Avery's room, Vanessa made a great production of fluffing his pillow and helping him sit up to eat his soup. He was going to live . . . and he forgave her!

Once Avery was comfortable and fed, Vanessa sat on his bed and entertained everyone with another story. The sick little girl on the cot also seemed to be doing better. But the father and son were still struggling. When Vanessa finished her tale of three puppies searching the barnyard for their mother, the children's mother began attending to her family.

Avery took her hand in his and gave it a squeeze. She turned to face him. "Please don't be . . . overwhelmed . . . by what I said earlier." Avery pulled his hand from her grip. "I don't want anything to ruin our . . . friendship."

Bringing his declaration up again, and the way he averted his eyes and blushed confirmed Vanessa's suspicions. His "care" for her was definitely romantic. But after forcing herself to suppress her attraction to him for so long, it was taking time to allow those feelings free rein. Plus, after Ned, she still wasn't sure she trusted her instincts.

But one thing was sure. She, too, didn't want anything to ruin their friendship. "Oh, Avery." She took his hand again. "Nothing ever could, I swear."

He didn't reply and his expression was hard to read, a little unfocused. How she enjoyed looking into his big, brown eyes. Too bad he hid them behind those glasses all the time. "Oh my goodness! Your spectacles!" She sprang from the bed and opened the drawer in the bedside table. "I bet you want them."

"They're here?" He took his glasses from her and slid them on. "I figured I'd just be half-blind until I got back home."

"Aavey! You're awake." Bess barreled into the room and wrapped her brother in her arms.

"You're . . . choking . . . me," Avery protested into the loose roll of wavy blonde hair covering his face.

Bess laughed and set him free. Stepping back, she rubbed her eyes with her fists and tossed a guilty glance in Vanessa's direction. "Sorry I didn't make it back last night." Bess spoke more to her brother than to her.

"How's Karl doing?" Vanessa remembered her own fright at seeing the hotel manager collapsed across his desk.

"Through the worst of it, it seems. Mrs. Juneau is a godsend."

Avery pressed his glasses up his nose. "Glad to hear it."

Bess nodded, then looked directly at Vanessa. "Thank you for staying with him."

"I wasn't going anywhere." She preferred not to think about Bess finding her on the hospital lawn, where only the hoot of an owl had stopped her from fleeing. Bess raised her eyebrow but said nothing.

Avery grabbed Vanessa's hand. "My guardian angel."

"Uh-huh." His sister's gaze floated down to their entwined fingers. "I . . . I'll go let Father know I'm back. See what he needs me to do."

"No." Vanessa pulled her hand from Avery's. "Take some time with your brother before he falls asleep again. I'll go see if your father needs any help."

Bess sounded wary. "All right . . ."

"Down, girl." Avery's eyes crinkled behind his glasses. "Vanessa and I agree. It was time for us both to leave the Enchanted Wood behind."

Moving closer to his side, Bess responded to him—but kept her eyes on Vanessa. "I just don't want to see you get hurt." The warning to Vanessa was unmistakable.

"Bess, I love you. But I can't have you fight *all* my battles." The firmness in Avery's voice relaxed Vanessa's shoulders and brought a smile to her lips. "Get out of here, Sis. You can both track down Father." He scooted down under the covers. "I need a nap."

"Don't hold having me as a sister against him," Bess muttered in Vanessa's general direction once they were in the hallway. "Hattie was always the charming one."

Sorrow over Hattie's death snatched Vanessa's breath away, so it took a moment for her to reply. "You're just protective. He makes me feel the same way." She suppressed a laugh. "When he's not protecting me, that is."

Bess gripped her neck as she rolled her head. "He's a grown man, and we're the exact same age, for crying out loud. I've got to stop treating him like a little boy."

Vanessa put her arm around Bess's shoulder. "He's lucky to have a sister like you, and I promise, I'll never hurt him."

"You better not." The raw vulnerability in Bess's eyes startled Vanessa before they both stopped, barely avoiding a collision with Mrs. Donnally and a teenage orderly. They were carrying a stretcher. A sheet-draped corpse. Vanessa's spirits fell back to earth. The nightmare wasn't over.

As she and Bess walked toward Dr. Nolen's office together in silence, she thought more about her relationship with Avery. She loved him as a friend. That was sure. But could she ever want him to kiss her . . . touch her . . . like she wanted Ned? She didn't know.

Her hands turned to ice. What if being friends wasn't enough for him? Vanessa glanced at Bess from the corner of her eye. What if she couldn't keep the promise she just made?

Chapter Seventy-Eight

Two weeks after she'd left the hotel with Irene and the wagonload of supplies, Vanessa strode up the hotel's circular drive for the first time. The leaves had nearly all fallen from the trees, leaving dark skeletons silhouetted against the gray sky.

She smiled at the sight of Mr. Seward and Irene's brothers loading bags onto the hotel wagon. Denis and Frank seemed as fit as they had before the flu, but their father was shrunken. Heartbreak had taken a toll.

"Hello there!" She waved as she passed. "Lovely to see you up and about!"

They waved back, but all three smiles were stunted. No one got away unscathed. Pleasure at seeing the Seward boys up and about gave way to the reality that they were loading luggage belonging to the last of the hotel staff.

A slight tremor shook Vanessa's insides as she contemplated her uncertain future. She'd been so busy at the hospital, just getting through the day was her entire plan. But now, things were calming down. The flu had peaked, at least in New Hampshire, yet she was dragging her feet about making new arrangements for herself. She was concerned about her lack of plans, yes. But felt nothing like the terror that plagued her when she first arrived at Twin Birch House, worried that the slightest mistake would lead to her immediate sacking. A one-way ticket to Boston's streets.

Closing her eyes, she took a deep breath. Fear, the beast that had stalked her since losing her family, had finally been slain.

Vanessa and Avery had not spoken of their relationship after the day he'd woken up and they'd discussed letting nothing ruin their friendship. Nonetheless, giving herself permission to consider him romantically was getting easier every day. Her boots crunched on the hotel's gravel driveway and her lips twitched as she recalled the morning she walked in on him splashing his face at the washstand. The droplets glistening on the smattering of hair on his forearms, and on his chest, and the peek she'd taken at the thin line of hair descending from his belly button into the mysterious land beneath his drawstring pajama bottoms. She had no trouble with the idea of kissing him now. He had returned home the day before, leaving a painful void at the hospital. But there was no doubt about it; Avery Nolen was the reason she couldn't bring herself to make plans for her future.

Vanessa found Mrs. Juneau in the head housekeeper's quarters, packing the last of her suitcases. She folded her arms in Mrs. Juneau's doorway. "So, you're off."

"We are." Mrs. Juneau tucked her hairbrush into her valise. "The worst seems to have passed in Boston, and we need to get to our posts before we're replaced. Come for your bag?"

"Yes." Vanessa sat on the edge of the stuffed chair. "Looks like my room's been closed up."

"Last guests left on Sunday. Irene has your things."

"And Mr. Fiske?" Bess had visited the hotel daily and reported that he was slow to recover.

"Strong enough to leave on this morning's train." Mrs. Juneau stopped packing and stood upright. "I was surprised you didn't ask for a recommendation to go to New York with him."

Vanessa shook her head, her belly developing a slight cramp. "That idea sort of fell by the wayside when everyone got sick. I never got a chance to talk to him about it." Had she made another false step? Been distracted by a different man, but made the same wrong choice?

"Ah, well." Her mentor resumed packing. "What are your plans?"

"Most of the married women have gone back to their families, so I'm sticking around to help at the hospital . . . until everything's back to normal at least."

Mrs. Juneau stopped to give her a careful look. "The Nolens are good people." She laid a folded shawl into her suitcase. "Sterling characters, every one of them."

"They are, aren't they?" Not only did she adore Avery, but Bess was also growing on her, and Dr. Nolen was a teddy bear beneath his gruff exterior.

"Been hit by the nursing bug after all that time at the hospital?"

Vanessa shuddered and shook her head. "Definitely not my calling."

"My offer still stands." Mrs. Juneau pulled her Royal Poinciana Hotel postcards from the mirror above the dresser and handed one to her. "Whatever you end up doing, stay in touch."

"We Home girls . . ."

The older woman laughed. "That's right."

Vanessa rose and they hugged. The normal human contact was a welcome relief after weeks of keeping distance from everyone.

Feeling loving arms around her once more, it occurred to her that Home girls might turn out to be the only family she would ever have. The thought made her squeeze Mrs. Juneau even tighter.

Vanessa glanced over her shoulder as she placed her clothes in the top drawer of Hattie's dresser. Dr. Nolen had been kind enough to invite her to stay until she figured out her next steps, but it was awkward to move into Hattie's place with Bess across the room, curled into a corner chair. "I'm perfectly happy to sleep on the couch . . ."

"Nonsense." Bess stared out the window. "Hattie doesn't need the bed anymore."

Now that things were calmer, Vanessa found herself thinking about Hattie and Mrs. Nolen more often. She could only imagine how much Avery, Bess, and Dr. Nolen were still hurting.

Bess swiped her hand over her eyes and waved toward the suitcases sitting next to her own matching bed. "Besides, I leave at the crack of dawn, so you're hardly putting me out."

"If you're sure . . ."

"Won't a bed beat those ghastly hospital chairs?"

"I can't deny it." Vanessa smiled. "I've never appreciated the ability to lie down as much as I do now."

Having won her point, Bess returned her gaze to whatever lay outside the window. "Thanks for what you did for my brother." She frowned and picked at her cuticles. "I don't always show my appreciation in the most appropriate way."

She and Bess hadn't spoken much after Avery began his recovery. Bess spent most of her time helping out on the hospital's administrative side. Irene and the other volunteers did most of the work with the remaining patients, while Vanessa had found her niche distracting the sick and their families with stories and simple games.

This time, it was she who waved Bess off. "Don't mention it. Least I could do when you and your father were killing yourselves." She covered her mouth with her hand. "That came out wrong!"

"Oh, relax, Vanessa! It's an expression."

"First time anyone's told *me* to relax."

Bess laughed. "If you're not careful, you'll end up as serious as Karl."

Sitting on the corner of the Hattie's bed, Vanessa wrapped her arm around the wooden bedpost. "So how are things going between the two of you?"

"What do you mean? He's a friend."

Vanessa leaned back. "It just seemed . . ."

"There's nothing between us." Bess stood up. "I'm leaving for DC in the morning and his life is in New York . . . or here."

"Okay." She was taken completely off guard by the violence of Bess's reaction. "I was wrong." Looking down at her hands, Vanessa touched her ring. *"Garnet,"* Mrs. Juneau had said the stone was called.

Bess strode to the door. "Supper will be ready in a half hour." She stopped in the doorway. "And I'm sorry about Ned. That couldn't have been easy." Then she was gone.

Vanessa resumed unpacking, pushing away the painful memories of her and Ned's last night together. She preferred to think of him smiling, in all his glory that first night on the dance floor. And of his breezy air approaching her at the pony corral, Cecile and Albert in tow. She shook her head. At least he'd spared her a loveless marriage.

Her hand stopped in mid-air over an open drawer. Marriage. Avery just might propose. He'd been looking awful moony. And she did care for him, deeply . . . and he'd treat her like gold. Better than Ned ever would have.

She lowered the folded blouse. The fairy's prophecy still haunted her. With everything that had happened, she knew she shouldn't give another thought to whatever the fairy said. Besides, most people had to decide who they should marry all on their own, without any magical guidance at all. But she couldn't help it. Part of her still yearned for that moment of recognition the fairy promised. To know she wasn't fooling herself again. To be certain Avery was the right man.

Chapter Seventy-Nine

"A very?" Vanessa walked into the Nolen's entry hall after spending the afternoon at the hospital. She peeled off her coat and laid her gloves on the side table, then froze. *This is what it would feel like to live here for real. To come home to him every day. To have a family again.* The intensity of her longing softened her knees.

"In here." Avery spoke from behind her.

"Oh!" Vanessa spun around. "You startled me."

He stood on the other side of the dining room table. It was set with candles, laid out with two places. The centerpiece was a giant jack-o'-lantern, a candle flickering behind its triangular eyes.

"Happy Halloween."

"Avery." Her throat clamped as she fought back a sudden wave of tears. "That's so sweet."

She couldn't remember anyone doing something special just for her. Birthdays were celebrated on the fifteenth at the Home. One cake for all the girls born that month.

"Since the village's Halloween parade was canceled."

"And you remembered it's my favorite holiday." Her gratitude was overwhelming and awkward. She had to remind herself this was normal. What happens in real families. The kind of thing people who care about each other do.

"With Bess gone, and Father staying away from the house as much as he can, I thought we might have a special supper." He smiled shyly. "Just the two of us."

Vanessa gripped the back of a dining room chair, her eyes sweeping over the candy corn sprinkled on the white tablecloth. "You cooked?"

He pushed his glasses up his nose. "The ladies from church brought another hot dish."

Trembling, she glanced back toward the staircase. "Give me a minute to wash up. I'll be down in a jiffy." Once she got to the landing and Avery had retreated to the kitchen, she leaned against the wall. She couldn't breathe. She pressed her palm against her sternum. Was this what love felt like?

By the time they finished their bowls of beef stew, Avery's face was flushed. Vanessa's belly pinched as she patted her lips with her napkin. What if he was having a relapse? "Are you alright?"

He nodded and pulled an envelope from his pocket.

"What's that?"

He laid it on the tablecloth between them. "A letter from the Selective Service."

Staring down at the official-looking envelope, Vanessa's stomach knotted even harder. "But . . . the war's nearly over." She grabbed for the table edge. "Everyone says so."

He put his hand over hers. "Guess they're not taking any chances. Law says they can keep us up to four months after peace is signed."

She turned her palm up and gripped his hand, her head spinning. "When do you go?"

"I report on Monday." His gaze drifted to the jack-o'-lantern. "Camp Devens."

"Monday?" She was on her feet, flying over to him. She threw her arms around his shoulders, and he pulled her onto his lap. There she found a spot more magical than the Enchanted Wood, curled up against his chest, her nose buried against his neck. He smelled of pine and Pears soap. Clean and fresh. "I don't want you to go." Who cared if she sounded childish? It was the truth.

With one arm wrapped firmly around her back, Avery stroked her head with his broad palm. "I don't want to go either."

With a sigh, she cuddled in closer. The pulse in his neck against her cheek and the strength of his arms around her back formed a world she never wanted to leave. Whatever thrill Ned provided, it was like a sparkler on the Fourth of July. Dazzling and bright, but sure to burn out quickly. What she had with Avery was more like the glow of embers in the hearth. Hot and steady, lasting forever if tended with care.

She reluctantly pulled away to look into his deep brown eyes, her face damp from her tears. "I love you, Avery Nolen."

With a crooked smile, he reached up to a tendril of hair stuck to her wet cheek, and brushed it behind her ear. "And I love you, Vanessa Perkins."

Would she ever see that earth-moving smile of his again? Or had it fallen victim to all the heartbreak and loss?

He lifted her off his lap. "Please. Take your seat." Still dazed from the bliss she'd found in his arms, she sank into her chair and patted her cheeks dry with her napkin. Clearing his throat, he rose and stood before her. She bit her lip when he lowered himself to one knee and pulled a square box from his pocket. "Vanessa Perkins, will you marry me?"

Dizzy, she stared as he pulled back the box lid to reveal a ring. The center stone was an octagonal sapphire, flanked by two smaller, octagonal diamonds. "It was my mother's, and Father offered it to me to give to you."

"It's . . . beautiful."

"I've loved you from the moment I first saw you in the woods, calling so desperately for Walter and Edna." He pushed his hair back with one hand. "I know you hoped for a wealthy man, and I may never be that. But I promise you, no one will ever love you as much as I do. That I can offer."

Staring deep into Avery's eyes, Vanessa found nothing but kindness and warmth. "You know something?"

"What?" His guileless voice brought tears to her eyes.

"You've got something better than wealth. You've got a heart of gold."

Mrs. Juneau's words echoed in her mind. *"Sterling characters, every one of them."*

"Oh, my goodness. Avery!" She leapt to her feet and spun in a circle, clapping her hands. "It's you. It's always been you."

He rose, clearly puzzled. "What's always been me?"

Vanessa bent over, laughing, remembering the fairy's cryptic words. "She never promised me a wealthy man. She promised a man of "true worth." A man of sterling and gold. And it's you."

He cocked his head. "I . . . don't . . ."

She grabbed his free hand and swung it back and forth. "You're a man of *sterling* character and a heart of *gold. You* are my man of sterling and gold. I just couldn't see it before."

Avery ran his hand through his hair, a little dazed. "I'm your man of sterling and gold?"

Vanessa's head bobbed up and down wildly. "Yes. Yes. It's always been you."

He dropped the ring box on the table, hugged her to his chest and lifted her off the ground, spinning her around the room as they laughed together. He threw his head back and shouted to the heavens, "I'm your man of sterling and gold!"

When he put her down, Vanessa gazed up at his dancing eyes. Still enfolded in his arms, she rested her hands on his shoulders and tilted her lips up to his. As his warm mouth pressed against hers, she closed her eyes. His kiss was different than Ned's. Less greedy, more tender. Yet there was an urgency in the pressure of his lips. Power in his grip as he pulled her against him. Ned's kisses were like delicious fruit. But Avery's was like a banquet, full of promise and undiscovered delights.

When they parted, both were breathless.

"So, you'll marry me?"

"Yes. Yes, I'll marry you."

And there it was. That smile that had won her heart the day they met. It, too, had survived.

He reached back and took the ring from the box, lifted her left hand and slipped it onto her finger. Together, they admired it glittering on her hand, then he gently pulled her to her feet and they kissed again. The salt of her joyful tears just made the kiss even sweeter.

When they finally broke apart, he took both her hands. "You can stay here while I'm gone, and we'll get married as soon as I get back." He let go of one hand and pushed his glasses up. "Or maybe we can get Reverend Tiller to marry us Sunday, before I go." He re-clasped her hand. "Which do you prefer?"

"When you get back." Vanessa spoke quickly, sure of her decision. "I want our marriage to start off with something happy. Not with you going away because of the war. And that way, Bess can be included, too."

He twirled a lock of her hair in his finger. "Of course. That's perfect. And this way, I'll have even more to look forward to when I come home."

Vanessa got a little teary again, thinking of the lonely months to come, worrying about him all over again. "I'll have to come up with something to keep me busy while you're gone." She scanned the dining room and entryway. "Make myself useful."

"I actually had an idea about that." He pushed his glasses up his nose. "Something I thought of in the hospital . . . listening to your stories."

"What idea?"

He held his hand out. "Come with me."

Her laughter had a nervous edge as she followed him up the stairs. "Where are we going?"

"You'll see."

They arrived at his door and her face warmed. He turned the knob and strode inside, but she lingered in the doorway. Still glowing from their kissing, it was awkward to be in his bedroom, with its faint, but alluringly musky scent.

He strode to his desk and turned his head, his eyes sparkling. "Over here."

Releasing her breath, she felt silly . . . and a little embarrassed. She might still be thinking about the feel of her body against his, but he clearly had other things on his mind.

She swept across the room to his side and gasped at the stack of watercolors on his desk. The one on top was of a skinny mouse wearing a tiny crown, standing before a hole in a stone wall stuffed with jewels. Next to the illustration were words written in careful block letters. ". . . collected gems instead of nuts."

"It's my story!" She turned to him in amazement. "One I told the children in your hospital room."

Nodding with a wide grin, he turned the paper over to reveal the next line with a darling watercolor of the golden-eyed cat obsessed with catching the mouse king. "I thought we might collaborate . . . if you like my drawings."

"Oh, Avery." Her eyes misted as she continued turning his pages. It all made sense. They would make storybooks together. It was what she'd been meant to do. And he had seen it and brought the idea to life. It was the most precious gift she'd ever received. Her throat was so choked, she could barely speak. "I . . . love them."

He wrapped his arm around her waist and nuzzled her ear. "Then write down more of your stories while I'm gone."

"I will." Smiling through her tears, she imagined holding the picture books they would create in her hands . . . reading them to their children. "I will."

Reaching out, he touched a painting of Willow tacked to the wall above his desk, his voice tinged with melancholy. "Maybe you could even write some new ones . . ."

Vanessa turned and slid her arms around his back as she lifted her face to his. "Between us, we'll share Willow with more children than could ever have visited her in person."

The gratitude in his eyes was more powerful than any words he could have spoken. Avery took her face in both hands and pressed his lips to hers. And in that kiss, Vanessa found the beauty of the Enchanted Wood . . . the rustle of the forest treetops . . . and the warmth of Halloween candles. She was finally home.

Chapter Eighty

"One hundred years?" cried the naiads from their pond. "That's not fair!"

"You were warned when you took Ezra." Lachima's voice was soft with regret as she gazed down at them. "Yet you took Ned."

The water nymphs avoided her eyes, expressing their displeasure with crossed arms and listless swirls. "But it's so lonely at the bottom of the lake. There's no one to talk to down there!"

"You've given us no choice." Morniero scowled. "You heard our mother. Even the weakest among us must be able to resist temptation."

Some of the water nymphs began to cry. "It's just so hard to go without men," a buxom brunette whined, her blue eyes wide and brimming with tears.

"And they're always happy to join us . . ." A wispy nymph with fine blonde hair pouted, her head cocked.

Lachima knelt by the side of the pond. "I know, my loves, I know. During this banishment, you must consider a true solution to your problem. I'm sure the wind sprites' offer still stands."

"To become the sylphs' consorts?" The nymphs snorted and rolled their eyes. "Lachima, darling." A zaftig nymph pushed back her black hair, streaked gray at her temples. "You've obviously never been with a man."

Tossing their hair, the naiads joined hands and dove beneath the surface as one. The pond calmed, leaving the lily pads to float undisturbed.

Considering the power of her connection with the humans, Lachima was grateful to be spared carnal attraction to them. The naiads weren't the only ones to be plagued by that curse. Such passion contained a heat that too often consumed the human . . . and occasionally burned the immortal as well.

She looked up at her brother. "No accounting for taste, is there?"

"At least they're consistent." He extended his hand. "And in fairness . . ." He chuckled. "The wind sprites are a bit lacking in substance."

Lachima slapped her brother's hand playfully before taking it. "At least the sylphs are cheerful." Her smile faded as she rose. "The lares have become so irritable since Irene stopped keeping their flowers fresh."

Morniero frowned. "Her mother must not have made it clear how important it is to keep those boys happy."

Upright, Lachima ran her fingers through her hair with a sigh. "I'm afraid you're right."

As they squeezed hands, bright light pulsed from within their chests, filling the Wood, then contracting just as quickly.

With a glance at their reflection in the pond, Lachima admired the beauty of her brilliant wings of sapphire blue fluttering alongside Morniero's butterfly wings of emerald green, etched in black and silver.

Then she flew off, her brother following right behind.

Hope you enjoyed *All That Shimmers*!

If so, I'd deeply appreciate an honest review. It doesn't have to be long or complicated and can make all the difference to helping other readers discover *All That Shimmers*, me, and my work. Thank you!

Leave a review on Amazon, Goodreads, and/or your favorite book retailer. Quick links to retailer purchase & review pages at **bit.ly/AllThatShimmers Page** or scan this QR code:

Want to know how the fairies and magical creatures got to Twin Birch House?

Sign up for my newsletter and get your *free* copy of ***Under Dappled Sunlight***. It's a prequel novelette to *All That Shimmers*!

Set in 1851, *Under Dappled Sunlight* is about a tenacious circus performer who must find a new home for the fairies who've bound her in their service or she'll lose her chance at freedom and true love with a handsome innkeeper building a grand hotel in New Hampshire's White Mountains. I still get misty when I read it.

As a newsletter subscriber, you'll also get introductions to inspiring women from history; fascinating bits of fantasy lore; pretty pix of my adopted city of Paris and my adorable doggie, Saylie; exclusive freebies for subscribers; updates on future releases; and more!

Get your ***free copy*** of *Under Dappled Sunlight* at **kadyambrose.com.**

Direct link with this QR Code:

Check out my historical fantasy book recommendations and more at **kadyambrose.com** and on social media. Find and follow me on **Facebook, Instagram, Tome** and **Pinterest** as @KadyAmbrose.

Happy Reading!

Kady

About the Author

Kady Ambrose is a historical fantasy author whose prior work has been published in short story anthologies and *Woman's World* magazine. When not writing historical fiction, she's known as Lynne Moses, a screenwriter, playwright, and writing consultant who taught story development in Los Angeles at UCLA Extension and elsewhere. She lives in Paris, where she and her husband are happily bossed around by their sweet little Yorkie-mix, Saylie.

Visit her at **kadyambrose.com** or via this QR code.

Acknowledgements

This is my first published novel and it has truly been a group effort. More people supported me along the arduous and fulfilling path to publication than I can possibly name—but I will be making an effort. To any I've accidentally overlooked, please know my gratitude extends to you as well.

The origins of the Twin Birch House world trace to my childhood spent visiting my grandparents in a forested mountain village that once hosted numerous grand hotels overlooking its pristine lake. By the time I arrived, the hotels were gone or shadows of their former selves, but their influence can be felt to this day. I want to thank Deda, Grandad, Mom, Dad, and my brother, Stuart, for creating genuine magic for me in that beloved village and the surrounding forests. I'm pretty sure I spotted fairies there once or twice, or in the woodland's dappled light, at least imagined them possible.

Any work of historical fiction requires an enormous amount of research, which I fortunately enjoy, sometimes too much! I specifically wish to thank those who were so helpful during my research trip to New Hampshire's White Mountains: Bryant Tolles, Jr., author of *The Grand Resort of the White Mountains: A Vanishing Architectural Legacy*, Bob Cottrell of the Conway Public Library and Conway Historical Society, Warren Schomaker of the Jackson Historical Society and the staff at the Omni Mt. Washington Resort, Mountain View Grand Resort, and Eagle Mountain House.

I also offer my most profound thanks to the Los Angeles chapter of RWA, for teaching me so much about writing and everything else about being an author, as well as for introducing me to so many writer friends I continue to cherish. Thanks to Veronica Blade, for being the very first to greet me at the door and for immediately becoming a lifelong friend. To Rebekah Ganiere, for taking me under your wing, inviting me to the Santa Clarita Writer's Group, and providing invaluable critique. To Allison Morse, for being ride or die, plus reading and commenting on every manuscript I've ever written. To Beverly Diehl, for inviting me to the amazing writers' group you founded; Cara King, for all those meetings talking about YA fiction, and Sarah Vance-Tompkins, for the treasured hours supporting one another on our writers' journeys.

Much of this book's first draft was written during NaNoWriMo, which I participated in with the help of Entangled Publishing's Smackdown boot camp. I want to thank our Entangled leader, Karen Grove, and my Smackdown team, CJ, Lacey, Michele, and Susan. Our check-ins really helped get me over the finish line.

I want to thank all you patient and generous critique partners who have read countless pages and provided much-needed and appreciated notes. Deepest gratitude to Bev and the others reading our pages aloud in Tony's office after hours: Bruce Bartels, Tony Faggioli, Vance Gloster, and Brian Liyama. And to Toni Floyd and the rest of the Santa Clarita Writers Group gathered at the Denny's off the 405. It was worth the drive in rush hour traffic. Thanks to Lea Shizas and Melinda Pierce at Editpalooza, and Allie Burton, Ashley Fuchs, Brenda Hiatt and Lisa Hood from the Yahoo YA-PF critique loop. And to Leslie Lehr, for your insightful critique and for being such an inspirational role model.

And then there all the beta readers for *All That Shimmers*, who graciously read and commented on entire drafts. My deepest thanks to Jamie Branker, Susan Berger, Katanie Duarte, Katharine Lotze, CJ Matthews, Bronwyn Mauldin, Lily Mercer, Kaitlyn Stone, Michelle Zeitlin, and my mom, Beck Ney, whose passion for reading and stories inspired my own.

But the journey wasn't complete once the manuscript was finished. Publishing required a whole new team, to whom I am also deeply grateful. Eternal thanks to editor extraordinaire, Raquel Brown, whose editing and proofing polished my rough stone (any remaining smudges are entirely my own responsibility). Profound gratitude to Alisha and the design team at Ebook Launch for the gorgeous cover art, and to Omar Faruk Sabuj for designing the beautiful imprint logo. Thanks so much to Randi Rayl for your blurb magic, Amanda Cummins for your sage advice on managing my social media, and to the brilliant Katie Meyers, for shining a light on the path toward getting the book into the hands of readers who would appreciate it most.

The writing and publishing journey is long and hard, and I couldn't have made it here without the support of Darius Garland and Sean Hemeon. You have become so much more to me than partners in a writing group. I also want to thank Karen Stewart Lueders for lifting my heart with your laughter and being an unflagging patron of my arts.

And last, but not least, I want to express my deepest gratitude to children, Michael and Annie, for giving me even more joy than writing does. And to my husband, Ben. Your emotional reaction to my work inspires me every day, and your constant encouragement to pursue my dreams has enriched my life far more than I could have ever foreseen when I said "yes." I'll love you all forever.

Book Club Questions

1. Would you recommend this book to someone? Why or why not (or with what caveats)? What kind of reader would most enjoy this book?

2. Did any part of this book strike a particular emotion in you? Which part and what emotion did the book make you feel?

3. Was there any part of the plot or aspects of the characters that frustrated or upset you? If so, why?

4. Did you highlight or bookmark any passages from the book? Did you have a favorite quote or quotes? If so, which ones, and why?

5. How did the author portray the historical setting and period of this book? Did you learn anything new or interesting about the time and place of the story?

6. How did you feel about Vanessa and Avery's chemistry and compatibility? Did you root for them or not?

7. How well did the author present the fantasy elements in the book? Did

they do a good job of explaining how it works and what its rules and limitations are? Did it make sense and fit with the story?

8. Were there any moments or themes in the book that resonated with your own life experiences or beliefs?

9. How do the book's setting and time period influence its central themes, and how might the story differ if these elements were changed?

10. How does the book address themes of love, loss, or friendship, and in what ways did these themes resonate with your own experiences?

11. How would you adapt this book into a movie? Who would you cast in the leading roles?